DEAD
MONEY

GRANT McCREA

DEAD MONEY

a Rick Redman mystery

RANDOM HOUSE CANADA

www.randomhouse.ca

Library and Archives Canada Cataloguing in Publication

McCrea, Grant
Dead money : a Rick Redman mystery / Grant McCrea.

ISBN-13: 978-0-679-31398-4
ISBN-10: 0-679-31398-2

I. Title.

PS8625.C74D42 2006   C813'.6   C2005-905119-1

Text and jacket design: Kelly Hill

Printed and bound in the United States of America

2 4 6 8 9 7 5 3 1

To my muse

1.

I'D BEEN AT THE WOLF'S LAIR til closing the night before. Not for any special reason. Just because. I dragged myself into the office. The place had a foggy, unnatural air. I sat down. The message light on my phone was blinking. It made my head hurt. I checked the voice mail, to make it go away. Nothing urgent. That was a relief. I deleted a few dozen e-mails. Maybe some of them were important. I couldn't really tell.

The phone rang. Please hold for Mr. Warwick.

Shit. Please hold for Mr. Warwick. The lard-ass can't dial four digits for himself. Has to delegate it.

Redman.

Yes, Charles.

I heard an unsubstantiated rumor.

They're the best kind.

Someone resembling you was seen in the elevator this morning.

Yes?

At ten forty-five.

Yes?

In sneakers.

Well, yes. I've got plantar fasciitis. Very painful. Something to do with tendons in the arches. Common in basketball players. Anyway, I change my shoes when I get to the office.

Well, I don't doubt you, Redman. I really don't. Well then. But we've got to think of morale.

Morale?

Yes. Morale.

All right then.

All right?

Yes. I'll think about it. Morale, that is.

Good. Good. You think about that.

Yes, I will.

Morale.

Yes.

Click.

Jesus. What was wrong with these people?

I'd never figure it out.

My stomach hurt. My head felt light and heavy at the same time. I thought about the hours of my shrink's time my conversation with Warwick was going to eat up, at two hundred dollars per. Time that could much better be spent talking about my sex life. Why I didn't have one.

All I could do was close my door. Pretend it wasn't there. This job. My life.

And call Dorita.

Guess what now? I said.

Don't tell me.

But I must. Listen here, darling. They're monitoring my appearance in the morning.

Who is?

Them. They. You know, the ubiquitous, omnipotent, omnivorous They.

I do. I know them well. Pesky.

Yes. Get over here.

In seconds she was at my office door.

Ricky? she inquired.

Her legs were impossibly long. Her back was army straight. Her breasts, voluptuous. To be desired.

But not for me. No. I'd thought about it, more than once. Something in my wiser self had held me back, appraised the situation and realized, as clear as vodka in a martini glass, that this was not a good idea. Not at all.

So, we were friends. And friends we would remain.

Dorita closed the office door behind her.

Why did I ever get into this business? I asked.

Because you're brilliant at it. Come on, Ricky, do I have to tell you that every day?

Well, yes. If you don't, who will?

You've got a point. Anyway, what's today's little crisis?

That damn Warwick again, what else? He thinks I'm bad for morale.

Dorita pulled out a cigarette and a platinum blowtorch of a lighter. The blue flame shot a good six inches toward the ceiling. She sat down, took a generous haul of the smoke, blew it decisively about the room.

That's a laugh, she said.

Of course it is. How can wearing sneakers in the elevator compete with five-page memoranda about how to train your secretary to stop wasting file folders?

They're a scarce resource.

Secretaries?

File folders.

So I understand. Damn, why did I ever get started in this business?

We already resolved that question.

That was a resolution?

As much as the topic merits.

I should have been a poker pro.

Yes, darling. And how does your poker bankroll stand today? Don't lie now.

Minus eighteen thousand. But that was tuition. I don't lose anymore.

That's some expensive school you went to.

Yes, well. I did some stupid things.

Nobody never loses at poker.

You know what I mean. I'm in control now. I almost never lose. Long term, it's a lock. I know that if I stay at the table long enough I'll be up at the end of the night.

Let's see. Maybe you could quit your job. Minus eighteen thousand times two – it's been six months, right? – that's minus thirty-six thousand a year. You could probably live on that. You'd have to cut back on those happy lunches at Michel's though.

That's what I love about you. Always a sympathetic ear.

The fact was, she *was* a sympathetic ear, in her twisted way. Or, rather, more than that. She was my eccentric anchor in the heaving seas of temptation. Had I been less embarrassed about it, had shared with her, somewhere along the way, my bad luck streak, and that my cure for it had been to raise the stakes to get back all that money quick, it never would have happened. Or at least it would have stopped somewhere short of eighteen thousand. She'd have kicked some sense into me.

I'd like to kill him, I said. I really would.

Warwick?

Who else?

That's quite a segue.

Isn't it, though? I rather liked it myself.

Drinks later?

Twist my arm.

Dorita left.

The image of her legs lingered.

2.

MY BACK HURT. My head hurt. I worried about these pains. What did they mean? Was I ill? Was it cancer? Cancer of the lower back? Hadn't heard of it. That didn't mean it didn't exist, of course. I made a mental note to look it up.

Why wait? I googled it. God bless modern technology. 'Lower back pain, cancer.' Several hundred hits turned up. Alarming. I opened the first. 'Cancer is a rare cause of low back pain,' I read.

I relaxed.

'But not unknown.'

I flinched.

'When cancer does occur in the lower back, it usually has spread from the prostate, lungs or kidneys.'

Jesus, I thought, I'm a dead man.

I called in Judy. Told her to make an appointment with Dr. Altmeier.

Five minutes later she buzzed me.

Next Monday at one, she said.

The pain went away.

Tomorrow I'd tell her to cancel the appointment.

I turned to the deposition of Lawrence Wells. The transcript lay unopened on my desk. It had been there for days. I resented it. It sat accusing me. Read me! it shouted, you irresponsible lout! The hearing's in two days! You've got to prepare a cross examination, fat man!

I wasn't fat, actually. A little rounded at the edges, perhaps. But the transcript liked the sound of it: fat man!

Well, I thought, I guess I've procrastinated enough. I picked up the transcript. I set my chair to optimum lean. I adjusted the lumbar support. I dove in.

Halfway through the first page, my mind began to wander. I thought about last week's oral argument before the Court of Appeals. Just as I was reliving my brilliant riposte to a particularly sticky question posed by the Chief Justice, my computer beeped three times.

Reverie interrupted. E-mails. All from Warwick. Damn.

I'd missed another meeting, it seemed.

Warwick loved meetings. Endless meetings packed to bursting with trivia. Secretarial evaluations. The need for new coffee machines. The latest seminars for junior associates. A new committee on office decoration.

With a heavy heart and a trembling hand – trembling not from trepidation, mind you, but from lack of sleep and excessive beverage consumption – I dialed Warwick's extension. While the phone rang I rehearsed my tale of incapacitating illness. Lower back pain. Of course. That would do the trick. Hell, it was almost true.

Mr. Warwick's office, chirped his terminally cheerful assistant, Cherise.

Hi, Cherise, I said.

Hello, Mr. Redman! she fairly screamed. I'll see if he's in!

A curious exercise, that. In light of the fact that her desk sat immediately outside his office door, one would think she'd be aware if he was in.

After a suitably pompous interval, Warwick's voice arrived on the line.

Redman, it said. Come to my office at once.

I composed myself. Rubbed some color into my face. I'd forgotten to shave. Fortunately, I'm blessed with the facial hair of a blond adolescent, so it wasn't obvious.

Warwick was sitting ramrod straight in his chair, chewing on an unlit cigar. Doing his best General Patton. I pulled back the visitor's chair a foot or two. I knew that in my condition a mere whiff of chewed cigar and cloying cologne would make me gag.

Well, he said.

Well, I responded, my wit taking wing.

You're not looking well.

I'm not well, I said. Lower back. I had to cancel the Lockwood deposition yesterday.

Indeed? he responded, with a skeptical raise of the eyebrow. Well.

I maintained a discreet silence. No point in pushing the issue. God knew what his spies had told him.

We've got a problem, he said.

Yes, we do, I thought but didn't say. His notion of what the problem might be was highly unlikely to agree with mine.

We had a meeting of the Executive Committee last night.

He paused. I waited.

Revenues are down, he said, giving me a Look.

He was concerned, the Look told me, that I had been insufficiently attentive to the problem of declining revenues.

So I understand, I said, trying to fill the conversational space. But it's a cyclical business. Things will pick up soon.

It's a cyclical business, he repeated, with a small impatient shrug. Yes. But we have obligations to the firm.

Yes, I said. Of course we do.

And we can't permit these fluctuations to get out of hand. Everyone here depends on that. We can't have big peaks and valleys.

I would think the peaks are okay, I said with an innocent smile.

Valleys aren't, he said grimly. So we have to smooth out the valleys. And when downtrends occur, the Committee must act. That's our fiduciary responsibility. To the partners. To the firm.

I was waiting to hear what all this had to do with me.

In '98, when things were going bad, we managed to find Gibson. To fill the gap. His billings were a boon to the firm.

Yes. I recall.

This year, there's no Gibson on the horizon.

That's too bad, I commiserated.

Yes, it is. So we need to take other measures.

I see.

We've drawn up a list.

A list.

A probation list.

Ah.

Yes. Now, Redman, I don't want you to take this personally. We go back a long way. And we all appreciate your abilities. You're a terrific trial lawyer. But that's only one part of being a successful partner. We expect everybody to carry their weight around here. And you do have to admit that you don't bring in the kind of business that your talents would indicate you should.

My gut clenched. Something with small sharp teeth was chewing on my gall bladder.

So we've put you on the list.

Warwick pushed out his chest. Gave me an imperious look.

He seemed to be expecting a response.

What was I supposed to say, exactly? 'Thank you, oh wise one, for tripling my psychiatrist bills and giving me less income to pay them with'?

What exactly does that mean? I managed to croak.

We're not asking you to leave, he said. But we're going to ask you to prove yourself. Over the next six months to a year. Probation, like I said, in a sense. We need you to work up to the level of your abilities, Redman. Get out there. Beat the bushes. Rustle up some business. Show the flag. Go to lunch with someone other than Dorita Reed.

That last was a low blow.

I see, I said.

And please, Redman. Start getting in to work at a reasonable hour. I personally don't care if you come in at midnight. But it makes a bad impression.

Yes, I said. Morale.

Exactly, he replied smugly, pleased that I had so efficiently imbibed that morning's earlier lesson.

Listen, Redman, he continued, look on it as an opportunity. We're not singling you out. There are eight others on that list.

I knew it wasn't my place to ask who my fellow probationists were. But I had an idea. List the partners with personalities. Multiply by those with interests beyond the profitability of the firm. Shake well. Don't stir. Might rock the boat.

If it works out, great, he went on. Welcome back. If it doesn't? Well. I think we can both just agree that your heart's not in it. Because I know you can do it. If you want to.

Yes, I said. Of course.

Why did I feel like a delinquent high school student?

Ah, I answered myself. Because I was being treated like one.

Though it was true, that last bit anyway. I could do it. If I wanted to. But it was a goddamn big 'if.' I'd never been a natural at the schmoozing game. The cocktail party chatter. Inviting prospects to lunch. 'Hey, keep me in mind, buddy.' It always seemed a bit too much like begging. I preferred to let my trial work speak for itself. Apparently it hadn't been speaking loudly enough.

Redman, Warwick then said jovially, as though none of the previous had occurred, as though we were all just good old buddies again. You have some criminal experience, don't you?

I hesitated. Criminal experience? What now? My adolescent shoplifting career? Weren't those records sealed? The pain in my lower back made a sharp comeback.

You do some pro bono stuff, don't you? he prodded.

The pain receded.

Sure, I replied. Mostly appeals. Death penalty appeals. The Case of the Red Car Door. I've done a couple of trials too. Manslaughter. Aggravated assault. Nothing special.

Well, I guess you're the best I've got, then, he said.

I refrained from thanking him for the vote of confidence.

FitzGibbon's son's in some kind of trouble, he said.

This gave me pause.

I want you to handle it, he said.

What kind of trouble? I asked.

Never mind what kind of trouble. Bad trouble. I don't know. Drugs. Murder. Grand theft auto. I couldn't make out FitzGibbon's voice mail. He sounded disturbed. Anyway, it doesn't matter what it is. Find out. Get on it. Handle it. Make it go away. Make him happy. Get some more business from him. It'll be the first step on the way to your rehabilitation.

I nodded obediently. Fine choice of word. Rehabilitation.

You'll be a hero, he said.

Warwick turned his chair to the window, signaling the end to the audience.

I turned to leave.

Oh, Redman? Warwick said.

I turned back.

Yes? I asked.

Lose the sneakers.

I got the hell out of there. I asked Cherise for the FitzGibbon particulars.

She gave them to me with a wink.

I had no idea what it meant.

3.

I WENT BACK TO MY OFFICE.

I called Dorita.

You won't believe this, I said.

Oh, shut up, Ricky. You already said that. I've got a client meeting in ten minutes.

Put it off. FitzGibbon's son's in trouble. Something serious. Warwick wants me to handle it. Oh, and I'm being fired.

Jesus, she whispered. I'll be right there.

In less than a minute she was at my office door.

Come in, I mumbled.

She flounced onto the couch. Lit a cigarette with her blowtorch.

You know, there's a rule about smoking in the office, I said.

Right, she said, tapping some ashes on the carpet. So what's this all about?

I told her about my audience with His Portliness. At the mention of probation, a moment's shock passed across her face. She quickly brushed it off.

Did they issue you an ankle bracelet? she asked breezily.

Listen, I said, I appreciate the effort, but this is too big for a joke or two. Let me digest it for a while. We'll talk about it tomorrow.

My, my, Ricky. You're getting soft in your old age.

Tomorrow, I repeated, with unusual resolve.

Okay, have it your way. So, what's this FitzGibbon thing?

I don't know anything more than I've told you. FitzGibbon's son, what's-his-name. He's in some kind of trouble. Not a speeding ticket. Something serious. I don't know what.

Jules. His name is Jules.

Right. But the thing is, why me? It's not like I'm a top-flight criminal lawyer. I'm a civil litigator, for Christ's sake. I just do the stuff on the side. Do my bit for the social fabric, all that.

My poor little paranoid bunny. Warwick just wants to keep it in the house. You get the boy off, we get more business from Daddy.

Yeah, well. That might make sense. But I can't help thinking Warwick's setting me up to fail. Rehabilitation. Jesus.

Well, I can't say that's utterly beyond the realm of possibility. But what are you going to do about it?

Do my best, darling. Just like always. Sad but true. Can't help myself.

That's the ticket, Ricky. Anyway, you know the old man hates his guts.

Who?

Jules. FitzGibbon can't stand him.

I'll ignore the fact that the 'old man' is in my age bracket. And I know. Or at least, so I've been told. But blood runs thick, darling.

If blood it is, in that shit's veins.

Well, yes. To tell you the truth, I don't know the guy very well. Met him at a cocktail party or two. Big red Irishman as I recall. Full of noise and spit.

That's the one. You're not going to have an easy time with him.

Meaning?

Meaning he's a major-league prick. He fired a guy for having a Snickers in the elevator.

Was he just holding it, or eating it?

What?

The guy with the Snickers. Was it unwrapped? Was he *eating* it in the elevator?

I don't know. What kind of question is that?

Well, if he was eating it, I could understand.

Sure, and maybe he was wearing sneakers, too.

Snickers *and* sneakers? Jesus.

You're right. I'd have fired him too.

4.

FITZGIBBON'S OFFICE WAS on the thirty-third floor of the Consolidated Can building. It was vast and modern, paneled in the sort of expensive blond wood that gave me a headache. Furnished in black leather and chrome. A large twisted ropelike thing reposed on the coffee table. I took it to be a pricey piece of Modern Art.

A much-too-well-manicured young man was sitting stiffly in the left-hand visitor's chair. His hair was expensively coiffed and lacquered. He looked like a salsa kind of guy.

FitzGibbon gave the kid a nod. The salsa guy moved to the less comfortable chair. On the way, he gave me a Look. I wasn't sure what kind of Look it was. But it was definitely a Look.

Security, FitzGibbon said.

Ah, I said.

I wondered what it was about me that seemed dangerous.

FitzGibbon himself had a set of perfectly sculpted New Teeth. Caps, I surmised. They would not have been out of place in a glass display case. In his mouth, on the other hand, they were a bit too big. They gave him a perpetual too-large grin. Which actually wasn't too bad an effect. Something about him, I'd heard, made young female subordinates' heels turn suddenly round, as they used to say.

He also had the Irish flush – which at a distance or in good lighting could have been taken for a Perpetual Tan – together with an Insistent Nose.

In short, he was a prize.

First of all, he said, in a deep voice that betrayed the excessive cultivation of the formerly uncultivated, I'd like to thank you for taking this on. It means a lot to me.

Not a problem, I said. It's my pleasure.

Not to mention that I hardly had a choice, I neglected to add.

Really, it does, he said, as though I might be doubting his sincerity.

I appreciate that, I reassured him.

I guess you know that Jules and I have had our problems, he said.

I've heard a few things.

Well, pay no attention. He's my son. I'm not going to let him twist in the wind.

Of course not.

Wouldn't look good.

He lifted up a large glass ashtray. Shifted it from hand to hand.

Bad for business, he elaborated.

I nodded. I struggled to keep my poker face.

FitzGibbon looked at the lacquered gent in the other chair.

The salsa guy was staring straight at me, scowling. Like I might spring up any second and spray the joint with slugs from a cleverly concealed Uzi.

I know, FitzGibbon said. You think I'm just another arrogant rich guy.

He paused. I did my best to maintain my neutral, expectant air.

Eight kids, he continued. My father left when I was five. Never gave us a dime til he died. Westchester to Hell's Kitchen. Mom died when I was sixteen. I was the oldest. I took care of the rest. Worked my ass off.

I nodded sympathetically.

It wasn't easy.

I can imagine, I said, sincerely. But didn't your father have to pay child support?

Those were different days, he said.

I waited for him to elaborate. He didn't.

I started my own business, he said. I'm not saying I was a genius. I'm no genius. But I built it up from scratch. Machine tools. Built it up. Branched out. Trucking. Taxi fleets. Whatever came along.

I nodded admiringly.

Didn't let anything get in my way, he said, giving me a new kind of Look.

It was the kind of Look that told me it wouldn't be wise to get in his way.

He let the Look linger for a while. I shifted in my chair. The room was uncomfortably warm. My hands felt sticky. I wiped them on my trousers, as discreetly as I could.

And I don't keep it all to myself, he said.

I see, I replied.

Sure. I'm active in the community. The mayor's antidrug task force. I'm the chairman. I fund the whole damn thing.

That's very admirable, I said.

I wondered why he seemed so anxious to impress me.

And then I got lucky, he said.

I raised my eyebrows.

I met Veronica. Beautiful woman. Fell in love with her.

He fixed me with a challenging stare.

I did, he said, with a touch of aggression. Whatever you've heard, we married for love.

The fact was, I'd heard nothing. I had no idea what the hell he was talking about.

So if I've still got a few rough edges . . .

His face went blank. He stared into space.

I took the unfinished sentence as my cue to make a contribution.

Well, I said, I can relate to that.

Really? he said, turning back to me.

Sure. I flunked out of high school myself, originally. Had to go back later, to get into college.

Jesus H. Christ, that a fact? You hear that? he asked, turning to Mr. Hairdo.

Mr. Hairdo didn't take his eyes off me.

It is, I said. Charles probably didn't tell you about that.

No, he didn't. Probably thought I'd be put off.

FitzGibbon pondered for a moment.

Warwick's a pompous ass, he said.

I smiled, involuntarily. Maybe this guy wasn't so bad after all.

My wife's the only reason he gets my business, he continued.

I see, I said.

She and Joan are close.

Joan Warwick?

They were on some conceptual art committee or something together. At the Modern.

Hence the ropy thing on the coffee table, I surmised.

His eyes wandered to the window. I could have sworn they misted up a bit.

I was beginning to wonder when FitzGibbon was planning to get around to talking about his son's little problem. I was also getting a little concerned about the drift of the conversation. I didn't trust myself not to blurt out some random comment about Joan Warwick's taste in men. For all I knew we were being recorded, for Warwick's later entertainment.

I decided to get to the point.

What do you know about Jules's situation? I asked.

He stared at me. He looked confused.

Jules? I repeated. Anything you can tell me about his situation?

Jules? he bellowed. Not a damn thing. I got a call from some public defender guy. Seems Jules didn't have the balls to call home himself.

Well, I said, I suspect he wasn't thinking too clearly.

It was FitzGibbon's turn to give me the raised eyebrow. Thinking I was making some reference to drugs, I surmised.

Stress, you know, I clarified. It's not every day you get arrested. I assume he's never been arrested before?

Not that I know of. But that isn't saying much.

His voice trailed off. He picked up the ashtray again. Gazed at it intently. As though it had some secret to reveal.

I kept my counsel.

He looked up at last.

All right, he barked. Head over there. Find out what's going on. Warwick says you're a top-notch guy. I'll have to take his word for it.

I was flattered. Sort of.

Apparently the audience was over.

I got the particulars from FitzGibbon's secretary. Jules had called from a lockup downtown. She gave me the address.

Mr. Security followed me out. Sat on the edge of her desk. Gave her a smile. Gave me a Look.

I felt like I was interrupting something. Something I probably didn't want to know about.

5.

I GRABBED A CAB. The plastic pine tree air freshener hanging from the mirror did little to disguise the smell of sausage and green peppers.

The jail was bleak. Outside, a prisoner in white coveralls was tending a tiny wilting garden. He gave me an obsequious smile.

Inside, I was ignored. I asked around til someone directed me to a large square woman. She ruled behind an elevated counter fronted by bulletproof glass. One look and she knew my type. The big-shot lawyer hired by someone's daddy. I asked to see Jules FitzGibbon.

Jules FitzGibbon? Harry, you got a Jules FitzGibbon back there? she shouted over her shoulder in a heavy New Jersey accent. It came out 'beck they-ah.'

I heard an indeterminate growl from the back.

Miss New Jersey turned back to me.

Nah, she said. They let him go.

Ah, I said. Well. I understand he was questioned here earlier. Is there someone I can talk to?

She gave me a withering look. Didn't answer.

I had an idea.

Hey, I said, is Butch Hardiman on duty?

Butch? she said. Maybe.

I took that for a yes.

Would you do me a favor and call him? Tell him Rick Redman's here?

She added a layer of skepticism to her cynicism. Picked up the intercom. Paged Butch.

When he came out, Butch had his big smile on for me. Butch was an old buddy. We'd been on opposite sides of a case or two. We understood each other. I asked him if he knew what was up with this Jules FitzGibbon. Told him I was the kid's lawyer.

Don't know much, he said. They brought him in on something. Not enough to hold him on it. Sent him home.

What's the 'something'?

Don't know, he said. Wasn't here when they brought him in.

You got an address for him?

I can get it for you. Ask around a bit.

Hey, I said. Appreciate it. We'll catch up next time.

Sure thing, buddy, he said.

Butch always made me feel good.

6.

IT WAS ALMOST IMPOSSIBLE to get a cab downtown in the afternoon. After ten minutes of futility a beat-up gypsy car rolled by. The driver gave me the 'you need a cab?' look. I leaned in the window to negotiate.

The guy smelled of anchovies.

I got in anyway.

The traffic was hell. Why should today be different from any other day? Hey. Not so bad. Gave me time to think.

I leaned back.

I thought about my life.

It wasn't entertaining stuff.

I thought about Melissa.

Some months before, we'd taken her to the Emergency. She'd fallen down, hit the bathtub with her head. Kelly had found her, lying on the tiles in a pool of blood as big as Lake Wobegon. Melissa had opened her eyes.

How was school? she'd said to Kelly.

She was that far gone.

Kelly had called me at the office. I'd interrupted my nap. Rushed home. We'd tried to get her into the car, but she wouldn't go.

There's nothing wrong with me, you prick, she'd yelled, blood spraying from her mouth.

So we'd had to call the cops. She'd liked that even less. They'd strapped her down. Loaded her into the ambulance.

She'd let loose with a few nouns and adjectives I didn't know she knew, before the EMTs shot something into her, and she got quiet. Kelly and I sat with her in the back, on flimsy fold-out seats. I felt too big, like an adult in kindergarten. Kelly's eyes were red from crying. I couldn't think of anything to say.

They kept her for five days. She'd lost a lot of blood. Had a minor stroke along the way. No permanent damage, they said. I wondered. I still wonder.

Kelly and I went to the hospital to pick her up. A nurse brought her to us in a wheelchair. She seemed small. Humbled. It was strange to see her that way. Disconcerting.

I'd never thought of her as small.

We were taken to see Steiglitz.

There was something too slick about Steiglitz. He had that George Hamilton thing. Bronze tan, set off beautifully against his pristine white lab coat. Sparkling, manicured teeth. Six foot five if he was an inch. Smooth baritone. Vaguely European accent.

Come to think of it, there was a whole lot too slick about him.

But he was good at what he did. The best, I'd been told.

He made us wait. Kelly sat on the green couch. I sat in the armchair. Behind the desk, a large picture window gave on to the East River, dark and languid in the rain. Brooklyn on the other side. A large windowless building dominated the view.

We all stared out the window.

We didn't talk.

There was nothing to say.

Steiglitz entered, filling the room with color and charisma. As if from another world. Large. Larger than life.

We were diminished.

He strode to the desk. Sat down. Looked us each in the eye, ending with Melissa.

Hello, Melissa, he said.

Hello, Dr. Steiglitz, she replied.

You've got a problem.

I know, she whispered.

He turned to me.

It's very simple, he said. When it gets to this point, there's nothing we can do.

He paused to let that one sink in.

As professionals, I mean. The best we can do is show you the way. Give you some tools.

Okay, I said.

She's not going to change.

Though he looked straight at her as he said this, he spoke in the third person.

Unless, he continued.

Unless?

Unless she hits rock bottom.

If this wasn't rock bottom, I asked myself, what was?

And even then, he said. Even then. There's no guarantee. This has gone very far. But I can tell you, with complete assurance, that if she doesn't hit rock bottom, nothing will change. Or at least, if she doesn't really, truly believe that next time, she's going to hit rock bottom.

He paused, but clearly wasn't finished.

We waited.

He looked straight at Melissa.

She'll be dead within a year, he said. Maybe two.

No emotion showed on his face. He was simply stating a fact. His voice was still the silky baritone of the late-night radio announcer.

Melissa looked at the floor.

I'm trying, she mumbled.

You're trying, he said, a note of sarcasm creeping in. All right. Let's examine that. What is the longest period of time you've gone without a drink? In the last year.

There was a long pause while she thought about that.

I quit at Christmas, she said at last.

Kelly looked up at me, brows knitted. If she had quit at Christmas, it was news to us. She'd been, if anything, more absent then than ever.

I didn't ask you when, said Steiglitz. I asked you how long.

He was slowly raising his voice. Playing the prosecutor. Melissa was so shrunken, so beaten down. I felt protective. I wanted to say something. But Steiglitz gave me a Look.

The Look said: Don't do it.

How long did you quit for? he repeated.

Three weeks, she said, barely audible.

Three weeks, he nodded. When did you stop?

Christmas Eve. I stopped on Christmas Eve. I wanted to be there for Kelly.

We could barely hear her. Kelly looked at her feet. Melissa hadn't been there Christmas Eve. She'd been asleep in Kelly's room. We'd eaten without her.

And when did you start again?

Kelly's birthday, she mumbled.

When is Kelly's birthday?

The fifth.

January fifth?

Yes.

I looked at Steiglitz, a question in my eyes. What did all this mean?

He ignored me.

How many days in three weeks? he asked.

He was boring in.

Twenty-one, she mumbled.

How many days between December twenty-fourth and January fifth?

She was silent.

How many, Melissa?

Thirteen, she whispered.

Twelve, Melissa. Twelve days.

Twelve.

Not three weeks.

No.

Not even two.

No.

She looked up at Steiglitz for the first time. She seemed strangely pleased. As though she had enjoyed his performance. Or perhaps it was relief. That somebody at last was confronting the Monster.

He looked at me.

So, he said.

Silence.

Rock bottom, he said.

What does that mean? Kelly asked, with a flash of impatience. What's rock bottom?

The street, he said.

The street?

She has to know that if she takes another drink, another pill, she's on the street. That's it. She's gone. You're going to disown her.

You're telling me to throw my wife out on the street? I asked.

Only if she has another drink. Or takes another pill.

He looked at me placidly. It occurred to me that he had had this conversation many times before. An infinite array of naive and loving husbands, fathers, sons. Anguished. Confused. Protesting.

I thought of all the homeless people on the streets I walked. They'd hit bottom, to all appearances. They didn't look too cured to me.

I suddenly felt very tired. I just wanted to go home.

He's right, you know, said Kelly.

She never failed to surprise me.

Melissa looked resigned. Steiglitz looked smug.

It seemed that everyone understood but me.

Steiglitz prescribed three Valium a day, for five more days. To ward off the DTs. Then nothing. Antabuse. AA. And patience. One day at a time. Not just for her. For us.

When we got up to leave, Steiglitz came around his desk. He shook my hand, and Kelly's. He turned and put his arms around Melissa, hugged her.

He was so tall, so manicured.

She was so small, so disheveled.

7.

JULES LIVED IN A CONVERTED FACTORY on the lower East Side. More factory than converted.

I rang the bell.

I rang it again.

I rang it a third time.

A sleepy voice finally responded.

Yeah? it said.

Jules?

Yo.

Jules, I said, I'm a lawyer. Your father sent me.

Hmph, he responded.

Jules, I said again, a bit louder.

Silence.

Do you think you might let me in?

Silence.

I was girding for more repartee when the door finally buzzed. I pulled it open just in time.

I took an ancient elevator to the third floor. Found Jules's place. The door was ajar. I invited myself in.

The loft was huge, asymmetrical. A balcony ran across one end. Bedroom up there, I surmised. The lower space was entirely open. The ceiling must have been at least twenty feet high. Exposed metal girders, painted primary colors. Blue, yellow, red. The effect was startling, but pleasant. The space was big enough to take the color. At the far end, tall arched windows, a spectacular view of the tenements across the street. A kitchen counter against the left-hand wall, underneath the balcony, piled with pizza boxes, takeout cartons, beer bottles.

A body was lying on a large tattered couch. My client's, I presumed. It had its back to me.

Sit up, I said to the back of its head. I need to talk to you.

It rolled over and opened its eyes. They were gray and out of focus.

Who are you? he asked.

A reasonable question, I assured him. I'm Rick Redman. Your father sent me.

He considered that information. He eyed me intently. His eyes were focused now.

Fuck him, he said at last.

I'd be glad to do that, if I get the chance, I said, attempting to curry favor. But right now he's paying me to represent you. And if I were you I'd take advantage of it.

He thought some more.

Fuck him, he repeated.

Okay, I said. Fuck him. Now let's get down to business. You're in some shit here. I don't actually know what kind of shit yet, but you can help me with that. I think it's safe to say it's going to take some work to get you out of it.

He sat up. He looked at me with curiosity. His eyes stayed gray. He looked down at his shoes. Standard-issue paint-splattered high-tops. Faux-camouflage overalls. Metallica T-shirt. Nose ring. Hair dyed an unnatural henna red. In short, the downtown works.

He's paying you? he asked.

Yep.

Why?

I looked for tracks on his arms. Didn't see any.

I don't know. Maybe because he's your dad?

That wouldn't explain it.

Well, it's all the explanation I've got today. Anyway, I'm not here to be a marriage counselor. I'm here to get you out of whatever shit you're in.

He considered that.

In that case, he said at last, I guess you're hired.

Good, I said, taking a seat.

Fuck him, he said again. This time the emphasis was on the first word: *Fuck*'m.

Okay, I said. *Fuck*'m. Right now, I need you to tell me what happened. Beginning at the beginning. Continuing to the end, which is right here right now. Then we figure out what to do about it. First thing, you didn't do it, right?

I didn't do shit.

Good. That's the right answer. Now, tell me all about what you didn't do. In other words, what happened?

Shit happened.

Yeah, I know. Shit happens.

He snorted.

So, what exactly kind of shit happened?

There was a fight.

A fight?

Yeah. A fight.

What kind of a fight?

A fight, man. A fight. What kind of a fight do you think?

I don't know. That's why I'm asking the questions. Listen, Jules, this is going to take a very long time if it keeps going like this. I'm not the cops. I'm your lawyer. I can't help you if you don't help me.

Meaning?

Meaning, can you just answer the damn questions?

He considered this for a while.

Okay, he said. You got a smoke?

As a matter of fact I do, I said, but I doubt they're your style.

I fished out my pack of ultra-light menthols.

Shit, he said. My brand.

For the first time, he'd surprised me.

I thought you'd be a Marlboro-type guy, I said.

Yeah, me too, he replied. But I like these. Maybe I'm half black or something. Or half a fag.

Right, I said, lighting his and mine, I guess I am too. So, let's get back to the story.

The fight story?

Yeah. The fight story. Who was fighting?

Me and this guy.

What guy?

A buddy of mine. Larry.

Larry who?

Larry Silver.

What were you fighting about?

Money.

What money?

Money he said I owed him.

How much?

Two grand.

Two grand? That's a lot of money.

That's a lot of money.

And you don't agree that you owe him the money?

Owed him. No. I didn't.

Why 'owed'?

What do you mean?

Why the past tense?

You don't owe a dead man money, do you?

It depends. But wait a minute. I guess we need to back up a bit here. He's dead?

Yeah. He's dead. What the fuck. They didn't tell you that?

They didn't tell me anything.

I'd been thinking simple assault. Aggravated at most. Plead it down. Make Daddy happy. Get back to the quiet life of litigation, drink and gambling.

Were there any weapons involved in this fight? I asked.

Nah. Hands. Feet.

How did he die?

I don't know.

He didn't die right there?

Shit no. Broke his nose maybe. That's all.

So how did he die?

I told you, I don't know. They found him later.

Who found him later?

I don't know.

Then why did you say 'they'?

I don't know. It's what you say.

Where was he when they found him?

I don't know. I don't know shit.

What did they find?

They found him dead, man. Shit. I'm getting a little tired of this crap.

Okay, okay. You don't know shit. All right.

He put out his hand for another cigarette. I gave him one. I took one for myself.

We smoked awhile.

Okay, I said. I'm going to have to get some information.

Sounds like it.

Before I go, just tell me the whole story again. What you do know. The fight. From the beginning. I'll stop asking questions.

That'd be good.

All right then. Shoot.

Larry came over. He was pissed. He said I owed him money. From the poker game.

Poker game. Hm. Maybe I had some expertise to bring to this case after all.

Two grand, he said. I said, Fuck you, man, I don't owe you no two grand. We settled up last night. I mean, he was too wasted to remember shit anyway.

And?

So he starts yelling and shit, all kindsa bullshit. I could tell he was wired. I don't know what he was doing, mescaline or something. He had that paranoid thing in his eyes. I couldn't even understand what he was saying half the time. So I told him to fuck off and come back when he came down. But that just got him more pissed off. He picks up a bottle, and he's waving it at me, a beer bottle, and he's saying he's going to kill me. So I dive at him, low, going to take him out at the knees. And then it was just punching and wrestling and shit, and I guess he let go the bottle at some point, 'cause he never hit me with it. And sometime in there I must've busted him in the nose, 'cause he's bleeding all over from it, and after a while we're just both all tired out, and we lie there for a while, breathing heavy, and I say, Shit, Larry, what the fuck? And he's, Fuck you, man, and he gets up and walks out, and he slams the door.

And that's it?

That's it, man. Next thing I know the cops are at the door, and they're telling me I killed the guy.

So you never heard from him after he left?

Nah.

Anybody see any of this fight? Hear it?

Shit, somebody had to hear it. There's fifty people in the building. It's lofts. It's an old factory building. You can hear everything. I hear the next-door neighbors fucking six times a night.

Okay. All right. I've got to go ask some questions. Don't go anywhere.

Yeah, sure. I'll cancel them plane tickets.

I started thinking I kind of liked this kid. Feisty little guy. I might even start to believe his stupid story, you gave me a little time.

8.

ON THE WAY HOME, I stopped at the Wolf's Lair. I took my usual seat next to the cash register.

I worked on a double Scotch, and the seventeenth draft of an article for *World Oil* magazine. I was bored.

I read the letter tacked to the wall behind the register. I'd read it before. A hundred times, at least. It was on the letterhead of a Dr. Fritzinger. It said:

Dear Thom,
Just a note to let you know your lab results were all
ok. Thanks.

Sincerely,

Natalie,

Medical Assistant

I wondered, as usual, what it was doing there, pinned to the cork above the telephone.

But I never asked. If I did, they'd probably figure I didn't get the joke. Whatever it was.

A young guy sat down next to me. Well, younger than me. He was maybe thirty-five. He ordered a whiskey sour.

Hey, he said.

Hey, I replied.

What's that you're writing?

An article.

Really? You a writer?

Not really. I'm a lawyer.

Oh, he said. So, what's it about? The O.J. case?

No, I laughed. I don't think they care too much about O.J. anymore. Old news.

Right.

It's just a little thing for *World Oil* magazine.

He leaned closer. I could smell aftershave.

World Oil? he said. Don't think I've heard of it.

I'd be surprised if you had. The circulation's only about three thousand.

Really?

He seemed genuinely interested.

So, why would you want to write an article for them?

It's a very rich three thousand.

Ah.

Very, very rich.

So, you're an oil lawyer?

No. Just a litigator. Sometimes oil companies are involved.

Right. So, what's it about?

It's about the difficulty of enforcing an arbitration award in Kazakhstan.

Ah. Interesting.

No, I said, it's not. But it looks good on the resume.

Ah.

I went back to my article. I looked for wrongly italicized commas. That's what you do when you get to draft seventeen.

The guy went back to his drink.

A few minutes later he leaned back in. The aftershave was musky, pungent.

I'm an actor, he said.

Really? That's great.

Not so great. I'm not working right now.

I'm sure something will come up.

It always does. But I'm in a dry spell right now.

That's too bad.

Last thing I did was a hair loss thing.

A hair loss thing?

Yeah. You know, one of those spray-it-on-your-bald-spot things. A commercial.

Right, I said, glancing at his long, full hair. Well, it looks very natural.

It was funny, he laughed. They tricked me out in a bald man hair-piece. Itched like hell.

Why wouldn't they just hire a bald guy?

I don't know. I guess I had the look they were going for.

I pondered that one.

By the way, he said.

Yes?

You need any carpentry work done?

Gee, I don't know. You a carpenter too?

Yeah. When I can't find work. But don't get me wrong. I'm good. I used to do it for a living. My former life. I'm not one of those waiters looking for a break. Like that one over there.

I looked around.

The one with the bow tie, he said.

Ah, I laughed. Him. Yes.

I'm not like that. I'm a serious guy.

Yes. I can see you've got some substance.

You can?

He was surprised. Pleased.

Kind of charming. Innocent.

So anyway, he said. I can do anything. Rough work. Fine work. Whatever you need. Just to tide me over. Til I get another gig.

Gotcha, I said. Right.

Maybe I can find something for this guy, I thought. Nothing big. Can't afford anything big right now. A little thing. A bookshelf, a table.

Well, I said. Let me think about it. There might be something I could use you for.

Great, he said, getting up to leave. Hey, I'm here all the time. Just drop by and let me know. Or leave a message with Thom.

Sure. I'll do that. Nice talking to you.

Jake, he said, putting out his hand.

Rick, I said, reciprocating.

His hand was warm. Dry. His grip was loose.

Funny. I'd never seen him there before.

9.

I GOT HOME BEFORE MIDNIGHT. An early night. I felt virtuous.

Melissa was still up. She was on the sofa, reading, reclining, legs curled beneath her. Black hair. Green eyes. She was beautiful. After eighteen years, I was still startled by it.

She had a smile for me that night. I basked in it.

What's up, love?

Nothing, she said. Just reading.

What?

Oh, nothing.

She was embarrassed. It was something about feng shui. Or pressure points. Anti-carcinogenic foot massage. She knew I'd laugh. Yes, darling, my liver feels so much better, now that you've squeezed my pinkie just so. Others have squeezed my pinkie before. But not in just that way.

She wouldn't find it funny.

She was fragile.

I sat next to her. I took her hand. Her fingers were long, patrician. Her skin was dry. There were small, eloquent lines at the corners of her eyes.

She was not so young anymore.

It bothered her.

I met a kind of interesting guy tonight, I said.

Really? she replied.

She sat up a little straighter. An unusual concession.

I was encouraged.

He seemed like a nice enough guy, I continued.

Oh?

I told her a bit about him. The carpentry thing.

'But don't get me wrong,' I quoted him, 'I'm good. I know what I'm doing.'

She laughed at that. A brittle sort of laugh.

I thought maybe I could get him to do a bookshelf. For the bedroom.

Sure, she said.

I'll invite him over.

Sure.

Her eyes returned to her book.

The audience was over.

I trudged upstairs.

10.

NEXT MORNING MY BACK FELT GOOD. I told Judy to cancel my appointment with Dr. Altmeier.

I gave Butch a call. Figured he might know a little bit by now.

Meet me later, he suggested. The usual hang.

Gotcha, I said.

I marked up some briefs. I took a three-hour lunch meeting with a bottle and a half of Corton Charlemagne. 1998. Not as good a conversationalist as Dorita, but it had a good nose and a long finish.

I took a nap. I made a few phone calls. I grabbed a cab. It smelled of sardines. The traffic was hell. I thought about the Case of the Red Car Door.

My client, Juan Perros, had been convicted on the testimony of one witness, his girlfriend, who hadn't actually seen him commit the crime. Now, I didn't know whether Juan did it or not. I still don't. But I did think that something wasn't right. It didn't pass the smell test. There just wasn't enough evidence presented to the jury to take a man's freedom away. It seemed clear to me that Juan was put away on the basis of nothing more than preconceived notions about guys named Juan from Brooklyn.

Jury verdicts are awfully hard to overturn, though, and I had to find something other than the fact that Juan's court-appointed lawyer had slept through large parts of the trial. That didn't make him any less effective than half the criminal lawyers in town.

I was lucky. I found Butch. It wasn't his case, directly. He'd been a minor witness. But he had a sense of justice that was, shall we say, somewhat more nuanced than that of many of his colleagues. And with his help I found the one thing that was guaranteed to spring Juan. Prosecutorial misconduct. Big, juicy prosecutorial misconduct. Up-the-wazoo prosecutorial misconduct.

When they'd arrested Juan, they'd taken pictures of his car. The car was a black Chevy Impala, just like the one that had been seen at the crime scene. But, as was plain to see from at least two of the photos, photos that appeared mysteriously in my e-mail in the middle of the night, it wasn't all black. It had a bright shiny red driver's side door that Juan had gotten from a junkyard to replace the original after he'd been sideswiped in a 3 a.m. drag race on Prospect Boulevard.

More importantly for the appeal, the prosecutor had never seen fit to share the photos with Juan's lawyer. And nobody at the trial ever testified that they'd seen a black Impala *with a bright red driver's side door* at the crime scene.

So there I had it: not only prosecutorial misconduct, but misconduct that, especially given the flimsy state of the evidence, had clearly had a material impact on the verdict.

So I got Juan out of jail. Whether he was re-tried and re-convicted, I don't know. I don't want to know. I don't want to know whether he turned around and murdered someone else, either. I felt ambivalent enough about the case as it was. I mean, frankly, the guy probably did do it. It made me remember why I hadn't gone in for criminal defense work in the first place.

But the case got me a little publicity for a time. SELFLESS CRUSADER FOR JUSTICE RESCUES INNOCENT MAN FROM PRISON. All that shit. I didn't bother enlightening the reporters. That I'd only taken on the case to fulfill a pledge the firm had made to the Bar Association. They would have ignored that detail anyway. Why let the facts get in the way of a good story?

More important, the case got me a friend. Butch admired what I'd done for Juan. And I appreciated what he'd done for me, at considerable risk to his career. We hung out a bit. He'd invite me to the weekly poker game with some of his guys once in a while, when they had an extra chair. Cops and goombahs. A fun crowd. We had a bond. An unspoken, unnamed bond that's shared by those who have walked the fine, fine lines of legal ethics on the edge. The place where nobody can tell you what the answer is. You have to make the call yourself, and live with it. With others' freedom in the balance.

That's why I knew he'd give me something. At least that he wouldn't brush me off with a quote from the manual. 'Members of the force are not to talk to defense attorneys without a member of the Departmental Legal Staff present,' or whatever.

11.

BUTCH'S HANG WAS THE VELVET DOG, across the street from the twenty-ninth precinct. Best to approach him there, where he'd be comfortable. A couple of drinks down and I'd be more comfortable too.

The place was full of noise when I arrived. Full of noise and beer and friendship. There were groups of two and three and four dispersed throughout the joint, each group enclosed in its own small world of warmth, shared experience and feeling.

I found a seat in the back. I ordered a Guinness. A meal in itself. Thick, meaty and nutritious. Carbs enough for a week.

I nursed it.

I thought about stuff.

The kind of sweaty camaraderie that now was all around me made me more than faintly uncomfortable. I'd missed the locker room thing. I'd spent my adolescence avoiding it. Cultivating contempt for sweaty guys who'd never heard of Dostoevsky. I was always smaller than the rest, and slower. Lacking killer instinct. Late to sport the hair and manliness you needed to compete for shower space and recognition.

I was on my second Guinness when I spied Butch, coming in the door, nodding and smiling, shaking hands and slapping shoulders. In his element.

I let him settle in. When he seemed as comfortable as a man can be, I contrived to sidle up to him.

Hey Butch, I said, good to see you.

Rick, my man, he said. How goes the battle?

It goes. It doesn't go. Shit happens. Then it doesn't.

I think I get the drift, he laughed. Sounds like my life, too.

I smiled. I put a hand on his shoulder.

Come on back, I said.

I nodded to my booth.

Sure, he said. Give me a minute. I got to talk to some guys.

I retreated to the back. Butch made the rounds. Some backslapping here, a little joking there.

He was a big guy. Broad-shouldered and black as Kenyan coffee, with a smooth shaved head that somehow made him look even bigger. But he also had that huge warm smile, and a soft side that he knew how to use to his advantage.

Ten minutes later, he made his way to the booth. He sat down.

So what can I do for you, my friend?

Butch did not stand on ceremony. It was one of the things I liked about him. No need to indulge in the tribal chitchat. Get to the point.

Hey, I said, I know you've got your rules. But I was hoping you could tell me what you can.

He gave me a knowing smile.

Hey, Rick, he said, you're not tight with Internal Affairs, are you?

Not on this one, I laughed. Next time maybe.

Okay, just wanted to make sure. Anyway, I don't mind telling you what I know, because what I know isn't much. I hear it's pretty cut and dried, Rick.

That may be so, I said. But I've got my job to do. The kid says he didn't do it.

Well, there's a shock.

I know, I know, I smiled. But I got to tell you, there's something very believable about him. He's an angry kid. But I don't see any guile in him.

You don't need guile to hit a guy upside the head with a blunt instrument.

All right. I know. I'm not going to convince you of anything.

You always were a wimp.

Just tell me what you can.

He gave it some thought. He ran his hands over his cleanly shaven head.

Okay, here's what I know. The guys have a fight. Sounded pretty damn vicious. A lot of thumping and banging and yelling. Then it all goes quiet. We got a time on that. One thirty-five a.m. Almost exactly an hour later, some homeless guy in an alley about three blocks away picks up a big cardboard box. Going to use it for a house or something. And under the box is the body of this kid. His face is half caved in. Blunt trauma. Kid's dead as a doorknob. They haven't found the weapon yet.

Nose broken.

Whole fucking face broken, Rick.

Any witnesses?

Not that I know about. Old lady in the building on the other side of the alley thinks she heard something. But she's vague about it. So far, nobody saw nothing.

So how'd they find Jules?

Somebody in his building called in a complaint about the noise. When they were fighting. Nobody'd got around to showing up by the time the body was found. But after that, somebody made the connection.

So it's all circumstantial. Not enough to arrest him on.

They usually are, my friend, Butch laughed. But yeah. Sort of. Brought him in, but couldn't hold him. Took them hours to get a warrant to search the kid's place. Got the wrong judge.

Albertson?

You got it. What's the probable cause, he says. Shit.

Well, there are two sides to that argument.

I guess, he smiled. They're doing tests now. The usual forensic stuff. Talk to me in a couple of days. The picture might be different.

Could have been random. A mugging.

Sure. Always possible. But it didn't look like it. Too vicious. Looked like something personal.

I asked whether they had tracked down Larry Silver's relatives, friends. Looked for folks with grudges.

Sure, he said. The family's in Kansas somewhere. Hadn't heard from him in two years. Nice old folks. Had Larry late in life. Couldn't understand what went wrong. His brother is twenty years older. Has a good job down at the feedlot. Comes to dinner every Sunday. Something just clicked in Larry one day, when he was fifteen or so. Gone wild, they said. Like a barnyard dog. Nothing you could do but stay away from him. And then he left town. Didn't tell anyone. Didn't leave a note. Never wrote. Never called. They'd just sort of written him off. Hoped one day he'd come to his senses. Give them a call. Send a postcard.

Friends?

The usual losers you get with a guy like that. Small-time dealers. Runaways like him. He'd lived in Riverside Park for a while. Stretched some plastic between two trees. Begged for quarters. Til some local punks rousted him out of there. Got lucky. Ran into somebody who got him a job. Flipping burgers somewhere. Didn't last long. Just long enough for him to get a little place in Williamsburg, pay a couple months' rent. Nobody really liked him much. He was a moody guy. Chip on his shoulder. But nobody really hated him either. They just tolerated him.

Not much to go on.

Not much.

I don't have the resources to reinvent the wheel, I said. Do me a favor, if you can, Butch. Just get the details on a couple of kids most likely to have information about him. Who knew him best. Who might know something. I might find something your guys missed.

Always possible, Rick. I'll see what I can do.

From most people, that would be a no. From Butch, it was a yes.

All right, I said. Hey, I really appreciate this, Butch.

Rick, I owe you. You know that.

Actually, I didn't know that. But I was happy to let him think so.

12.

I REMEMBERED DORITA. Damn. I'd completely forgotten we'd arranged to meet the night before.

I called her up. Begged for forgiveness.

If you'd remembered, she laughed, I'd have fallen off my chair.

We arranged to meet at the Monkey Bar. For the first time I noticed the pun. Monkey bars. Hah.

Despite the name, it was more upscale than the Wolf's Lair. More Dorita's style. Plush sofas. Indirect lighting. Colored drinks.

I spied Dorita in the corner. She'd snagged our favorite spot. A small banquette, largely blocked from view. It made it hard to hail a waitress, but it helped the conversation. You felt you were alone.

I ordered a Scotch, Dorita a cosmopolitan. Her drink was pale red and pretty. A cherry in it. She crossed her legs. They were pale and pretty too.

I was thinking, I said.

You were thinking.

I was.

Dangerous.

I was thinking that I really ought to give up this racket.

Here we go again.

No. I mean it. I really do.

But you can't afford to.

There's the problem.

Don't you owe the IRS a half a million?

Well, yes. Rehab's expensive. Fifteen times in rehab is fifteen times more expensive. And not tax-deductible.

Then stop dreaming.

There's always bankruptcy.

Talk to Mort, darling. They never let you go. A tax debt never goes away. Bankruptcy or no bankruptcy.

I've heard that.

It's true. Talk to Mort.

But that would only matter if I had a job, some assets.

Oh. I see. Hit the road? Beg for quarters? You're too old for that, Rick. And anyway, you're not that romantic anymore.

You'd be surprised.

Yes. I would.

Anyway, the idea is, I could play poker for a living.

Rick, your brilliance is exceeded only by your naïveté.

I guess you're right.

The Gang of Eight had a meeting.

My fellow probationists?

Right.

I wasn't invited.

I'm not surprised, Ricky. You're such a goddamn recluse.

True, true. And I wouldn't be in this mess if I weren't. Believe me, darling, I try.

I know you do. You should call up Martin. Tell him to include you. It's like a support group. They're all helping each other. Getting together to drum up new business.

I'll think about it, I said, in a tone intended to close the topic.

So, she said, picking up the cue, tell me about your visit with Jules.

Interesting kid. I kind of like him. Feisty. Doesn't take any shit. A kid his age, you'd think he'd be terrified. But he isn't. He's quite cool about it.

That could be interpreted two ways. At least.

Yes. You're right. And I'm not sure I believe his story.

Okay. But did he do it?

I don't know. And I'm not sure I want to know. I'm not sure he told me the whole truth, and nothing but. In fact, I'm quite sure he didn't. And he may well have done it. But he's not evil. If he did it, I'm guessing, there were circumstances.

She asked me for the details.

There aren't a whole lot of details yet, I said. What I know isn't too helpful. The kid's story doesn't buy him much. It's not a whole lot more substantial than 'I didn't do it.' But they don't have any physical evidence to tie him to it. Still less an eyewitness. But there's all this other stuff going on. Between Jules and Dad. Weird stuff. I can't shake the feeling that they're all playing some kind of game. At my expense.

Wow. You're even more fucked up than usual today. Tell me more.

I recounted my meetings with FitzGibbon and Jules, my talk with Butch.

Intriguing, she said. Lots of loose ends. I guess there's enough for you to play Philip Marlowe for a few more days.

So come play with me.

Now you're talking my language.

Not that. Butch gave me a couple of names. Let's check them out.

Good old-fashioned PI spadework?

Exactly.

Could be fun.

Or not.

Worth a try.

Okay, there's a Sarah Fishlin. Apparently she'd been Larry's girlfriend for a while. Actually made it through a semester at Brooklyn College one time. Very high-functioning, for this crowd. She's a stripper now. You take Sarah.

Sure. Clearly my type.

And I'll take Serge. Reportedly a dealer on the neighborhood level. Larry might have bought from him. They knew each other, anyway.

That sounds vague enough.

You never know.

All right. Let's check them out tomorrow. White Stallion at seven, compare notes?

The White Stallion. Decent food, good wine list.

Couldn't say no.

13.

BUTCH HAD GIVEN ME AN ADDRESS for Serge in Williamsburg. I took the subway. Get me into the proletarian mood.

It wasn't the funky part of Williamsburg, the land of mediocre poets and art-house filmmakers who couldn't afford Manhattan. It wasn't even the upwardly striving immigrant Williamsburg, which in any case was largely indistinguishable from the funky bits. It was bombed-out Williamsburg. Empty lots choked with trash and hopelessness. Crumbling buildings that might once have housed a thriving sweatshop or two. Rows of shabby two- and three-family tin-sided houses. Graffiti so old you figured even the vandals had fled the place long ago.

I found the address. Boarded-up windows. Broken concrete steps leading to a steel-reinforced door. A casual glance and you might think the place was abandoned. But the steps were cleaner in the middle than at the edges. If you looked from the right angle, in the sunlight, you could make out a boot print or two. On the door, two ancient heavy-duty locks. Scratches in the grime around the keyholes. Someone with a shaking hand had been there, not so long ago.

I banged on the door. I listened for movement. I thought I heard a footstep. I couldn't be sure. I banged again. Nothing.

I looked up and down the street. Not a soul. I felt exposed. I turned to go.

A muffled voice stopped me.

What do you want? it said from behind the door.

I told the voice I was a lawyer. Not the cops. A private lawyer. Looking into a case. Nothing to do with him. Just had a few questions.

The voice asked me to wait a couple of minutes.

Okay, I said.

More than a couple went by. I sighed. Slipped a twenty under the door. A minute later, the door opened a crack. A long pale face peeked out. Stringy hair. Dark rings around reddened eyes.

Yeah? it said.

Serge?

What's it to you?

I took that for a yes.

Keep the twenty, I said. No obligation. But I'd like to talk to you. Just a few minutes. You don't have to tell me anything. Just listen to the questions.

It gave me a good long look. Pronounced itself satisfied. Unhooked a couple of chains. Let me in. Didn't say a word. Went down a flight of stairs.

I followed.

We were in a basement. It was lit by candles. As my eyes adjusted to the dark I looked around. There wasn't much to see. Stone walls. Concrete floors.

Serge sat down cross-legged on a cushion on the floor. The guy was junkie thin. He was wearing a tattered Adidas tracksuit. His bare feet were black with grime. A gold chain around his neck glinted in the candlelight. It seemed utterly out of place.

I sat on the floor next to him. I refrained from pulling up my trousers to preserve the crease. Might have sent the wrong message.

He looked at me without a trace of interest.

Serge? I said.

I got an almost imperceptible nod in reply.

I'm Rick.

Congratulations.

I'm trying to help out a guy.

A guy.

Guy named Jules FitzGibbon. I'm his lawyer. You know Jules?

Maybe.

They think he might have killed somebody.

No shit, said Serge, flat and uninterested.

You knew that?

No.

Okay, well. Murder. Serious stuff.

No shit, he said again, in the same flat voice.

Yeah. They say he killed Larry Silver.

No shit?

This time he added the question mark. I was making progress. Pretty soon we'd be best friends.

Yeah, I said. You knew Larry Silver?

Maybe.

What do you know about him?

He's a guy, he said. Guy who hung around.

Serge and Jules must have gone to the same elocution school.

He have any enemies? Anybody might want to kill him?

I don't know, man, said Serge.

He was warming up a bit.

Can you tell me anything else about him?

He was just a guy. Hung around. I don't know anybody liked him much. I don't know anybody wanted to kill him, neither.

He have any friends you know of?

He had a girlfriend, for a while.

You know her name?

Nah.

Sarah?

Don't know.

Was he into drugs?

Serge almost smiled. Didn't say anything.

Listen, man, I said. I'm a lawyer. I'm not a cop. I'm here right now. I got eyes. Don't worry about it.

Serge thought about it.

Yeah, he said.

What was he into?

Whatever was around. You know. Tree. Meth. Whatever.

Did he sell?

When he had some money to buy, he'd sell. What he didn't do hisself.

I'm thinking that wasn't too often.

You got that right.

Did he and Jules know each other?

Sure. Everybody knows everybody.

Anything special between them? They hate each other? Hang together?

Nothing special I know about.

You know anything about a poker game, a few days ago?

Poker? Shit, no. I don't play no poker.

Not you. A game that Larry and Jules were at.

Nah.

Anything else you can tell me? I asked. About either of them?

Serge sat and thought. And thought. I rolled my eyes. Pulled another twenty out of my pocket. I placed it neatly on the floor in front of him. He eyed it. He thought some more.

I think they had some kind of a deal going, he said. One day. Once.

What kind of a deal? Dope deal?

I don't know. Maybe.

Anything you know about it at all?

Nah. Not really. Larry saying something about how they had something going. He was going to get some money out of it.

Some kind of poker scam? I persisted. They going to take somebody for some money?

Could be. I don't know.

Anybody else you know might know something about it?

Nah.

I asked a few more questions. I didn't learn anything more. He was a slug. A cipher. He couldn't even make stuff up if he wanted to.

I got out of there.

The light and air of the outside world startled me. I squinted. My eyes slowly adjusted. I took a deep breath. A whole bunch of tension I hadn't known was there slid out of me.

Jesus H. Christ, I said to myself. I thought *I* had problems.

14.

WHEN I GOT TO THE WHITE STALLION, Dorita was already there. We compared notes. I told her about Serge. She told me about Sarah.

She's quite a number, she said. Purple hair. Mouth on her like a rabid carp.

A rabid carp? You're outdoing yourself.

I'm just getting started.

I was afraid of that.

She talked up a storm. But she didn't say much.

You must have got along famously.

Have you noticed how pointy these shoes are?

Sorry.

You'd better be.

I am. Truly. Abjectly. As sorry as those shoes are pointy.

That sounds like just about the right amount of sorry.

I like it when things work out like that. Can we get back to Sarah?

I found her in a bar downtown. Ratty couches. Black light. Candles. Nice.

She was smoking a clove cigarette.

Ugh.

Indeed. She was a little uptight at first. The cops had talked to her yesterday. Seems she wasn't too happy about that. Not a big fan. Didn't have anything to tell them. On the other hand, she didn't have much to tell me, either.

Did she admit to being Larry's girlfriend?

She didn't exactly deny it. She didn't like the word. But she lived with him. Some dank little studio off Delancey Street. She was with him the day he died, earlier on. She didn't know anything about Jules. Or any money Larry owed him.

Not a whole lot of help.

No, but she did tell me a bit about the guy. Sounded like a snake.

A loser kind of snake.

Not a great snake success. But he was always looking for a scam. Always thinking the next one was going to be the big one. They'd be set for life.

The usual.

Sure. He was talking about how if his parents were rich he and Sarah could pretend he was kidnapped, get a ransom out of them, disappear with the money. But his parents are some kind of farmers or something.

So I've heard.

They wouldn't get far with a goat and some chickens.

I guess they could ride the goat out of town.

Into the sunset.

Sure.

I mean, she seemed to find him sort of sexy, in a loser sort of way. I got a bit of S&M flavor, from the way she talked about him. He had a mean streak. Had his share of incidents. Big scar on his stomach he said came from a knife fight. Never been arrested, though. Or so she said. Strangely enough, for a guy like that.

What about the poker angle? She know anything about this poker game?

Nothing specific. He played poker. Went off to a game once in a while, usually all night. He'd come home after the sun had come up. Sometimes he'd have a bunch of cash. More often tapped out.

Did she know who he played with?

Just 'the guys.' You know.

Not inconceivable that he and Jules had cooked up some kind of poker scam. Ripped somebody off. Made an enemy. Or argued over the spoils.

One doesn't exclude the other.

Could be either. Or both.

But if it happened, she didn't know anything about it.

Or wasn't saying.

Or wasn't saying.

And I suppose whoever they ripped off might have followed Larry to Jules's place, waited outside. Followed him. Bashed in his head. When the moment seemed right.

Well. It's not impossible.

You don't seem entirely convinced.

What's to convince? It's not inconsistent with what we know. But there's not much positive in support of it, either.

But you don't think I'm off the deep end?

Not any more than usual.

Thanks, babe. I knew I could count on you.

Let's talk about sex.

You know I hate it when you do that, I said.

Let's do it anyway.

I'd rather go dancing.

Then let's go dancing.

I was being ironic.

So what?

You know I can't dance.

You can watch me.

Yeah, that'll be fun.

Why does nobody know how to eat pussy anymore?

Come on.

Really. Why not? Don't you have a theory? You always have a theory.

Did they used to?

Darren did.

Yes. But he was Australian.

I could get past that.

That's not what you said at the time. And anyway, wasn't he the one with the button dick?

That was a problem.

I would think.

It was so embarrassing.

Imagine how *he* felt about it.

That's what I mean.

Sad.

Shocking.

You still haven't gotten over it, I'm sure.

And he was so pretty, too. What a waste.

And so dumb.

But oh, he could eat pussy.

Overcompensation, I guess.

Yes, well, she said. If you're going to overcompensate, there are worse ways.

Skeet shooting?

Fast cars.

Random anger?

Bar fights.

Homicide?

Compulsive eating.

All of the above?

I think I dated that guy.

Listen, honey, all this sex talk makes me depressed.

Poor baby.

I mean it.

You really ought to drop this martyr thing, Rick. Get yourself a girl-friend.

I can't do that, I said.

Why not? Everybody else does.

I just can't.

Come on, darling. Give in to it. Lust can be fun.

Lust. I'd felt it all the time, an age ago, or two it seemed. Resisting temptation had never been my long suit.

But now, there was nothing to give in to.

So I gave in to Dorita. We went to a joint she loved. In the meatpacking district. Transsexuals. Bikers. Investment bankers. In short, the usual Saturday night crowd. We drank. She drank more. She danced on the bar with the other exhibitionists. Flirted with the bartender, a blonde named Erika. I watched. Attractive women all around. I wished I knew how to flirt.

I stood against the wall. I smoked a whole pack of cigarettes.

It was a lot like high school.

Dorita started talking to a muscular guy with a deep tan and a leather jacket. She stood very close to him. He put his hand on her waist, leaned in to whisper something in her ear. His teeth sparkled. She laughed.

Time for me to leave.

I left.

Dorita didn't seem to notice.

I didn't mind. I knew that she'd say sorry later. That she'd mean it. That it didn't matter, in the end.

Outside it had begun to rain. I hailed a cab. The back seat smelled of wet newspapers and stale chewing gum.

At home, the lights were out. I groped my way upstairs. I didn't want to turn on any lights. Wake Melissa up. Have to deal.

Let Steiglitz deal.

15.

MONDAY MORNING MY TEETH HURT. Why should today be different from any other day? I asked myself. Every day they hurt. I grind them in the night.

Two hours of tossing and grinding hadn't rested me. I smoothed my suit. I'd slept in it. It would have to do.

I unlocked the pill drawer. Paxil, 30 milligrams, to bring the anxiety down. Wellbutrin, 150 milligrams, to jack the initiative back up. Another 75, slow release, to keep it going. Valium, unprescribed, to take the edge off. Prilosec, 30 milligrams, for the reflux.

None of these had any perceptible effect. It was only when I didn't take them that I felt it. In spades. Bricks on my shoulders. Pains in my gut. Darkness all over.

Thank God for chemistry. I was a walking talking lab rat, but at least I wasn't miserable. Well. At least I wasn't as miserable as I used to be.

I went downstairs. Melissa was on the couch. Face up, mouth open. She looked dead. I was used to that. It was the dry skin, I think, that created the effect. The first few times I'd noticed it, I'd been afraid. I'd woken her up. But it was no longer fear I felt, when I saw her this way. A mild dread, perhaps. Curiosity.

In the kitchen, Kelly was eating breakfast. Scrambled eggs and toast. Maple syrup. Too much of it.

Kelly was my consolation.

I worried about her weight, though. Much more than she did. In fact, she professed not to care. I didn't believe it. Though knowing Kelly, I should have. She wasn't given to mendacity.

She was on the wrestling team. The boys' team. There was no girls' wrestling team.

She was very strong. I'd noticed it years before, when she was young. I'd told her so.

You're so strong, I'd said, it's amazing.

I knew, as a father will, that it was my remark, so long ago, that had inspired her to test her strength against the boys. I was proud of it. And afraid. Proud that my daughter would think my opinion so important as to manifest it in her life. Afraid at the power I wielded. That I might wield it badly.

Curious to think of the childless few. Their simple lives.

What are you up to today, love? I asked.

Nothing.

It was endemic, this nothing thing. What are you doing? Nothing. What are you thinking? Nothing. What are you reading? Nothing.

Take all these nothings, I said, put them in a big brown bag. What have you got?

Nothing in a bag, she replied, deadpan.

I laughed so hard I dropped the milk.

Jesus Weinstein! said Kelly.

Jesus Weinstein? I asked, grabbing paper towels.

Yes?

What the heck is that?

Mr. Weinstein. He's my Tech teacher.

I think I knew that. And?

Well, the other day in class he's writing on the blackboard. He writes down a bunch of stuff. Circuit diagrams and stuff. And then he says—You know how his hair is red and sits on top of his head like roadkill?

I remember that. At least, I remember you telling me that.

Well, now it looks like bad-fitting roadkill.

Okay.

And he says, this is your Bible. It's the Bible of electronics.

What? His hair?

If by 'his hair' you mean 'the stuff he wrote on the blackboard.'

Ah.

So now we call him Jesus Weinstein.

I think I'm following you, I laughed.

And that's what we call Jesus, too. Jesus Weinstein.

I guess that's the part I don't get.

If you don't get it, I can't explain it to you.

Okay.

I mean, why not?

Right.

We've got it. Why not use it?

Right. I'll remember that, next time I write the tuition check.

Kelly laughed her sweet, infectious laugh.

Melissa appeared in the kitchen doorway. Rumpled. Bleary.

What's all the laughing about?

Just joking around, Mom.

Melissa frowned, went to the fridge. Opened the door. Leaned over and peered in, as if shortsighted.

Which she wasn't.

Where's the milk? she asked, irritated.

Most of it's on the floor, said Kelly.

Melissa scowled at me. I still had the sopping paper towels in my hand.

I shrugged, like an embarrassed schoolboy.

You're such a clumsy fool, she said.

Serious. Grave. A doctor giving her patient the bad news.

She was still beautiful.

I turned away and sighed.

Oh come off it, Mom, said Kelly, lightheartedly.

Did you walk the dog yet? was Melissa's answer.

Not yet, Mom. I'm eating breakfast.

Good God. How many times have I told you he can't wait for your dithering all morning? I'll be picking up dog crap all day again. Always the same. Every bloody day.

The dog had been a mistake. Kelly was a cat person, like me. I'd had cats all my pre-Melissa life. Loved cats. Aloof, but intense. Relaxed, but ready to attack when necessary.

Just like me.

Sure.

When Kelly was small, she'd insisted on a pet. Of course, I'd said. Bad enough to be an only child. The least we could do was get her a companion. But Melissa was allergic to cats. A sign I should have heeded, long before.

So we had a choice: a hairless cat, or a dog. Kelly went for the dog. It was a bichon. Cute and cuddly. As close to a cat as we could find. Purebred, unfortunately. Cost me a cool fifteen hundred.

Kelly loved the dog. I tolerated it. Melissa hated the thing. Nobody walked it. It shat all over the house.

Melissa's voice rose as the dog rant escalated. Her face turned hard. But she didn't look at Kelly. It was as though she were alone. Talking to herself. Angry and alone.

I felt it in my teeth. My knees. My lower back. The pain. To see her like this now. Aging. Angry. Alien.

I'll go buy milk, I said, and slunk out of the room. The corner store was not so far away. I'd take the damn dog. What did it cost me? Less than a confrontation would, for sure.

Day in, day out, the anger.

It hadn't always been like this. I remembered other times. Law school days. The Blue Bar. Low ceiling. Pale blue walls. Odd lights in unexpected corners, throwing blue shadows. Bryan Ferry singing 'Avalon.' Cold and at the same time warm.

She had been brash, funny, fearless. Domineering. Beautiful, of course. But needy, underneath all that. And smart as hell.

I fell in love.

I thought that she did too. We lived life as the joke we arrogantly thought it was. We were smart enough to get away with it. For a while. We joked with Marco, the owner of the Blue Bar, in a pink dress, shining Day-Glo in the blue light. We exulted in our difference from the crowd. From our fellow students, fearful of failure. We both knew we'd never be the life of the party. But we'd make our own. Melissa, me and Marco. There were rarely any other customers in the place. The joint must have been a front for something, we'd speculated. We couldn't figure out what, though. Marco seemed so innocent.

Then, in her apartment, she'd succumb. Tie me up, she'd say. Take me hard. Show me who's a man. She'd wanted to be dominated. Submissive. At my mercy. Deliciously against the grain. It struck a chord in me. A deep, discordant chord, full of danger and promise. And yearning. The Tristan chord, it was, brought to life.

When it was over, we'd collapse into each other's arms. We'd put on Bruckner's Eighth. We'd kiss for hours, and hold each other tight. The power of our love seemed endless.

What had happened? Had I missed something? Had this Melissa always been there, this new Melissa, angry and vindictive, waiting to leap out, lash out and tear apart our dreams? I'd seen no sign of it, back then.

There were the pills, of course. The green ones, purple, orange, white. The vodka that washed them down. Stolichnaya from the freezer. But substances alone could not be all it was. It made no sense. It must always have been there. The anger. Hiding. Waiting. The pills and vodka only helped it show itself.

16.

WHEN I GOT TO WORK the elevators were down. Firemen slogged about the lobby, heavy with rubber clothes, oxygen tanks, large axes. Bomb scare, someone said.

A sign from God. Fuck the Lockwood hearing. I'd call the court. Plead natural disaster. Unforeseen contingency. Death and destruction. Lower back pain.

I called the other side. Pled my case. They agreed to an adjournment. We called the judge's clerk.

No problem, he said.

It worked.

I was free.

I figured I'd drop by FitzGibbon's office. See what I could see.

I grabbed a cab to the Consolidated Can building.

The cab smelled of stale cigarettes, and distress.

I negotiated the three security checkpoints. I found myself on the thirty-third floor. FitzGibbon was in.

The salsa guy was there, sitting like a stiff in his usual spot.

Furniture. It comes in all shapes and sizes.

FitzGibbon was leaning back in his chair, feet on the desk. He had on a pair of what looked to be very expensive snakeskin boots. And a seersucker suit. I hadn't seen one since New Orleans.

I told him about my talk with Jules.

FitzGibbon didn't ask me how Jules was. He didn't ask me whether there was anything he could do to help.

Instead he leaned forward, looked me in the eye, and said, Hey, as if the thought had just occurred to him, you don't think he's innocent, do you?

I tried not to look too surprised.

It's not my job to make that judgment, I said.

He leaned back in his chair.

I admire that, he said. I really do.

Well, I said. I'm doing my job.

Mmm, he said, and looked off into the distance.

He leaned forward again. Gave me a long and searching look. Didn't say a thing.

The guy was not normal.

Or maybe he was trying to get me rattled. Sizing me up. See how I handled it.

Either way, I decided not to push the envelope, yet. Probably not prudent. To alienate the firm's biggest client, fishing for dirt.

I'd like to come back and talk to you some more, I said. After I've got a little more information. I want to dig around a bit.

Sure, he said, the toothy smile growing larger. Anything for a lowlife.

I returned the smile.

There was another long pause.

You look a bit like Harrison Ford, he said.

Ah, I said. Thank you.

I wasn't sure it had been intended as a compliment, but I couldn't think of anything else to say. All I could think about was how to get the hell out of there. Before things got even weirder.

It's been a pleasure, I said, and got up to leave.

But it wasn't going to be that easy.

Redman, he said as I reached the door.

I turned around.

I assume you've got some good Trusts and Estates people?

New business, I thought, switching to rainmaker mode. This could be going somewhere. Maybe Warwick had been right.

Sure, I said. We're a full-service shop.

I've got a little something I'd like somebody to take a look at.

Just give me an idea what it's about, I said, so I can set you up with the right people.

I was thinking of Dorita. T & E was her specialty.

Well, he said, it's a little delicate. But I guess you're my lawyer, right? Attorney–client privilege and all that?

Strictly speaking Jules is my client. Though of course you're paying the bills.

Are you sure? he said, looking none too pleased.

There's no reason you can't be my client too, I said. So long as there's no conflict.

Conflict? Why would there be a conflict?

I don't know. It depends on what it is.

Let me tell you, he said, just between you and me.

I wasn't sure that it could be just between him and me. For one thing, Mr. Hairdo was in the room. But I let him talk.

You know that Jules and I haven't always got along.

Yes, I said. I think you mentioned that.

I took him out of my will.

So I understand.

You don't judge me for that, do you?

It's not my job to judge, I said, truthfully.

I have my reasons. If you knew them, you wouldn't judge me.

I'm not judging you, I said, not entirely truthfully.

I was, in fact, judging him. But I promised myself not to bill him for the time.

The thing is, he said, he's got some trusts. From his grandfather.

I had wondered how Jules could afford a loft in Manhattan. I'd put it down to rent control.

Your wife's father? I asked.

He got that vacant look again. He looked at Mr. Hairdo. Mr. Hairdo looked back. If something was communicated between them, I sure didn't know what it was.

FitzGibbon turned back to me.

Mine, he said. Dad felt guilty, at the end, I guess. He left us some money. Put some in trust for the future grandchildren.

Ah.

Very substantial trusts.

Ah.

The income isn't much. But when Jules turns twenty-five, he gets the capital.

I see.

It bothers me.

It bothers you.

Yes. I'd like to talk to somebody about it.

I was starting to get the picture.

Well, I said, that would seem to present a pretty stark conflict.

How so? he asked obstinately.

Jules is my client, as I said, even if you're paying. And what you're talking about certainly doesn't sound like it's in my client's interest.

His face darkened.

It's for his own good. The kid's never going to come to anything as long as he can suck off grandpa's tit.

Ignoring the bizarre metaphor, I stuck to my guns.

That may well be true, I said. I don't doubt you. But that's not a judgment I can make. Like I said, I'm not in the business of judging.

You're in the business of getting paid by me, goddamn it.

His neck bulged with purple veins. I saw my nice new business flying out the door. But there were lines that even I was not ready to cross.

Yes, I said, you are paying the bills. I agree. But frankly, if you insist on this as a take-it-or-leave-it proposition, I'll have to say no.

He glared at me. His neck throbbed.

It was a stalemate. I'd played it right. He was a tough guy. Tough guys admire toughness.

Listen, I said, here's what I can do. I have a buddy, a very smart guy. A pillar of the T & E bar. He's got his own firm. I'll refer you to him. He'll do a good job for you.

FitzGibbon didn't look entirely mollified, but he nodded his large red head.

All right, he said. Have him call me. I'll have him checked out.

17.

I WENT BACK TO THE OFFICE. The bomb scare, or whatever it was, was over.

I thought about FitzGibbon's last remark. I wondered whether he'd had me checked out too. And if he had, what he'd found.

I called up John (Don't-Call-Me-Jack) Kennedy. He and a buddy had spun off a small Trusts and Estates boutique. Wills. Old ladies. Trusts. Tax shelters. Helping the rich stay rich. John was very good at it. He had the perfect blend of perfectionism and schmooze. And a closet full of designer bow ties.

He was a touch over-sensitive about his name, however. I took a childish glee in exploiting it.

Hey, Jack, I said.

Don't call me Jack, Dick.

You won't be so rude to me once you hear what I'm calling about.

I'll be the judge of that.

Really, I mean it.

Okay, okay, shoot. You got some work for me. You'll never let me forget it.

Right on both counts. But even better than you think. Listen up. We've got a big client. *Big* big. Eamon FitzGibbon. CEO of Consolidated Can. You know him?

I know of him.

Good. Big, fat, red-faced, Irish charm. But most important, rich as Croesus.

That I knew. Even us T & E guys read *The Wall Street Journal*.

Especially you T & E guys.

Especially us.

Right after you finish with the *Times* obits. I know. Anyway. He needs some help. Estate stuff. Maybe some tax stuff. Doesn't sound like much. But as sure as A leads to P with an ampersand you can make something big out of this.

I don't doubt it. Sounds good.

Don't doubt me. I can't give you any details. Privilege, you know. Do a conflict check. Actually, I can tell you this much: it's more than privilege. Dark-glasses-and-trench-coat stuff. Keep it quiet, okay? We'll get together. Compare notes. Later. Just make him happy. We'll go places, Jack.

Don't call me Jack.

That's my boy. Keep him happy, okay?

You said that already. You can count on me.

I know that. That's why I called you, and not one of my other asshole T & E buddies.

I'll try to ignore the ambiguity in that last.

Excellent.

All right.

All right.

18.

I COULDN'T SLEEP. Again.

I went downstairs to the kitchen, avoiding the living room on the way. I warmed myself a glass of milk on the stove. I always warmed my milk on the stove. The microwave made it taste strange. Like someone had peeled an onion over it.

I would have added some Scotch, but we ran a dry house. Except for Melissa's statutory AA bottle. The temptation talisman. They're supposed to keep one in the house. To show that they can live without touching it.

No smoking in the house either. No substances, Dr. Steiglitz insisted. I had to sneak out back. Maybe I should quit, I often thought. It's bad for you, I'd heard.

I took my warm glass to the bedroom. I lay down. I turned on the TV. CNN. The Albanians were protesting in Macedonia. Fascinating. I watched blankly. I drank the milk slowly.

The milk didn't do it for me.

I gave in to it. I had no choice. I got up. I smoothed the creases from my suit. I sucked in my gut. I said, okay, that's you, in the mirror there. That's you. You're good-looking, sort of. Accomplished. Compared to most. You have nothing to fear. Get back to the bar.

And so I went. I glanced into the living room. Melissa on the couch, reading. I went out the back door. Around the side of the house. Down the block. Back to the Wolf's Lair.

I sauntered through the door. It felt like I had never left. I looked around, surveying my territory. I sniffed the air, to see if any strange dogs had left new spoor.

I didn't see Jake.

I felt a vague and unexpected disappointment.

Thom behind the bar. His welcoming smile.

The usual?

Can't say no.

Make it a double?

Thom knew my predilections.

Twist my arm, I said.

Thom poured my drink, wiped the counter clean. The Scotch was warm and comforting. I took a magazine from the rack. *The Economist.* What's happening in Armenia. The Minister of Justice announces court reform. Good luck.

Two stools down, an older guy. I'd seen him there before. Long gray hair. Ponytail. Kodiaks. Pall Mall non-filter. Thick hands. Thin lips. A worldly air. A working man. A poet. I remembered his name. Hal.

Hey Thom? I asked.

Rick.

You know this Jake guy?

Sure, he said. Been around here quite a bit lately.

Says he's a carpenter.

So I hear.

You know anybody can tell me if his work's any good?

Not really, Thom said. But I can ask around.

I'd appreciate it, I said.

Hal turned to me.

Hey, man.

Hey, Hal.

What's up?

Nothing much.

What brings you here?

I don't know. Conflict. Disaster. Depression.

More laughter. The dark warm mahogany of the bar. The cool brass rail.

Hey, you were talking about Jake? asked Hal.

Yeah.

Kind of weird, that guy.

Weird? How so?

I don't know. Just something about him. Something in his eyes. The way he looks at you.

How's that?

Like you're not there. Like he's thinking of something else.

I hadn't noticed that.

Look for it, next time. You'll see what I mean.

I made a mental note.

Hal went back to his beer, I to my double. The Scotch began to do its work. The warm seeped slow and dreamlike into my extremities. I drank the rest. I sat awhile. My brain slowed down. I smiled, paid Thom, ambled for the door.

Now, I thought, I can sleep.

19.

MELISSA WAS ON THE COUCH, legs curled beneath her, head askew. Sleeping. I stood, wondering. Daring to wonder. What would it be like to make love to her? I'd forgotten. And anyway, my recollection, if I had one, would have been misleading. She was a different person now.

If I disturbed her she'd be angry. Her sleep had not come easily, since her return from the hospital. What little rest she got was precious. To her, and to the rest of us. When she'd had some sleep she was less difficult.

I found a blanket, spread it over her. I leaned over. Braced myself on the sofa arm. Looked into her face. The face I loved. I took a chance. I kissed her forehead. Her eyelids fluttered, but she did not wake.

A victory.

I turned away. I crossed the room. I went upstairs. The stairs were steep. My feet were heavy.

Exhaustion. The house was full of it.

20.

I SLEPT. I WOKE. It was black outside. I willed myself back to sleep. I woke again. The sun was up.

My feet were clammy. I could tell I smelled. I made myself take a shower. I avoided the mirror. Last time I'd looked, I'd seen small veins sprouting on my nose. I'd tried to console myself. Just the Second Law of Thermodynamics at work. Entropy. All things tend toward a state of maximum disorder. There was nothing I could do about it. It was a law. And I was a lawyer. I was bound to uphold the law.

I trudged to Kelly's room.

Wake up, I said. It's a beautiful day.

I know, she mumbled, turning over and putting a pillow over her head, I can't wait til I'm awake.

Oh, all right, I said. I guess you've earned a late morning. I'm not sure how.

For being me, she mumbled.

That'll do, I said.

At the office the air was heavy and gray. I answered some calls. I read some faxes and e-mails. I delegated some trivial tasks.

I had to get out of there.

I made an appointment to see the Assistant District Attorney in charge of Jules's case. Some hotshot young guy, I'd been told. I knew I wasn't going to get much out of him. But it was a good idea to feel him out. See which way the wind was blowing.

The ADA's office was at the end of a long narrow corridor in an old gray building in lower Manhattan. The door was closed. The receptionist asked me to wait outside for a few minutes. While he finished a phone call.

There was nowhere to sit. I amused myself by examining the bulletin board. It was plastered with the usual bureaucratic detritus. Badly photocopied wanted posters. Employee of the month announcement, eight months out of date. Tattered menus from the many local take-out joints.

The office door opened. The ADA waved me in.

Hi, he said. Russell Graham.

He shook my hand with a firm grip. He had a strong chin and a Roman nose. A generic name. I could tell he was going places.

He shared a small room, replete with the usual government-issue squalor. Battered gray filing cabinets. Ancient oak swivel chairs. Ink stains. Piles of dusty files that looked as if they hadn't been consulted since the Great Depression. And, speaking of depression, a rumpled colleague, asleep with his head on his desk, his nose dangerously close to an ashtray overflowing with chewed cigar butts.

Russell, I said loudly. Pleased to meet you. Rick Redman. I'm representing Jules FitzGibbon.

The rumpled fellow lifted his head. Rubbed his eyes. Looked around in confusion. Scuttled out the door.

Russell gave me a rueful smile. Made no comment.

Good to meet you, he said.

You might change your mind about that later, I said.

He laughed good-naturedly.

How can I help you? he asked.

Well, frankly, I said, I don't know anything about this Larry Silver case. I'd be happy to hear whatever you're willing to share with me.

There was a pause while he thought about that.

There's not much to tell, he said. It seems to be pretty straightforward. At least six neighbors heard the fight. The kid is found dead in the alley an hour later. Blunt trauma. That's about it.

So I gather Jules is a suspect?

I think you can assume that.

Stupid question, I guess, I said with a grin.

He didn't return the smile.

Any other suspects? I asked.

I'm not sure that I'm at liberty to tell you that.

I understand.

At the appropriate time.

Yes.

What about physical evidence?

You know, I'd like to help you. Or at least, I'd like to help you within the constraints of my duty to the State. Now, it's no secret to you, I'm sure, that Mr. FitzGibbon, the father, is rather well connected. In fact, he's the chairman of and biggest single contributor to the mayor's antidrug campaign.

So I understand.

Of course, that would never affect the way we prosecute the case. But, well, you understand.

I wasn't sure I did. I tried to say so as diplomatically as I could. With a questioning look.

Let's just say, said the ADA, that I'm likely to be weighing my words perhaps a bit more carefully than I would in other circumstances.

I understand, I said. Of course. But if there's anything you can tell me. About any physical evidence. That you're at liberty to reveal.

I'm sorry, said Russell Graham, ADA, with a sorrowful shake of the head that seemed almost genuine. But there's not much to say. We're doing the usual forensics. You'll get them when you're entitled to them.

If and when.

If and when, he smiled.

I was just wondering, I said. If Jules did it, why would he leave the body right there? In an alley? Right after a loud fight that everybody in his building must have heard? Doesn't really make sense, does it?

Crimes of passion, said the ADA with a hint of irony. People aren't always thinking too clearly.

Crimes of passion?

They were in the middle of a fight. Uncontrolled anger. People don't act rationally. Or maybe he was trying to hide the body, put it in the Dumpster, and somebody came along. Scared him away.

All right. I see you have your theories. All I can say is, he says he didn't do it. So I'm not sure there's anything more to talk about. Right now, anyway.

I understand.

Clearly he did. And clearly this wasn't going anywhere.

I'd been hoping for some kind of response. Something about the kind of plea that might be available if the kid got charged. A crime of passion, after all. He'd said it himself. Not first degree. Plead it down to manslaughter. Depraved indifference. Whatever. I sat for a moment, waiting for Russell Graham, ADA, to say something that might go somewhere.

His smile was obliging.

No words followed.

Damn, I thought. This guy's no fun.

I had to get *something* out of him before I left.

Could I ask you one favor? I said.

Ask away.

Well, if you do end up charging Jules, down the road?

Yes?

Let's not do the perp walk thing, okay? Handcuffs and all that? I can bring him in.

Well, said the ADA evenly, I'll certainly take that into consideration.

I appreciate that. I'll be in touch.

You know where to reach me.

I left the building with a spring in my step, bursting with pride at my show of wit and investigative acumen.

FitzGibbon's kid was in good hands.

21.

I CALLED JULES. He was home. On the way to his loft I stopped to look at the alley where the body had been found.

It was a normal alley. Apartment buildings on either side. A tall metal fence blocking egress at the far end. Razor wire on top. Garbage cans. Wind-blown trash. A Dumpster. The smell of motor oil and rot.

The body had been found propped up against the Dumpster, at the far end of the alley. There was no bloodstain now, if there had ever been. Blunt trauma. Not necessarily a great deal of blood. Anyway, there would be crime scene photos. I'd try to get a look at them later.

There were four doors leading off the alley, three on one side, one on the other. All were of the metal kind. No visible handles. They could only be opened from the inside, it seemed.

I made a note to check out where the doors led.

Fire escapes clung to the side of each building. They were the type with a retracting last flight. Nobody without a ladder could climb them from the outside. The bottom flights were in the retracted position. They looked in working order.

I surveyed the scene.

No way out, for Larry Silver.

I could smell the fear.

I looked more closely at the metal door on the left. It had an abandoned air. Long shoots of weeds grew through the cracks in the asphalt in front of it. Not a door that had been used for months, at least.

I looked at the doors on the other side. Same thing. Emergency exits, probably.

I went back to the Dumpster. Got down on my knees. Peered underneath.

Two green eyes peered back.

I hope you don't have rabies, I said to them, and tossed a pebble in their direction.

The cat skittered off.

I had an urge to apologize.

I went around the Dumpster.

The cat was sitting contentedly on top of a stack of graying two-by-fours. It was black, with a white spot over one eye. White front feet. Damn cute. It didn't look like an alley cat. No scars. No scabies. Clearly it belonged to someone. Maybe it was lost. It had a collar. Perhaps its address was on the collar. I felt obliged to find out. Take it back to its home.

Sorry, I said.

It stared at me. I approached it slowly. It sat and stared some more. A street cat would have hissed, spat, run away. This one stayed. Watched me creep up on it. Cocked its head to one side.

When I got within a couple of feet, the cat took one last look at me. Sprinted away.

Damn, I thought. Another metaphor.

I left the alley. Turned right. Three blocks to Jules's building. The downstairs door was ajar. The elevator wasn't working. I climbed the stairs. I knocked. I heard voices. One was sharp, female, not pleased. The other was Jules. Some argument going on. I couldn't hear the words.

I knocked again.

The voices stopped. A minute going by. Metal machine music starting up. From somewhere inside.

The door opened. Jules was wearing baggy jeans slung down low, Union Jack boxers underneath, half exposed. And nothing else. If you didn't count the tattoos. Japanese, they looked like. And a large leonine thing on his chest. An odd pattern of scars on his belly.

Hey, he said.

Hey, I replied, trying not to stare at the scars. Is this a bad time?

Nah, that's just Lisa.

As though I should know who Lisa was.

She's pissed I didn't tell her you were coming. She'll get over it.

Okay, if you're sure, I said.

Sure I'm sure.

He didn't ask me in, exactly. He just turned and walked to the couch. Threw himself on it. As much invitation as I was going to get, it seemed.

I took a seat in the beanbag chair opposite Jules. The music grinding and shrieking from somewhere upstairs. I looked at the bookshelf next to the sofa. Tattered paperbacks. *Shōgun. The Man With No Name.* DVDs. *Kill Bill,* both volumes. *Reservoir Dogs.* A set of nunchuks. *Nunchaku,* I recalled, in the Japanese. Kelly had taught me that. She was way into anime.

Fuck you, too! I heard a voice, pitched high over the drone and crunch of the music. Fuck you too fuck you too fuck you too . . . !

I looked up. The owner of the voice was on the balcony. She was tiny. Hennaed hair, one side shaved higher than the other. Nose ring. Sleeveless T-shirt. I couldn't quite make out the tattoo on her shoulder. Something with a dragon, I thought.

I assumed that the imprecations weren't aimed at me. I turned away. Jules ignored her. A door slammed upstairs. She was still screaming.

Domestic problems? I asked lightheartedly.

No sweat, he said. She forgot her meds. Her mom's bringing them over. Then she'll be all right.

Ah. Can she hear us down here?

Not over that stuff, for sure.

Because if she hears us, the conversation's not privileged. Do you know what that means?

Sure.

His indifference was not reassuring.

It means it's not legally private, I said. The DA can ask either of us, or her, what was said.

I said she can't hear us, man.

He didn't say it unpleasantly. Just reciting the facts.

All right, I said. I'll take your word for it. Listen, I'd like to ask you a bit about your family.

The hell my family's got to do with it?

To tell you the truth, I'm not sure your family has anything to do with it. I'm just going to ask you some questions. I don't know if they'll turn out to be relevant or not. But they might. Depending. So it's important for me to ask you. It's kind of my job.

Whatever, he shrugged.

All right. Let's start with your father.

My father? What about him?

I didn't respond. I wanted to see what he'd volunteer. It's often a good technique. And not only for shrinks.

He looked at me from his reclining position. I gazed back at him, in my most professionally passive manner. Suddenly, he sat up. His eyes widened.

What? he said. You think *he* killed the prick?

Do you think your father could do such a thing?

He considered the question.

Wouldn't put it past him, he said evenly.

Why? Did he even know the guy?

He'd do it for fun. Or just to bug me. Or frame me for it.

You mean that?

Sure I mean it. Why wouldn't I mean it?

Sometimes people say things they don't really mean.

Not me, he shrugged.

Well, all right. But do you mean to say that you actually have any reason to think your father might be involved in this?

You're the one who brought it up, he said defensively, giving me a Look.

The Look said: You sure are stupid.

What are you so angry at each other about? I asked.

Ask him.

I will, but I'd like to hear your side of the story too.

He sat for a while in thought.

It's about my mom, really, he said at last, with a reflective air.

Really?

Yeah.

How so?

When he threw her out, he wanted me to hate her. Like he did. He was pissed when I didn't.

Wait a minute, I said. I'm not sure I understand. When I talked to your dad, he went all misty-eyed over your mother.

Who?

Your mom.

He gave me a withering look.

Shit, he said, you really don't know dick, do you?

Maybe not. But I'd like to learn.

You talking about fucking Veronica?

Ah, I said, starting to get the picture. She's not your natural mother?

No fucking way, lawyer guy. Nothing natural about that bitch.

I think I'm beginning to understand.

You don't understand dick, he repeated, shaking his head.

Well, I said, looking to regain some lost ground, I'm trying to get all the facts. Then I can start trying to understand a bit better.

Shit, he said. Who the fuck doesn't know that slut's not my mother?

Me, it seems.

Thinking that maybe humility worked best with the kid.

He seemed somewhat mollified.

So who *is* your mom, Jules? I asked.

My mom's my mom, he replied, helpfully.

What's her name?

Lily.

Lily. I like that. Kind of old-fashioned.

Right, he said, unimpressed.

I decided to make him do some work for a change.

Well? I asked.

He thought for a while.

When he threw her out, it was really bad, he said.

How so?

There was so much screaming, and stuff.

Did he hit her?

I don't know. I was upstairs. But it sounded like something awful going on.

And then?

And then, after she was gone, he wanted me to hate her. He wanted me to hate her like he did. But I didn't. Why would I want to hate her? She was my mom.

Was?

She's dead. She died. He killed her.

He killed her?

Yeah, I mean, she had nothing to live for, right?

I hear you.

She fell apart.

He turned away. He was trembling. Crying, it seemed. Though he was doing his best to hide it. I went over to the kitchen area, looked in the fridge for a soda or something. There was nothing but beer. Shelf after shelf of beer. Foster's. Heineken. Molson. Beck's. You name it.

Mind if I have a beer? I asked. You want one?

Sure, he said, answering both questions at once.

I found a couple of Anchor Steam in the back. Brought them over.

Whether it was the beer, or the fact that I'd brought it over for him, Jules warmed up. Started telling me stuff. Maybe it was the memory of his mother. He certainly seemed to have adored her. And that, it appeared, had been the problem. The divorce was highly acrimonious. She'd had an affair. The old man was a vengeful bastard. There was a pre-nup. The litigation had gone on for years. Meanwhile, her boyfriend dumped her. Not so interested, once she'd become effectively single and, more to the point, poor.

Lily had gotten thinner and thinner. Her hair had begun to fall out. She'd stopped caring for her appearance entirely. She'd show up in court in a tracksuit and sneakers.

FitzGibbon was determined to make sure Lily didn't get a dime of his money, and wasn't shy about spending it to get what he wanted. He had three lawyers working more or less full-time on the divorce. And they weren't just ordinary lawyers. He'd hired one of the most prestigious, and expensive, outfits in town. You could fit my entire firm in their lobby.

When the trial finally came around, FitzGibbon needed Jules to testify to what an awful mother Lily had been. And she hadn't been the best, the most attentive parent, Jules admitted. She was self-absorbed. A poetic soul. She relied too heavily on the plentiful hired help. She'd had more than one boyfriend on the side.

But she loved Jules. And he loved her. So when it finally came to trial, he'd refused to testify.

FitzGibbon was not a man who was used to hearing the word 'no.' It was that word, too often spoken, that had gotten Lily kicked out of the house in the first place. And here was her son – FitzGibbon's too, to be sure, but that didn't seem to be part of the equation – standing up to him. It was almost too much for a man to bear. So out the door went Jules as well. Along with any hopes he might have had of inheriting Daddy's riches.

But Jules had the trusts.

And he had his mother back.

Though that didn't last long. Within months of his moving in with her, she was diagnosed with tuberculosis. It was the drug-resistant kind, and it ravaged her. Right before Jules's eyes. She died two months later.

FitzGibbon did not attend the funeral.

Jules told me all of this in a rush, hardly taking a breath. It was as if he'd been waiting for years. For someone who'd listen.

When he was finished, we sat in silence.

I didn't know what to say.

I went into the kitchen for another couple of beers.

We drank them slowly.

I'll do whatever I can for you, Jules, I said. Not just legal stuff. Whatever I can do.

He looked up. He nodded. I got up. Shook his hand. Got out of there.

So there it was. FitzGibbon had omitted a few details from his little biographical speech. Veronica was neither his first wife, nor Jules's mother.

An objective observer might have thought those facts important.

FitzGibbon probably had his reasons for leaving them out.

Maybe they were innocent.

I doubted it.

But what did any of it have to do with the blunt instrument in the alley?

Something, I felt.

But nothing that I could see.

22.

THE BEST THING ABOUT THE WOLF'S LAIR was its lack of success. Never more than seven or eight people in the joint. Except on Saturday night. I tried to stay away on Saturdays. For some reason, the college crowd showed up. Chatty misfit girls. Surly misfit guys. The socialized ones went to Armando's, down the street. Armando's had a DJ. They danced til dawn. The Wolf's Lair crowd sat, stood or staggered. No dancing there. No doubt they all had two left feet.

I know I did.

Tuesdays, on the other hand, weren't a problem.

I took my place at the bar.

Hal was in his usual spot, two stools down.

Hey, Hal, I said.

He looked up from the notepad he was scribbling on.

Rick, he said.

I've got a question, I said.

Fire away, boss.

What you said about Jake, the other night?

What I said about Jake?

Something about him not looking you in the eye?

Did I say that?

Something like that, you did.

I don't remember that, man. Sorry.

Oh.

I was a bit bewildered. He'd said it with such sincerity.

I turned back to the book I had brought with me. Sklansky. The Bible of Texas hold'em. I was on my sixth pass through it. My second copy. The first had disintegrated from use. Cigarette burns, spaghetti sauce, bathtub water. This one bristled with colored tape flags. Every second line was highlighted, underlined, highlighted again in a different color. You read, you played, you reread. You played some more. Suddenly, something you'd only digested in the abstract took on a life. You'd played that hand last night – you knew that situation – and here it was, on the page. Maybe not the very same cards, the very same bets. But the situation.

A hand on my shoulder. I turned my head.

Jake!

Yo Rick!

At least you remember my name.

Well, yeah.

He looked puzzled.

You got one leg up on my wife in that department, I explained.

Really?

That innocence. Charming.

He saw the book. The forest of tape flags.

Whatcha reading?

Sklansky.

I held the book up.

You're kidding.

I am not. You know Sklansky?

Shit. He's my brother. My right arm. Shit. You play?

I try.

Oh man. I got to get you to my game.

You've got a game?

Sure, I've got a game. I've got a helluva game. Hey, you serious?

Do I look serious?

He looked at the tattered remains of Sklansky.

Yeah. You look serious. Okay, listen, this game is very cool. Actors. Artists. Very successful people. I got to get you there.

Well, sure, I said. What's the buy-in?

Five hundred. No limit.

I think I can handle that. How do I get in?

I've got to work on that.

Hm. Mystery. Impediments. I liked that.

What is this, the Masons? I asked. You need the secret handshake?

James Mason?

No, the Masons, I laughed. You know, the Masonic Lodge, all that?

He looked blank.

Charming, like I said.

Hey, he said. You hear about anybody needs a little carpentry work done?

Actually, I said, I've been thinking about putting a bookcase in my bedroom. That too small a job for you?

Nah. I'll take anything I can get.

Great, I said. Why don't you come by, look at the space. Give me an estimate.

Sure. Just let me know when.

Let's make it Thursday night, I said. Say around eight?

This Thursday?

Right.

Uh, okay.

Some other day better for you?

No, no. Thursday's fine. Thursday's fine.

We got down to poker talk. We talked about semi-bluffs. Semi-bluff raises. How to play a maniac. What to do with two maniacs.

Find another table, he said.

Be happy, was my opinion. Stay right there.

Poker is a solitary occupation. You don't reveal your thoughts to anyone you might be playing later. Which is to say, anyone at all. But there was something about Jake. His innocence, his enthusiasm. And,

I guess, the fact that there wasn't a whole lot else we could talk about for more than two minutes.

When I finally left the bar, hours later, my feet didn't quite find the ground. I stumbled. A little lean left, a list to the right. I had to focus to stay upright.

I didn't usually let myself get drunk. Normally I was in control. I'd developed a prodigious capacity over the years. I knew when to stop. To slow down. I could feel it coming. The cotton-ball brain. The tongue less limber. The quips a little lame. Too quick to laugh. Too easy. Got to keep it hard. Keep the line. Don't cross the line. Drink water for a while.

This time I'd let it go a bit. One too many single malts.

I staggered down the street in the snow. I tripped on my own front stairs. I laughed out loud. Laughed at myself. It took a clumsy try or two to get the key into the lock.

Shit. Sometimes it felt good to let it go.

23.

I SAT ON THE EDGE of the bed. I looked at my feet.

Kelly had my feet. A younger, softer version. We liked to sit together and admire each other's feet. It was one of our special things.

I tried to feel tired. But it wasn't sleep I needed. It was consolation. I sat at the computer. I cruised some porno sites. Chatted with a cyber whore. Thank the Lord for cable modems. She wore a silver sequined G-string. She had the handcuffs ready. She was my friend. She could give me what I wanted, she said.

It didn't take too long to find out that it wasn't true.

Enough of that. I'd get my consolation from the poker site.

I'd been flipping channels one night. I'd come across a poker show. The World Series of Poker. Binion's Horseshoe. Las Vegas. Guys in shades. Mountains of chips. When the field got down to two, women in bikinis dumping piles of cash on the table.

Right away, I was hooked.

I'd read a bit, when I was young. Don't open with less than two Jacks. That's all I remembered. That was draw poker, anyway. Nobody played draw poker anymore. Too much skill. The better players always won. The lousy player had to win sometimes, to keep him coming back. The ideal game combines the right amount of luck and skill.

Texas hold'em has that balance. I don't know who thought it up, or how it got the name, but the game is perfect. The strategy is deep enough that very few can play it really well. Long-term, the better player wins. But on any given hand, any given night, the luck is such that anyone can win. Dead money can play the ugliest of hands, bank his whole roll on an inside straight on the river, the last card dealt. And it would happen. He'd fill that straight. Bad beat, the other guy would tell himself, and anyone else at the bar, later, who would listen. It would happen often enough. Dead money could most naturally succumb to the delusion. That feeling of omnipotence that every card shark feeds on.

I sat down, logged on.

I played for hours.

I loved the rhythm of it. The back and forth. The artificial swish of cards being dealt. The click and clack of chips being bet. The site designers did a great, hypnotic job. Most of all I loved the charge you got from winning. The best was when you won with garbage cards. Nothing in the world like a bluff that worked. Two Three off-suit. Pick your spot. Play it like Aces. Watch the suckers fold. Take the pot. Yes.

I started with two hundred dollars. It went up. It went down. At one point I was all in, every cent I had in the pot on a heart flush draw. Five of hearts on the river. Bingo. Back to one-fifty. That was the start of the rush.

I rode the rush, and nothing mattered for a while. I ended up with fifteen hundred dollars. Every night as good as that, and I could quit my day job.

Yes. Now I could sleep.

24.

A THICK MANILA ENVELOPE sat on my desk. It had come from FitzGibbon. I knew what was in it. Old files. Trust deeds. Wills. Correspondence. Maybe a legal opinion or two. I was supposed to forward it to Kennedy. Normally, I'd call in Judy, tell her to seal it, send it to John. Hand delivery. Private. Confidential. To be opened only by addressee.

That was the right thing to do.

But, I said to myself, pulling the envelope toward me. Wait a minute. Jules is my client. Not his father. Daddy's just paying the bills. I don't have any fiduciary duty to him.

Actually, I didn't know for sure if that was true. But I wasn't about to look it up. And I wasn't about to call up Tightass Bob Shumaker, the firm's resident Ethics Guru, and ask him. Bob's answer was always the same: if it feels right, it must be wrong.

A peek. A quick look. Who would that hurt? Jules, it might help. Jules was my client. I owed it to him to take a look. It wasn't just curiosity, prurience. There might, there just might, be something in there that would help Jules. Information: it's the stuff of litigation. Jesus, it's the stuff of life itself. Without information, where would we be? Even the sloth, the slug, the amoeba, they operate on information. At a minimum, where the food is. Why was I any different?

The beauty of poker, I mused, the envelope heavy on my desk, is that it's a game of incomplete information. Like quantum physics. No matter how powerful our computers, our detection methods get, the best we will ever do is predict the probability that a given electron is in any given place at any given time. And poker's exactly like that. He who divines most consistently the missing pieces of knowledge – the other players' cards – is the master of the game. The old lady next to you in Vegas. The old lady who lifts her cards to her face each time, like she's seen in the cowboy movies, giving you a millisecond peek at her hand. Ignore the input? Be a good boy, turn your head away? Lean over to her, whisper a word of warning? 'Ma'am, please keep your cards on the table. Watch how the others do it . . . you're giving your cards away'?

No, you wouldn't, would you? I didn't think so. You might stop short of taking her money, if you wanted to be a stickler about it. But you'd keep looking at her cards. For the edge it gave you on the others.

I opened the envelope.

Just a quick peek.

Trust deeds. At least a dozen. Most were old enough to have been typed. High-class bond paper. Ancient paper clips. I paged through them. The usual mumbo jumbo. Whereas. Heretofore. Thus is it said. And the Lord God made it so.

I flipped through the documents. Ah, there it was. The grandpa trust. To Eamon FitzGibbon. Daddy hadn't entirely disappeared, had he. Twenty million. Jesus. Daddy had been rich as Croesus too. And never shared a dime with his family before his death? It seemed inconceivable. And to any grandchildren, a cool twenty million too. Vesting at the age of twenty-five. Until then, a modest allowance. Enough for the loft. Not much more. To be administered by Jones & Pogue, Attorneys at Law. Never heard of them.

I put the papers back into the envelope. What had I learned? I asked myself. Nothing I hadn't already known, really. The amounts involved. A little shocking. But nothing that was going to help Jules stay out of jail.

Shit. Maybe it had been just prurience. Had I risked violating a sacred trust for nothing?

This wouldn't do.

I opened the envelope again.

Maybe I'd missed something.

Page upon page of ancient legal cant about dead people. Long-gone enough to be meaningless, most of it. And then, near the end, I saw what I had overlooked the first time.

Damn. Damn. Damn.

Somebody had a motive.

25.

KELLY WAS OUT AT THE MOVIES with her friend Peter. Peter was loud and funny and fat, and Kelly and he were inseparable. I didn't think that they were anything other than friends. Peter's predilection for classic films and opera was one reason. Another was that Kelly had never expressed the slightest indication of romantic interest in him. In anyone else for that matter. She was a mysterious thing. On the other hand, I was humble enough to reserve judgment.

I had seen her in the living room before she left. She was standing in front of the mirror, inspecting what I took to be invisible pimples.

I don't know what you're looking for, I said. You have the most flawless skin I've ever seen.

If by 'flawless' you mean 'pitted and pocked with ugly zits.'

Oh, come on, Kelly. I mean it. You're gorgeous.

Dad, she said, without turning from the mirror, you're in denial.

She shouldered her purse. Jack the Pumpkin King on it. Sauntered to the door. Gave me a mischievous wink.

Like I said. A mysterious thing.

After she'd left, the house became a quiet place. Melissa read her self-help books. Fell asleep for a while.

The Wolf's Lair beckoned. I resisted it. Maybe I could draw Melissa out a bit more. The other night had been encouraging. I cooked a small but tasty meal. She was up to joining me for it. An unexpected if not unalloyed pleasure. We didn't talk much. When we did, there were many pitfalls to avoid.

I preferred the silences, if the truth be known.

During one of the long barren stretches of the evening I went into the study, closed the door.

My cell phone rang. 'Private number,' it said. I ignored the call. I had a rule. If somebody doesn't want me to know who they are, I don't want to talk to them.

But there was the phone. In my hand. It seemed lonely. I called Dorita.

Ten o'clock at night? she said. Don't I ever get a break?

I'd prefer to think, I replied, that a call from me constitutes a welcome relief from your otherwise humdrum existence.

Of course, of course. Nothing to do with escaping from *your* dreary life, I'm sure.

Of course not. Life at home is an endless round of witty discourse and gay parlor games.

I knew that. So what tears you away from the latest raucous game of charades?

I was thinking about FitzGibbon.

You have my sympathy.

Thanks. So anyway, I've been thinking. I guess the whole downtown thing must rankle the old man. He's way into this antidrug crusade. But is that really enough to explain it? I mean, he's disowned the kid. And he's only a kid. Why not try to help him? And Daddy's nose hasn't always been clean itself, has it? You don't get to where he is from where he started without cutting a corner or two.

Sure. But that's a different kind of bad. He can relate to that. If the kid was an embezzler, he might actually be proud. I think it's more that the kid repudiates everything Dad's spent his whole life working for. Wealth. Prestige. Club membership.

Yeah, sure. I can see that. Anyway, I've got something that might lead somewhere.

Do tell.

But I can only tell you if you promise that it stays right here.

In your bedroom?

I'm in the study. But you know what I mean. Between you and me.

Are you suggesting that you can't trust me, Rick? I think I'm going to have to reevaluate our relationship.

Sure, sure. We'll do that later. I just need to make sure you understand. I'm not really supposed to have this information.

Mum's the word, darling.

Okay. FitzGibbon sent me the trust documents, to pass along to Kennedy.

Yes?

I took a peek.

Bad boy.

I *am* a bad boy. I actually do feel a bit guilty about it. But hey, whatever I have to do for my client, right?

Right. So what did you find?

There are conditions.

Yes?

That have to be fulfilled. Before Jules gets the money.

And?

And one of them is that he not have been convicted of a felony.

My, my.

Exactly my reaction.

So Daddy might have another motive.

It can't be about the money. He's got more than he knows what to do with.

Yes, but keeping Jules from it. I wouldn't put it past the bastard.

Mysterious are the ways of the human heart.

Or bile duct.

Spleen.

Keep me in the loop.

You can count on me, I said.

26.

I WAS PUZZLING over the last corner of the *Times* crossword, and trying to think of an excuse for missing the monthly partners' lunch, when the phone rang.

Rick, it's John.

John?

John Kennedy.

Jack!

Don't call me Jack. Rick, this is really getting old.

The fun thing about Kennedy was that he really had no sense of humor.

All right, all right, I said. What's up?

I've got something I've got to talk to you about.

That would explain the phone call. Talk away.

Not on the phone. Meet me for lunch.

Ouch. Sounds serious.

It is serious. To me.

Okay, Moran's at one?

One-thirty. I've got to check out a few things first.

All right, I said. One-thirty at Moran's.

Excellent. I had my excuse.

I noodled about til one. There were many important decisions to be made, in many important, high-paying cases. But I wasn't up to that. My head was fogged up, entangled. I didn't know which way was up. Which confusing message was worth examining in more detail.

I thought about the trust deed. Who would get the money if Jules didn't qualify? Would it devolve by operation of law? To FitzGibbon, as the surviving parent? Would he be disqualified himself, having disowned the kid? Damn, law school had been so long ago. I needed some Trusts & Estates advice. Strictly speaking, I shouldn't ask Dorita. Because of the conflict. We were partners in the same firm. My client was her client. I had already compromised her enough by bringing it up at all. Maybe I could pry something out of Kennedy. I doubted it. But it wouldn't hurt to try.

Moran's looked the same as it had for eighteen years. The theme was black and green and Irish. The pool table was still small and warped, the dartboard skewed but ever popular. James behind the bar was cheerful, full of a joke you'd heard before but didn't mind hearing again. The bar itself was still as long, as dark and as packed with heavy-smoking Guinness-slugging regulars as ever.

The only real difference, I noted with chagrin, was in the visage of the distinguished attorney in the mirror. Much more gray, not only of hair but demeanor. And I wasn't sure the facial symmetry the new haircut provided was worth the extra freight. $225, style by Jacques, blow-dry included. Oh well. Kelly liked it. That was all that mattered. Give it a smile, I told myself. That's better. You look five years younger. No? Okay, four. Two? Never mind.

When Kennedy arrived, he insisted that we move to a table. To me this was an affront to James, my second-favorite bartender, and I apologized to him.

James was gracious.

You gentlemen have some business, he insisted. Please, take the corner booth.

Kennedy's bow tie was black with tiny white dots. Very elegant. I refrained from making a bow tie joke. I saw from his face that the usual banter would be unwelcome. I waited. He played with a small pile of cardboard coasters for a while. I sipped my drink.

He finally looked up.

What am I going to do with this new client you so kindly referred to me?

Well now, I said, I don't know. Make money? Squeeze him for all he's worth? What, is there something I don't know?

Make money. Yeah. Thanks. I think I could have figured that much out.

Hence my surprise at the question, I said. What's with the long face?

Shit, Rick, I go to lunch with old ladies for a living. I've never had to deal with a guy like this before. Frankly, he scares the hell out of me.

Cuddly old Eamon FitzGibbon? What's so scary about him?

I don't know if I can give you any facts.

Then I can't help you, my man.

Listen, I can't talk about privileged stuff. You know that. I mean, it's even worse than that. You've got a conflict. That's why you sent him to me in the first place.

True, true. But you've got to give me something to go on.

Well listen. There's this. I checked into the guy a bit. I talked to people who've dealt with him before. They've told me a few things. I mean, the guy's capable of anything.

Such as?

I don't want to go overboard here, Rick. But just to take an example. I called up a buddy of mine. He'd been on the other side of a deal with FitzGibbon. He'd reneged on some payments. And my buddy sends his partner over, to try to broker a deal. Seventy cents on the dollar, or something. And FitzGibbon's being a real hard-ass about it, won't give an inch. All polite and joking, but not giving up a thing. And my buddy's partner's getting up to leave, and FitzGibbon says, 'By the way,' and my buddy's partner says, 'Yes?' and FitzGibbon says, 'Where I come from, the word *contract* has more than one meaning.'

Ouch.

But that's not the end of it, Rick. Next week, my buddy's partner? He's hit by a car. Right in front of his house. Hit-and-run. He's a paraplegic now. They never found the driver.

Jesus.

I mean, coincidence, maybe. But.

I hear you. But listen, what's this got to do with you? God knows what some of your old ladies might have gotten into in their heyday. What was that movie, *Arsenic and Old Ladies?*

Old Lace.

Yes, Jack, I know. It was a joke.

He managed a wan smile.

Come on, man, buck up. Even if that story's true, and frankly it sounds apocryphal to me, the guy pissed FitzGibbon off. But you're on his side. You're a schmooze. You won't piss him off. Nothing to worry about.

Kennedy was silent.

I gave him an under-the-eyebrows look.

All right, all right, he said. I guess I ought to lighten up.

Good, I said. Now let's get down to something more meaningful. Golf on Sunday? You can take me to your club.

It's the middle of winter, Rick.

Right.

And anyway it's my sister's birthday.

Your sister's birthday? Jack, you've got to get your priorities straight.

I know, I know. But my mom will kill me if I don't go. You know how it is.

Actually, Jack, I don't. But that's all right. I can try to imagine it.

Shit, Rick, don't rub it in. And stop calling me Jack.

On my way back to the office I pondered the implications of this new FitzGibbon story. Did it mean anything? I doubted it.

But maybe.

Everything was Delphic. Equivocation, ambivalence, ambiguity.

Just as it should be, I could hear Dorita say.

Just as it should be.

27.

WHEN I GOT HOME THAT NIGHT I got the silent treatment. I didn't know why. Melissa got ideas in her head. Instead of airing them and working out whatever problem she was having, she'd do the silent thing. If I asked if anything was wrong, she'd say, 'No, no, nothing at all.' In a tone that clearly said the opposite.

No amount of insistence would make her open up.

So I'd long ago stopped trying.

She'd always been like that.

But as with so many other things, it had gotten worse with time.

The doorbell rang. Melissa scuttled upstairs.

It was Jake, coming over to see the bookcase space. I'd forgotten about my invitation. But I was glad to see him. Maybe his presence would brighten the evening.

I ushered him into the living room.

Jake looked about the room nervously. I could see that he was a little taken aback. Our house wasn't lavish, by New York standards. But there was furniture. There were carpets. Things on the wall. Everything arranged for aesthetic effect. For a young man from a humble background, one still living hand to mouth as he waited to become a movie star, it probably looked pretty darn alien.

Melissa will be down in a sec, I said. I think you'll like each other.

He looked terrified at the thought. Stage fright, I guessed.

He leaned in toward me. Aftershave. The scent reminded me of the night I'd met him at the Wolf's Lair.

Melissa returned. She'd put on a dress I hadn't seen in years, black and red and seductive. She launched into her best hostess routine. She came across the room, arms outstretched.

I've heard so much about you, she said, with a touch too much enthusiasm, and kissed him on both cheeks.

She grabbed his hands. Held him at arms' length. Admired him. Like he was a visiting prince.

It was a role she knew well, but one she hadn't played in a good long time. There was something forced about it. Fragile.

Jake looked uncomfortable. I was sure he wasn't accustomed to the ways of the upwardly striving upper middle class.

Welcome to our home, Melissa said, expertly dimming her smile from effervescent to charming and slightly flirtatious. Can I offer you a drink? I'm sorry to say we don't keep alcohol in the house. But tea? Iced tea? Orange juice? We have just about anything else.

That's okay, said Jake. I don't need anything.

Are you sure?

Yes, I'm fine.

Sit, sit, she said. Make yourself comfortable.

He sat nervously on the armchair, perched forward.

We made small talk. Melissa asked some polite questions about his acting career. He replied in short sentences.

Lots of auditions, mostly, he said. Close calls. Small local repertory. Nothing big yet.

He kept looking over at me. As if for help. He was not the jovial Jake I knew from the Wolf's Lair. He was an overmatched child.

Well, I thought, take the drunk out of the bar. Tell him there's no booze around. God knows what you'll get. I was reminded of mornings waking up in a strange apartment after a fine night of casual sex. The morning made everything different. There wasn't a daylight protocol.

I took him upstairs, showed him the space where I thought we might put the bookcase. He became all business. He'd brought a tape measure. He handled it with a practiced nonchalance.

Sure, he said. No problem. I can get some nice maple. It'll match the molding. I'll sketch it out for you. Twelve hundred, say?

I was a little taken aback. I had expected five, maybe six hundred.

I figured you wanted it first class, he said apologetically. I could use pine, stain it red, he added, without conviction.

No, no, I said. Let's do the maple. Twelve hundred is fine.

I didn't want to be an ungracious host.

Back in the living room, there were a few more minutes of overly polite conversation. The weather. The latest Brad Pitt vehicle. Jake was clearly anxious to leave. Melissa asked for a cup of tea. Jake declined again. I went to the kitchen to make the tea. I warmed myself a glass of milk.

When I returned Jake was sitting on the couch next to Melissa.

Good, I thought. She's actually relating to somebody.

Got to be going, said Jake.

Okay, I said, a little surprised. Nice of you to come over.

Melissa looked relieved. Jake looked relieved. I felt relieved.

Melissa rose. Jake got up. Cheeks were kissed. I took him to the door.

Uh, listen, he whispered on the way. I wonder if I could ask you a favor?

Sure, I said, wondering what he thought I was doing, hiring him to build a bookcase I didn't really need.

I'm a little short, he whispered. You think you could front me a couple hundred?

Gee, I said, I'd like to help you out. I really would. But I'm tapped out this week. Nothing I can do. Sorry.

I shrugged.

It didn't feel like a convincing performance. I wasn't sure I wanted it to be.

Hey, he said, that's okay. That's okay.

He left. I returned to the living room.

He's sweet, isn't he? she said.

I guess, I said.

And kind of cute.

Right.

It was an odd thing for her to say. Quite out of character.

Her smile was forced. Like a child caught doing something bad.

28.

I HAD A HEARING in the Lockwood case. Some poor kid had died of a rare form of brain cancer. The grieving parents, understandably, needed someone to blame. They sued our client, a local manufacturing company. Unfortunately for them, there was no known cause, environmental or otherwise, for the disease. So proving causation was going to be a problem. We'd made a motion to exclude some crucial expert evidence about groundwater contamination. Without it, without the veneer of objectivity of a professionally disinterested expert witness, the other side would have to rely on the testimony of a weasel-eyed company engineer named Cecil Crepe. I kid you not. And although it was pronounced 'Crep' and not 'Creep,' I was not at all sure that a jury would attend to the distinction. So I wasn't about to let them have their expert without a fight.

I took Vinnie Price with me. Vinnie was my favorite associate. He was an up-and-comer. A spit-polished young man with a burning ambition and a way with a client.

These shortcomings were redeemed by a wicked sense of humor.

When we arrived in court Vinnie and I were introduced to the learned counsel representing the plaintiff, a man named Trumbull. A pillar of the local Episcopalian church. Trumbull had thick mats of hair growing out of his ears. In state court, you sit side by side at the same table with opposing counsel, the dais in between. So each time Trumbull got up to speak, we had an unobstructed view of the vegetation. Moss, it was. It was like thick moss on a rotting tree trunk. It was a marvel of nature.

There were probably many other notable things about him. He may even have been a powerful advocate. But all Vinnie and I could talk about later was earwigs.

The judge had decided he'd hear from the expert before deciding the motion. Usually these things are decided on the papers, and oral argument from the lawyers. So we were already ahead of the game. I was looking forward to cross-examining the guy.

Cross-examination is an art and a science. Perhaps a little sport as well. You need laser-like focus on the only goal. To manipulate, bully or seduce the target into saying things he doesn't want to say. There's an infinite variety of techniques. The key is to adapt them to the target and the situation at hand. That ability is what separates the world-class cross-examiner from the merely competent. Anyone can recite the standard questions. Do the routine song and dance. Elicit the testimony they already knew was in the bag. But the masters of the trade, those who have the talent, the cojones and the will, they can push that envelope. Identify and maximize the weakness of the witness.

Everybody, even the slickest and the smartest, has a weakness.

Many times, it's ego.

This guy had a big one.

He was good, but after a couple of hours of sparring I managed to maneuver him into testifying that a pool of contaminants in the groundwater – 'DNAPL,' if you really must know, dense non-aqueous phase liquids – wasn't actually 'touching' the water, because not 'all of it' was in contact with the water. Now, I knew what he meant to say. He meant that the contaminants weren't all mixed up with the water. But I didn't care what he meant. I was quite happy to use what he said. I swept my arm through the air, my index finger alighting on the dais in front of me.

Am I touching this dais? I asked, raising my eyebrows.

He sat and stared at me for a while. Damn it, I could see him thinking, I have to say no.

And he did. He had to say no, because all of my finger was not in contact with the dais, nor was all of the dais in contact with my finger. So, by his definition, I wasn't touching the dais. He had to say no, or take back what he'd said before. Either way, he was going to look like what he was – a well-paid flack.

He said yes.

The judge had had enough.

Witness excused, he said.

It was sweet. As always when we won, I left the courtroom pumped, elated, full of myself, high-fiving with Vinnie and crowing about my skill.

Vinnie, I said, let me know when my honorary Ph.D. in groundwater science comes in.

You'll be the first to know, boss, he said.

It's what kept me coming back to the office. The once-a-month or sometimes better chance to be the star on the judicial stage. To have my words, my oh so eloquent words, slice through the air and puncture the pretensions of whatever inflated excuse for an argument or a witness the other side had dared to drag into the courtroom.

If only the feeling would last. But it never did. If it got me through the day it was a major event. Some days, it didn't get me through the cab ride back to the office.

This was a good one, though. I was still humming a happy tune when I strode past Judy into my office. I was about to pick up the phone and summon Dorita, to regale her with my tale of splendiferous advocacy, when Judy interrupted.

Mr. Warwick wants to see you, she said.

The sonofabitch, I thought. He won't even let me enjoy myself for ten minutes.

There wasn't any reason to put off the inevitable. The magic of my morning's victory had vanished the moment I'd heard Warwick's name. I trudged the length of the thirtieth floor, smiled at Cherise. She nodded me in.

Redman! Warwick said, with uncharacteristic warmth.

Charles, I said.

Everyone called him Charles. We all pretended to an informality we never actually felt in his presence. In return, he called everyone by their last name. It was a territorial thing, I think. Though I wasn't sure exactly how the metaphor worked, I knew it bore some quite precise relationship to dogs pissing on lampposts.

I was just talking to FitzGibbon, Warwick said. He seems quite smitten with you.

I'm glad to hear that, I said, ignoring the homoerotic choice of phrase.

Good job, said Warwick. This could be the start of great things for you.

I forced a smile.

Thanks, I said. I'll stay on it.

Excellent, he said. We'll have that morale problem licked in no time.

I gave that one a pass.

On the way out, I gave Cherise a wink. I figured I owed her one.

To the uninitiated, that brief conversation might not have seemed so bad. But in reality it was fraught with import. Venom. Spleen. Fear.

Morale, shit. The only morale Warwick gave two shits about was his own. And his morale was fed by power, nothing else. The right to squash, humiliate and defile with boundless guile and glee.

I don't know, maybe he had a good side. I just hadn't seen it for a while.

What made it worse, we'd come up in the business together. Worked side by side in the trenches. Reviewed documents in dingy conference rooms for days on end, until we fairly bled to death from paper cuts. Drank at the same bars. Chased the same women in those same bars. We'd actually had some fun together, back then.

It was hard to imagine now.

I called Dorita.

It was too late to crow about my morning triumph over the moss-eared man. But at least I had Warwick to bitch about.

Dorita wasn't in her office.

That only left one thing.

29.

SHEILA SPECIALIZED IN ADDICTION. Junkies, drunks, cokeheads, aspirin freaks, whatever. She got a lot of cancellations.

I called her up. Her three o'clock had OD'd, so she had a slot for me. I decided to walk over. It was a nice day.

Her office was in an upscale building in the east seventies, otherwise residential. You'd never have known the office was there. I supposed most of the residents didn't. I was quite sure that the lunching ladies with Pekingese I passed on my way into the building would have been quite scandalized to know that back behind their very own marble-floored palm-plastered lobby, eight hours a day, fifty-five minutes at a time, sat, weeping, whining and rationalizing, scores of the city's most hopeless slaves to substance.

The doormen, on the other hand, certainly knew. They knew everything. And being even more snobbish than their tenants, though also professionally discreet, they never failed to give me a tiny nod and a subtle sneer. Which I invariably returned.

I didn't have to wait. The door was open. Sheila was in her recliner. I always called her Sheila. I liked the name. It reminded me of old Jack Lemmon movies. I knew she didn't approve, though she never said so. But whenever she left me a voice mail she never said, 'It's Sheila'; she always said, 'It's Dr. Schwartz.' And I would always make it a point to begin my return voice mail with, 'Hi Sheila, got your message.'

That was the extent of my rebellion, though. We actually had a very good relationship.

I hoped so, for two hundred bucks an hour.

We talked about Warwick. She nodded sympathetically. She said the right things. What a terrible man, she said.

She made me feel better.

We got down to work.

You were telling me about your father, last time, she said.

Yes, of course, I said. Father, Warwick. Not subtle. But possibly effective. Yes, I was twelve.

When he died, I meant. He was thirty-seven. Keeled right over. Face in the lasagna. I wasn't there. I heard about it later. Aneurism, they said. I envisioned a dark-clawed beast, stalking the unwary in the night. The dreaded Aneurism. The reality was simpler, more insidious. A vessel burst, the bleeding uncontrolled. Invisible.

After that, only women. Mother, sister, wife, daughter. I'd never had a son. I didn't have a brother, either, anymore. My brother died. But don't feel sorry for me. I barely remembered him. I was four. He was three. He'd had a fever. They took him away. He never came back. It was really only from stories I was told that I remembered him at all. It was years after the fact that I began to miss him. To regret.

Twelve years should be enough, I said, to have generated one fond memory.

You would think, Sheila said.

But I don't have any. Not one. No hugs. No kisses. Not a pat on the shoulder. Not a good word. Nothing.

That's terrible.

Her sympathy was palpable, genuine.

Not really, I said. I mean, he didn't beat me or anything. I didn't grow up in a war zone. I have all my limbs. People endure worse things. And even if he lacked the skills to love a child, he did leave me something. He went to work every day. A real job. In the copper mine. Not a pussy job like mine. He never missed a day. Never complained. If he'd been sick a day in his life, he sure didn't let us know about it.

He set an example for you.

That's what I'm saying. Something in me always makes me slog ahead. Never give in. Keep on keeping on. And I know what it is. It's what he gave me.

But there's more to being a parent than setting an example, Sheila said. It would have been one thing if you had gotten some love from your mother.

Right, I laughed.

My memories of my mother were far more vivid. Most of them involved humiliation. But Sheila and I had been through all that.

It's a terrible thing, she said. It's a huge gap in a person's life. I don't know if you can ever fill it.

I liked it that she'd say such things. I was quite sure that they weren't in the shrink manual.

I don't know either, I said.

Really, I thought, wasn't all this the worst kind of self-indulgence? Who the hell had nice parents? Warm, loving, *Leave It to Beaver* folks? Nobody I knew, that's for sure.

I changed the subject.

There's something to be said for displacement, I said. It's the differentiation. I read an article about it the other day.

Sheila leaned forward.

I loved the way she always seemed interested in what I had to say. So what if I was paying her to be interested? So what if she probably acted just as interested in the turgid tales of all those addicted idiots, every stupid recidivist story of stopping and starting and telling the wife and kids they're sorry and starting again and puking blood in the airplane bathroom and passing out and not remembering a thing the next day and wondering where the hell that big gash on their forehead and the stuffed penguin came from, sounding exactly the same after a while from every pathetic one of them? So what?

I liked it anyway.

Children, I continued, the theory goes, contrary to the popular conception, go out of their way to differentiate themselves from their siblings. People are always surprised. My, they say, how different Johnny is from Joe. But it's actually not surprising at all. It's the natural order of things.

I was on a roll.

Differentiation is a strategy designed to maximize parental attention, I went on. A Darwinian world like any other. Your older brother already has a lock on, say, freestyle Frisbee. You can't compete. He's had three years' practice before you were born. So you take up tennis. Occupy the tennis side of Mommy's brain. Find a vacuum. Fill it.

There's a lot of truth to that, Sheila said.

Yes, I said, but here's the problem: You grow up. You become a lawyer. And then what? Who do you compete with for attention, wealth, success? All those things that stand for love in this society? A bunch of goddamn lawyers, just like you. And in that world, anybody the slightest bit different is viewed with suspicion, fear, hostility. Contempt. Who does he think he is, wearing sneakers to work? It's everywhere. Christ, they spy on you.

Warwick, she said.

Back to Warwick, I laughed.

Of course, I mused aloud, without this competition to be the best of a bunch of folks just like you, we would never have a genius. The one who transcends it all. By taking sameness through the looking glass. Newton. Darwin. Shostakovich. But meanwhile, the rest of us pay the price. Anonymity. Wage slavery. Disgust. Despair.

But some people don't feel that way, she said.

I suppose that's right. Or at least not as strongly as I do.

Not nearly.

Not nearly.

Next time we'll explore that.

Okay, I said.

My time was up. I was always agreeable about the fifty-five-minute rule. Some people were offended. But I used to drive a cab. I understood how a meter worked.

30.

I CHECKED DORITA'S OFFICE. She was furiously typing something. So concentrated that she didn't notice me in the doorway. Or so I thought.

I quietly installed myself in her burgundy velvet armchair.

Hi, Ricky, she said, without slowing down or looking up.

Hi. Hey, did you have a rough childhood?

Nah, not me, she said, the keyboard clattering away. Rabbi father, mom a junkie hooker. The normal suburban thing.

I didn't believe her, of course. Any more than I had the other seventeen times she'd invented a set of mismatched parents in response to a question about her past. Bikers, bankers, doctors, child molesters, thieves and poets. They'd all had their moment hanging from a branch on her invented family tree. I wasn't sure whether she did it to protect herself from some truly awful family history, or because the truth was so benign, so uneventful, that she was ashamed of it.

Either way, it was always entertaining to ask the question. To see what she'd come up with next.

Stop that, I said.

What?

She looked up at last.

Enough with the typing. I'm more important.

Oh, all right, but if I lose my train of thought I'm making you finish it later.

It would be my pleasure. Though I couldn't hope to emulate your limpid prose.

Limpid? she snorted, closing the door and lighting a cigarette. Have we been attending the book club meetings again?

No, no. It's just a word that always comes to mind in your presence.

I'm not sure how to take that, she said, flopping theatrically into her high-backed leather executive chair, putting her stockinged feet up on her desk.

Don't. You don't have to take it. Anymore.

I won't. I'm not going to take it anymore, damn it!

We paused. We smiled. We were very pleased with ourselves.

Where were you earlier? I asked.

Lunching with some ladies, what else? What's it to you?

I needed you.

Why should today be any different from any other day?

Yes, but this time I really needed you. Lucky my shrink had a cancellation, or you might be calling an ambulance for me right now.

Why for?

I told her the story of my small triumph in court that morning. My subsequent deflation at the hands of Warwick.

Warwick again, she said.

Warwick again, I agreed.

Ricky, Ricky, Ricky. You've got to get over this thing you have with him. You've let him inside your head. You don't have to do that. He's obnoxious enough from the outside.

Easy for you to say. You didn't grow up in the business with the prick. And get professionally eclipsed by him.

That's just what I'm saying. Who gives a shit? What price has he had to pay for that?

Not one I'd be willing to pay.

Precisely. You made your choices. They were the right ones. Live your life.

Damn. If you'd been here earlier today I could have saved myself two hundred bucks.

You'll get my invoice in the mail.

I've got a little T & E problem for you, darling, I said, throwing caution to the winds.

I'm back on the team?

You never left it.

God, you know how to make a girl feel good.

If only. Anyway, say I've got a trust deed. It leaves x gazillion dollars to my father, another gazillion to me. But I don't get it until I reach twenty-five. And there are conditions that have to be fulfilled before I get the money. So, I turn twenty-five, but one of the conditions hasn't been fulfilled. Who gets the money?

Are you pretending I don't know what you're talking about?

Yes.

Well, it's pretty lame.

I know. But given the circumstances, I don't have much choice.

Those nasty conflicts issues.

You got it.

So. To answer your question. It depends on a lot of things, my dear boy.

I knew you were going to say that.

Of course I'm going to say that. If life were simple, we wouldn't need lawyers, would we?

Good point. So, what does it depend on?

First, whether the condition can be fulfilled later, and whether the gift is worded in such a way as to allow later fulfillment.

Let's say it's irrevocable.

An irrevocable trust?

No, no. The condition. The fact that the condition isn't fulfilled. Say it says you can't collect if you've been convicted of a felony. And you have.

That again.

This is purely hypothetical.

Right. Well, I suppose there could be cases where that wasn't an irrevocable event. It gets overturned on appeal. You get a pardon. It depends on the wording, though. It always comes back to that. Did you get the language?

No, I didn't. I'm working on that, I lied.

The fact was, I couldn't remember. And anyway I hadn't turned the page. Could have been all sorts of other clauses I hadn't seen.

Let's keep it simple, I said. Let's assume the conviction stands. I want to know who gets the money.

This is as simple as it gets, Ricky: it depends. I've got to see the language.

I don't have the language. Right now.

Then it's very hard to answer the question. Because there can be express provisions for that. If there aren't, then the law is complicated. Heavily fact-dependent. Most of the time, though, it would go to the nearest relative. Whoever would inherit the donor's estate upon death, if the gift hadn't vested yet.

FitzGibbon.

Oops.

I didn't say that.

Right. Anyway, could be. But let's get the language. Can't you just call up your buddy Kennedy?

I'm sure he won't give it to me, I said. It's a client confidence. Kennedy's a real stickler for that kind of stuff. He won't bend any rules. I mean, frankly, if I were Kennedy I wouldn't give it to me either.

Then we've got a problem.

I know.

Ricky, you've got a client here. And he's not about to lose a lousy couple million. The kid could go to jail. And soon.

Good point.

So what are you going to do about it?

I don't know. I was hoping you'd have an idea or two.

My God, Ricky, do I have to do everything for you?

Well, not everything. But most things.

Jesus, she said, lighting another long thin cigarette.

She took a good haul. Blew a river of smoke to the ceiling. Looked me in the eye.

Okay, she said, let's get down to it. Hit the pavement. Examine the paper trail. We need more data points.

Data points? You're kidding me, right?

It's just shorthand, Ricky. The point is, the more you know, the more you know.

Can't argue with that. Okay, data points. Such as?

The usual stuff. Credit card records. Bank accounts. Telephone records. Did the deceased have a cell phone?

Who the hell doesn't?

Phone records are always interesting. We should get everybody's.

God's in the details.

And the more details you have, the closer you get to seeing the face of the Almighty.

Yeah. Data points. The Almighty. I'll see what I can do.

Redemption awaits.

So much better than rehabilitation.

31.

JAKE'S BIG GAME. I was looking forward to it. Something different. Something new. Something less Delphic than daily life. I reserved a limo, put it on the office tab. Research, I told myself. If I was going to be the house criminal lawyer, I had to get to know the criminal element.

Eighth and thirty-eighth, Jake had said. Not a nice neighborhood. In the civilized parts of the city, your eyes relentlessly were drawn to street level: the lights, the signs, the people. The store windows, with their stuffed rabbits and silk dresses. Here, at 10 p.m., there was none of that. Solid metal shutters put the doorways and the windows far beyond reach. The buildings were uniformly dirty gray. Monoliths. Nothing to see. Your gaze drifted upward. It wasn't pretty up there. Broken window panes. Dirt. The grime of ages. No doubt the upper parts of buildings were as squalid elsewhere in the city. But here you saw it. You looked up. You noticed.

The limo driver had let me off at the corner. There were no numbers on the buildings. I saw no open doorway on the block. Was this the right block? Was there really such a place? Had Jake led me on, led me into some . . . setup? I hardly knew the guy, after all. What was it that Hal had said about him not meeting your eyes? Was I too naive? Would meaty guys with hairy palms grab me from behind, take my wallet, my watch, my life? Who's that dark and dangerous-looking fellow on the corner, anyway?

Foolish thought. Too elaborate a ruse, for such a paltry goal. I looked again at the corner. Nobody there. The hulking brute was gone. Or hadn't been there at all.

My cell phone rang. I jumped two feet. 'Private number.' I ignored it. Damn. I'd almost had a heart attack.

I found the door at last. Dark gray. Flush with the building. Hard to see.

Just push, Jake had said.

I pushed.

Inside, the space was small, old and dank. The walls were papered with ancient flyers. 'Massage therapy: Call Helga.' 'Blues bassist wanted for trio.' 'Sofa for sale, slightly soiled.' Love for Sale, I said to myself. Johnny Hartman. John Coltrane. Good. This is good.

A low chuckle startled me. Apparently I'd been talking out loud. I turned around. There was a guy with a do-rag, hanging out. I hadn't noticed him. Weird. He was sitting on a kitchen chair, in the corner. What was he doing there? He certainly didn't look like a watchman. He chuckled again. I hoped it was a friendly laugh.

I nodded to him, pressed the button for the elevator.

The elevator took forever to descend. The do-rag guy was silent. I felt like I should say something. Strike up a conversation. But I couldn't think of anything to say to a do-rag guy in a tiny fetid lobby at ten at night. Lobby? Much too grand a word. Sinkhole, maybe. Death trap. For the second time, I wondered if I'd come to the right place.

Finally the elevator arrived, with much clanking and wheezing. I stepped in. Room for one. Two in a pinch. Random graffiti. 'Jumbo D. sucks cock.' I made a mental note. You never could tell what might turn out to be important.

Fourth floor. Step out. Turn right, left at the end, past the men's room door, from under which a sharp rank odor seeped. Three more doors. The red one. Laughter, shouts from inside.

I knocked once.

Twice.

Silence.

A voice.

Yeah?

It's Rick.

Rick?

Jake invited me.

Oh yeah. The voice grew fainter: Jake, your bud's here.

The sounds of chains and bars. The door opening. A heavy velvet curtain. The smell of mildew. The room lit deeply orange.

I was through the looking glass.

The place was tiny, windowless, rank with reefer smoke. Guitar cases, well-traveled steamer chests. A mammoth equalizer on a stand, a drum kit. A loft bed, rack on rack of CDs. Amps, a beer keg in the corner. A green felt poker table in the middle of it all. And that orange light.

Rehearsal space, it seemed. Rock 'n' roll tricked out for poker night.

It felt warm, and like a dream of childhood.

Introductions. Mike, Jonesie, Jake, Riverstreet, the Dane, Andrea. And the other Jake.

Yeah, said Mike, two Jakes. Straight Jake and Drunk Jake.

My Jake was Drunk Jake. He looked at me with bleary eyes.

Rick!

Jake. How's it going?

Never better, Rick. Take a look.

A mammoth pile of small-denomination bills sat on the table in front of him.

Andrea laughed. A woman's laugh. I liked that. Nicely out of place. Andrea. Slim, long-faced, all angles. Her arms delicate and muscular, all at once. Leaning forward. Open to inspection. Seductive. Between the sleeveless top she wore and jeans, the bottom of a tattoo. The apertures of a violin, or cello. Man Ray. A living Man Ray photo.

I was in love already.

Hey, man, take a seat, said Drunk Jake.

The seat across from Andrea was free. Mike on my right, my Jake on my left, Straight Jake next to him.

We're playing hold'em, Drunk Jake said, leaning close to me, whispering with a whiskey breath. See that guy, Jonesie? Famous actor. You recognize him?

Really? Don't think so. What's he been in?

Just made his big breakout. *Nine Times on Sunday.* Seen it?

No.

Fact was, I'd never heard of it.

I took Jake's word for Jonesie's budding stardom. For Straight Jake's one-man show in Berlin, Riverstreet's stock market killing, and the other morsels he slurred my way.

It was true that everyone at the table seemed to exude a certain self-confidence. An aura. A charisma, if you will.

When Jake told them I was a lawyer, it got the predictable response.

Okay, I said, so I'm a lawyer. So shoot me. No, wait. Sue me.

That got a laugh.

Listen, I said, now that I had an audience, it's not true, all that stuff they say about lawyers. Or actually, it *is* true, but it's only true about a certain type of lawyer. Plaintiffs' lawyers. Ambulance chasers. Champions of the dispossessed. Bullshit artists. Most lawyers, actually, are more uptight than your great-aunt Gertrude. Won't take a piss without clearing it with the Urination Committee.

You say? said Mike.

I do. They're very fearful people. Not risk takers. Don't ask a question you don't know the answer to. That's the cardinal rule of cross-examination. It's built into the system. Fear. Fear of the unknown.

Shit, I never heard that before, said Jonesie.

Of course not. Why would we publicize it?

He's got a point, said Andrea.

I usually do. Points are my thing. Getting to the point. Talking points. Pointed remarks. Singularities.

I was warming up.

Andrea took the bait.

Ah. Singularities, she said.

Points with no dimension, I replied.

Are there any other kind?

Infinitely dense points.

The point of it all.

She nodded as she said it, and dealt me pocket Queens.

I felt a surge of euphoria. And it wasn't just the cards. Here was a crowd I could relate to. I could let my mind and mouth run free.

I bet twenty bucks. I was in early position, but I had a good feeling. Besides, I wanted to project the right table image. Aggressive but selective. If somebody called me down, saw my Queens, even if I lost the hand I'd still have made a point. I make a big bet, I've probably got a hand. I could use that later, bluff a few pots.

As it was, Riverstreet raised me from the button. It was a pretty automatic call. The only question was whether I should re-raise. Feel him out. Anything other than a pair of Aces or Kings and I would be the favorite. If he came over the top on me, I could be fairly sure he had them, get out before I got in too deep.

I re-raised.

He just called.

The flop came all rags. I bet out again. Riverstreet took his time. Looked me in the eye. If he had a hand, he was doing a good imitation of someone who didn't. He raised.

I went with my gut. I figured him for Ace King, Ace Queen, maybe a middling big pair like Tens. He was figuring me for the same, hoping to push me off the pot.

I re-raised.

He mucked his cards.

I'd made my point.

I'd tripled my stake in one hand. But then I lost a few. These guys weren't amateurs. They weren't averse to slow-playing a monster hand. Check-raising an over-optimistic middle pair. Varying their strategy to keep you off balance. Players. No doubt about it.

I came close to tapping out. Got lucky with a full house on the river to survive. Boat on the river. Maybe that's how it got to be called a boat. Or how the river got its name. Which came first? It was hard to say. A boat to float you on the river.

The question seemed way too interesting. I was caught in a blur of beer and joints and laughter.

The beer was warm. I drank it anyway. Red plastic cups. Like you get at the ball game. I breathed the smoke. I had no choice. The room was thick with it. As the night went on my head got fuzzier. I folded a Seven Three off-suit in the big blind. Nobody had raised. I could have played for free.

Uh, you shouldn't have done that, said the Dane.

The Dane was tall and blond and young and well-meaning. I could have, should have said, 'Oh, sorry, didn't realize I was in the big blind.'

But I didn't. The guy irritated me.

Hey, I said, though I said it with a smile, hold'em is my game. I know what I'm doing.

If you knew what you were doing, he said patiently, you wouldn't have folded. You could have seen the flop for free.

Yeah, well, fuck you, I said.

I meant it as a joke. Tough-guy talk. But it didn't come across that way. He looked surprised, taken aback. I sank into my chair.

The flop was Jack Jack Six.

Oh my God, I said sarcastically, unable to stop myself. Why did I toss my pair of Sixes?

Sorry, said the Dane, contrite. I was just trying to help. I didn't know if you knew the rules.

I'm sincerely grateful, I said. Really, I am. I appreciate it. But fuck you anyway.

I was on a roll.

After that I lost another pot or two. I played too loose. I didn't want to seem a churlish guest. Maybe if they took my cash they'd invite me back next time, despite my bad behavior.

The cards started coming bad again. I couldn't catch a draw to save my life.

Cold cards, they say. You just can't hit a thing. When you do get dealt a pair, or a couple of nice connectors, Ten Nine suited, and you chase them to the river – correctly: there's been some betting; you've got the odds – you know the deck will deal the other guy his card, not you.

That's where the Zen comes in. The master of the game just flows with it. Okay. I'm here. The weather stinks. The beach is closed. My girl-friend left with Moe. Let's see what I can salvage. Here's a good book. A quiet bar. Chat up the waitress. Wait for my luck to change. Wait it out. It will end, like everything else. As sure as chickens come from eggs your luck will change. Just minimize your losses til it does. Take what the cold cards give you. Steal a pot or two. Don't ask for more.

My stack dwindled. I tightened up. I didn't play a hand for an hour. I started watching, taking notes.

It was Mike's game, it seemed. He lorded it over the table. When someone breached etiquette he'd fine them. Five bucks for betting out of turn. Ten for gloating. The misdemeanor jar grew stuffed with bills.

The idea was to play one hand at the end of the night for all the mis-demeanor cash. It was a lure, to those who otherwise might leave, to stick around until the dawn came through the window. If there had been a window. The saddest loser would hang around, for a shot at that last pot.

It was 2 or 3 a.m., I'd lost track, when the final hand came round. One hand of hold'em for a pile of crumpled beer-drenched cash stuffed in a peanut butter jar.

It wasn't really poker, playing one hand for all that dough. Just really rolling dice. So much money had accumulated from the fines that it dwarfed most any bet that you could make. It didn't matter what cards you had. I looked at mine. Jack Ten again, unsuited. Could be worse.

Two bets up front, the Dane re-raising. Normally I'd fold, but with that jar in view I wouldn't dream of it.

I'd sunk a couple hundred in the game so far. I was weary and annoyed, upset that I'd let myself lose control. The Dane hadn't spoken to me for hours.

The flop came Nine Queen Queen. Andrea went all in. Three Queens, for sure. She knew enough to know that bluffing wouldn't work. What the hell. I pushed the rest of my money in. An open-end straight draw. I'd take the chance. No matter what the odds, and they weren't that bad. With that much money in the pot it would be foolish not to try.

The rest all called as well.

Drunk Jake, who'd long before collapsed from excess booze and substances, lay sideways like a fetus on the floor.

I call, he slurred, although, seeing as he hadn't been awake for at least an hour, he'd not been dealt a hand.

Everyone was in. We turned over our cards. Andrea's three Queens. The Dane had a flush draw, clubs. The turn was a Two of diamonds – no help to anyone. The river came, and lo, the Eight fell. The Eight of hearts, not clubs. There it was. I'd made my straight. The Dane had busted out. The jar was mine. I leapt up. I crowed. I laughed. I felt a fool.

But there's nothing like winning.

I stuffed the stash into my jacket pockets. I picked Drunk Jake up by the armpits, dragged him out. I flagged a cab. I managed to elicit just enough inebriated mumbling to figure out Jake's address. Three blocks from my place. Convenient.

The cabbie smelled of cabbage and chipotle. He'd never heard of Jane Street, and didn't speak a word of English. I directed him with gestures.

By the time we got there Jake had revived enough to say, Hey, let's have a drink.

I'm not sure that's a great idea, I said.

Oh, come on, he said. I had a good nap. Let's party.

I looked at my watch. Almost four. I shrugged. What the hell. I was already fucked for tomorrow.

Come on up, he said.

Okay, I said. Just for one.

32.

I DON'T KNOW WHAT I EXPECTED his apartment to look like, but whatever it was, it wasn't what I got. The place was bare. As bare as a place could be and still have an inhabitant. The walls were white. The furniture was black. All of it. Couch. Chair. Table. Kitchen counter. A black-and-white existence. A couple of paperbacks next to the bed. I couldn't make them out, but they had the look of airport books. Thick, cheap and designed for maximum throughput with minimal effort. In the kitchen, on the counter that served for a kitchen, one plate, one glass, one fork, one spoon.

'Ascetic' was the word that came to mind. The only thing missing was the crucifix over the bed.

Jake motioned me to the couch, found a bottle of Scotch somewhere, and another glass.

A plastic glass. I laughed, as though this was a very good joke.

Jake handed me my Scotch, sat on the matching black leather armchair, across from me. He seemed strangely sober.

So listen, man, he said, I think we should talk.

Okay, I said. Let's talk.

Because, he slurred, we got a connection, you and me. We need to explore it.

Oh shit. I guess he hadn't sobered up as much as I'd thought.

You got any ice? I asked.

Should be some in the freezer, he said.

I got up to get it.

Listen, he called after me, my life hasn't been easy, you know.

I did not know that, I said, involuntarily adopting the Johnny Carson inflection.

Yeah, he continued, apparently not catching the irony. Things are all fucked up.

I found the ice. The ice tray was black. It made the ice cubes look dirty.

I mean, he said, there's stuff you don't even know.

What do any of us know? I asked.

Jesus on a stick, he said, you got a point.

He pulled out a tin box, rolled a joint. Lit it, toked it, handed it to me.

I'd had enough of the stuff already, second-hand. It made me stupid.

My mind would race in circles. But I didn't want to seem rude. I took a hit. I handed it back to Jake.

You know, he said, sucking in and holding a major lungful, sometimes you got to ask yourself.

Yeah, I said, thinking, Right, sometimes you do, man, and then thinking, Shit, I hate this shit, I just said to myself that I thought that ... what? What did he just say? Whatever. I just said to myself that he was right, and I don't even know what he said. I hate this shit. Get me out of here before I start thinking I know what he's talking about.

You got to ask yourself, he continued, as my refried brain picked up the thread, what's better? You tell the truth, you let it all out, or you don't. You keep it all in.

Right, I said, wondering if he had some Led Zeppelin.

You got some Led Zeppelin? I asked.

Sure, he said, yeah. All right.

He wandered to the stereo, picked through a pile of CDs scattered randomly on the floor, put one in the player. All of this taking an eternity and a half.

'Black Dog,' it was, and I sank into it. Yes, this was what you needed, at times like this. Every note and wail crystal clear and powerful, an echoing orgasm of meaning you knew you'd never remember later but it didn't matter, right there right then. Damn, this was some good shit he was smoking.

Yeah, he said. The thing of it is, do you know, or don't you know?

What?

Do you know or don't you know?

Know what? I asked, searching the swirling notes for the genesis of the question. It seemed like so long ago the conversation had started that I'd need an anthropologist to sort it out.

Shit, man, he said, his voice getting loud and angry, you can't tell me you don't know.

Know what? I asked, feeling strangely as though I'd asked the question before.

About the thing that makes me me, he said, that makes you you, that makes the whole thing so fucked up you won't even open up to it.

Okay, I thought, the fucker's off the deep end. He's hallucinating. Sure as hell he isn't talking to me. And I don't see anyone else in the room. Maybe there is, though. Someone only he can see.

I don't know shit, I said, steering it back onto the epistemological plane.

Yeah, he said. And I can't tell you, either.

He fixed me with an accusing stare.

One day, though, he said.

The guy was having some kind of psychotic episode, drug-induced or not. And I had enough of that at home, thank you very much.

I got the hell out of there.

33.

WHEN I WOKE UP next morning, I realized I still had my shoes on.

Does it get any more depressing than this? I thought.

On the other hand, I mused, it was very efficient. Take a piss. Brush the teeth. Pop the pills. Out the door.

Saved time.

The pills didn't kick in right away. I made a mental note. Check into the effect of vast quantities of booze and cigarettes, and a touch of dope, on the effectiveness of meds.

I amended the note. Forget it. I knew the answer.

Kelly was in the kitchen. I sucked it up. Acted normal.

Where's Mom? I asked.

My room.

Asleep?

Yep.

Okay.

Kelly busied herself with her omelet. Diced the garlic, the pancetta. Grated Emmental, ground some peppercorns.

Kelly was very particular about her omelets.

She sat down across from me while it cooked.

Dad?

Yes, angel child?

She smiled.

About Mom?

Yes?

You shouldn't be so hard on her.

Hard on her? Kelly, I'm not hard on her. I do everything for her.

Yes, you are. You're hard on her.

What are you talking about? Jeez. Do you have any idea what she's put us through?

A foolish question, I realized at once. Kelly rolled her eyes.

Yes, I do, she said. I do. But she can't help it.

Well, I don't necessarily agree with you there. She's helping herself now, isn't she? Since she got back? She's trying really hard.

That's not what I mean. Of course she's trying. But that's just the point. She *wants* to get better. But it's not easy.

You think I don't know that?

No. You know that.

Then what's your point?

The buzzer on the stove rang. Kelly got up to turn off the burner. She put on her cow-shaped oven mitt to put the pan in the oven, to briefly brown the top.

Kelly loved her cows. We'd gotten them on a whim one day, at Ben & Jerry's. They'd been hanging on the wall, with other oddities for sale. Absurdly overpriced oddities. But we couldn't resist the cows.

I think I'm very patient, angel child.

You're patient, Daddy. You're patient. But your patience shows.

My patience shows.

Yes. It shows. She sees it. She sees you being patient. Holding it in. It's like she's some cancer patient and nobody wants to tell her it's terminal. They whisper about it, thinking she can't hear. But she hears it. She sees it. It hurts her.

I was taken aback. The truth be told, I'd long ago stopped ascribing ordinary feelings to Melissa. She'd become a task, a puzzle, a conundrum. A burden, a challenge. Anything but a person, really. And Kelly knew it.

I felt ashamed. And angry. God, how much could this life expect of me? As it was, I felt my life was held together with rotting string and brittle masking tape. One trip, one fall, one more jolt and it would fall apart. Like a house of cards.

Okay, was all I could say. Okay. I get you. I'll try. I'll try harder.

She hugged me for that. She kissed my cheek.

There was nothing sweeter.

34

DISGUST.

Guilt.

What had I done?

I must have done something, to make me feel this way.

What was it?

I decided to walk to the office. To purge myself.

The day was cold and windy. Gray clouds and spits of rain. I buttoned my jacket. The cold wind in my face was bracing. I walked down Fifth Avenue. I took in the famous canyon of buildings, stretching all the way to the harbor. It was a magnificent thing, in its way.

Strangely empty at the bottom end.

I wasn't sure I'd ever get used to that.

I thought of people falling. Husbands, wives, sons and daughters falling.

I thought of the cold water of New York Harbor.

Breathless.

At work things were normal. That is to say, depressing. The same complacent, driven faces everywhere. The endless slough of information thick and unavoidable. A fax, red-covered for urgency. Must attend to right away. Don't ignore. An e-mail, in Alert mode. Must read, respond. Keep the process going. The telephone message slips. Calls from clients, colleagues. The whole preposterous, endless wheel of verbal commerce and pretense converging on my desktop every day again.

I needed a break.

Instead I got a call from Warwick.

Or rather, Cherise, summoning me to His Pomposity's chambers.

He wanted to know how the Jules case was going. He was meeting with FitzGibbon later. Needed some talking points. Warwick was a fiend for talking points. We often speculated, Dorita and I, whether Cherise prepared him a point-form list of things to say to hookers. Not that we had any direct evidence that he patronized hookers. But he seemed the type. In fact, we wouldn't have been at all surprised to find out that he had a dominatrix stashed away somewhere.

I shuffled and dissembled. I didn't want to tell him that I had a line on something. Something possibly exculpatory. That there might be someone with a motive to frame the kid. That it might be the firm's foremost client. That Kennedy thought he was not just strange but dangerous. Knowledge is a hazardous thing. It would be particularly stupid to put it in the hands of Warwick. So I gave him the bland version: It didn't look good. The cops, the ADA were treating it as open-and-shut. They'd charge him soon enough. The best that we were likely to do was appeal to sympathy. Emphasize his youth, the circumstances. Plead it down.

Warwick nodded, as though this was what he'd known all along.

All right, he said. We've got to manage expectations.

Yes, I said. I think FitzGibbon's got to be prepared.

Warwick looked at me with uncharacteristic admiration. As though I'd just discovered something deep and interesting.

It occurred to me, at that moment, that Warwick might not be the only one setting me up to fail. That maybe it wasn't FitzGibbon's confidence in Warwick, or the firm – certainly not any confidence in me – that had gotten me the assignment. It could be, I thought with alarm, that for FitzGibbon it was the very fact of my inexperience, my presumed incompetence, that recommended me.

Shit.

Yes, Warwick said. Well. Now that I think of it, that's probably a job for you.

Managing FitzGibbon's expectations?

Yes.

It figured. If a messenger was going to be shot, it wasn't going to be Warwick.

I knew I had no choice. I asked the obligatory question.

Do you want me in the meeting?

Yes, that's a good idea, he said, as though I'd just come up with a brilliant new notion. I'll make an excuse halfway through. Take an urgent call. Then you can brief him.

Excellent. Not only was he throwing me to the wolves, he didn't have the stomach to watch the resulting carnage. Afraid his pristine shirt might get splattered with entrails.

Okay, I said. I'll be there. Three o'clock?

Three o'clock. The Franklin Room.

The Franklin Room it is, I said, with as much good cheer as I could muster.

Good. You can meet the twins.

The twins?

Yes. Ramon and Raul.

He said it with a raised eyebrow. As though I should be intimately familiar with these twins.

I'm sorry, I said. Perhaps I've missed something. Ramon and Raul?

FitzGibbon's kids. You're not telling me you've never heard about them?

No, I don't believe I have. Ramon and Raul? Ramon and Raul *FitzGibbon?*

Yes, he said with a slight smile. Adopted, I think. Kept their first names.

Ah, I said, as though this cleared it all up.

It didn't clear up a thing.

But it did remind me that I had a case to work. I went back to my office. I called up Vinnie Price. Told him to get me whatever he could on Jules FitzGibbon and Larry Silver. Credit card data, assuming either of those losers had a credit card, which I doubted. Telephone records. Bus tickets. Laundry receipts. Whatever. I gave Vinnie the name of a contact I had at a small PI outfit, in case he needed help.

I knew if there was anything to find, Vinnie would find it. Which would nicely relieve me of the obligation of thinking about it. If he turned up a big pile of paper, I'd send it on to Dorita. It had been her idea, after all.

35.

THE TABLE IN THE FRANKLIN ROOM was highly polished. The newer leather chairs were neatly arranged around the table. A fine selection of hors d'oeuvres was prettily arrayed on the sideboard. The firm's best vintage Burgundy reposed in a crystal decanter. Most tellingly, Warwick was already in the room.

In short, a major client was expected.

Warwick's solo presence was not an unalloyed pleasure. Small talk was out of the question. I decided to use our happy little time together to press for a bonus for Vinnie Price.

This is not the time, Warwick responded testily. They'll be here any minute. And in any case I would prefer it if you stuck to the procedures.

Before I could launch into a tirade about the vacuous and petty nature of the bureaucratic procedures in question, there was a knock on the door. Patricia, our mouselike receptionist, peered in.

A Mr. FitzGibbon and a Mr. FitzGibbon for you, sir, she said, addressing only Warwick.

Send them in, Warwick directed, ignoring a golden opportunity to make fun of Patricia's simplicity. Not something I'd have overlooked, were I running the firm. A brace of FitzGibbons? I would have asked. A matched pair?

Moments later FitzGibbon père entered the room, full of red-faced bluster and bonhomie. The real FitzGibbon. The paradigm.

Immediately following came the pale reflection.

I'd like you to meet my son Ramon, FitzGibbon said, with just the hint of a smile.

Pleased to meet you, I said, extending my hand to Mr. Security.

I'm sorry Raul couldn't be here too, said FitzGibbon to Warwick. Other business.

Warwick nodded.

A deeply understanding nod.

Ramon took my hand with obvious reluctance. The touch was brief. His grip was wet and weak. I noticed a handkerchief peeking out from his right jacket sleeve. A germophobe, I guessed. I watched to see if he tried surreptitiously to unsleeve the handkerchief and wipe his hand. But I was distracted by Warwick. He was busily seating the guests, pouring the wine and passing the hors d'oeuvres with a grandly false air of festivity. If the handkerchief was unsleeved, I didn't see it.

Moments later, FitzGibbon's in-house counsel arrived. Marvin Threadgill, Esq. A tiny, well-appointed fellow. Polite to a fault. Good at what he did.

It was hard not to dislike him.

There followed an hour or so of back and forth. Threadgill and Warwick talked about investments. Projects. Tax shelters. Other business matters that I knew less about than I let on.

FitzGibbon looked as bored as I felt.

I did my best to participate. From time to time Warwick would call in a tax associate. A securities lawyer. To explain an arcane point or two.

They would stand uncomfortably during their audience, eyeing the food and wine. Feeling diminished. Until Warwick was through with them, which he indicated with an extra-loud 'o-*kay* then' that never failed to send them scuttling from the room.

I was about to fake an attack of gout when we finally got to the reason I was there.

I've got to take a call from the Governor, said Warwick to FitzGibbon. I thought Rick could take a moment to give you the update on Jules, nodding at me and sidling for the door.

No, no, said FitzGibbon, Charles, please. The Governor can wait a minute or two.

FitzGibbon winked at me. Warwick sat back down, with an almost imperceptible grimace.

There was much I could have said, but the presence of Ramon made me uncomfortable. I could argue that FitzGibbon was our client, for attorney–client privilege purposes, since he was paying the bills. But Ramon unquestionably was not our client. Anything I said, then, was not protected. The cops, the ADA, a judge could ask, if they knew to do so, any question they liked about what was said in that room.

And I certainly wasn't about to ask Ramon to leave. FitzGibbon and he seemed joined at the hip. So I felt obliged to give the sanitized version. Which was probably the wiser course in any event.

There's not that much to tell you, at this point, I said. Clearly they're convinced that he did it. He hasn't been charged yet, but it seems like that will happen any day. I sounded out the ADA. They don't seem interested in a plea. But Jules isn't either. He continues to insist that he's innocent. Fortunately, there's no physical evidence or eyewitnesses to tie him to it. But the circumstances certainly are suggestive. I'm not going to tell you it's going to be easy. We have our work cut out for us.

There was silence from the FitzGibbon side of the table. I thought I saw a slightly ironic smile on FitzGibbon's face. But it could have been the teeth. Ramon kept looking around the room. For assassins, I presumed.

Warwick felt obliged to fill the silence. Well, Rick, he said, a little too cheerfully, why don't you tell Eamon the progress you're making in your investigation?

FitzGibbon nodded absently.

I'm looking at a few things, I said. But frankly, I don't want to raise expectations, or mislead you in any way. So I'd prefer to save the details for when I have something more concrete to tell you.

Warwick gave me a dark look. He'd given me my opening to impress FitzGibbon with how diligent and skilled I was. I'd dropped the ball. I could just hear him afterwards: Rick, he'd say, you have to pay more attention to the dynamic in the room. They were looking to hear something from you. That man pays the firm a great deal of money. He expects exemplary service. Blah, blah, blah.

That had not been my take on FitzGibbon. I had read things in his face. Boredom, mostly. Vacuity. But the desire for some self-serving blather about the great job I was doing wasn't one of them. And anyway, I didn't care. I had a job to do, damn it, and I was going to do it right.

We escorted our esteemed guests to the elevator, executed the obligatory round of hearty handshakes, which Ramon deftly managed to avoid.

I went to my office. I looked at the pile of message slips. The blinking message light.

I ignored them.

36.

WHEN I GOT HOME, I was treated to an unexpected sight. Melissa and Dr. Hans Steiglitz were seated together on the sofa. He was holding her hand. Her eyes were red. He was speaking earnestly to her in a low voice.

When I came in, he looked up.

Mr. Redman, he said in his mellifluous way, smoothly getting up and striding toward me, his hand outstretched.

I took it, reluctantly. I noted the silk hankie in his breast jacket pocket. Worse yet, that it matched his tie.

Rick, he said, *sotto voce,* putting around my shoulder an unwelcome arm that perfectly complemented the uninvited use of my first name. Would you mind giving us a couple of minutes alone? I just need to wrap this up. Just a second or two.

Wrap *what* up? What kind of nerve does it take to ask a man to leave his own living room so that you can be alone with his wife?

Steiglitz kind of nerve, I concluded.

I saw Kelly in the doorway to the dining room, frantically signaling for me to join her. Without saying a word to Steiglitz, I peeled his tentacle off me and went to her.

What's this all about? I asked.

Shh, she said, closing the door behind us. It's all right. I mean it's not all right. But it's okay. I called him.

You called him?

I found Mom with a bottle, she said. Right after I got home. She was trying to hide it under the kitchen sink, and I couldn't believe it, I thought she was doing so well, and it was three-quarters empty, and I don't think the dog drank it. I could smell it on her, and see it on her face. You know.

I knew.

I called you right away, Daddy, she said, tears appearing in her eyes, but they said you were in some important meeting. I didn't know what to do. I called Dr. Steiglitz. She kept asking for him.

Kelly could see from the look on my face, bewildered and angry, that her explanation was not assuaging me.

Since when do famously successful shrinks make house calls? I asked.

I don't know, Daddy. I guess maybe they do. I just called him to ask him what I should do. Should I take her to the hospital? What should I say to her? Should I be angry at her? I was so confused. And he said, 'I'll be right there.'

The tears were streaming down her face. I was too angry to pay attention.

Since when do shrinks make house calls? I repeated, looking at the door to the living room.

I was in a rage. I should have been grateful, I suppose, that this famous doctor was there, giving my wife hands-on personal treatment at the first hint of a relapse. But something about him, about his silky manner, about the way Melissa shrank and groveled in his presence, gave me the creeps.

I went back to the living room, prepared to tell him to get the hell out of my house.

Steiglitz got up and most unctuously excused himself. Had to go. Needed at the hospital. So sorry to disturb.

As we reached the front door, he said in a whisper, I'll call you tomorrow with a report. For now, I'd suggest she not be left alone.

Slick enough to anticipate me. Slick enough not to touch me, this time. No handshake. No tentacle over the shoulder. Just got the hell out of there.

Smart bastard. I might have hit him in the nose.

I turned to Melissa. She was huddled in the corner of the sofa, knees to her chest, arms around her knees. Cheeks streaked with mascara.

Melissa, I said.

She stared straight ahead at the wall.

All the angry energy left me. An unutterable weariness descended.

Let Steiglitz deal. Let that scumbag deal. More power to him.

I slunk out of the room, went upstairs. Turned on the computer. Logged on. Anything. Anything to get me away from this.

Kelly appeared in the doorway.

Daddy, she said, what's going on?

Nothing's going on.

Okay, she said, with a hint of anger. Be like that.

She left. She closed the door quietly.

She knew. She knew I needed to know she was angry at me. And she knew I needed to be left alone. And she knew how to make both happen at the same time.

But something broke in me that night. The last tie to Melissa. The last thread of hope. That I could be the one to bring her back to life. That we could once again see life through shared eccentric glasses, and laugh.

37.

THE MORNING WAS DRAB. I was confused. Disturbed.

When I'm confused and disturbed, I call Sheila. Well. When I'm even more confused and disturbed than usual, I call Sheila.

I called Sheila.

She answered the phone. I was taken aback. This was a rare and pleasant event. I didn't have to sit through her minutes-long voice mail message, reciting the triage of telephone numbers: in an emergency, call . . . in case of urgent need, call . . . Subtle distinctions, but apparently understood by her clientele.

Don't tell me, Sheila, I said. Your ten o'clock didn't show up?

You are correct, she said.

Coke? I asked. Barbiturates? Compulsive masturbation? Run-of-the-mill alcoholic?

Silence.

I'll be right over.

I grabbed a cab. It smelled of ginger and anise.

I told Sheila about the night before. Steiglitz. Melissa. Weirdness. How I'd allowed myself to be overcome instead by what strangely felt like jealousy. And how embarrassing it was, to feel that way. About a doctor, however oleaginous, who not only was there to help my wife recover, but was doing so on his own time. Who had demonstrated again and again, if one sat back and took the more objective view, that he, and only he, of all the people who had treated her, could put his finger on the pulse of her addiction. Could actually get a reaction from her.

Yes, said Sheila, but is that so hard to understand? You've failed her, in your eyes. He hasn't. Yet, at least. It's hard to face. You resent him. You hate him for being the man you can't feel yourself to be.

She may have been right. But I wasn't ready to talk about how much of a man I couldn't feel myself to be.

I wanted to talk about good and evil.

Shrinks hate that topic. Hovering behind the notion of good and evil is the death of their profession. If we all went back to confession, they'd have nothing to do.

So we segued into the shrink-authorized version: Why was I so obsessed with it? Why was I so obsessed with whether or not I was a 'good' person? What the hell was wrong with me anyway? (That'll be two hundred dollars, please.)

One could put it down to the usual claptrap about the affectionless childhood – if nobody loved me I must have been bad. And I haven't gotten any better. So I must still be bad. I'll spend the rest of my life trying to prove otherwise. To my long-dead parents.

And that was probably true.

But what did it buy you?

Or it could be that the tattered shreds of whatever conscience (superego, please) I had left were desperately trying to dam the flood of narcissism that threatened to engulf me.

But what was that, other than a different way of saying the same thing?

Narcissism is widely misunderstood, Sheila said. Most people think of it as overweening self-regard. Love of one's own reflection. But that's not it at all. Narcissism is, in fact, a form – perhaps the very definition – of self-loathing.

Narcissus drowned himself, didn't he? I asked.

Exactly.

I recalled a passage from Norman Mailer's biography of Picasso. Mailer – himself no stranger to the notion of self-regard – explained, as I recalled, that the narcissist simply regards nobody's feelings as paramount to his own.

It's that simple.

It's the midway point, I said, between the saint and the psychopath. The one who doesn't credit others with any feelings at all. And the common wisdom has it backwards there, too, doesn't it? Most people think of the psychopath as *un*feeling. In fact, the opposite is true. The psychopath has raging feelings, insatiable desires. It's the rest of us who are emotional ciphers, in his mind. What was it that Ted Bundy said, with a shrug? There's a million brown-haired girls out there in the world; who's going to miss another one or two?

Or three dozen.

And it's the fear, I'm guessing, of descending to that state that drives a certain type of borderline narcissist, like me, to his obsession with 'goodness.'

Which notion Sheila deftly used to steer me off the abstract plane.

That might explain all the strong women, she said.

How is that connected?

You've always needed a woman.

I can't deny that. But that hardly makes me unusual.

But more particularly a strong-willed woman. One who will tell you what to do and think, in no uncertain terms. Because you can't trust yourself to make those decisions.

Yes. Melissa had been like that, once. Long ago.

38.

I CALLED UP RUSSELL GRAHAM, ADA. Maybe I could scare up a little more intelligence. Not likely, but worth the try. It seemed to me that there was all sorts of stuff going on here. Tangled relationships. Hatred.

Vengeance. Anger. Drugs. There had to be some tortured paths to follow, see where they would lead. Maybe he'd see it that way too.

There was only one way to find out.

I asked for a bit of his time, and a look at the crime scene photos.

I got lucky. Somebody had copped a plea. He had a free hour.

I grabbed a cab. It smelled of broiled octopus and seaweed. It made me hungry. I resisted the urge to stop off at a sushi joint.

Russell Graham, ADA, made me wait again.

Warwick was the same way. When you were granted entrance to the august chambers, he'd sit with his back to you, reading e-mails. Just long enough for you to imbibe the crucial fact that you were nothing to him. A speck. A mote. Worthy of attention only at his whim.

Like I said, this Russell Graham kid was going far.

After the suitable interval I was nodded in to the dusty, weathered room. This time his sleepy colleague had absented himself in advance. I sat on a creaking metal chair. Russell Graham sat, poised and professionally correct, behind his army-issue metal desk.

I guess you won't mind if I take a look at the photos? I said.

I do not, he said with exquisite politeness. In fact, I've had some copies made for you. He pushed a manila envelope across the desk. I glanced in quickly. Photos all right. I'd examine them closely later. Didn't want him to read anything into me, watching me look at them.

I decided to get right to it.

What about these twins? I asked.

There was a moment's pause. The ADA looked into my eyes. His look was searching. Not impolite. Earnest. Ambiguous. Well chosen.

The twins, he said at last. The adoptive brothers. Yes. We've checked them out.

And?

An interesting story, all of that.

He said no more.

Interesting, I said, yes. Any connections, you think, to the Larry Silver thing?

Another pause.

Haven't found any, he said.

Ah. But you've interviewed them?

We've talked to anyone who might have information.

I took that for a yes.

Seriously, I said, just between you and me . . .

He laughed a good-natured laugh, which I ignored.

. . . just between you and me, doesn't the whole thing strike you as a bit of a snake pit?

What whole thing? he asked disingenuously.

The twins thing. The mother thing. The whole thing.

I was being deliberately vague. I didn't want to tell him anything he didn't already know.

He reciprocated.

Ah yes, he said. It's an interesting family.

Don't you think there might be some rather tangled motives in all of that? Stuff worth following up?

We follow up whatever seems appropriate to follow up, he said, a testy edge creeping into his voice.

Well, can you tell me anything about these twins? Without revealing any trade secrets, of course.

He gave me a wan smile. Thought an inordinately long time. I pulled out a cigarette. Lit it. What the hell. I figured I was entitled. He wrinkled his nose slightly, but didn't protest. That was good enough for me.

They're curious, he said at last.

Curious?

Yes. Curious.

In what way?

He thought again. I could almost see the wheels spinning inside that handsome head.

They've certainly taken full advantage of their position, he said.

In what way?

The phone rang. The ADA looked me in the eye while he answered it.

He nodded his head once or twice.

Okay, he said into the phone. I'll be right there.

He smiled apologetically.

The audience was over.

I bowed to the inevitable. I very politely excused myself. He very politely excused the interruption. I understood, I assured him. It's the nature of the business.

The elevator ride to the street seemed to take forever.

Damn. The guy could have given me a bone. Dropped a crumb.

39.

I NEEDED TO GET OUT OF TOWN.

I popped into a record store. Picked up a couple of Allman Brothers CDs. Grabbed a cab. Curiously, it had no smell. I directed the driver to the local Avis shop. Rented a generic pale blue car, with Utah plates. I'd hit the road. A good long drive would give me time to think.

On second thought, I didn't want to spend that much time with myself.

I called Butch.

Butch, I said, let's hit a casino.

I hope you don't mean what it sounds like you mean, he said with a laugh.

No, no. Let's go play poker.

Ah. Poker. I'm tempted.

Come on. Take the rest of the day off. I did. If I can do it, you can do it.

I'm not sure that's always true, he chuckled. But today, it just might be. I don't have a whole lot on my plate.

I'll pick you up in ten.

Man. You've got a serious Jones on.

I do. Come protect me from myself.

Okay. But I'm charging my usual rates.

No problem. I'll take it out of my winnings.

I picked up Butch. We hit the road. I asked him to drive. I wanted to look at the pictures.

I figured we'd go to one of those new Indian reservation casinos. I'd never been to one before, but they were popping up everywhere. We could do our bit for the indigenous peoples, and scratch that poker itch.

I was pretty sure I knew which one was closest to the city, and what road to take. I wagered there'd be signs as we approached.

Once we were on the road I asked Butch if there were any developments in the Larry Silver case. That he could share with me.

Not really, he told me.

I pulled out the manila envelope. Looked at the crime scene photos. Offered them to Butch.

Nah, he said. Seen them before.

It was the usual grisly stuff. The left side of the kid's face was caved in. Okay, right-handed perp. That really narrowed it down. I made a note to check Jules. We get lucky, he's left-handed. Blood soaked down Larry's shirt. Stopped and pooled at the belt-line. He was sitting down when he got whacked. Another interesting detail. Maybe. Nothing much else.

Murder weapon? I asked.

I'm not supposed to tell you that.

Come on, Butch. They find anything?

He didn't respond.

I peered at the photos. Turned them this way and that. The wound was ugly. But symmetrical. Rounded. Narrower at one end.

Baseball bat? I asked.

Butch glanced at me. Didn't say anything.

Baseball bat? I repeated.

He looked at me again. Winked.

I wasn't sure what it meant.

There were signs for the casino, but it still took us hours to find the place. Once you got off the thruway you had to thread your way through rural roads and small towns, and in the end a forest. Twenty minutes of trees and the road opened up, and there it was: a string of behemoth casino buildings, stark, banal and insistent, in the middle of nowhere.

Not your father's Indian reservation.

Inside, we navigated miles of not so tempting kitsch. Trinket shops, arcades, three zillion tacky restaurants and the usual array of glittering machines designed to take your money all night long. We found the poker room, way in the back. They didn't want to advertise the game. The margins were too low. It was the only game you didn't play against the house, which meant that though the take was regular – a small percentage of each pot was raked – it was not spectacular. Never would be.

Three in the afternoon. The few active tables were full of lifers. The yellow faces and stale banter of guys who'd played each other every night and day for years. Just keeping busy til some fish swam up.

Once I sat and played a hand they'd all converge like sharks on chum.

Butch had no fear. He sat down. Bought in for five hundred. Gave me the wink and the nod.

I, on the other hand, I told myself, am not that stupid.

I wandered back through noisy corridors. They beckoned me at every step to spend my hard-earned cash on things I didn't want and needed less. Blow-up alien dolls. Ten-dollar plastic amulets. Tickets for the second coming of some washed-up third-rate crooner.

I resisted the temptations. I found the hotel desk. Checked in for a nap. Butch was a big boy. He could take care of himself.

The elevator to the rooms was hard to find. They'd hidden it in a corner. Back behind the Indian trinket shop. They didn't want you in your room. You couldn't spend your money there.

The bed was hard. The TV didn't work. There was no mini-bar. I fell asleep.

I had a dream. I was pulling at my ear. The ear came off in my hand. I looked at it with curiosity. Turned it over in my hand. On the back were buttons. Ah, I thought, in my dream, so that's how they're attached.

I drifted slowly awake. I touched my ear.

It was there.

There were no buttonholes.

I had no idea what time it was. My watch said seven o'clock. Morning or evening, I wasn't sure. The window in the room overlooked an atrium. No help there. Until I looked up. Skylights, black as pitch. Evening, then. A winter night in paradise.

I smoothed the creases from my suit.

40.

IT SEEMED FIVE MILES to find the poker room again. I stopped for coffee and a Danish. The Danish was obscenely sweet, the coffee thin and odorless.

I found Butch. It wasn't hard. He hadn't left his seat. The table had become highly promising. Two guys in Hawaiian shirts and shorts, red-faced and pounding bourbon shots. One long-haired guy, steaming. Cursing every card as it was dealt. Guaranteed irrationality on tap. It's what you dream of. A brace of young depressed compulsive losers there as well.

Heaven.

I sat down.

Deal me in, I said.

It was a five-ten limit game. Not huge, but you could win, or lose, enough to make you notice. I started slow, conservative. Taking time to educate myself about the players' tendencies. Mr. Longhair jamming every pot with hope and desperation, trying to recoup his long-lost stake. The depressives on the other hand played slow. Agonizing over every bet. Tight and passive, they call it. Plum pickings. Any time you felt like taking their money, you just put in a big bet. If they didn't have the nuts, they'd fold like origami. If they had the cards, they'd gleefully re-raise, their childlike excitement so apparent on their sallow desperate faces you'd have to be a brick to fail to notice.

Not to say there weren't some good players at the table too. Butch. Me, maybe. A woman to my left. Small and feisty. I liked that. I liked the worn suede boots she wore, zipper on the side. I liked the tear in the knee of her jeans. I liked the hand-knit driving gloves, the crumpled visored khaki hat. I liked her large and succulent mouth, her watchful eyes. I liked that she chewed gum with unselfconscious vigor. That she threw her chips into the pot the same way.

With all the dead money at the table, it didn't take long to double my stake.

Once I'd taken a couple of easy pots from the sallow pair of desperados, they wandered off to recoup at the slot machines.

I wished them luck.

I meant it.

I had a small rush.

Poker players live for the rush. The statistics guys tell you it's all random. And yes, you can grasp that. But, like saying love's a chemical affair, it might be true, but it doesn't come close to describing what it's like to be there. When you know, you just know, the next card will fill your boat. Full house. Give me your money. And the rush can run and run, hand after hand of mammoth cards in the hole and improbable draws on the end. Until, as suddenly as it started, you hit a wall. Bricks in your face. Wake up. Back to normal. Fold, fold, fold.

The key is to recognize the rush when it comes. Loosen up. And when it ends, go tight again, before you lose it all.

Every poker player knows the rush. Even the bean counters, the statisticians. A rush by any other name is still a rush. The master of the rush is the master of the game.

But it's a truism that most decent players can maintain their A-game only for an hour or two. Success, especially, tends to weaken your resolve.

I was no exception. I started loosening up. Feeling cocky. Playing non-suited connectors for a raise. Forgetting to vary my play. Even tourists will pick up your habits after a while. I was duly punished a couple of times, most embarrassingly by one of the Hawaiian shirt guys. Lost half of what I'd gained, on busted draws. Retrenched. Went back to tight aggressive. Got back to double.

The hours went past like a river in the rain. The dawn came through the skylights. It seemed like I had just sat down when I looked up and half the tables had emptied. As the high-limit tables broke up the pros drifted over, looking for small fish to fry. The game got tough. Butch was up a grand. He could play with these guys, with a cushion like that. I stayed awhile, to see if I could hold my own with them. A glib young Asian guy with shades and a thin mustache slow-played a boat and caught me napping. Just calling with two pair instead of raising or getting out. He and the dealer bantered like old friends. A grizzled bent-backed veteran sat down. He and the Asian guy traded unsubtle gibes about the fishing season.

It didn't take me long to figure out the fish was me.

I folded a few hands, until I finally got something worth playing. Ace Queen off-suit. A good hand. Not a great one. A hand that could get you in trouble, especially in early position. I raised. The old guy re-raised. The Asian guy called. Everyone else folded. I had a bad feeling.

The flop came Queen and rags. It's the flop you want with that hand. If an Ace comes, you can get out-kicked by someone with Ace King, which is exactly the type of hand the old man might have re-raised me with. But with the Queens, I couldn't get out-kicked. I had the Ace. And if an Ace came now, well, Aces up can win a lot of money. So I was feeling better.

I put in a bet.

The old guy raised, and the Asian guy re-raised. Hell, I thought. What was going on here? It was a rainbow-flop – the three flopped cards were different suits – and far enough apart that straight draws were unlikely, the more so because of the pre-flop action. Someone could have the same hand as me, of course, which would be a pain but not a disaster. The big problem was if someone had flopped trips. I eyed my two opponents. Could one of them have played that way pre-flop with a small pair, hit the trips on the flop? Sure.

Damn. I didn't know what to do. And I was taking too much time thinking about it. Giving them a read. I always try to take the same seven seconds to make my move. Fold, call, bet, fake an angina attack, whatever. Keep the tells to a minimum. But I was well over ten seconds. I could feel them figuring me.

I folded my Queens.

The old guy and the Asian guy checked it down. Showed their cards. Junk.

That was enough for me. They were very good. Or colluding. Or both.

I got up and stretched. The pros encouraged me to stay, eyeing my remaining chips. I declined.

Butch gave me a Look. The Look said: Hey, man, you're a pussy.

The office beckoned. A three-hour drive awaited. It wasn't going to be an easy day.

Come on, I said. I got to get to work.

Butch heaved a sigh of friendly exasperation.

We cashed our chips. Butch had a healthy wad. I hadn't done as badly as it felt.

Hey, I said, I did you a favor. Those guys were going to eat us both for breakfast.

Speak for your own self, said Butch.

I grabbed an acrid coffee from the kiosk by the door. I tipped the valet an absurd amount from the chips I'd kept.

They're only made of clay, I told Butch.

He shook his head in mock despair.

We got into the car.

My first instinct, on settling into the well-upholstered seat, was to lean it back and sleep. I fought the feeling, shifted slowly into drive. I drove. I felt empty. My stomach growled and hurt. I hadn't eaten all night.

My mind wandered with the road. Against my better inclinations, I started talking about Warwick.

He was not a man you reasoned with, I told Butch. Warwick was a man you obeyed or defied. There was no middle ground. The last time I'd tried to reason with him, I'd learned my lesson.

I'd come to the defense of a junior lawyer who'd been accused of having too much fun. Some associates had gone out partying one night, after a long day of combing through hundreds of boxes of financial documents. They'd had some drinks. Things got a little out of hand. Unfortunately for the young fellow in question, somebody had a disposable camera, and took a few shots of him blearily, and apparently incompetently, trying to impress his favors on a female associate. She was herself possessed of considerable, shall we say, charms. Which charms were rather well displayed, in at least one of the photos.

I was Chairman of the Hiring Committee at the time. Sometimes better known as the Firing Committee. Warwick called me into his office. Showed me the pictures.

I laughed. Silly kids, having a little fun.

Warwick found my laughter inappropriate.

What we see here, he said, is highly unprofessional behavior.

Charles, I said. They're just kids. Need I remind you of some of the more entertaining evenings we had as juniors?

He looked genuinely puzzled. It struck me that in fact he did need to be reminded – Warwick had a prodigiously selective memory. But as soon as I began describing a certain hot-oil wrestling incident of fifteen years earlier, he cut me off.

Those were different times, Redman, he barked. There are potential liabilities here.

Charles, I said. Last I heard the girl hadn't complained to anyone.

Be that as it may, he replied in his flat stentorian voice, the firm has a responsibility to react forcefully and expeditiously to such incidents.

Why should this guy be punished out of proportion to the event? I asked. Just because he was unlucky enough to have been with someone who had a camera? Worse things happen every night of the week, I'm sure.

We cannot fail to act when we have acquired reliable information, he pontificated. To do so could set a precedent, or be used as evidence of a firm policy of disregarding such incidents.

Don't you think this is a bit hypocritical? I asked. A whole bunch of our partners are married to former associates, Charles.

We cannot allow the values of the past, even if we personally share them, to undermine the well-being of the firm.

I felt like I was talking to a badly programmed automaton, and was about to launch into a screed about his lack of humanity when I noticed on his desk a piece of paper filled with neatly regimented point-form sentences. I belatedly realized that he'd been glancing down at his desk regularly as he spoke.

Egad, I thought. Talking points.

He'd been reading from a script.

I hadn't been talking to a human being. I'd been talking to a piece of paper.

Butch laughed long and loud.

With an evil as overweening as Warwick's, I said, driving mechanically toward the office, there must be a pre-existing pestilence, germinating in some organ or another. The spleen, probably. The gall bladder. Some eighteenth-century thing involving bile. I'm confident that whatever it is will kill him someday. I'm just not sure I can wait that long.

I got some friends, said Butch with a laugh. Anatomists.

Anatomists?

Sure. They specialize in certain bones.

Bones?

Sure. Kneecaps. Like that.

Sure, Butch, I chuckled, have them call me up. We'll do lunch.

For a moment, just a moment, I thought it might be a real good idea.

41.

THE OFFICE, WHEN I FINALLY GOT THERE, seemed a touch unreal. The light was too bright. The furniture shimmered in the fluorescence, vague, unfamiliar. My colleagues had a vulpine air. I saw an accusation in every glance. I tried to avoid them. I closed my office door.

All I wanted to do was sleep. I eyed the sofa on the far wall. It threatened to seduce me. I fought to resist its charms. Its soft cushions. Its inordinate length. Room enough and then some for a tall man, say six foot two, to lie upon. To sleep. To dream.

I shook myself. I had a job to do.

What next?

I figured it was time to talk to Jules again. Get his take on the twins. Find out why he didn't tell me about them. An innocent omission, perhaps? Never came up?

Sure.

At the loft I rang the bell. Nobody answered. I rang again. I waited. I rang a third time. A small, thin voice came through the speaker. Yes?

It's Rick Redman, I said. Is Jules there?

No, the voice said.

Maybe I could come in and wait for him?

No, said the voice.

Charm school. A wonderful thing.

Is this Lisa? I asked.

There was a long pause.

What do you want? the voice asked.

It's Rick, I said. I'm the lawyer. Helping Jules. Would you mind letting me in? I won't bother you. I'll just hang around. You can throw me out any time you want.

Another long silence.

The buzzer rang.

I pulled open the door. I found my way to Jules's door. It was ajar. Nobody in sight. I called Lisa's name. No answer. I invited myself in. I found an Anchor Steam in the fridge. I sat down on the beanbag chair. Brown corduroy. Nice. I sipped the beer. It was cold. It felt good.

Lisa appeared. She was eyeing me from the other end of the huge room. She looked as small and frightened as a misplaced mouse.

Come and join me, I said.

Unh unh, she replied, shaking her head.

Why not?

You're the lawyer.

We're not all bad. In fact, as lawyers go, I'm not bad at all.

You were hired by Jules's dad.

I confess. But Jules is my client. I'm acting for Jules. If his dad asked me to do anything that wasn't in Jules's interest, I'd refuse.

Right, she said sarcastically.

No, really. Join me over here. Give me a chance.

She came over gingerly, without taking her eyes off me.

As though I might leap up any second, smack her with a broom.

Sit, sit, I invited.

I felt a touch presumptuous, acting as though this were my home, not hers.

But she sat down.

You been seeing Jules for a long time? I asked.

She looked at me for a few seconds. I thought I could see a tear forming at the corner of one eye. She nodded slowly.

How long?

Three years.

I detected a need to talk, to confide. I knew I had to be careful, not to scare her off. But if I did it right, she might have something useful to say.

You from New York? I asked.

Long Island.

Really? I have a lot of friends out that way.

Silence.

You going to school?

I was going to F.I.T.

Ah, I said. I always wondered about that name. Fashion Institute of Technology. You'd think they might have come up with something a little more, I don't know, artsy.

Silence.

You said 'was.' Did you graduate?

No. I dropped out.

You didn't like it?

She shrugged.

What made you quit?

Long pause.

I needed to take care of Jules.

Does Jules need taking care of?

More than you know.

How so?

He's very fragile.

She uncrossed her arms. A good sign.

Are you afraid he's going to hurt himself? I asked.

The tear reappeared. She nodded.

Is that what you were fighting about, when I came over?

Her eyes widened.

How did you know that? she asked.

I didn't. It was just a thought. So that was it?

Yes, she whispered.

She hung her head.

Geez, I said. I didn't realize it was that bad.

He's had it very hard.

I know. He told me.

He did?

She looked surprised.

He did, I said.

The tears began to flow.

I don't know what to do, she said softly, wiping at her cheeks. I feel like I have to be with him every minute of the day.

Really?

She looked up sharply.

To make sure he doesn't hurt himself, she said. He cuts himself, you know.

I didn't know that.

On his stomach. He's got scars all over. He's got this Japanese sword. It's sharp as a razor blade.

I remembered the scars. The books. The nunchuks. The kid had a samurai fetish, evidently.

Are you worried he's really going to hurt himself?

What do you think?

Has he seen somebody about this?

She laughed a mirthless laugh.

Jules? You got to be kidding. He never wants help from anybody.

If I suggested somebody, do you think we could talk him into seeing them?

Never, she said. He's Superman, you know. Not the comic book one. The other one.

Nietzsche?

That one.

The superman in his cave? Waiting to come out and conquer the world? Needs no help from anybody?

That's the one, she said.

Super fucking Samurai Man. This was one dangerously messed-up kid.

She got up. I figured she was going to the bathroom, to cry a bit, or whatever. I got up too. To get myself another beer. But as she passed by she turned and pushed me back into the chair. Swung her leg over me, feline quick, sat facing me on my lap. She put her arms around my neck. She put her face on my chest. It happened very quickly. I was confused.

Did she need a fatherly hug? I put my arms around her. She was tiny and soft. She was crying. She felt very warm against me. I felt too large. Awkward. She lifted her face to mine.

It's going to be all right, I said.

She put her mouth on mine. It was small and soft and wet and tasted like need.

I felt a stirring that I hadn't felt in years.

Oh God, I thought, tell me the nightmare is over.

But not like this.

I pushed her back.

Lisa, I said, I'm sorry. I want to help you. But this isn't right. We shouldn't be doing this.

I know, she said, suddenly calm and with an air of wisdom that startled me. But I wanted to taste you.

She had a little girl's voice. But she wasn't any little girl.

She smiled a tear-stained smile. I returned her smile.

Okay, I said. You've tasted me. Now I think you'd better get back to that couch. Before Jules walks in.

Oh, he'd be okay with it, she laughed, lifting herself off me and going to the kitchen. Do you want a beer?

Sure, I said.

I was dizzy with the sudden changes of mood. Four, I could count, in less than half an hour.

This was one interesting girl.

Jesus, I reminded myself, she's not more than five years older than Kelly.

The front door opened. Jules was home.

Anxiety. Disappointment. Fear. Relief. How was Lisa going to act? Would she tell Jules? Had I irretrievably destroyed my objectivity, my credibility? Could I get her alone again sometime?

Hey, said Jules, as though my presence was expected. What up?

I came by to ask you a few things, I said. And tell you a few.

He flopped down on the couch.

Lisa bite your head off yet?

Not at all. She's been very nice.

Not too nice, I hope, he said, shooting her a Look.

I'm always too nice, according to you, she said from the kitchen, projecting her voice across the vast loft space.

That's a fact, he said, and turned to me again. What up? he said.

He had a strangely confident air, for a young kid under suspicion of murder. One who, I had just learned, had a frightening propensity for self-mutilation.

Tell me about the twins, I said.

He fixed me with a level stare.

What about them?

Why didn't you tell me about them? Let's start with that.

Why should I?

I don't know. It seems like it might be a detail worth knowing.

They got nothing to do with this.

I don't know that. I don't think you know that either.

Shit, man, I try not to think about those little slime-buckets, okay? It didn't come up.

What's so slimy about them?

You met them?

One of them.

Then you don't have to ask.

I guessed he was right.

Lisa brought over a couple of cans of Heineken. I took both, tossed one at Jules. He caught it clean. With his right hand.

Lisa vanished. Upstairs, I presumed.

Did you see either of them that day?

Who?

Ramon and Raul.

What day?

The day Larry was killed.

Them? Nah. Why would I have seen them?

Just asking. What about your father? Did you see him?

I try to stay as far away as possible, he sneered.

Tell me about the poker game.

What poker game?

The one where Larry said you lost two grand to him.

I told you, man, Jules laughed. The guy was wired. Wasn't no two grand.

Well, who else was at the game?

Shit, man, whose side you on anyway?

I'm on your side, Jules. I'm your lawyer. Everything you tell me is privileged. I couldn't tell anyone about it even if I wanted to. I'm just looking for somebody who can maybe corroborate your story.

He looked me in the eye, his lips curled in a good imitation of someone who didn't believe a word I was saying.

What difference would it make, somebody says I owed him, says I didn't?

He had a point, I supposed. If somebody confirmed that he did owe Larry, all that would prove was that Larry had been right about the debt. Perhaps hurt my client's credibility a bit. That wasn't my goal. If they said there was no debt, all it meant was that Jules was right. Either way, it wouldn't change the fact that Jules and Larry disagreed about it. That they had a fight. And it wouldn't say a thing about whether Jules chased Larry to the alley.

Listen, Jules, I said, I'm just trying to get all the facts here. You don't need to keep answering my questions with questions.

Okay. Yes, no, maybe.

I'm trying to help you, Jules.

I know. Sorry. Whatever. Sorry. Sometimes I just say shit, you know? It comes into my head. If I don't let it out, it stays there. It fucks me up.

All right, I said. I understand. Listen, maybe you need someone to talk to. I could put you in touch with somebody. Somebody who's real good to talk to.

You're kidding, right?

No.

Jesus, man, I don't need no fucking talk buddy. I just need a high-caliber rifle and a clear field of vision.

That's not going to help anything, Jules.

He gave me a hard glare. Then he laughed.

I know, he said. I was just pulling your chain.

I wondered.

42.

BACK AT THE OFFICE, I called up Vinnie Price. To see what he'd come up with. Not a lot, it turned out. He'd got the records. Jules didn't have a credit card. No surprise there. Neither did Larry Silver. Less surprise there. He'd got Jules's and Larry's cell phone data, sifted through it. Not much there to catch the eye, so far. Except, maybe, a few calls from Jules's cell phone. Calls to FitzGibbon's office. Four or five of them, in the days just before Larry Silver's demise.

Curious.

I thought about what that could mean.

I didn't have a clue.

I needed to clear my head.

Nah. I needed a drink.

Not mutually exclusive, I told myself.

I called Dorita.

She talked me out of it.

I admired her for that.

But I had to get away from the office glare, at least. We went to Starbucks. I had a tall something. She had a mucho grande skinny low-fat vanilla no-foam latte. Or something.

I told Dorita about the Lisa thing.

You pushed her away? Dorita asked in dismay.

Of course I did. What do you take me for?

Even more of a pussy than I thought?

Oh come on. Can you imagine the complications?

Mmm, yes. Delicious.

You're crazy.

I thank you for the compliment.

I think we should get back to business.

Let's get some paper. Make a list of all the facts. The suppositions. Draw some lines and arrows. Make a chart. Charts help me think.

You know, I think we should do that. But not right now.

What do you want to do now? Whine about your awful wife? I mean life?

Well, yes. I do.

Okay. I guess you have to take the warts with the frog.

Nice metaphor.

Thank you again. But first, I want to know more about the chickie.

Lisa?

That's the only chickie I know about. Are there others?

Not that I can think of.

That's a relief. Only so many chickies I can handle in one day. So tell me about her.

What's there to tell? I told you everything already.

Is she cute?

Oh for God's sake, does it always have to come back to that?

Yes. Is she cute?

Sort of. In a pierced and tattooed kind of way.

Describe her for me.

Come on.

Go ahead. It'll be good for you.

Jesus. All right. She's very small. Maybe five feet. Pale and thin, in that junkie kind of way. Green eyes. Very pretty green eyes. They give her an innocent look. Her hair is shaved off on one side. Heavily hennaed. Rings and stuff inserted here and there. Dragon tattoo on right deltoid.

Nice.

It is. It's a very nice dragon. Not a frightening dragon. A C.S. Lewis kind of dragon.

Did he have dragons? I thought that was a lion.

I don't remember. But you know what I mean.

Aslan.

That's right. Aslan. But maybe there was a dragon in there somewhere too.

Okay, go on.

Isn't there always a dragon?

Sure. There's always a dragon. Get back to the subject, smart guy.

I think that sums her up pretty well. She's a bit of a type. Tries very hard to cultivate the bad girl look. But she's not fooling anybody. Very vulnerable. She's afraid.

Afraid of Jules?

Just generally. She's fearful. I'm quite sure she's had a traumatic childhood. I'm guessing abuse by the father. It fits with how she acted today. From what I've read.

Needs Daddy's approval.

And comfort.

Some kind of twisted comfort.

Yes, but that's how it works, you know.

I know. So tell me, you weren't tempted? Even for a moment?

Of course I was tempted for a moment. Maybe even two. I'm a man.

In some senses of the word.

It was a challenge, that last.

I had never really confided in Dorita. Nothing very private. Our friendship was one of banter and innuendo. But always that tension, hovering over every bit of repartee. Why we'd never consummated it. That's what made it fun. One of the things that made it fun. That and all the things we shared. We always got each other's jokes. That was rare, and to be treasured.

It was fragile, that tension. Break through it and you couldn't predict what might happen. Perhaps you fall in love. Live happily ever after. But more likely, much more likely, the magic disappears. The delicate bubble bursts. You see that there was nothing more than air inside. And even that has dissipated. To the clouds.

Back to dreams.

I don't know what made me forget that. Some need, I guess. A need for consolation, for commiseration not artificially enhanced by two hundred dollars an hour.

I blurted it out. I didn't give myself time to think it over. To second-guess.

I couldn't have done anything with her even if I wanted to, I said.

There was a wide-eyed pause.

Ricky, she said softly, are you saying what I think you're saying?

Unfortunately, yes. And now I'm not at all sure I should have.

Of course you should have. I'm not going to take advantage. I swear. Right here on this empty coffee cup. I swear I'll never make a single joke.

I think you just did.

Sort of. But that'll be the last one.

Okay. Nothing I can do about it now anyway.

Sure there is. Talk about it.

There's nothing to talk about.

How long has this been going on?

Years. Since the first time Melissa went into rehab.

How odd.

Yes. A funny coincidence.

Sure.

Or whatever.

It's not physical, is it? I mean, they have drugs for that.

No, it's not physical. I don't have to go to a doctor to know that. Though I did. I went to all the doctors. There's nothing wrong with me. Physically.

Oh dear.

Oh dear, I repeated. Anyway, you can imagine how uncomfortable this conversation is making me. So maybe we can drop it now?

Dorita looked at me sympathetically. It was a new and strange experience, that look. I didn't know quite what to make of it.

All right, she said softly, but we're coming back to it soon.

Please.

No, we are, she said, in her don't-mess-with-me tone. We're going to fix it.

Ah. You are an arrogant young thing. If only it were so easy.

I admit to the arrogant bit. But I'm not so young anymore. And we *are* going to fix it.

I'd like to take you up on that. But I don't think we should be jeopardizing our thing with this. I shouldn't have brought it up.

I have powers that you can't even guess at, darling.

I have no doubt of it, and I'd love to see you demonstrate them. But maybe on someone else. I'll watch.

You'll need protective glasses.

Listen, I appreciate the offer, but frankly I'd rather you helped me with my poker game.

Not my field, I'm afraid.

Not that way. Come to the casino with me. Just hang around. Keep my spirits up.

Jesus, that's a job for Hercules. Anyway, I thought you had meds for that. Your saintly shrink. The miracle worker.

Now don't you start on Sheila. She saved my life, you know.

I know, I know. My competition. Anyway, tell you what. Next time you're going to throw another stack of cash away at the casino, call me. I'll be your, what do they call them? Your sponsor. Pull you back from the abyss.

Please, baby doll, no AA jokes. I get enough of that at home.

I'm sure it's a laugh riot, darling.

You're too kind.

I'll try not to step on wifey's toes again.

Damn. It was hard to keep that girl away from the edge.

43.

I WAS A BIT SURPRISED when Jake invited me back to his game. Maybe I hadn't made as much of an ass of myself as I'd thought. Or the rest of them had been as drunk as me, and hadn't noticed.

I asked him if I could bring my buddy Butch along. With him there I'd be more likely to behave. Jake checked with Mike. It was okay. They'd squeeze him in.

I didn't tell him what Butch did for a living.

The game was in the back room of an arty little joint in the Village. The Dane wasn't there. I was relieved. The rest of them were there. Jonesie, with a cowboy hat, two diamond earrings. Maybe he really was a famous actor. Andrea, in a black leather bustier and very red lipstick. She made me nervous, in a nice kind of way. High school nervous. Unworthy of talking to such an enticing creature.

Mike was in the captain's chair, looking fierce in a shirt with Chinese characters that he claimed said 'death to transgressors.' Riverstreet, looking sharp in a blue pinstripe with thirties-style pleats. Straight Jake, all Armani and carrying a large black portfolio. Preparing a grant proposal, he said.

Early on, the banter was loose and the play desultory. Just a bunch of players having a good time. Butch fit right in. He always did. He was that kind of guy.

There wasn't much check-raising, no big bluffs, at least that I was able to ferret out. And Drunk Jake stayed relatively sober.

The feel of the game turned when I took Drunk Jake for a big pot.

It was heads up. The flop came Jack of hearts, spade Ten, spade Three. I bet my Ace Jack. Pair of Jacks, Ace kicker. Pretty good hand. Jake called. The turn was a third spade. I bet, Jake put in a big raise. I called, feeling a little queasy about it. Jake's confidence was palpable. He could have the flush. But the pot was big, he could be bluffing, and my Ace was the spade, so. I had a twenty-five-percent chance of improving to the nuts, the best possible hand, even if he hit the flush. I hung in. Swallowed hard. And saw that fourth spade hit on the river. Jake stared at it. You could read him like a *New York Post* headline. He knew that card could be big trouble. He looked at me. I smiled. He shook his head.

He checked.

I bet big.

He stared me down. He looked at me for a long time. Wondering. Calculating. Going back over the previous rounds of betting. Had I been getting the odds to try to outdraw him? If I wasn't on a draw, could I have something big enough to have stayed in the pot? There was a Ten on board. I could have pocket Tens. Trip Tens was certainly enough to play with.

I was still smiling at him. He didn't know if my smile was real or manufactured. I could just be happy, to have hit my Ace-high flush. But I wouldn't want to show him that. So maybe I was bluffing, trying to make him think I had it. Or maybe I had it, knew that he'd know that I'd know that he'd know that I wouldn't want to show it but might be bluffing, and was . . . well, you get the picture. Poker's not an easy game.

In the end, he couldn't take the chance. That I'd gleefully turn over a pair of fours while pulling in his money. If I had the spade Ace, he could say I was lucky. Outdrew him. If he folded and I didn't have it, he'd look a fool.

He called.

I showed my spade Ace. He looked away.

Fuck, he said. I knew it.

He turned over his spade King Queen, threw them into the middle of the table. He got up, walked to the beer keg, drew out a pint into a plastic cup. Sat back down.

This was a new Jake. Normally he took the beats good-naturedly. He was drinking less this time. He wasn't playing the buffoon. He was playing well. You could feel his ambition.

He wants to crush me, I thought.

I was game for the challenge. I knew it was foolish. Poker isn't like high jumping, or tennis. You don't draw on extra reserves of energy and suddenly transcend your opponent's performance. There's too much luck involved. Like that last hand. I'd played it right. And over the long haul I'd make money playing that hand that way. But on this night, this one iteration, that spade might well not have fallen. In fact, the odds were excellent that it wouldn't. Four to one, in fact, a little worse. But tonight, it fell. And the other cards on the other hands for the rest of the night would also fall as they would, with no regard for anyone's ambition or resolve.

But we're all human. So Jake's reaction to the beat wasn't unusual. I didn't hold it against him. In fact, I invited it. It pleased me. Because it was dangerously close to a tilt. When a player gets so angry at a beat or two, or three, that he begins to play irrationally, recklessly, making big bets against the odds as though to bully you out of the game, he's on tilt.

You can make a lot of money from a guy on tilt.

But Jake wasn't on tilt. Not quite. He was focused. Determined. He played cagily. Tight. But mixing it up a bit. Taking a small pot on a bluff, he showed me his Ten Seven off-suit. He wanted me to know I couldn't peg him just for tight. A bit of unpredictability goes a long way.

But I outplayed him on that night. Caught him big a couple more times. I slow-played trip Sixes against his Aces. Just checked, called his bets. Checking and calling is bad poker, most of the time. And he should have known that I knew that. Had he stopped to calculate, he'd have known that I didn't have the odds to be on a draw, waiting for a straight or flush card to hit. So my calling had to mean something else. The slow-play alarm should have gone off in his head. But it didn't. I bet big on the end. He called, thinking I was bluffing. I won the pot.

More important, I won the ego battle.

He got darker after that. A couple of hands later I was looking at a small straight draw. I was in the big blind. Everyone folded around to Jake. He raised me in the blind. I looked down at a suited Seven Eight. A drawing hand. Not a good heads-up hand. But I felt like gambling. I was getting to see a pretty cheap flop.

The flop came Five, Six, King. Rainbow. But now I had the draw. And the flop had hit Jake. Or so he wanted me to believe. He put in a big bet, stared me down.

I just called. The odds said to fold. I only had eight outs: four Fours and four Nines. No flush draw. And pairing any of my cards wouldn't do it for me. Not if he had the Kings. Or better. And even if I hit the straight it wouldn't be the nut straight. He could have a better straight draw. Maybe that's what he was doing. Maybe he was on a semi-bluff. Had nothing now, but enough outs to a straight to make it profitable. Because I would fold enough times. Add those to the times he hits the straight, and you've got a profitable bet.

I figured him for the Kings. It was just a feeling. But you learn to go with your feelings. Separate a hunch from wishful thinking. Too many times I'd argued myself out of a hunch at the table. Found out later I was right.

I didn't see him on the semi-bluff. The bet wasn't quite big enough.

He'd have wanted me to fold without even giving it a thought. Especially in this aggressive mood.

Kings, then. Not a huge kicker. Not Ace King. He would have raised more pre-flop with that hand. I figured King Queen. I was almost sure of it.

Something about the situation felt just right. I wanted to fool with him. I flat-called.

A tiny flash of doubt crossed his face. More weakness. He didn't understand my call. The situation would indicate a raise or fold. He knew I was doing something funny. But he didn't know what it was.

I had him halfway there.

The turn card was an Ace.

Excellent.

I stayed calm. If he bet, I had him.

He looked at me.

He looked at me for a long time.

He pushed in another big bet. Double the first.

Raise, I said, without a pause.

Goddamn, he said. I knew it.

He'd figured me for the Aces.

He folded his Kings.

Love them semi-bluffs, I said, showing him my busted draw.

He said nothing.

I saw in his eyes something that I hadn't seen before.

Rage.

Butch leaned over to me.

Jesus, he said, careful. This guy could hurt somebody.

44.

I TRIED TO SLEEP.

It didn't work.

I went downstairs to warm some milk.

I glanced into the living room.

Melissa wasn't on the sofa. She was on the floor. Face down. One arm limp across the ottoman. One bent behind her back. An unnatural position for sleeping.

But she wasn't sleeping.

She was unconscious.

There's a difference, I'd learned.

I didn't stop to try to pick her up. I was too angry. I'd seen this pose before. She'd had the local drugstore bring some pills. Or come across the hiding place of some forgotten flask of vodka. Perhaps she'd even given in and breached the ultimate taboo, the talisman. It didn't matter which. Whatever it was, we were back at the starting gate. Again. It hadn't been an aberration. Tomorrow I'd try to deal. She'd tell some lies. She'd had a cold. It was cough medicine.

I didn't have the energy to care. Let Steiglitz care. Let Steiglitz deal. I needed sleep. I climbed the stairs. I lay down. I slept.

In my dream the fog had eyes. The fog had eyes to see through me. Through the fog I could see nothing. Nothing but the fog around me. The fog had a mouth. A face. A name. Hello! The face was Jake's. Jake laughed. He put his arm around my shoulder. Bought me a drink. I felt grateful. The fog had lifted. I turned to him.

I had my arm around a woman. Her name was Lola. Tall. Slim-waisted. Muscular. A snakelike thing. It broke my grasp. It got away. Escaped.

I woke up feeling strange. It was six in the morning. Too early to get up. I tried to place the feeling. I wasn't just hungover. Or anxious. It was something more specific. After a while it occurred to me: unsatisfied. I felt unsatisfied.

I lay in bed for a while, thinking about what it meant. To be unsatisfied. It was different from being dissatisfied. Dissatisfaction implied a goal. Something expected or desired that hadn't come to pass. Something specific. Being unsatisfied was different. It was an emptiness waiting to be filled. With something. Anything. Anything, that is, that would fill the emptiness.

But what that was, what that could be, I didn't know.

45.

EIGHT O'CLOCK ARRIVED at last. I got up. I took off my wrinkled suit. I put on shorts, a golf shirt. There wasn't a chance in hell I was going to go to the office.

Barefoot, I went downstairs. Kelly was in the kitchen. Her eyes were red. She knew.

What are we going to do? she asked.

I don't know, I said. I don't know.

I sat at the kitchen table. I put my head in my hands. I smelled of nicotine. My chest was tight.

Did you call Steiglitz? I asked.

I got his voice mail.

Did you leave a message?

I told him that we've got to get her back to the clinic.

More money. More post-tax money. For what? To give her another chance to torment us with false hopes and promises? Jesus. How much of this could we take?

I was trying to choke down a scalding cup of coffee when Steiglitz called back. Kelly answered the phone. He said we could bring her to the clinic. He wouldn't be in today. But he'd see her tomorrow.

At least they could keep her off the stuff til then.

Kelly went to her bedroom, where Melissa was hiding. I drank another cup of coffee. I cleaned the kitchen. I put in a load of laundry. Kelly was gone for half an hour.

She'll do it, she said on her return.

She'll go to the clinic?

Yes.

Just like that?

What do you mean, just like that? I had to sell my soul.

I'm sorry to hear that. We'll have to get you a new one.

I got a small smile for that one. She was resilient. She'd handle it. Hell, she'd handle it better than I would.

What did she say? I asked.

Never mind what she said. She said she was sorry. She made a mistake. She'll never do it again.

That's depressing.

Yes, it is.

Should I go and talk to her?

She doesn't want to see you. She's too embarrassed.

I wasn't certain how that made me feel. There was a kind of relief. That I wouldn't have to deal with her. Too many emotions. Loud, insistent and inconsistent emotions. I needed a rest from emotions. But it was also a rejection, of a sort. She didn't need me anymore.

But had she ever?

Everything I'd ever thought or felt about Melissa was suspect.

I called an office limo for them. I asked them to send Christof. He'd take good care of Kelly.

I went to my bedroom. Booted up the computer. Nosed around some paleontology sites. Sometimes old bones can be comforting.

I heard the limo pull away.

The bones weren't doing it for me.

I had to get away.

I called Dorita.

46.

WE AGREED TO MEET at Trois Pistoles, a nice French bistro near the park. If the mood struck us, we could take a stroll after lunch.

We ordered a nice but inexpensive bottle of Burgundy. We had steak frites. Dorita was a demon for steak frites. For any kind of steak. For meat. Red meat. Red bloody meat. When the waiter asked her how she wanted her steak, she made her usual scene.

Rare, she said. And I mean rare. With a capital R.

Certainly, madame, the waiter said.

No, she said, I don't think you understand. Make it all caps.

Certainly, madame, he repeated.

Twitching, she said. I want it twitching.

Pardon me, madame?

If I can't taste the fear, it's too well done. Get it?

The waiter looked around for help.

Oh, never mind, she said.

Certainly, madame, he replied.

After he had left us, no doubt to regale the kitchen staff with tales of the tall, slim lady and her lust for blood and fear, I got right down to business. I didn't want to give Dorita a chance to go personal. I'd been having serious second thoughts about revealing my secrets to her. I was not at all sure that our thing could survive. I'd seen a face of Dorita – the kind and sympathetic side – I'd always suspected but never confirmed was there. The dissonance between it and the jolly misanthrope I'd grown to know and love was highly disconcerting. It meant complication. Ambiguity. Doubt. In other words, the very things that defined my marriage. That I'd used my friendship with Dorita to escape.

I wanted to get back to being Nick and Nora, sexually ambiguous detectives.

We talked about Jules. I brought her up to date. The phone records.

That's an interesting detail, she said. I thought they weren't on speaking terms.

So they've both told me. But it reminded me of something FitzGibbon said when I first went to see him. Something about how Jules didn't have the balls to call home. I mean, if they weren't even talking to each other, why would he have expected Jules to call him?

Hm. Something to ask him about.

Jules?

Either or both.

No doubt. I'll have to think about how to approach it, though. Clients don't normally take it well, when they find out you've been surreptitiously looking at their phone records.

There's that too.

We searched for benign reasons for Jules to be calling his hated father.

Asking for money? I suggested.

Possible.

Forgiveness?

Unlikely.

Threatening him?

Much more plausible.

But with what? The kid's a small-time loser. Daddy's a big-time player.

I told her about the samurai connection.

Jesus, she said. Sounds like the kid needs a shrink real bad.

No kidding. But he thinks he's Superman. Don't need no help from nobody. You know.

Denial.

The alcoholic syndrome.

I guess you'd know about that.

I guess I wouldn't be the only one in the room.

Sure. You got me. But you're not his shrink, you're his lawyer. What do you care? I mean, he did or he didn't, right?

I'm not in the 'he did it' business, darling; I'm in the 'he didn't do it' business.

Thanks for reminding me. So, what else?

I told her about my conversation with Kennedy. His fears about FitzGibbon.

My, she said. Maybe Daddy *is* more than just an obnoxious blowhard.

Could be. But.

But.

Well, say we do a little investigating. Turn over a few flat rocks. Find some slimy things.

Crawling things.

Slugs.

Centipedes.

Rot.

Ugh.

We find out FitzGibbon's more than just a fatuous dickhead.

He's a psychopathic fatuous dickhead.

He set up his son.

He killed Larry Silver.

And framed poor Jules.

Right.

And then what? I asked.

He goes to jail.

He goes to jail. Right. And?

You're a hero.

Am I?

Sure. Front page of the *Post.*

Get an agent.

Book deal.

Movie rights.

Syndication.

You'd better be right.

How so?

Think about it, I said.

I gave her the under-the-eyebrows look.

Ah.

Right.

The firm just lost its biggest client.

I'm not on probation anymore.

No, you're not.

Instead, I'm fired.

You're fired.

And so are you.

Darn, she said. Aiding and abetting. You're right.

And even if by some miracle we're not fired, the firm goes under anyway.

Fifteen million in billings.

Up in smoke.

Unless the twins hire us. Having inherited the business.

Yes. That might happen. They'll be so grateful. That we've incarcerated their dad.

I see your point.

We sat in silence for a while. Contemplating the ramifications. The imponderables. The tangled web.

Oh, fuck it, Dorita said at last.

In what sense might you mean that?

The usual sense. The 'fuck it' sense. Fuck it. Let's do the right thing. Let's do it right. The consequences be damned.

They're unknowable anyway.

We can only calculate the probabilities.

Let's not go there. Too complicated.

It's so much simpler.

What is?

To do the right thing.

Indeed.

Yes. Do it right. Do our job. Hell, Warwick handed this crap to you. How can he complain, just because you do it right?

And anyway, who says FitzGibbon did anything wrong?

He could be innocent, I suppose.

Of this, anyway.

Of this.

Sure. Maybe the maid did it.

Or that old lady next door.

The one dressed in the Anthony Perkins outfit.

Hmm. You hadn't told me about her. Are you holding back on me again?

I could see Ramon in that outfit. And speaking of the twins again . . .

Ramon, Raul, she said. Trips right off the tongue. I wonder if FitzGibbon made up the names too?

You'd think he'd have enough imagination to come up with 'Carlos' or 'Pedro.' Something that started with a different letter.

Yes. A viable theory. We'll keep it on the list.

Good. I like to think I'm making some kind of contribution to the enterprise.

Oh please, darling. You're the boss. Isn't that enough for you?

The boss? This is news. When was the title bestowed?

Just now, she said with an indulgent smile. I knew it would make you feel better.

You were right. I feel much better.

So, you were saying?

About those twins. I think we ought to dig around a little. I mean, why did FitzGibbon keep that bit of information from me?

Did it ever come up?

Well, one would think, when discussing wills and trusts and mothers and sons and things, that it would be natural to mention, at least, the existence of two potential heirs. Besides, one of them was right there in FitzGibbon's office. FitzGibbon said he was Security.

Ah. That is indeed curious. Or not. Would someone normally introduce his son to a perfect stranger?

Perhaps not. But it would be more believable if he'd said nothing. Why say he was Security?

Maybe he is.

Part-time job for Daddy Warbucks?

Right.

But still. And somehow Jules never mentioned them either. Which I find even stranger.

Had other things on his mind, I guess.

Maybe. But he was awfully defensive when I asked him about them.

Why would *he* want to hide them from you?

I'm not saying he did. But it's a possibility. Have to keep it on the list. No evidence to exclude it. Implausibility is not a criterion for removal. Many things seem implausible, until more facts are in.

Quarks.

Not the first example that comes to mind, but yes. Quarks.

The indeterminacy of the quantum world.

Right. Although right now I'd prefer to stay on a somewhat less rarefied plane, thank you.

Oh, all right. I thought you liked that kind of stuff.

I do. I do. But right now I'd like to keep playing unsophisticated gumshoe, if you don't mind.

I don't mind.

Okay. So. My point is, we know a lot of stuff. Some of it makes perfect sense. Is irrefutable. Or close to it. There's a body. It's homicide. Jules and the former owner of the body had a fight earlier. Not long earlier. If he's convicted, he'll be out of luck on the trusts. FitzGibbon hates his son, and would be happy if he lost the trusts. All of this seems clear enough. At least enough to serve as a starting point. But we don't have enough information to put everything together. To make sense of it all. Even to have an idea whether we're wasting our time. That Jules just did it. Too bad. Work the plea angle.

Agreed.

So, the more information we can gather, the better. The closer we can get to at least achieving that critical mass of data that will tell us whether our efforts have a reasonable chance of bearing fruit.

I love it when you get into professorial mode.

Sorry, I didn't mean to.

It's so sexy.

Please don't go there.

Sorry. But you left something out.

Yes?

Data points.

Jesus, I said, you're relentless.

47.

WHEN DORITA LEFT, I missed her. This was not good. This was not how carefree friends were supposed to feel. Damn. What was I doing to myself? My life was already complicated enough.

I was confused.

Well, I sighed, since I'm confused, there's only one thing to do.

I called. She was free. This was good.

I walked there.

I needed the exercise.

Halfway there my cell phone rang. 'Private number.' Jesus.

This time I answered.

I heard a clattering sound. Some muffled grunts. Then the line went dead.

Just what I needed. Crank calls. I resolved to go back to ignoring private numbers.

Sheila was wearing a suit.

My, I said, you're looking very corporate today.

She usually wore her quasi-hippy gear. Sandals. Baggy flowered top of some kind. Jeans, or something between hospital workers' greens and silk pajamas.

She smiled, ignored my comment.

Okay, I said. On to matters more germane.

I wanted to talk about this Dorita thing. I wanted to talk about how radically I needed to sublimate – or was it how radical was the sublimation I needed? – when the need that needed to be sublimated was itself so radically submerged. But I couldn't. For some reason it didn't feel right. I didn't feel ready. Not that I thought that Sheila would react in some inappropriate, some disabling way. Just that I didn't think that I was ready to handle facing up to it. Getting up front and personal with my own personal Monster. Couldn't do it. Not that day.

We talked about the strange and liberating coldness that I felt in the face of Melissa's relapse.

There's got to come a point when you recognize her responsibility for her own condition, she said. That it's not your doing. You're like the child who blames himself for his parents' divorce. It's not your fault. And you don't have to live in hell forever. She's created that hell. Not you. And only she can un-create it. You've done what you can do. It's time to sit back. Let nature take its course. Or Melissa. If she's ever to be rid of this, it won't be because of anything *you* do or say. It has to come from within herself.

Sheila rarely went on at such length. But I'd lobbed her an easy one. And she'd hit it out of the park. Yes, of course. That was what I had been feeling. It wasn't cold, unfeeling evil. It was resignation. It was taking back my life. And it was okay.

We talked about work. My increasing disillusion with the gamesmanship and intellectual squalor of office life.

She made the usual sympathetic noises.

The sympathetic noises helped. But they weren't quite enough. We talked about tinkering with the meds. Increasing my dosages. I refrained as usual from telling her about the extra Valium I'd stolen from one of Melissa's many stashes. Not because she wouldn't understand. Because she might tell me about some deadly side effect. Of mixing it with all that other stuff. Then I'd have to give it up.

I'm thinking of quitting the legal biz, I said. Become a professional poker player.

Really? That's interesting.

Interesting? I thought you'd disapprove.

Why would you think that?

Don't you addiction people think of gambling as just another species of the beast? Wouldn't you be afraid I'd succumb? Make my life even more ruinous than it already is?

Your life isn't ruinous. You know that. And yes, it can be an addiction. A very destructive one. But I don't see you as a gambling addict. I think you're too calculating. Actually, I see you more like one of my other clients. He quit a very successful investment banking career and opened his own poker room. Right here in the city. He's doing very well. And he's happy. More happy than he ever was making five times the money.

That's positively inspiring. And you think it's okay? Isn't running a poker room illegal?

I wouldn't know. But you know I don't make those kind of judgments.

The moral agnosticism of the shrink profession never failed to give me pause. It didn't seem to fit, somehow. Perhaps it was some residual connection my subconscious made between therapy and confession, but I always expected Sheila to show some disapproval, however subtle, when I told her of my less savory actions and thoughts. But she never did. She was very consistent that way.

Well then, I said, I'll keep it on the agenda. I wouldn't know how to start, though, to tell you the truth. Which I always do, you know.

Know how to start?

Tell the truth.

Ah.

But not all of it.

She smiled her warm smile.

You wouldn't be you if you did, she said.

I shook my head in admiration. She knew me better than I knew myself.

Of course, that's what I was paying her for.

Anyway, as I was saying, I continued, to tell you the truth I wouldn't know where to begin. But I can do some research. How hard can it be? Can't be harder than what I do now, can it?

I would think not. We know that anything you apply yourself to you can do.

Sublimation, I said.

Sublimation?

She raised an eyebrow.

That's what it is, isn't it?

What what is?

This poker thing.

Maybe, she said.

Sometimes she liked to go into mysterious mode. Let me figure it out. Old-style shrinkification. But she saved it for special moments. When she knew I was close to something. When she could sit back and let me break out. Open a new door. Take a new step.

How far I still had to go. Before I could just sit in a chair, in the sun, sipping an iced coffee, and think, wow, it's a beautiful day.

Damn, I said, you're good.

She smiled her indulgent smile.

Did she like a compliment, like the rest of us? Or did she put it in a box, with the rest of my neuroses, neatly labeled? 'Rick Redman's compulsive aggrandizement of therapist: overcompensation for lack of parental objects of veneration in anal stage,' blah, blah.

Who knew? Who cared? Hey, it made me feel better.

Surely that was enough.

48.

I CALLED BUTCH.

I asked him if he knew about the twins.

Sure, he said. Job one is track down the family. You know that.

Of course. It's just that their existence seems to be something of a secret. In certain circles, anyway.

Could be. I don't know about that. But we tracked them down pretty quick.

Okay. You interviewed them, then?

Somebody did.

I meant the institutional you.

Right. Not much there. I heard they and the kid didn't get along too good. But that's just hearsay.

Anybody ask where they were that night?

Sure. You always ask.

You do?

We do.

One does.

Right. They were at some club. Some exclusive kind of place.

You know the name of the club?

The White Swallow.

Don't think I know that one.

I'd be surprised if you did. A little upscale for you, I'd think. Besides, you're way too old.

Really? I guess you'd be in a position to make that kind of judgment.

Butch laughed. I laughed.

He gave me the address of the club, the name of the owner.

The place wasn't far away. I grabbed Dorita. We walked over.

When we got to the address, I figured I had written it down wrong. There was no sign proclaiming the existence of a club. The street number was crudely painted on a metal door.

Dorita pointed out that this was exactly what you'd expect to find at an exclusive, known-only-to-the-plugged-in-few dance and debauchery joint.

If you say so, I said.

We knocked.

No answer.

I stepped back from the door. From that vantage, I realized that the crudeness was feigned. The numbers were shaped to resemble a bird in flight. A white bird.

Yep, I said. This is the place.

We knocked again.

The door opened a crack. A small thin man with a pencil mustache peered out. Can I help you? he asked. He had a heavy eastern European accent.

Is Anfernee here? I asked. We have a business proposition for him.

The thin man looked suspicious.

Wait here, he said.

It must have been ten minutes before he returned. Time enough for a smoke, anyway. When he finally came back he opened the door wide.

Come in, he said. Mr. Wallender will see you now.

I wanted to ask him where he'd left his hunchback, but thought better of it. Dorita looked like she wanted to say something similar. Or, knowing her, worse. I jabbed her in the elbow, gave her a stern look. She got the message. Reluctantly.

Igor led us through a maze of black-painted corridors, into a large octagonal room in which a dozen or so heavily sweating workers were variously hammering, sawing, humming and wallpapering under the direction of an elegantly high-strung Cole Porter look-alike. If Cole Porter had had a North African mother. The smoothest milk chocolate skin I had ever seen. An elegant slightly curved nose. A fabulously expensive silk shirt. And an air of absolute entitlement that made his warm, sympathetic brown eyes seem strangely out of place.

Anfernee Wallender thrust out a limp hand, as if to indicate that ring-kissing would not be out of place. I was tempted to crush it with a Manly Squeeze, but refrained, remembering that we wanted information from the guy.

Rick Redman, I said. And this is my colleague, Dorita Reed.

Most pleased to meet you, said Wallender. I understand you have some kind of business proposition for me?

Not exactly. Actually, I just used that to get by your assistant here.

I looked around for Igor, but he seemed to have vanished into the darkness.

Igor. Yes. He's very protective.

You're kidding, right?

Kidding?

His name isn't really Igor, is it?

Sure. It's like 'John' in Russia. Very common.

Wow.

Wallender looked puzzled.

Never mind, I said.

Dorita suppressed a giggle.

I must let you know, said Wallender. As you can see, I'm very preoccupied here. We have to get this room ready for the VIP opening tonight. And there's a great deal left to be done. If you don't really have any business to discuss . . .

He said this in a sincere, apologetic tone. He looked frankly into my eyes. I could feel the pull of the professional facilitator. He aimed to please. You wanted to like him. You wanted to accommodate his needs.

Yes, I said. Sorry about the little ruse. We won't take much of your time. We're investigating an incident. We just have a few questions we'd like to ask you.

An incident? he said, raising his eyebrows.

A murder. A homicide.

Good Lord. What could such a thing have to do with me?

Nothing to do with you, I assured him. But maybe something to do with some people you know.

Lucious. I knew I never should have brought him back. What's he done now?

I don't know who Lucious is, I said, but I don't think he's the person we're interested in. Do you know Ramon and Raul – I paused involuntarily at the incongruity of the last name – FitzGibbon?

The Fitz brothers! Wallender exclaimed. Of course. They have something to do with this?

His mouth hung open in a convincing show of incredulity.

How is it that you know them? Dorita asked.

I could feel her itching to take over the conversation.

Um, perhaps I should know who you are, Wallender said. Are you with the police?

No, Dorita said. We're just lawyers.

Oh. Are you representing the Fitzes?

No, I said. We're representing someone else. Did the police not talk to you about this?

Not me. He paused. His mouth opened, closed.

Ah, he said. I remember now. Yes. I wasn't here. They talked to Igor. I see.

Who might it be? he asked. That you represent?

Nobody you would know, Dorita said.

All right. I think I understand. Am I to take it that you're not at liberty to reveal the identity of your client?

That's correct, I said.

This seemed to reassure him. He returned to the topic of the twins.

They're one – two – of our best customers, he said. More than customers. Friends. Part of the fabric of the place. They were here at the inauguration. They pitch in. It's like the Club is their second home. They've been intimately involved in the renovations. They have very good taste.

He paused, perhaps suddenly aware that he was babbling.

So, he said, surely they're not implicated in some . . . crime?

He said the last word after a long pause. As if the notion required a serious screening before admittance.

I'm not saying that, I said. Not at all. We're just trying to put together facts.

Okay, he said, not entirely convinced. What facts can I provide you with?

Let's start with whether they were here the night of February 18th.

Oh dear. I don't know if I can tell you that. I'm not so good with dates. I'll have to check my calendar. Although I can't guarantee you that will help.

Give it a try, I suggested. You really don't have anything to lose.

I wasn't sure what I meant by that last. Apparently he wasn't either. He gave me a quizzical look. Went into a small room in the back. To check his calendar. Or maybe to call up some guy named Luigi and his lead-pipe-wielding minions to come and break my kneecaps.

Fortunately for my figure-skating career it turned out to be the former. Wallender came back with a smile and a nod.

As it happens, he said, we had a private party here that night. For an old friend. Tenth anniversary. Of his divorce. So I can tell you that they were here. They wouldn't have missed that party for the world.

I see, I said. Do you remember when they left?

Oh, I don't know. These things tend to go on all night. Maybe five or six, they left.

Are you sure about that?

Pretty sure.

Is it possible that one or the other left for, say, half an hour?

Well . . .

Wallender smiled, shrugged.

Listen, I'd love to keep chatting, he said, but this is a very big night for us. We're opening the new VIP room. The Dalai Lama will be here. And a thousand things have already gone wrong, of course. Everything was supposed to be ready a week ago. I'm a tad overwhelmed.

The Dalai Lama. Jesus.

Wallender seemed to be sincere. Although since he also appeared to be a man whose vocation was to exude sincerity, I wasn't sure that meant anything.

Well, I said, thanks for your time. Can we speak to you again at a later date, if necessary?

Of course, of course. Any time. Juan, please, that wallpaper is crooked! he shrieked at a muscular young man on a ladder. We're going to have to redo the entire wall!

We'd lost him.

I tried one last question as we turned to leave.

By the way, I called to him, how do you come to know the twins?

Oh, goodness, said Mr. Wallender, they've been around the club scene forever. They helped design this place. He's . . . they're very sophisticated. I can't really say when I first met them. Juan, come down here right now! I've *got* to talk to you.

He shrugged an apologetic shrug at us, and scampered over to give Juan a wallpaper-hanging lesson.

We left. I suggested that we drop into a local pub for a quick pint of Guinness. Clear the perfume from our heads.

I suppose, Dorita said, Mr. White Swallow could have called the twins when he went into his office, asked them whether they wanted to have been there that night.

Possible. He certainly seems to think highly of them.

Or wants us to think he does.

Yes. Well. I don't know what we expected to find out, to tell you the truth. But anyway, it's one more fact to add to the list.

What's that?

That we don't know if they could have been near Jules's place.

That's a hell of a fact.

Best I could come up with.

Anyway, you're right, Dorita said. He wasn't exactly unequivocal about it.

Or forthcoming.

Nor.

Nor. If you insist. I mean, the cops talked to Igor, but Igor didn't tell his boss what they talked to him about?

And anyway, they're twins, remember? Couldn't one of them have been gone for a while? Without anybody noticing?

Sure. *The Patty Duke Show.*

Right.

Dorita began humming the theme song.

Well, I said. Another theory for the pile. But there's a small piece missing before we can give that one any credence.

What's that?

I've only met one of them. I don't know that they're identical. Or even similar.

Ah. Good point.

For all I know, Raul's got a handlebar mustache.

Or some other hideous deformity.

49.

I STOPPED BY THE HOUSE on my way to the Wolf's Lair. To see Kelly. Get the report on Melissa.

Steiglitz had seen her that morning. The prognosis was poor.

There was nothing new about that. Every relapse after the first one made the ultimate chance of recovery worse. It had long been approaching zero.

They were sending Melissa home. There was no point in her staying at the clinic. They needed the bed for more promising cases. Steiglitz had repeated to Kelly the advice we'd heard before. She's got to hit bottom. She touches another drink, throw her out on the street.

I knew I wasn't going to do that. No matter what. I just didn't have it in me.

I didn't want to be there when she got back. But I hated to leave Kelly alone in the house. I talked her into calling up Peter, asking him over. Usually she didn't take much convincing, but on this night she seemed determined to wallow in it. Fear. Disappointment. It took me half an hour and a threat to call Peter myself, but she finally gave in.

I decided to wait til he got there. To make sure.

He barged loudly into the house without knocking, as usual. He'd dyed his hair in purple and gold streaks. He was wearing a T-shirt that said 'I'm like a superhero, but without powers or motivation.'

I'm writing a book, he announced. It's called 'Quentin Tarantino Is God.' It's all about how Quentin Tarantino is God.

I laughed.

Kelly laughed.

I loved the sound of it.

I knew I'd done the right thing.

They decided to watch episodes of *Family Guy* on DVD. More laughter. Maximally therapeutic. I was even tempted to stay. Watch *Family Guy* with them. Kelly loved it when I did that. I always laughed so hard. It was infectious. It made everything seem even funnier.

But I just couldn't bear the thought of dealing with Melissa. Yes, it was heinous, I agreed with myself. To leave it to a child. But really, Kelly was more an adult than this old man. She reminded me of that, from time to time. When she caught me smoking. When I yelled at Melissa. Lost my temper.

I needed my Wolf's Lair too. I needed a Scotch, real bad.

That clinched it.

I bade Kelly and Peter good evening. I added the usual useless imprecations about bedtime, and not eating in the basement.

I wanted everything to seem normal.

The Wolf's Lair didn't feel normal, though. Not its usual inviting self. I looked around. The bar was still mahogany. The rail was still brass. Thom was still smiling and warm. The regulars were scattered about in their usual poses. But it didn't feel right. The stool felt hard, uncomfortable. The Scotch tasted watery. My stomach hurt.

It felt like I wasn't in control of anything anymore.

I knew the 'anymore' part was illusory. I'd never been in control of anything. Certainly not Melissa. Or her Monster. Especially her Monster. Though I may have fooled myself otherwise, once. For a short time. Maybe.

My professional life had always been, would always be, in the hands of others. Even if I quit, or got quit by Warwick, I still wouldn't be in control. Even if I opened my own shop. I'd always be at the mercy of the market. Of clients.

On top of that chilling realization, I knew that Kelly was getting to the age where, no matter how much she loved her dad – and I had no doubts on that score – she was becoming her own, independent person. I couldn't really tell her what to do anymore. I didn't want to. It wasn't right. I could no longer think of her as an extension of myself. A thing I'd probably done to a fault, in the past. Contributed to her reclusive tendencies.

Damn, it was hard being a parent.

Hal was at his usual spot, two stools down.

Hey, he said.

Hey.

Did you ever get a chance to play in Jake's game?

I did. Twice, actually.

How was it?

It was all right. Interesting bunch of characters.

How'd you do?

The first time, I was down all night. Won the big hand at the end. Got back in the black. Next time, I was ahead all night.

Good.

Yes. I like it better that way.

Hal laughed.

I went back to my Scotch.

Hey, said Hal.

Hey.

Did you check out that thing I told you?

What thing?

The thing with his eyes.

I looked at him, raised my eyebrows.

How he looks at you like you're not there.

No. I didn't notice that.

Hal went back to his beer.

Hal, I said.

Rick.

You're deeply weird.

I am?

Yes, Hal. You are.

Well, I guess I am.

Two Scotches and the *Times* crossword puzzle later, Jake came in, brushing snow off his shoulders. He was wearing a plastic raincoat. I hoped it had a lining.

Hey, Rick, he said.

Hey, Jake, I replied, looking at his eyes for signs of vacancy.

They looked pretty normal.

He sat down beside me.

You've got a head start on me, he said.

I guess I do, I agreed.

Give me a double, he said to Thom. Got to catch up with Rick here.

Thom laughed, poured him a double.

We talked a little poker talk.

The World Series of Poker had been on TV. We talked about our favorite players. There was a whole culture of hold'em. Books, magazines, Internet chat rooms, websites. I recognized some names. The old guard. Amarillo Slim. Everyone's heard of him. TJ Cloutier, former football player. Tough, solid, fearsome. I knew Ken Smith. He'd been a strong chess player, too. Smith had died a couple of years ago. Now there was a bunch of guys I'd never heard of. Phil Hellmuth. Arrogant, petulant, brilliant with a big stack of chips. Phil Ivey, young, imperturbable. You never knew what he had. And all the rest. Johnny Chan, Men Nguyen (say 'Wynn'). A multicultural panoply of fearless card mavens.

About four double Scotches in, Jake asked how Melissa was.

I paused. I remembered the ache in my gut. The poker talk had taken my mind off my problems. I wasn't too pleased to have Jake break the spell.

It wasn't his fault. He didn't know.

She's fine, I said.

There must have been something insincere about how I said it. Jake gave me a quizzical look.

Let's go smoke a joint, he said.

A joint? I laughed. I don't know. Last time it weirded me out. I'm very sensitive to it, for some reason.

C'mon. Take a chance.

Jesus. I don't know.

Come on. Just a toke or two.

All right. If you insist.

I'd never been very good at resisting peer pressure.

We went out back. We smoked a joint. My mind started looping in circles. Everything I said repeated itself in my head. I was a walking echo machine.

I needed a few more Scotches. To calm it down.

I started babbling. Baring my soul to my buddy Jake. At the point when you start throwing your arms indiscriminately around the shoulders of people you barely know. Sharing your darkest secrets. The alarm system shut down.

I told Jake what had happened with Melissa. How depressed I was. How much I loved my daughter, and worried about her.

Maybe it was the novelty of the guy thing. Whatever.

She's in treatment? he asked.

Kelly? No.

No. Melissa.

In a manner of speaking.

I told him about Steiglitz. His pessimistic prognosis.

At least you have your work, he said to the back of the bar.

Hah, I said. Not a consolation.

I told him about Warwick. Probation. Stress. Anxiety. Fear of failure. Loathing of my colleagues. Most of them, anyway. I didn't mention Dorita. Some things were sacred.

I knew I was out of control. Drunk. Stoned. But whatever. It felt good to share it with someone. He seemed to be listening, if only with one ear.

You seem preoccupied, I said.

He turned to me. His eyes were vague. He was looking through me. I glanced at Hal, down the bar. He was writing something on a napkin.

I've had my issues too, Jake said.

Haven't we all, I said. Listen, I don't mean to bore you with all this stuff. We all have problems. I shouldn't complain. My daughter's wonderful. I'm a successful lawyer. Don't listen to my whining. I've got all my arms and legs. Hell, I'm not even missing a digit. The world is full of people worse off than me.

No, no, he said. I didn't mean it that way.

I suddenly saw how sad a person he was. I felt a wash of sympathy. He was my buddy. My soulmate. We understood each other.

I guess that's why I became an actor, he said.

Right, I said, pretending to know what he meant.

So I could live in an imaginary world, he amplified. The real world was so fucked up. Is so fucked up.

You said it.

My father was a creep.

I didn't say anything. He was gearing up to tell the whole story.

We all need a confessor.

His father was a drunk, he told me. A mean drunk. He beat Jake's mother. He broke Jake's leg when Jake was eight. Kicked him. Because Jake had skipped school. Jake's sister was older. Didn't want anything to do with the family. Jake thought he knew why. His father had abused her. Snuck into her room late at night. Unspeakable things.

Dark, said Jake, it's all darkness.

There were tears in his eyes.

50.

WE WEAVED DOWN THE BLOCK. I thought I'd lost my keys. I checked every pocket twice. Jake giggled. The third time round, I found them. In the first pocket I'd checked. Jake giggled some more. It took me five tries to get the key in the lock. When I finally succeeded, I looked around. To see if my new best friend wanted to come in for a nightcap.

He wasn't there.

I was puzzled.

The dope, I mused. It slows down time. I'd probably been fiddling with the keys for ten minutes. He'd wandered off.

I shrugged.

I opened the door as quietly as I could.

I stumbled. I hung on to the banister. I kept myself upright.

Melissa sat up on the couch.

Who's there? she said.

Sorry, I said, it's me.

Come here, she said.

I staggered to the couch, fell down into the cushions.

She opened her arms.

My God, I thought, what's happening?

I kept falling.

51.

I WOKE. I was naked on the bed. It was the middle of the night. Someone was hammering a rusty spike into my right temple. Someone was boiling vinegar and dirt in my stomach. A small deceased rodent was rotting in the back of my throat. I went into the bathroom. I felt like throwing up. I held it back. I looked in the mirror. I didn't like what I saw.

I went back to bed. I tried to sleep. It didn't work. I tried to read. Something about Zeno's paradox. How you can never get from A to B. Because you always have to get halfway first, then half of that. And halfway to there. And on into infinity.

I closed my eyes again. The room slowly revolved. The blackness came.

As I drifted off to sleep, I thought of Steiglitz.

He entered my dreams.

He's in the park. Kelly is there. She's young. She's a small child.

He's playing with my daughter.

She looks afraid.

52.

I WENT DOWNSTAIRS.

Melissa was sprawled on the couch. She was on her back. Her mouth was open. She was snoring. A line of saliva drooled from the corner of her mouth, forming a pool on the sofa cushion.

I stood and stared.

I went back upstairs. I took a shower. I made it hot. Very hot. Maybe I was scalding myself. It felt a bit like that, through the gray metal fog. Perhaps I'd end up red and peeling, in monstrous pain. I took some comfort in the thought.

I walked dripping from the shower. I threw myself naked on the bed. I closed my eyes. I tried to reconstruct the night before. I remembered Jake. Our conversation. That I'd said too much. His revelations. His sadness. Our awkward stumble down the street. His vanishing. Where had he gone? I didn't trust my memory. Melissa, beckoning me. And then? I wasn't sure. Could it have been? That she'd have welcomed me like that?

She was bent over the coffee table, face down, legs apart. I was holding her hips, lifting her in the air. I was strong. I was hard. I pulled her up. I dragged her across the room. She moaned. She wanted more. Take me hard, she said. Show me who's a man. I propped her up against the mirror. I took her. Took her hard and long. I was taking out the misery of years. She wanted it. She begged for more. Hurt me, she said, tears and mascara streaking the mirror.

I threw her down. I left her there. It felt right.

Had that been me?

I didn't know.

I wasn't sure I wanted to.

I shook my head. Get a grip, I told myself.

I tossed on some clothes. I didn't take the trouble to look for something clean.

I dragged myself downstairs. She was still there. On the sofa. Her mouth hung open.

I averted my eyes.

I didn't want to see.

53.

I SAT IN MY EXPENSIVE ergonomic chair. I looked at the phone. It beckoned me. I was receptive to its charms. This was curious. I usually shunned it. I picked it up. I made some phone calls.

I knew from decades on this planet, and hundreds of hours on Sheila's black leather couch, that when I worked like this, picked up the phone, made calls, it meant the weight was lifting. The serotonins were uptaking, or being inhibited from uptaking, or re-uptaking. Whatever it was they did when they did it right. I didn't know why. I never did. It was random. But I wasn't going to complain.

The twins. There was something about them. I couldn't put my finger on it.

I tracked down a guy I knew. A guy who knew a guy who knew the twins. Set up a meet. Hound Dog Bar and Grill. Downtown and dirty. Perfect.

My source was Sammy Quantrill. Former FBI. Made a living tracking stuff down. Maybe a few other things on the side. Things you didn't want to ask about. Came in handy to know a guy like that. I'd used him before. He didn't come cheap. But he was usually worth it. The guy he knew was Joey. A club guy. Owned a piece of one or two. Did a little enforcing. Only when needed.

Sammy and Joey were at the bar when I came in.

Sammy and Joey, I thought. They could start a vaudeville act.

Hey Sammy, I said instead. Good to see you.

Sure, he said. Rick, this is Joey.

Pleased to meet you, Joey, I said, extending a hand.

The same I'm sure, said Joey, with a heavy dose of Brooklyn irony. His hand enveloped mine. I admired the pinky ring, the heavy gold bracelet.

I hear you know something about these twins, I said. Ramon and Raul FitzGibbon.

Sure. I know some stuff.

So what you got?

I don't know a whole lot direct. But I heard stuff. They got some rich daddy. Brought them over from the slums, Mexico City or somewhere, adopted them. They got some classy spread near the Park that Daddy bought them. Some penthouse thing with a huge deck on the roof. Private elevator. Servants. The works. Right next to the Museum.

They do anything for a living?

Joey snorted.

They try, he said. They're party boys. But Daddy keeps pushing them. Get a job. Do something. Pisses him off. He came from nowhere. Worked his way up. Thinks they should too. He's a controlling son of a bitch.

Never would have guessed, I said. So what do they do?

They think they're some kind of designers now.

They ever do any real work? I asked.

One of them set up shop for a while as some kind of investment guy, I heard. Thought he could be a Wall Street type. A smooth operator. Got some old farts to pony up some cash. Got creamed. Lost all the old ladies' dough. Daddy bailed him out before the lawsuits got started.

Was that Ramon or Raul?

I don't know. Probably Raul. Ramon's too stupid to fake it.

What do you know about Ramon?

Ramon I know from around. Got a vicious gun habit. He collects them. Lugers from World War II. M1s. Uzis. Whatever. Worth a shit-pile, the collection. Thinks he's some kind of a cowboy. Took some survival course down in South Carolina somewhere, off in the hills. Thinks he's a tough guy now. Started up some security outfit. Far as I know, Daddy's his only client, though. Everybody else knows he's too stupid to spit and shit at the same time.

So, FitzGibbon hadn't made it up. He really was Security.

It seemed like there was always just enough truth going around to make me doubt my doubts.

54.

WHEN I GOT BACK TO THE OFFICE I started a set of four-by-six file cards. On each one I meticulously wrote one and only one piece of information. I cataloged them by verifiability. One pile of substantiated facts – FitzGibbon had adopted Mexican twins. One for facts for which there was some evidence – there were some trusts, exact terms and consequences to be verified. A pile of hearsay only – Ramon's gun collection. A pile of suppositions contradicted by other evidence – life made sense. A stack of wild speculations – anything made sense. I put a different-colored sticker on each card, depending on the category. The stickers were removable, so something could easily be shifted from one category to another.

It took me hours. I felt good. I hadn't been so organized in years. I usually delegated this kind of work. Relied on my guys to tell me what was important. But this was different. Everything was slippery. Evanescent. Changeable. I had to be on top of it all. And anyway, I couldn't trust anybody with it. I thought about Warwick's reaction if he knew I'd listed his major client, and the firm's, as a potential suspect in a murder case.

When I'd assembled the cards I tacked them on the wall in descending order of certitude. I stood back. Gazed at my creation.

Didn't tell me a thing.

I needed to clear my head.

I logged on to the poker site.

I rarely played poker in the office. Warwick had his tentacles everywhere. He'd find out. Give me shit. But I was starting not to care. I'd take the chance.

I played aggressive but selective. I got into the zone. I felt the power. Life was good. There was a future. I went to a high no-limit table. I put it all on a pair of Sixes.

Doyle Brunson, twice world champion, believes in ESP. Now, I don't believe in ESP, really. But then, there have been times. There have been times when I just knew. I just knew, with the certainty that foments revolution, that the next card out was going to be a Six. Make my trips. Three Sixes. Take their money.

It happened. Two thousand bucks in a nanosecond.

Yes, life was good.

I logged off. Sat back. It took wisdom, I told myself, to step away. Take your wad. Sit back. Enjoy it. Play later. This went against the sages' advice. When you quit or when you stayed made no difference, they said. Take the long-term view. It's a lifetime gig, my man. The next hand has as much potential as the last. No more, no less. It's like flipping coins. A hundred heads come up, two, three, five hundred. What are the odds of heads coming up again? Fifty-fifty. Just like always.

I didn't believe it.

I understood it. I could not refute it. I just didn't believe it.

Dorita stuck her head in the door.

What's this? she asked.

I'm wallowing in poker madness.

No, this.

She pointed to the cards on the wall.

I'm organizing the Jules data.

She walked over to the wall. She looked over my masterpiece. She stood back. She lit a cigarette.

There's a rule about smoking in the office, I said.

Right, she said, tapping some ashes onto the carpet.

Computers are great, she continued. But sometimes file cards are better.

The screen is bigger, I said.

You can see it all at once.

Right.

Although.

Although?

It still doesn't speak to me.

Nor me, I said. Except in a whisper.

There's a whisper?

There is. Keep it up, it says. Keep adding pieces. And if you're a very good boy, I'll tell you something. Something good. Something satisfying.

Wow. That's one hell of a whisper.

I know. I think I'll keep it on the payroll.

55.

THE PHONE RANG. I picked it up.

Redman, I announced with authority.

I was in control. I was ready for battle.

Daddy! Why in Jesus' name didn't you wake me up!

I'm sorry, love, I said. I thought maybe you deserved a day off.

Oh God, she said. Oh Daddy. Come home. Come home now.

What's the matter, precious?

Never mind, Daddy. Just get the hell home, okay?

56.

WHEN I GOT THERE it was clear that it was bad. Ambulance. Two squad cars. Flashing lights. Serious faces. A large square cop confronted me, jaw set. He needed a shave.

Can I help you, sir? he asked, with an unhelpful air.

This is my house, I said. What's going on? Is somebody hurt?

His look relaxed to one of pity and concern.

I'm afraid there's been an incident, sir, he said.

Incident? What the hell did that mean? My first thought was of Kelly. Was she all right? But she had called me. She hadn't sounded hurt. Just frightened.

Strange that the obvious thought did not strike me first. That something had happened to Melissa. I can't explain it, even now.

The square-faced cop escorted me into my own living room. The room was filled with people. People in white, people in blue. People snapping cameras. People taking notes. And there, in the middle of it all, on the couch, Melissa. The same pose as that morning.

Oh God, she'd been gone the whole time. Or going, which was worse.

I'd blithely walked on by, slammed the door, lost in anger and embarrassment. While she lay dying. Right then. Right there. And I had known. Somehow, I had known. God, I had known. And I'd done nothing.

A stabbing pain started in my stomach, shot through my spine, into my teeth and jaw. A disabling pain. I fell to my knees. Nothing made sense. I knew the pain wasn't physical. It was the pain of loss. Blame. Confusion. Thoughts and fears rampant in my head.

I could feel the people around me, shifting uncomfortably. I had trouble breathing. The pain was in my lungs, my throat. I gasped the words: Melissa. What did you do?

A woman kneeled, put her arm around me. I felt her body against mine, soft beneath the lab coat. It felt good. Real. Corporeal. But not enough. Nothing would be enough. My breathing slowed. The pain began to ebb. But not completely.

I knew that it was there to stay.

The guilt made way for anger. What did you do? What did you do to me? What did you do to Kelly? My God, Kelly! Where was she? I stood up. Where's my daughter? Before the words were formed I saw her, head in hands, in the armchair across the room. I went to her, leaned over, kissed her forehead. She looked up. Her eyes were red. Her face was swollen, yellow.

The pain came back in force.

To see my angel child in such a state.

57.

THEY TOOK MELISSA AWAY. They took their pictures first. Put bits of things in plastic bags. Marked them up with black indelible pens. Asked me question after question. I answered. I was polite. But I didn't, don't, remember one thing I was asked. One thing I said. I was on automatic pilot. I was busy building walls. The only thing I wanted was my Kelly in my arms. They kept taking her away from me. To ask her questions too.

I just wanted them all to leave.

When they finally did, I put my arms around Kelly. We were both too tired and numb to say a thing. I fell into a sleep, as deep and dark as black on black. I did not dream. I did not think.

That's what nirvana's like, I think the Buddhists say.

I never wanted it to end.

But of course it did. Light came through the curtains. I woke up. My stomach hurt. Another day to face. I had no choice. I had to face it. For my angel child, if nothing else.

And there was precious little else.

They'd taken Melissa to the morgue. I supposed normal people called their friendly neighborhood funeral director. Or something. Somebody.

I didn't.

Melissa had no family, no friends to call.

And anyway I didn't want to have anything to do with it.

I wanted to pretend it hadn't happened.

I slept.

I woke.

Damn it. They were going to cut Melissa up. Cut her into little pieces. Recite her bits and pieces into a handheld tape recorder. Collect them, bag them, test them. Defile them. Put them all back into a pile. Sew it back inside of her.

I couldn't stand the thought of it.

I called the coroner's office. I asked for Dr. Nathaniel Jones. The Chief Medical Examiner. I knew him only well enough to nod at in the hallway. I don't know what I thought I was going to accomplish, talking to him. I wasn't thinking much, really. Action just seemed better than sitting and thinking. Brooding. Imagining. Any action. Action to push the darkness away, if only for a little while. To give me time. To give me time to wash it all away. To dull the edges.

Dr. Jones was not a friendly man. He was a tall ungainly thing with a peculiar crown of white hair that gave him a Caesarean air. He never smiled. Never reacted to anything, beyond a small twitching at the corner of his mouth, a slight frown at the corners of his eyes. I could picture him sitting imperially at his desk as he took my call.

Once he was on the line, I had no idea what to say.

I'm Richard Redman, I said.

Hello, Mr. Redman, said Dr. Jones.

My wife died yesterday.

Ah, yes. I'm so sorry for your loss, said Dr. Jones, without a hint of conviction.

I guessed he said that a lot, in his business. It got to be a chore. A bore.

I paused.

He cleared his throat.

Have you begun an autopsy? I asked.

Not yet.

Good.

Good?

Because I don't want one.

Pardon me?

I don't want one.

I'm sorry, sir. I don't understand what you're saying.

I don't want an autopsy.

There was a pause. Dr. Jones cleared his throat again.

Mr. Redman, he said, I have the utmost respect for your feelings. But I'm afraid that this is not an issue that it is in my power to decide. Nor is it yours. This is a matter for the police. The District Attorney.

A deep-seated anger arose in me. The numbly bureaucratic mind at work again. It was everywhere.

Listen, Dr. Jones, I said. She didn't believe in it. She didn't believe in funerals either. Or services. She just wanted to be cremated. Right away. Cast to the winds.

Right away? he asked. Is this a request she put in writing?

No. She's my wife. She was my wife. I know what her feelings were.

Well, Mr. Redman, I understand. I understand. I'll have someone call you.

The simmer turned to a boil.

Someone call me? Aren't you the one in charge of the bodies down there? Who the hell are you going to have call me?

I'll have someone call you, Mr. Redman. Good day.

Click.

I sat back. I got up. I paced back and forth. I felt like a jerk. Why had I done that? I hadn't the slightest idea what Melissa's beliefs were about funeral arrangements. It was me. I was trying to burn it away. Purge the guilt. The deadening sorrow. The responsibility. Jesus. Wasn't there more I could have done for her? All along the way? Yes. Of course there was. Every step of the way. Seen it coming earlier. Battled it more. Loved her more. Mostly that. Got out of my goddamn own mind a little more.

I went into the kitchen. I got some ice. I took the talisman from its sacred niche. What the hell. Might as well put it to good use. I poured myself a tumblerful. I drank it down.

It was eight-thirty in the morning.

The phone rang. It was a Detective Harwood. I didn't know him. He wanted to come over for a chat. Sure, I said. Come on over.

I hung up the phone. Oh Christ, I thought. What have I done? They think I'm trying to dispose of the evidence. But how could they? Who in their right mind would be so stupid as to call up the coroner's office to ask them to assist in disposing of the body? I laughed a small dry laugh. Me, I guess. I could see their thinking. A man consumed with grief can do some irrational things. Or a man consumed with guilt.

Harwood was an older guy. Short. Balding. Rumpled. A guy who'd been around. He wasn't the bullying type. More the sardonic type. He'd seen it all. He wasn't taking any shit. He asked a lot of questions. I answered them. The theme was pretty basic.

Where was I that night?

In the bar. Then home. In the house with the deceased.

Had I had anything to drink?

Lots.

Drugs?

No.

Any arguments recently?

No. We hardly talked.

Really?

Yes. She was a recovering alcoholic. And pills. Whatever. She didn't have much to say these days.

He perked up at that.

Who was the last person to see her alive?

Me, probably.

Interesting, I could hear him think. Very interesting.

He warmed up as we went on, though not a lot. He can see I'm not the type, I let myself think. Maybe I'm acting like you're supposed to act. Whatever that is.

But he never lost his wary, cynical air.

The questions went on too long. He asked the same question one too many times. I lost my temper, just a bit.

Listen, I said, I know you've got a job to do. But it's an overdose. It's been coming for years. Anybody who knew her can tell you that. Talk to her doctor. She wanted to die. She couldn't handle living. It was just too much for her. I'm not saying I can tell you why. I don't know why. And I should have known. I should have found out. But I didn't. And now she's gone. It's bad enough. Can you just leave me alone now? Please?

Mr. Redman. I understand that you're upset, he said calmly. But we have to follow procedures. We have to establish the cause in the proper way.

Establish the cause? Come on.

You never know, Mr. Redman. Death is a funny thing.

A laugh a minute, I said with a sneer.

He looked hard at me. I backtracked.

I'm sorry, I said. I'm a little emotional.

I could feel his distrust fill the room. Like carbon monoxide. Silent. Odorless. Deadly.

I could understand it. I knew that whatever I'd been feeling inside, however normal I'd been acting, no grief, no weakness, beyond that brief flash of anger, had made an appearance. I should have been reacting more, I supposed. Hysterical. Crying. Defying the Gods.

But my stony demeanor meant nothing. It's how I deal with adversity. I knew that. But he didn't.

I wasn't about to tell him, either. You don't say that kind of thing to a guy.

My throat constricted. I had to hold inside the twelve emotions that competed for attention.

Harwood asked a few more questions. Wrapped it up. Gave me one last searching look. Left.

Finally.

I poured myself another Scotch.

I drained it down.

It felt awfully good.

It was ten o'clock in the morning.

I began to understand Melissa a little better.

58.

I SLEPT A LOT. Sunday morning came. I found myself staring blankly at the toaster. I didn't know how I'd gotten to the kitchen.

There was no way I was going to get through this without Sheila.

I made the phone call. For the first time, I paid attention to the triage of numbers. I called the red alert one. A service answered. The voice was flat. Uninterested in my problems. We'll pass the message to the doctor, it said.

I got lucky. Sheila called me back within the hour. I told her I had an emergency. Had to see her. No, I didn't want to tell her over the phone.

I guess she heard it in my voice. She asked me to give her half an hour. Meet her at her office.

She was in her recliner.

One thing in life, at least, I could count on.

I told her that Melissa had died. I filled in some details. I didn't tell her everything. I didn't tell her about Harwood. I didn't tell her about the night before.

Oh dear, she said more than once. That's terrible.

I didn't feel better.

Of course I wasn't going to feel better, right away. It was a process. I had to go through it. Blah, blah, blah.

A long silence.

There's something I've always wanted to talk to you about, Sheila said.

Okay, I said.

I'd like to talk about why you married her.

I stared at the air conditioner behind Sheila's desk. I looked at the clock above it. It sat next to a book. *The Challenge of Pain*. Ronald Melzack. I almost laughed. It was about physical pain, though. I'd read it once. In college. I didn't remember much about it. One idea was that pain was not some absolute, measurable thing. Everyone felt it differently. I looked back at the clock. Still twenty minutes left. Shit. I didn't want to be there.

Which was strange. Normally I wanted to stay as long as possible.

Things were different, now.

I looked at Sheila.

Why you married Melissa? she reminded me.

I've often asked myself that question, I said.

You have?

Yes. Mostly because . . . because when I think about it, I don't really know her. I didn't really know her. I've never really known her. At all.

You knew enough to marry her.

I knew I loved her.

Yes. And maybe that's enough. But as I recall, you hadn't even met her parents.

That's true. I still haven't. She wasn't speaking to them.

Or any other members of her family.

If any. She never mentioned any others.

You don't even know where she was from, do you?

Illinois, I think. Or Indiana. Something with an *I*.

Ithaca?

Could be.

That's sort of my point.

I get your point. But what's the point? Of your point.

Don't you think it's a little unusual?

What's unusual?

To marry someone you know almost nothing about?

Unusual? Probably. But I'm an unusual guy. I kind of like that about myself.

You are. And there's nothing wrong with that. In itself. I'd just like to explore this particular aspect of your . . . difference.

Explore away.

Did the thought ever occur to you, any time before the marriage? That maybe you should know a bit more about her?

No. I mean, I don't think so. I was never so terribly close to my own family, you know. Of course you know.

Yes, I know that.

She just made me feel so good.

In what way?

I remember the nights in her apartment. It was tiny. Just enough room for a bed and the TV. And a small bedside table. And the kitchen, at the end of the room. The window looked out onto a brick wall. Two feet away. And it was always overheated. The apartment. So we took our clothes off. As soon as we got there. And lay on the bed. And drank wine. Cheap wine. But good wine. Stuff I hunted up. An unknown Rhône or two. Some esoteric stuff from Spain. And smoked cigarettes. Listened to Tom Waits. And I would read her poetry. Mine. T.S. Eliot. Dylan Thomas. Stuff that moved me. And it would move her. And her skin was so soft. And I'd think, This is what heaven must be like. Really. That's what I'd think. That's how it felt. I know it sounds stupid.

No, it doesn't sound stupid. It sounds sad.

Sad? How does it sound sad? Is going to heaven sad?

Not if it really was heaven. But it wasn't. It wasn't sustainable.

Well, you've got that right.

The pursuit of bliss.

Yes.

That's what it is.

Yes.

But bliss is not for us.

Us mortals.

No. Bliss is for the Gods.

Yes. I know. I know.

I hung my head. What a fool I was.

We had it for a while, I said.

Yes. And then?

Yeah. Then. If it wasn't hell, it was a reasonable facsimile.

That's what it is, you see? Pleasure and pain are relative concepts. If you weren't capable of that bliss, you'd never know it. And you'd never feel the pain of its absence.

Sure, but what's the point? We should all live within a tiny emotional range? B to C? No high Fs? Now that's a life worth living.

No. No. I'm not saying that. I'm saying that you have to recognize those highs for what they are. Moments. Glimpses of heaven. Luck. Not what you can expect from day to day. Or even ever again. It's part of the art of living.

Now *that's* sad.

Yes, she said. In a way. In a way it's sad. That heaven's not here on earth. But that's part of growing up, isn't it? Coming to terms with that fact?

Sure, I said. Sure. I've just never been sure that I want to grow up.

I know, she said. I know.

59

I WENT TO WORK. I knew I didn't have to. The firm always gave you two weeks, no questions asked, when a family member died. But Kelly had gone to school. She didn't want to stay inside and brood. The thought of being home alone, picking scabs, didn't appeal to me either. Action. Activity. It was the only thing. To keep the seconds from turning into hours. To keep from thinking about things. Things that didn't bear thinking about.

On the way to the office I took a detour to the alley. Maybe it had some secrets it would be willing to give up. To a widower.

The Dumpster was gone. The fire escapes were still there. The metal doors closed tight. Not telling me anything.

No surprise, really. The police surely had already combed every square inch. No secrets left for me to find.

I went over to the metal door on the left side. I stared at it. It wanted to tell me something. I sat down on the broken asphalt. I waited for the door to speak.

The weeds had grown a bit. The rust perhaps had spread a millimeter more. I couldn't tell.

I lit a cigarette.

I felt like crying.

I held it back.

The door wasn't talking. I upbraided it.

Talk to me, I said.

It sat in Buddha-like indifference in its rusted frame.

Talk to me, I said. I know you're hiding something. Sure, *you* don't care. You'll be here long after the rest of us are dust motes in this alley. If we're lucky. But *I* care. Come on. Throw me a bone.

The steel door spoke.

Patience, it said.

Patience, I repeated. Okay. I'll see what I can do.

I sat another minute.

It wasn't going to give me anything more.

I went around the corner. I walked the three blocks. I rang Jules's bell. No answer. Nobody home.

I rang again.

No answer.

I waited five minutes.

My cell phone rang. 'Private number.' I ignored it.

Patience.

I rang again.

I waited another five minutes.

Nothing.

Mission accomplished. Don't quit your day job.

I went to the office.

I endured the gauntlet of sympathy-wishers. They were surprised to see me. I didn't feel like explaining. I felt badly that I found no solace in their stilted efforts to help. I knew they meant well.

Dorita came by. She declined to make the usual noises. She just gave me a hug. A good long hug.

We didn't say a word.

It was enough.

I sat and stared at the wall. No thoughts intruded.

There was a knock on the door. I turned my head. Warwick. It startled me. I couldn't recall another time he'd come by my office. Normally, you got a call from Cherise, summoning you to His Chambers for an audience.

I'm sorry, he said.

He actually seemed to mean it.

Thanks, I said.

If there's anything we can do.

No, no. I'm dealing.

You don't have to be here. Take as much time as you like. We can cover for you.

Thank you, Charles. I appreciate that. But I'd rather be here. Passes the time, you know.

I understand. Well, like I said, anything we can do.

All right, I said. Thanks.

He left.

Hell, maybe he was human after all.

How confusing.

There was a message from Vinnie Price. He wanted to talk about the Futterman case. I had nothing else to do. I called him in.

I gathered Vinnie hadn't gotten the news. Which was all to the good.

He wanted my advice. He'd been working on the Futterman case for six months. High-profile. An honor to be selected. But he'd encountered a thorny ethical issue.

I knew that if he'd come to me about it, and not Uptight Bob Shumaker, Firm Ethics Guru, it was not a run-of-the-mill problem. Not your everyday thing. Not amenable to solution by reference to Shumaker's encyclopedic knowledge of the Canons of Ethics and the vast and impenetrable body of cases and commentary that adhered to them like leeches on flesh.

Vinnie Price explained the problem. We were representing the wife of a certain high-profile actor, model and sometime disco maven. His wife was rather well known herself, and notoriously high-strung. Now, it seemed that the actor had invited a few people over to his palatial penthouse apartment on the Upper East Side for an evening of fine wine, good food and witty repartee. One of the guests had been a young protégé of his, one Michael Millar, an aspiring leading man.

According to Millar's version of events, as recited in the complaint he later filed in State Court, the actor's wife, our client, had lured him onto the roof deck of the penthouse, where she suggested it might be pleasant to perform oral sex on him. Millar, anxious to make the right impression on his hosts, acquiesced.

The night then proceeded apace. Much alcohol, and perhaps the odd gram of a Schedule I substance well known to fabulously wealthy overachievers, was consumed by all. There was dancing. Laughter. General frivolity. And all went home in guarded limousines, as a gray dawn descended on Manhattan.

The next day, Millar arrived on the set of a reality-show pilot in which he had been awarded a small but highly visible part, feeling rather good about himself. He had ingratiated himself with the high-powered couple. He'd had a good time too.

Then the police arrived.

After the guests had left the night before, it seemed, the actor had confronted his high-strung wife, our client. Someone had made a salacious comment. He wanted to know the truth. What had transpired on the roof? he asked. At first, the flustered lady had denied any knowledge of the episode. But when confronted with some evidence, consisting of a whitish stain upon the custom-designed calf's leather settee reposing on the roof deck, eminently susceptible to DNA analysis, she confessed: Millar had forced himself upon her.

The actor then contacted the local constabulary, not forgetting to put in a side call to a prominent politician of his acquaintance, and the wheels of justice were set in motion. Millar was confronted on the set, handcuffed, patted down and shoved into the back of a squad car. At the station, he was read his rights, and told that he was being charged with second-degree sexual assault.

Then the fun really started.

According to Millar's complaint, three burly officers of New York's Finest then proceeded to strip-search him, probing orifices that he wasn't sure he'd known he had, and, most egregiously, making raucous fun of the size of his member. Which, he hastened to explain, right there in the complaint, was merely shrunken to near invisibility by fear and consternation. Under normal conditions, he insisted, it was a healthy size and circumference. But nevertheless.

All of this I had heard before, in more or less detail, but Vinnie had more to say. Our client had devised an imaginative line of attack on Millar's accusation that she had forced herself on his unsuspecting manhood. Not possible, she'd told Vinnie. Had it been a voluntary act, she averred, she'd have swallowed the evidence. To do otherwise was to risk damaging the exquisite leather covering of the aforementioned settee. Only irrational emotion brought on by the traumatic event of Millar's forcing himself upon her could have impelled her to eject the dangerously caustic fluid upon its delicate surface.

Although caught up in the excitement of the story, and laughing so hard that I'd almost forgotten that I was actually profoundly depressed and confused, I did not neglect to ask Vinnie what ethical issue had arisen in these circumstances.

The problem is this, he said. Our client keeps telling me how attractive I am.

Well, I said, you can't blame her.

I don't blame her, of course. But she's asking me out. She wants to take me to dinner. Dancing. Meet her girlfriends.

Oh dear.

Yes. I just don't think that I can keep working on this case, Rick. But I know how important it is to the firm. High-profile and all. We can't just fire the client. But if I recuse myself—

So to speak.

So to speak. If I recuse myself, I'm afraid that she's going to do something drastic. She's a bloody nutcase, Rick.

Well Vinnie, let's not rush to judgment. She's been severely traumatized.

He gave me a wry smile.

Anyway, I continued, it's a great story. But I don't feel qualified to opine on the ethical problem. Hardly at all. That's a call that only one man can make.

Oh shut up.

Yes. Bob Shumaker.

Jesus.

Glad I could help, I said.

Vinnie left my office laughing. I was left to ponder whether he had made the whole thing up. Either way, I thought, he's a good kid. Wish I'd had a son like that.

Wrong thought. Sons. Mothers. Daughters. Wives. My shoulders slumped. My stomach hurt. I worried about Kelly. I had to get home.

But that half-hour with Vinnie had told me one important thing. I'd been right. Action. Activity. Each minute of laughter was powerful enough to erase an hour of self-loathing.

Maybe I could get through this.

60.

I GOT A CALL. Not a call I could ignore. Much as I would have liked to.

It was Laura Cochrane. She was the Assistant Coroner. In charge of the actual work. I was surprised. Not badly so. An old friend, Laura. An expert witness, long ago. The Johnson case. Mississippi. Dog days. Death. The death penalty.

I didn't believe in it. I don't believe in it. So sue me. The State, in all its majesty, killing people. It isn't right. The ritual. The hood. The rope. The rifle. The cigarette. The straps. The hood. The chair. The gurney. The arms spread wide and strapped to it. The last meal. Billy Ray Rector, saving his dessert for 'after the execution.' The needle. The countdown. Finality. Who's to pull the switch?

It doesn't make a difference how you do it. Not a damn. The result is the same.

And everyone has their excuse. 'It's just my job.' 'I had to do it.' 'If not me to pull the switch, then someone else will do it.' Who? No matter. Someone. Who tells them that? Who tells each cog and wheel and joint and bearing that together make the big machine that says 'Not me'? It wasn't me made the decision, it was him, or her, or them, and yes, the system, them, the people, all of them.

The State. The will. The people. Jesus, what was that? Nobody with a gram of blame, of responsibility. We'd rather drink ourselves oblivious than think, Oh yes, that's me, I'll be there too, I'll be as nothing, as the man on the gurney there, like him, dust and ashes, it won't make a damn bit of difference, me or him, whatever we were blamed for, tried to do or failed, we'll both be dead as doornails.

I felt fairly strongly about it.

Laura was in private practice then. She'd volunteered, like the rest of us. She'd done her best. Come up with a theory. We'd pinned our hopes on it. Our client, Johnson, a sad and schizophrenic man, had been there. We couldn't deny it. He'd confessed. He'd stabbed the knife into the bodies of the man, his wife, the children. But, our psychologist had testified, he didn't mean to do what he'd so manifestly done. And even if he had, Laura had concluded, the bodies had been corpses long before he'd come into the room. Done in already by the depredations of his friend. All Gavin's fault, it was, that nasty young and angry Gavin, who'd told him that he had to cut them all.

You've got to do it, Gavin said. You've got to do something too.

She'd testified. She'd done her best. If the victims had been already dead, how could Johnson be a murderer?

She'd tried. It hadn't worked. I couldn't criticize. She'd done what she could do.

There's something about being at trial. In the trenches. Even more so when a life is at stake. The bonds you form last a lifetime. Sometimes more. I still went every year to Miklos Kariakin's grave. To say hello, and thanks. For all he taught me as a young and eager lawyer. For the all-nighters we pulled together, early in my career, in the defense of the indefensible. The bullshit sessions over bourbon and potato chips in cheap hotels in faraway places. Shreveport. Texarkana. Mobile. My death penalty education. My introduction to the life of hard-ass no-holds-barred trial work.

Sifting every piece of paper. Covering every angle. Being way over-prepared, for every witness and contingency. Litigation is the art of over-preparation. The art of never having to say later, Damn, I should have asked him that. So that the one time in a thousand that an otherwise random comment of Officer Brunson, in his statement made in 1987, contradicted what he said on the stand today, fourteen years later, you had it there. It was in your head. It was on a piece of paper. And you knew just where that piece of paper was.

So, Laura and I had bonds that never would break. But she also had a job to do. Cutting up my wife, for one. So first, I was surprised, to get a call from Laura. I didn't want my friends involved in all of this. Still less exploring my late wife's anatomy.

But then, in some strange way, it seemed inevitable.

Whatever was the fate the Gods decreed, I'd live with it.

It would be a couple more days, Laura told me, sympathy in her voice. They had to run some tests.

She was sorry. So sorry.

From her, I accepted it. She was an empathetic soul. She wasn't just mouthing the words.

It was a consolation. Of a sort.

61.

I CALLED BUTCH. To see if there was any news. Any new fact I could busy myself writing onto a four-by-six card, and tacking to the wall.

There wasn't much. The case wasn't exactly first on anybody's list, he said. Everybody still figured the kid had done it. Nothing had been found to suggest anyone else. They'd done the tests on everything found in the alley. Cigarette butts. The cardboard from the box. Larry Silver's second-to-last resting place.

If they're so certain, why haven't they charged him? I asked.

I'm not sure you want to hear the answer to that, he said.

Shit.

What happened? They got something off the cardboard box? Prints? DNA?

You know I can't tell you that, Rick.

Cardboard fucking box, I said. When they kill me, I hope they use something a little less déclassé to cover up the deed.

I was full of good cheer.

They'd searched the Dumpster, of course. Nothing there to cast suspicion. Only that it didn't seem to have an owner.

Hard to see how that might mean anything, I said.

Yeah, he said.

But I wrote it on a card anyway. You never knew how things might fit together later.

Butch's situation was too delicate now. I couldn't push for anything substantive. So I took a stab in another direction. I told him about the trust papers. That they might point to a motive. Of someone other than Jules.

Interesting, he said. I'll see if the guys got wind of that.

No. Don't do that yet. I need to see them first. See if there's anything there.

You haven't seen them?

I got a glance at them. I didn't get a chance to study them. A buddy of mine's got them.

I told him the story. Of FitzGibbon. What I'd got from Kennedy, so far.

Wheels and wheels, he said, getting the metaphor slightly wrong.

That's what I'm saying, I said. There's so much stuff here to follow up on. But your guys don't seem to see it. They're still treating it like a bar fight or something.

Hey, Rick, give them some credit. They're not trying to railroad the kid. It's just that nothing substantive has come up that leads anywhere else.

I can't say I've got anything substantive either. But there's a lot of trails to follow. I don't have the resources to follow them all.

Then stop telling me I can't use the stuff you're giving me.

I can't do that yet. Shit, I know we're in a tough situation here. Your interests aren't necessarily mine, right? I mean, we both want to know the truth. But if the truth is what I hope it isn't, I don't want you to know that.

Jesus, Rick. Can I have an hour or two to untangle that sentence?

You know what I mean. I can't just be letting your guys loose on stuff til I have a good sense of where it's going. I've got to see that trust language, for starters.

Would your buddy let you have a peek?

I don't want to ask him. I don't want to put him in that position.

You're a man of honor. But we knew that. So I guess at this point, the only thing you can hope for is that it mysteriously appears on your desk?

Right.

I see.

Anyway Butch, I really appreciate your talking to me. Taking a risk.

Nah. Don't worry about me. I'm bulletproof.

I admired his confidence. But I wasn't necessarily convinced. I had enough guilt already for one lifetime. If I got Butch fired, I didn't know what I'd do.

62.

JUDY BUZZED ME. Call on line two. I picked it up.

Mr. Redman? a familiar voice asked.

Here, I said.

This is Russell Graham, it said.

I felt a stab in my lower back. I knew what was coming.

We're going to have to bring him in, he said.

Well, I appreciate you calling me first.

Silence.

I'll get him, I said. Two hours okay?

All right. More than that, though, and we'll have to go pick him up.

I understand, I said. I'll arrange it.

Damn. They'd pulled the trigger. I'd been hoping for a little more time. Time to figure something out.

Shit. Maybe there was nothing to figure out.

I called FitzGibbon's office. To tell him he was going to have to put up some bail money. I was hoping I wasn't going to have to argue with him about it.

A voice answered the phone. Not FitzGibbon. Way too refined.

May I speak to Mr. FitzGibbon, please? I asked.

I'm afraid he's indisposed, the voice said.

Ah, I said. Well. This is extremely urgent. I'm sure he'll want to know about it immediately.

Perhaps I can convey a message, the voice said.

May I ask who I'm speaking to?

Raul FitzGibbon.

My, my. The mysterious Raul. Well, he had a good telephone manner. All right, I said.

I explained the deal.

It will be taken care of, he said, with a smoothly confident air.

63.

THE ARRAIGNMENT WENT CLEANLY. We were in and out of there in two hours. Probably a record. Raul had been right. Daddy had smoothed the way. The bail was already taken care of.

I walked outside with Jules.

Don't worry about it, I said. We're going to take care of this.

I'm not worried, lawyer guy, he said.

Sure, I said to myself. Little tough guy. Well, he might be in for a lesson or two, before this was over.

The preliminary hearing was two weeks Wednesday. Sixteen days. I couldn't guarantee he'd still be out on bail after that.

Damn. Two weeks and two days. I had a lot of work to do. What had I done so far?

Precious little.

Jesus.

The kid's life was at stake.

I had to get my act together.

I didn't share that thought with my client.

Wouldn't be prudent.

64.

I WENT HOME EARLY, to spend some time with Kelly.

Jules wasn't the only kid who needed me.

Peter was there. His T-shirt said: 'I may look funny, but I'd kick your ass at *Jeopardy.*'

Hey Dad, he said.

Peter liked to call me Dad. He thought it was funny. It probably wasn't, really. It was all in the way he said it. Like an eager toddler when Daddy comes home from work. So I laughed. Like I always did.

Dad, he said loudly, and took me by the elbow. I've got something to show you.

He winked at Kelly as he steered me to the kitchen. She smiled.

It was nice to see she could.

I'm staying here, Peter said once we were out of earshot.

It wasn't a request. It was a statement.

Okay, I said.

She needs distraction, he said. Entertainment. It goes against my nature, but I'll do my best.

Sure, I said, missing the joke.

Til she gets over the worst of it, anyway, he said with a suddenly serious air.

Back in the living room, Peter asked Kelly for a pair of scissors.

Why? she asked.

My shoelaces are uneven, he said, pointing at his feet. They must be punished.

Kelly brought the scissors. She hadn't laughed yet, but the smile was back.

Peter sat on the floor, fumbled about with his shoes for a moment.

Phew, he said. That's better. Kelly, come tie my shoes.

What? said Kelly. Why should I?

You *un*tied them.

I did not.

Okay, I lied. But haven't I told you my theory about shoe-tying?

No.

It's the most intimate thing a man and woman can do together.

Kelly laughed.

There was a poker game that night. I didn't want to go. Peter talked me into it. We should try to be as normal as possible, he said. I couldn't argue with that. And, I suspected, he was probably thinking that it would be better for Kelly if my gloomy face was out of the house for a while.

And he was probably right.

65.

THE GAME WAS IN A WAREHOUSE by the water. They never played the same place twice. It was a rule.

The space was huge, black, smelled of oil and axle grease. Someone had rigged three spotlights in the rafters far above, aimed them at the very center of the vast expanse, illuminating in three intersecting circles the green felt poker table, seven high-backed chairs and a rococo side-board packed with bottles of tequila, rum and wine. An oasis of light that made the surrounding darkness palpable. Like a massive black beast crouched around the tableau. Ready to swallow the unwary.

Jesus, I said, who's your set designer?

Friend of Jonesie's, said Andrea. You like?

It's a goddamn work of art.

The guy's a genius, said Jonesie.

You won't get an argument from me, I said.

As I took my seat I gazed around at the surrounding blackness. It was like we were sitting on a comet deep in space.

Drunk Jake wasn't there. Straight Jake was there. Wearing a fedora and suspenders.

Dressed for success, I said.

He smiled.

Andrea had on a slinky flapper dress.

I wish you'd told me it was a costume party, I said, to nobody in particular.

It isn't, said Andrea, without elaborating.

Where's Drunk Jake? I asked. Coming later?

He called in sick, said Mike.

Drunk Jake's absence seemed strange. I'd come to think of it as his game. But it wasn't his game. It was Mike's game. And Mike was there, in the dealer's chair. Wearing a green eyeshade.

The first hand was dealt. Seven Two off-suit. The worst possible hand. You couldn't even get lucky and make a straight with those two cards. I mucked them.

It was a harbinger. I kept getting rags. The cards were cold as the grave. Not a welcome image. But there it was.

I played with no enthusiasm. I had no focus. I didn't really care. I'd just donate my cash to these nice folks.

I tried to keep my side of the banter up. I feared the uninvited question, should my bereavement show. I didn't want to be the damper on the flame.

Andrea had a little yellow plastic duck.

Planning on taking a bath? I asked.

It's my travel duck, she said, smiling.

Your travel duck?

Yup. It comes with me everywhere.

I'm going to have to get me one of those.

Everyone laughed. It hadn't seemed that funny. Maybe they'd found out about Melissa, somehow. Were trying to humor me.

I tried to play a bit. With the cards coming cold, the only way to win was to get aggressive. Bluff a bit. Stay ultra-sharp and look for weakness, tells, indecision. But I didn't have the energy.

I went back to donating my money.

I left early. I didn't stay to try my luck with the penalty jar. Winning it would only have made me feel guilty.

As I left, I looked up into the endless blackness above.

I am but a worm, I thought.

A plaything for the Gods.

66.

WHEN I GOT HOME Kelly was still up. Peter was asleep in the basement, she said. They'd played chess for hours. She'd won all the games. He was sleeping off the emasculation.

In my day, I laughed, sixteen-year-old girls were not supposed to know the word 'emasculation.' Still less use it in a sentence.

Bad luck for them, she said.

Kelly was the ideal mix of sweet and sour. I thought of her trip the year before. She'd gone to Thailand with a group from school. To minister to AIDS orphans in the countryside. I'd saved all her e-mails. Printed them out. Tacked them to the wall.

The orphans are sooooooooooo cute. I want to take
all of them home. But I'll settle for my six favorites.

But now the sweetness was suffused with sorrow. I could see it. How hard she had to struggle to maintain her sense of self. To not succumb to unadulterated grief. She didn't want to do that. At least in front of me. She was too proud to lose control.

I hoped she had the sense to cry her heart out when I wasn't there.

Daddy, she said gravely once I'd sat down. We have to have a funeral.

Oh dear, I said. Do we have to talk about this now?

By which you mean 'at all.'

She was right.

Okay, I said. Why?

Funerals are for the living, she said.

I'm not sure I agree entirely. But let's say I do. I'm living. I don't want one.

But you don't count. You're a curmudgeon.

It was hard to argue with her logic.

Who does? I asked. She alienated everyone she knew. Who's going to show up?

I regretted saying it before it got out of my mouth. Tears appeared in Kelly's eyes. She glared at me.

Mommy had a lot of friends, she said. They'll be there. You keep avoiding the house. You don't take the phone calls. You don't know.

Damn it. This was unfair. She had encouraged me to go to the poker game.

Who are all these people who've called? I asked.

Everybody, she said.

She recited a list of names. Most I'd never heard before.

Amazing. That so many old friends long cast aside in favor of the Monster would care, would call. Commiserate. Show up.

I was helpless in the face of Kelly's onslaught.

All right, I said. We'll have a memorial service, okay? I still think she'd have wanted cremation.

The tears came back.

The word. *Cremation.* The reality of it. The finality.

I went to Kelly. I put my arms around her. We hugged. She cried.

I must confess I cried a bit myself.

It was good to have company.

67.

LAURA CALLED ME TUESDAY MORNING. Woke me up.

Hi, Rick. How are you holding up?

Not great.

I'm sorry, Rick. Stupid question.

I didn't reply.

I felt that I was being mean. But I didn't have the energy to be polite.

Listen, she said, there are a couple of things I'd like to talk to you about.

I'm all yours. Ears. I'm all yours and ears.

I think it would be better to talk in person.

Her voice was soothing.

Okay, I said. Whatever. How about lunch?

I'm not sure I have time for lunch. Can you come by the morgue?

Hard to pass up *that* invitation.

I'm sorry. It's just the office to me. Sometimes I forget.

No, no. Just joking. Sometimes I think of my office as a morgue too. Come to think of it, most days.

She didn't laugh. She had a sweet soft way with a laugh, and I wanted to hear it.

But I thought I heard her smile.

I promised to show up.

It took a few minutes of concentration to remember. What the last few days had brought. What the day would bring.

I shook my head. It hurt. I contemplated turning over. Putting the pillow over my head. Going back to the soft and unpredictable world of dreams. Who knew what wonders might await me there? But. I had an appointment. At the morgue. Jesus.

I hauled myself out of bed. I dragged myself into some barely presentable clothes. I opened the pill drawer. At least I didn't have to lock them up anymore. Life was handing me small consolations.

I took twice my normal doses. I didn't bother calling Sheila to ask. A little self-medication. Nothing wrong with that. I'd only get her endless voice mail message anyway. And I had to do something, to get me through this glorious day.

I left the house.

When I got to Laura's office, she was not alone.

Rick, she said, nodding to a rumpled gray thing on the couch, you know Detective Harwood?

Yes, I said, we've met.

He nodded. I nodded. He didn't extend a hand.

There'd been a change since he'd been at my house. His hostility had grown. Thrived. I saw contempt. Something had tipped him over.

The fluorescent light didn't flatter him. He had the pasty skin, the bored demeanor of the lifelong cop.

The couch had seen better days too.

You didn't tell me we'd have company, I said to Laura.

An effort to lighten the suddenly somber mood.

Laura smiled uncomfortably, shuffled some papers on her desk. I tried to see what they were, but the angle wasn't good.

The metal desk was gray. Like the metal chair in which I sat. Like the feeling in the room.

We have some results we'd like to share with you, Rick. From the autopsy.

I didn't want to hear. Whatever it was that had killed Melissa made no difference to me. Overdose, heart attack, ennui. She was gone. She'd never really had a chance. Whatever those demons were that she'd so skillfully concealed from me had gotten her in the end.

Fire away, I said.

Well, the first part is what we thought, Rick. What you thought.

Yes?

Alcohol, 0.4. Off the charts, for you and me.

Speak for yourself, I said, half-heartedly attempting another joke.

She didn't smile.

Not unusual in a long-term alcoholic, she said. But there was lots of other stuff.

She began to read from the report. They'd put together the blood results with the pharmacological detritus. Pill containers. When she'd got them. What was left in them. They figured she'd ingested, at a minimum, 50 milligrams of Xanax; 800 mg Effexor; 100 mg Ambien; Adderall 225 mg.

A listener less inured to the ways of the chronically addicted might have marveled at the quantities. Wondered how she could have stayed alive long enough to take it all.

But I knew better.

That doesn't sound like all that much, for her, I said.

Laura looked at me sadly.

Well, we don't know that, Rick. And even if it were, it's rolling dice. Every day your body survives that kind of abuse is a minor miracle. One day it can catch up with you. It *will* catch up with you.

It would have been depressing, if I wasn't already as down as a man can be.

My extra doses weren't doing a thing for me.

But, Laura continued.

But?

There was something else.

That wasn't enough?

There's no easy way to put this, Rick, so I'll just say it.

Please do.

There was semen, Rick.

Semen?

This was not a word I had expected to hear.

What? Semen? Where?

Where you'd expect it to be, Rick.

Her incessant repetition of my name was beginning to get on my nerves. I knew it was meant to soothe. To placate. Establish rapport, empathy. But it was pissing me off.

That's impossible, Laura, I said sharply. Come on. Lab contamination or something. We haven't. We hadn't. In years. Jesus. Two or three at least.

Yes, she said. I understand that you had said that. Actually, that's why it seems to be an issue.

I didn't remember telling anyone that. But then, I didn't remember much about that day. Nor, I suddenly remembered, about the night before that day.

Something vague and ugly came back to me. But no. No way. That had been a dream. A drunken hallucination.

Not one that I was about to share, with my good friend Harwood in the room.

So what the hell is this? I said. How is this possible?

That's something we might have to look into, Rick.

Jesus, I said. Jesus H. Christ. She didn't have a boyfriend. She didn't have the energy to have a boyfriend. She could barely get off that goddamn couch. For Christ's sake, she never even left the house.

Laura didn't respond. The weary eyes of Detective Harwood fixed on mine. I hung my head. I couldn't return his gaze. I felt an unaccountable guilt. Or maybe it was shame. Because something was going on here. Had been going on here. And I didn't know what it was. I didn't have a goddamn clue. And it had been my job to know. I'd let Melissa down. Again. I was only beginning to learn of all the ways I'd let her down.

Or maybe. No. Not that. It couldn't be that. Jesus. I was a happy drunk. Depressive, sure. But homicidal?

Laura finally spoke. Not you then, Rick?

I lifted my head. I was very, very tired.

No, Laura, I said, with as much dignity as I could muster. Not me.

And you have no idea who?

Jesus, Laura.

I slowly shook my head.

Harwood hadn't taken his eyes off me.

And, said Harwood.

It was the first word he'd spoken.

I turned to face him. He had that sardonic look. The one that grizzled cops habitually wear. You're going to lie to me, it says. Everybody does. Always.

He looked at Laura, raised his eyebrows.

Laura cleared her throat.

And, she said. There were signs of . . .

Signs of what?

Signs of . . . forcing.

She said the last word softly.

What? Forcing? Rape?

Forcing. I'd rather say forcing. Rape has all sorts of . . . connotations, that aren't necessarily apparent here.

A strange calm descended over me. I'd reached my limit. My emotional life shut down. It could not take any more assaults.

It gave me a certain clarity.

I don't understand, Laura, I said. I just don't understand. There was no evidence of . . .

No. No forced entry. No broken furniture. No disarray.

Except the disarray that was Melissa's life. Our lives.

Kelly was there, I said.

Upstairs. Yes. In her room.

So, how? How could something have happened?

If we knew that, Rick . . .

Harwood turned his hound-dog eyes on me again.

Jesus, I said, shaking my head.

It was a calculated response. Harwood's stare was unrelenting. I felt obliged to be as convincing as possible.

So, Harwood said. We need to do some further investigation.

Yes, I said. I understand.

Harwood lit a Marlboro. The smoke made me choke. I coughed. He lifted his eyebrows. As if some comment was expected of me.

I couldn't think of one. What was the appropriate thing to say, I asked myself, in this situation? They didn't teach you that in law school.

We need your permission for a few things, said Laura.

Sure, sure. Whatever.

There was a long pause. Harwood smoked. I wheezed. There was something intensely irritating about his passive smoke.

Like what? I asked. You've already ransacked the house.

You know, DNA things.

DNA things? You're kidding me, right?

I'm sorry, Rick. I was trying to get to this gently. We'd like a DNA sample from you. We could get it in other ways, of course. But I thought it better to be upfront about this.

You're kidding me, right? Laura? You're kidding?

I felt foolish at my stammering.

Harwood chimed in.

She's not kidding, Rick.

I tried to remember when I'd asked for his opinion. When I'd told him he could call me Rick. He'd said it with distaste. A curl of the lip. Too much emphasis. She's not kidding, *Rick.*

I looked straight into his eyes for the first time. They were yellow, like his face. He blew some more smoke at me.

Clearly this was the beginning of a beautiful friendship.

Fuck you, Harwood, I said.

I hadn't meant to say it. Just to think it. But it came out.

He didn't flinch. I guess he'd heard worse.

It won't be hard to get a warrant, he said, in a bored tone.

I may not have been much of a criminal lawyer, but I knew enough to figure he was right. *Cherchez l'homme.*

I turned to Laura.

This is really humiliating, I said.

I know it is. Listen. It's just routine. You know how it works. We want to eliminate you as a suspect. Officially. Get on to the real investigation. No distractions.

Suspect? It wasn't even clear there'd been a crime. Jesus, I thought. There must be something else. Something they're not telling me.

Harwood didn't look like a guy who wanted to eliminate me as a suspect. He looked like a guy who wanted to beat me with a rubber hose.

He got up and left the room, treating me to a sardonic smile.

I'm sorry, Laura, I said. I can't do that right now. It just doesn't seem right.

Laura shook her head.

Rick, I don't really understand why you're doing this. But I'm not going to argue with you about it. I know you're going through a lot.

I appreciate that.

She changed the subject. We talked a few minutes about the old days. But my heart wasn't in it.

I wasn't even sure my heart was still in my body.

I took my leave. Laura got up to escort me to the door. I could feel the tension in her as she walked me out. She wanted to commiserate. To give me a reassuring hug. But she couldn't do it.

Wouldn't be professional.

68.

WHEN I GOT TO THE OFFICE there was a message on my desk. I was to go to Warwick's office without delay. What a pleasure. What an excellent way to continue this marvelous day.

Bob Shumaker, Ethics Guru, was with Warwick in his office.

This was not a good sign.

They both had Serious Faces on.

Rick, said Warwick.

Now I knew that this was big trouble. Warwick hadn't used my first name since the Reagan administration.

I'm not going to beat about the bush, he said. I'm going to get right to the issue. Dispense with the formalities.

I wondered how many semantically identical clichés he was planning to generate, before he got to the point.

We think you should take a leave of absence, he said.

He looked at Shumaker. Shumaker nodded.

I opened my mouth to respond. To say that I didn't want to take a leave of absence. That I needed to keep busy to stay sane. But Warwick didn't give me the chance.

This has nothing to do with your coming in at eleven-thirty, Rick. We understand that you're under a lot of stress. This is a terrible thing. But there are other factors to consider.

My view was not being solicited. I stayed silent.

A Detective Harwood was here this morning, said Warwick.

Damn. He moved fast.

Warwick looked at Shumaker. Shumaker nodded. As though the fact that Harwood had been there needed independent confirmation.

Strangely, it wasn't Warwick I wanted to kill. It was Shumaker.

And frankly, Rick, said Warwick, some of the things he had to say were a mite disturbing.

I raised my eyebrows.

He says you're refusing to give a DNA sample, Rick. That they're going to have to get a warrant for it. That you want to have a cremation, right away.

He paused.

Harwood. That stupid prick.

I had nothing to say.

Rick. This doesn't make a good impression.

I refrained from telling him that it was none of his goddamn business. What I chose to do with my wife's remains.

And of course we've got to think of morale, he said.

There it was.

We just can't afford to have this kind of distraction around here, Rick. So. We're asking you to take a leave of absence. Just until all of this is cleared up.

I bit my tongue.

Sure, I said. I understand.

It'll be good for you, Rick. Clear your head. You've got a lot to deal with.

I had a few choice things to say to that. But I didn't bother. There was no percentage in it.

I got up to leave. I had to get out of there. Before I did something I couldn't take back later.

There's one other thing, he said.

What now? I thought. He's going to cut my compensation too? *Unpaid* leave of absence? I sat back down. My back hurt. I was getting a headache.

FitzGibbon wants me to keep you on his son's case.

I raised my eyebrows. They were getting a workout.

I tried to talk him out of it, Warwick continued, but he seems to have developed quite a liking for you.

There's no accounting for taste, I said.

It's a no-lose situation for us, said Warwick, showing no sign of having caught the irony. For you. He appears to think the kid is guilty. He probably is, from what I hear. So you don't have any pressure to get him off. You just need to keep FitzGibbon happy. Go through the motions. Plead it down if you can.

Sure, I said, ignoring Warwick's tenuous grasp of an attorney's duty to zealously represent his client.

You can work from home, continued Warwick. And if you need some help, you can have it. Anyone you want. Just let me know. I'd suggest Herman Walker. He had two years in the Brooklyn DA's office. Sharp kid. Could be useful.

I pictured spending time with Herman Walker and his matching tie and suspenders.

I'd like Dorita Reed, I said.

Reed? he asked. She's a T & E lawyer, for God's sake.

I trust her. She's got judgment.

Warwick looked irritated.

You did say 'anybody,' I reminded him.

Yes, I did, he replied, with a shake of the head. All right. Take Reed. You won't need her full-time, will you?

Not as of now.

If that changes, let me know. We need her around here.

I will. I might need Vinnie Price a bit too.

Warwick shook his head with a frown. But he didn't say no. I took it for a yes.

I got up again to leave. Warwick looked at Shumaker.

Shumaker nodded.

Approval. We all need it.

69.

I STOOD FOR A LONG TIME staring out my office window. Below me were rooftops. Manhattan rooftops. Ancient wooden cisterns. The occasional evergreen tree, struggling to provide a contrast to the impossibly thick accretion of concrete, steel and artificial space. I saw it all around. I saw it from space. How thin it was from there. How God with a shovel, a spade, a can opener, could peel it off and toss it in the sea, if he so wished.

How fragile it all was.

I saw a woman on a rooftop. She wore a long brown overcoat. She stood at the edge of the roof. She had something in her hand. I couldn't make out what it was. She didn't move. She was thinking, too. She'd been hurt, like me. Hoping to take some solace from the view. Letting her imagination create a world from a detail on the horizon. Yes. That could be me. Living there. In that building, way up north. The thirty-third floor of that building there. There'd be children in that home. Happy, playing children. And paintings on the wall. And phone calls from friends. A life. A place.

A home that gave her more than pain and dread and solitude.

My father spoke to me.

A man did not give up.

I shook myself. I resolved to do my job. I had a client. My client needed me. He sure as hell needed somebody. Soldier on, I said. Be right. Be good. The rest will take care of itself.

I wasn't sure I really bought into it. But I couldn't resist it, either. I didn't have much choice. I wasn't suicidal.

I loved my misery too much to give it up.

I sat and thought.

Strange, I mused, that FitzGibbon would insist that I stay on. If he was involved in something, it could only mean he figured I was incompetent enough to cause no harm. Not beyond the realm of possibility. Though I preferred other theories. That he wasn't. That he could see that he needed a man of my sterling abilities to get his only natural son out of this mess.

The problem being, of course, that everything pointed to the opposite conclusion.

I gathered up my four-by-six index cards, with the scribbles and lines. I untacked them from the walls. I put them in my jacket pocket. I took the elevator down. I went out the revolving door. I walked down the avenue. I stopped at Michel's. Last time I'd be there for a while. I sat at the bar. I had a steak. Onions fried in butter. Fuck cholesterol. A glass of Australian Shiraz. Another. Three. I placed the cards on the bar, in groups of five. I looked at them. I read the words. I followed the lines. I wrote in the margins. I drew more lines. I'd stolen some colored pens from the office supply closet. A man of action thinks ahead.

When I got bored with the colored pens, I made a list:

- Larry Silver is dead.
- His body was found in an alley three blocks from Jules's loft; blunt trauma to the head; his body had been covered with a cardboard box.
- The perp was probably right-handed, and Larry was probably sitting down when he got whacked.
- Jules is right-handed.
- He smokes my brand.
- Larry Silver was a lowlife and a snake, a penny-ante drug dealer, a small-time scam artist with pretensions to more.
- In other words, he probably deserved what he got.
- Jules is a bit of a nutcase; he disfigures himself; has some kind of samurai fetish; might be suicidal.
- He has a girlfriend, Lisa; she is a nutcase too.
- But rather sexy, in a tiny green-eyed junkie kind of way.
- She has a dragon tattoo.
- Jules has a lion tattoo.
- Absolutely nobody is telling me the truth, the whole truth and nothing but the truth.
- But then, isn't that always the case.

I thought. I pondered. I came to a conclusion.
I didn't know a fucking thing.

70.

I DRIFTED IN AND OUT OF SLEEP. I stayed suspended in that dreamy state. To live a half-life, suspended between dream and blissful blank sleep, alive and not alive, I mused. Maybe death was something like this. Dreaming, I thought, not for the first time, might be practice for the afterlife.

I finally dragged myself out of bed. Out of the house. It was closer to eleven o'clock than ten. I felt vague and dirty.

At the corner, waiting for the light to change, I remembered. Where was I going?

Things were different now.

I walked back to the house. I sat on the couch.

It made me uncomfortable. It was someone else's couch.

I got up.

I sat in the armchair.

I considered the options.

I couldn't go to work. I couldn't stay in the house. The ghosts would suck me dry.

There was only one option. I packed up the laptop. I stuffed my index cards into the computer bag.

I went to Starbucks.

I was surprised to find one of the big plush armchairs free. I plugged in the laptop. I set my papers on the chair. To discourage interlopers. I went to the counter. I ordered a tall skinny latte. I smiled at the fellow at the cash. I cooed at some babies in strollers. I nodded at my fellow lap-top geeks. I eavesdropped on some chatter from the three girls studying for the bar exam. I took my coffee to my chair. I fired up the computer. I thanked the Lord for wireless access. I checked my voice mail, e-mail. Nothing urgent. I opened the *Times*. I sat back. I looked around.

Hey, I thought. This isn't half bad. I could get used to it.

I was halfway through the *Times* when the laptop beeped. E-mail. I opened it up. It was from a name I didn't recognize. There was an attachment. Virus warnings went off in my head.

My cell phone rang. I picked it up. It was Butch.

Don't delete it, he said.

What?

Download it.

Okay.

Butch hung up.

I downloaded the attachment. Opened it up. PDF files. I took a look. Scanned documents. Old. It didn't take me long to recognize them. The trust file.

Shit. Had to love that Butch.

I spent a few hours reading musty documents. Without the must. This time I had the luxury. It was my only case. What else was I going to do? I plowed through it all. Every page. Every dusty word of every convoluted clause of every will and trust deed, until I got back to the FitzGibbon trusts again. 'Twenty million dollars to his issue, upon reaching their maturity.' An old-fashioned word, 'issue.' Babies issuing from the womb. Women as vessels. From which issued the fathers' progeny. Very quaint. I could hear the protests, if someone used it now.

I called Dorita. Gave her my new office address. She said she'd come by later. But only after five. She had stuff to do.

Damn. Stuff to do. Never thought I'd feel a twinge of jealousy at those words.

I was edgy. All those lattes. I didn't want to leave my comfy chair. Some pregnant woman would purloin it, the second I got up. But I had to get out of there. Take a walk. Air out the pores. Come back at five. Where to go, though?

Might as well drop in and see how the client's doing. Sure. Why not?

Jules was there. I was a little disconcerted. I didn't really have anything to talk to him about. I didn't want to ask directly about another sibling, the phone records. I wanted to do some more research first. Never ask a question you don't know the answer to. Besides, I thought, suddenly seized with fear, what if Lisa had made up some story? Exaggerated my role in her attempted seduction? Made him hate me, because I'd pushed her away, or for whatever twisted reason? Who knew the depths of the female mind? I'd be another pawn in a new and different Futterman game.

I thought of going home.

Jules opened the door. Turned his back on me. Sprawled on the couch.

Everything seemed normal.

I sighed a provisional sigh of relief.

So, Jules said, you solve the case, lawyer guy?

No. But I've learned a few things.

Spit it out.

He had a new and disconcerting arrogance to him.

Nothing I've confirmed, I said, warily.

Jesus, he said. I think I'll tell Dad to stop paying you.

Are you talking to him?

No.

Then that'll be a little tough.

I have my ways.

More power to your ways, I said. You got a beer?

Jules snorted. In a you-got-me-there kind of way. Went to the fridge.

I took this to be an excellent sign.

He brought me an Anchor Steam. One for himself. He sprawled back on the couch.

You seem very relaxed, I said.

Shouldn't I?

For a guy charged with murder.

He fixed me with a stare.

I didn't do nothing, he said. Why should I be worried?

No reason. Kind of a stressful experience, though, I would think.

I guess, he said, taking a pull off the beer.

Smoke? he said, pulling out a pack of my favorites.

I took one. He lit them both.

Something had happened. The lost boy in him had vanished.

I drank my beer. Tried to bond a bit. Talked a bit about the Rangers. The atmosphere was as conducive as it was going to get. I plunged in.

Listen, I said, there's one thing.

Yo, brotha.

I was talking to the ADA. You know, the Assistant District Attorney?

Yo, you think I'm stupid?

Actually, no. I think you're a very bright guy, Jules. I just wanted to make sure you knew what I was talking about.

I always know what you're talking about, lawyer guy, he said, taking a good haul off the beer.

He told me about some phone records, I lied.

He gave me a straight-ahead look.

Calls from your cell phone.

And?

To your father's office.

Silence.

Four or five of them. In the days before Larry Silver's murder.

Jules narrowed his eyes. Looked straight at me.

And?

Well, given how you and your dad don't seem to be talking to each other and all, the ADA thought it was a little strange.

Strange.

Yes. Strange.

He took another big slug off of his beer.

Whose side did you say you were on? he asked.

Jules. You don't seem to be getting it. I've tried to explain to you. I'm your lawyer. I'm on your side. All the way. No questions asked. But if I'm going to do my best for you, if I'm going to defend you to the best of my abilities, I can't be flying in the dark. I need the facts. I need all the facts. Then I can take the facts and turn them into a story that the ADA will buy. I can't be going to him with a 'Shit, I don't know what that's all about.' Because then he'll be making up his own story. The story he makes up might not be so good for you. And I'm telling you, Jules, right now. That's just what his story's looking like. Not too damn good.

Jules laughed.

Sure, dude, he said. I hear ya.

He still seemed way too calm. I waited.

Nothing.

The preliminary hearing's in two weeks, I said.

He looked at me.

I'd gotten his attention, at least.

You seen that show? he asked. The one with the puppets making phony phone calls?

Uh, yeah. I've seen the commercials for it, anyway.

It got me some ideas. Call up the old man. Get him a little crazy.

Ah. I see.

Just fooling around with the old fart.

Yeah. I get it.

I was lying again. I didn't get a thing. I certainly didn't believe his lame-ass story.

Okay, I said. Just wanted to check that out.

Sure. No sweat.

I got up to leave.

The street outside was cold and empty. I wondered. What had turned Jules from scared and confused to this caricature of cool? He and Daddy were somehow in cahoots in this thing? Jesus. But that couldn't be. It conflicted with just about every other piece of evidence I had.

71.

THERE WAS A POKER GAME that night. I resolved to go. I resolved to be a man. I resolved to win.

I called Butch. He was into it.

It was at a social club in Hoboken, across the river. Neon sign in the frosted window. Hudson County Men's Club. Peephole in the door. A big lunk with a homemade haircut opened it.

We're here for the poker game, I said.

The Lunk nodded, opened the door.

We walked in.

It was a picture from long ago. Linoleum floors. Hideous fluorescent light struggling through decades of dust and dead flies. Wooden fold-up chairs. Mary Mother of Jesus on the wall. In the corner the regulars were playing gin rummy. Beefy unsmiling guys with a lot of black hair and a way with a lead pipe.

They ignored us.

I wondered how Mike had talked his way into this place.

I didn't ask. No percentage in it.

I sat down. Everyone was there. Butch. Mike. Straight Jake. Drunk Jake. Andrea. Jonesie. Even the Dane had made an appearance. I smiled and shook his hand. He gave me a sheepish nod. I realized that he had been more mortified than me. He'd stayed away the last few games out of embarrassment.

It goes to show. There's always someone more fucked up than you.

I played aggressive. I jammed the pot. I bluffed like hell. I hooded my eyes and glared the others down, my head slightly tilted in contempt. I said little. I drank a lot. I had no qualms. I had no inhibitions. I didn't care. I was doing it for my father, my brother, my self-respect.

I won and kept on winning. I could see the dismay grow on their faces.

Butch ran out of high fives. He ran out of cash.

I can't compete, man, he said.

He called a cab.

It made me strong. They'd never seen a thing like this. I was in the zone. The slightest sign of weakness I could smell as clear as rotting fish. I pounced on it. I smelled the strong hands too. I picked up cues. I folded in odd places. I showed my rags when I'd jammed them out of a pot. I showed my Aces when I folded them to a straight. I had them on the run. Confusing. Unpredictable. Dangerous.

Andrea was losing too, like all the rest. But her dismay turned gradually to admiration. She leaned over, joked about the new aggressive me. I could smell the sexuality as strongly as the cards. I'd become a dog. A wolf. A snake. A door was opened to a new and feral world. My nether regions stirred.

My God, I thought. I've become a man again.

I won the last pot too. It was inevitable. It was a rush for the ages. I gathered up the cash. I stuffed it in my pockets, inside, out. I'd taken everybody's money. They looked at me with awe. They weren't angry. They were amazed. My pockets bulged. I grabbed Drunk Jake around the neck, dragged him into the night.

72.

IN THE STREET the cold air hit me in the face like a slap from an angry woman. The temperature had taken a dive. A sharp wind was howling up the street. A rusted fire escape was twisting with it, making strangely beautiful metal music. I wanted to shout to the heavens. I wanted to challenge the Gods to a chess game.

Drunk Jake was drunk. He slipped on a patch of ice, lay in the street. He was giggling. I dragged him to the curb, just ahead of a barreling Denali. Jesus, I thought, that's a big fucking vehicle. I began to sober up. Jake didn't. I hauled him to his feet. I put my arm around him, held him up. We staggered comically toward the PATH train to Manhattan. I was hoping for a cab to pass, before we had to be subjected to the underground's indignities.

At Bloomfield Street we stepped over a guy passed out on the sidewalk. We paid no mind. Just another obstacle on the road to becoming a man. But he took offense. We had awakened him. From a most important dream, it seemed. He crawled to his feet.

Hey, he yelled, the fuck you think you're doing?

I'm trying to rescue my frigid friend here from the ravages of the evil drink, I said. The devil rum. A concept you might well want to attend to, I added, eyeing his vein-lined face and trembling hands.

I was confident that the inebriate wouldn't follow a word of it.

Fuck you, the degenerate responded. Quote Shakespeare at your peril, shitbag.

Ho, ho, an *intellectual* walking dead pile of drunken pus, I said, strategically ignoring the fact that Shakespeare had nothing to do with it.

He must have mistaken my friendly tone, for he immediately launched himself at me, all hundred pounds of desiccated liver and grime-encrusted flesh aimed at my midsection like an RPG from the ninth circle of hell. I stepped aside, losing my grip on Drunk Jake's armpit. Jake staggered to a lamppost and held himself up by sheer force of will. The homeless bag of bones fell face-first into the gutter, reaping a visage full of dirty snow.

I laughed. Our dead-end friend gathered himself and launched another pathetic attack. I could see that he was going to take some convincing. I batted him upside the head as he came within arm's length, knocking him sideways into a wrought iron fence, sending him sprawling once again.

This time he lay there for a moment, catching what little breath his ravaged lungs made available to him, and cursed me from the prone position.

You piece of whale shit, he said, I'll Melville your ass from here to Nantucket.

Gad, I said, you're a literate piece of crap. Get up and I'll buy you a drink.

Stick him, Rick, kick his fuckin' head in, yelled Jake from his position at the lamppost.

C'mon, Jake, I responded, my words slurring for the first time, he's a fellow traveler. An angel sent from Dante for our delectation. Let's buy him a drink.

All the bars are closed, Jake said, more cogently than could have been expected. Kick the shit out of 'm.

I'm not sure that our good friend here should be the victim of the mere contingency that it's after closing time, I replied.

The angry hobo was not appeased. He gathered himself up and took another run at me. He was hunched over. I detected a glint of metal in his left hand. A lefty, too, I thought admiringly. A creative thinker. I landed a heavy uppercut to his sternum. He collapsed in a silent heap, and bothered us no longer.

Pity, I said. I was looking forward to some interesting conversation.

Fuck that, said Jake, let's find a cab.

As luck would have it, one tooled by at just that moment. We flagged it down.

Manhattan, I said to the driver.

He smelled of stale cigarettes, and Jersey City.

73.

AS I APPROACHED HOME I knew that I had to shed the macho skin. Kelly'd be awake. She'd be worried. In the midst of all of the bravado I'd neglected even to call her to tell her I'd be late.

I was deflated. I felt like a shit. I thought of my unconscious friend on the Hoboken sidewalk. Jesus. I probably should have called an ambulance.

But mostly I thought of Kelly. How I was going to explain this to her.

When I opened the door she was there. Standing in front of me. Arms crossed.

Where the hell have you been? she asked.

Out, I said. I had stuff to do.

I'm glad *you* believe that.

I looked at her. My angel child. My consolation. I didn't want to lie to her. No, goddamn it. Whatever the price, with Kelly I'd be honest.

So I told her the story of my night.

She alternately smiled and frowned. She understood, I thought. Sort of.

Then the hard part started.

I talked to Detective Harwood, she said.

Who?

Detective Harwood. He's investigating.

Jesus. He talked to you?

Yes.

Where?

Here.

He came here?

Yes, she said, with a hint of defiance.

What right did he have to come here? What right did he have to talk to you without me here?

I don't know, she said with a hard curl of the lip. You're the lawyer, Daddy.

I sat and thought. Tried to place myself in the context of earlier that day. Before the manly thing had caught me in its spell.

He seemed very nice, she said.

Nice?

Yes. He seemed to want to know the truth.

I guess that makes him nice.

Nicer than most.

Right. Okay. What did he want?

I told you. He wanted to know what happened.

What did you tell him?

The truth, Daddy. What do you think I told him?

I felt weak. I felt dizzy. I was having trouble following.

Let's talk about it tomorrow, I said.

No. I mean yes. Fine. But there's something we have to talk about now.

What?

He said you wouldn't give a DNA sample.

Oh God. What business did he have bringing that up with you?

She looked at me with accusing eyes.

It's insulting, I explained.

Insulting, she said, with a disdainful air.

I thought about a bottle of Scotch. I'd finished off the talisman, but there had to be another one, stashed somewhere in the house.

They're just doing their job, Daddy.

I know, I said, resigned.

Some macho guy. Brought low by a sixteen-year-old girl.

I sat and thought. Kelly didn't take her eyes off me. Waiting for a verdict. Damn. Was it really pride, that made me refuse? How sure was I that I'd had nothing to do with it? I'd convinced myself. Consciously.

That the memory, the dreamlike state, had been indeed a dream. Or the recollection of a dream. A confused recollection bred by excess substances and guilt and, God help me, perhaps a touch of wishful thinking. But I hadn't done it. Hadn't done a thing. And even if I had – that doubt again – so what? I hadn't killed her. If she'd killed herself, as a result? Was that my responsibility?

Probably, damn it.

But not legally.

Not murder.

I'd rot in goddamn hell. But I wouldn't go to jail.

Okay, I said. I'll do it. For God's sake. I'll do it.

All right, she said, and became herself again.

She gave me a small sad smile. A hug.

God, how I needed that.

74.

THE MORNING WAS UGLY. In eighteen different ways. Not counting the blotched and pallid face that met me in the mirror.

I slapped myself. Enough goddamn self-pity.

Or was it self-loathing?

What was the difference?

I made a mental note. To explore that with Sheila.

I called Dorita.

Meet me at my office, I said.

Dorita floated into Starbucks on a ridiculous velvet skirt. Red. Splayed about her like a tutu.

You're going to love this, she said, in a tone that said I wasn't.

Great, I said. More bad news. That's what I crave.

Remember the Gang of Eight?

My fellow probationists? The ones whose meetings I keep forgetting to get myself invited to?

That's the one. Well apparently they actually did something.

And what, dear girl, did they actually do?

They brought in some business.

All of them? Together?

Sort of. They drew up a plan. They called everyone they knew. Set up lunches with all their contacts. Invited in some outfit to give them lessons in how to pitch business.

Jesus. They got serious.

They did. And the funny thing is, it worked.

Really?

They already got six new matters in the door.

You're kidding.

I'm not. And Warwick is crowing about it.

What the hell does he have to do with it?

He's taking all the credit, of course.

For threatening to fire us all?

The probation thing. A masterful stroke of management, he says. Lit a fire under them.

Shit, I said. It wasn't really Harwood, was it? All Warwick needed was an excuse. To get rid of me.

You were the only one who didn't participate, Rick.

They never invited me, goddamn it.

You never asked, Ricky. Doesn't exactly show initiative, does it?

Yeah, yeah. Shit. I'm doomed.

There's always hope.

I'm close to concluding that there is not.

Is not?

Always hope.

Oh dear.

I sat and thought about my fate.

I resigned myself to it.

It was time to get down to business.

Time's running out, I said. The preliminary hearing's in less than two weeks.

Let's get to work, then.

What next?

Sounded like you had something in mind.

I don't. Sue me.

Jesus. Okay. Let's go talk to the twins.

Sure. We can appeal to their sympathy. Tell them I'm in danger of being fired. They'll confess.

Just talk to them. Get to know them. God knows what information they may have. Maybe without even knowing it.

I suppose.

All right, then. Pick one.

I'll take Raul. I'm not sure I've exactly ingratiated myself with Ramon.

All right. I'll take Ramon.

But there's just one thing.

What?

I don't have any idea where he is.

Oh ye of little faith, she said.

She fished into her purse. Pulled out a pack of matches. Handed it to me. Inside, a telephone number.

Cell phone?

Little faith, but quick off the mark.

She strode out of Starbucks. She looked good from the rear. Hell, she looked good from every angle.

75.

I LOOKED AT THE PHONE NUMBER. What the hell was I going to say to this guy to get him to meet me? What was I going to say to him if he did?

For lack of something more creative, I decided to try the truth.

I dialed the number.

A voice answered. A smooth voice. Smooth, but not friendly.

Raul here, it said.

Raul?

Here.

Ah. Raul, we've never met. But I was hoping you might have a few minutes to chat.

Chat?

He said it as if it were a word he hadn't heard before.

Talk for a few minutes. Place of your choosing. I'm buying.

Who are you?

I'd forgotten that bit.

I'm Rick Redman. I'm a lawyer. I'm representing your brother.

My brother doesn't have a lawyer.

He hung up.

Well, I thought. What was that all about?

I sipped my coffee.

Oh. Maybe he'd misunderstood.

I called back.

Raul here.

Your other brother, I said quickly. Your adoptive brother.

Long silence.

Raul?

Yes?

Jules. I represent Jules. Your father hired me. We spoke briefly the other day. About the bail.

And?

And I'd like just a few minutes of your time. Like I said, wherever you like. Whenever's convenient.

Long pause.

Okay, he said.

All right. Thank you. I really appreciate it. I won't take much of your time. Where would you like to meet?

Here.

Happy to do that. If you would be so kind as to tell me where 'here' is.

My place.

Could I have the address?

He gave it to me. Park Avenue. The bachelor pad. I was looking forward to seeing it.

I'll be there in half an hour, I said.

I grabbed a cab. The driver smelled of shawarma and aluminum foil. On the way I called up Laura. Made an appointment. To have some living part of myself purloined.

She was pleased.

I wasn't.

The twins' place was a standard Upper East Side fortress. Massive block construction. Elegant multipaned windows. In every one a very fancy set of drapes. Uniformed doorman. Red jacket. Epaulets. Obsequious air.

Rick Redman for Raul FitzGibbon, I said.

He's expecting you, he replied.

My. The personal touch.

Mr. Epaulet led me to the end of a narrow marble corridor. There was a single elevator there. In the elevator there was one unmarked button.

Nice to have your own.

I pressed the button.

The elevator rose.

It was silent, smooth. A sleek ride.

The elevator opened silently, right into a large, opulent living room. The walls were upholstered in burgundy silk. The furniture was lavish. Old. Polished to a moneyed glow. The drapes were heavy gold brocade, and closed. The room was lit by innumerable small lamps. Every surface seemed to have one.

A faint sweet odor permeated the place.

A pretty woman wearing a maid's costume straight from central wardrobe urged me to sit on a massive dark green couch. I sank into it at least a foot.

When the time comes, I thought, it's going to be hard to get out of this thing.

Please, sir, can I get you something? asked the maid.

I had expected some kind of foreign accent. I got Texas. Well, you can't be right all the time.

She had a nice bit of cleavage going though.

I'll have a Scotch, I said. On the rocks.

Live dangerously, I thought. Hell, you already are.

Miss Texas brought me a Scotch in a giant snifter. I stuck my nose in it. Smoke. Peat. Laphroaig. Had to be. The guy had good taste in single malts.

Raul entered.

He was an elegant sonofabitch, too. I had to give him that. He was dressed in black. Italian suit. Highly polished black shoes. Black silk shirt. One of those deep, deep tans that don't seem real. His hair looked like it cost more than my car. If I had a car.

I saw the family resemblance, but it wasn't striking. Non-identical, I concluded. One theory out the door.

I struggled to stand up. The couch enveloped me. He smiled a charming smile.

No, no, he said, don't get up.

His English was cultivated, flawless. No Spanish accent. I didn't know why I'd expected one. They'd come here young, I reminded myself. Been here at least a decade.

He walked over, extended a hand. His grip was firm and dry.

He seemed less like his brother every moment.

He sat in the matching armchair across the room. He looked absurdly far away. Like I'd have to shout for him to hear me.

There was some idle chatter. I complimented the decor. Asked about the paintings on the walls.

I understand you had something to do with the White Swallow, I said.

Raul smiled.

Yes. We helped out a bit.

We?

Ramon and I.

Really? Is this a sideline of yours?

We're trying to turn it into a real business, actually. Father's been very supportive.

Is that a fact? How would you make a profit with this business, if you don't mind my asking?

His smile grew broader.

People love to talk about themselves. Raul was no exception.

We have some skills. Some people are willing to pay handsomely for them. Up to now we've been giving out free advice. To people we like. Our friends. But we decided it was time to make a profit from it.

Great. I'm a big fan of free enterprise. What kind of advice?

Club advice. How to run a club. How to make a place popular with the right people.

Oh, I get it. Yes. That could be quite lucrative, I imagine.

We're hoping so.

That's really interesting, I ruminated. Can you give me an example of the advice you plan to sell?

Well, said Raul with a wry smile, the whole idea is to charge for the advice. If I start giving it out free, it defeats the purpose, doesn't it?

Sure, sure. I understand. But I'm not in the club business. I don't even know anybody in the club business. And anyway I promise it won't leave this room. I'm just curious, that's all.

Okay. But you've got to solemnly promise.

Sure. I'm a way solemn guy.

He grimaced slightly. But gave in anyway.

I'm sure you've noticed, he said, that most bars, particularly high-end bars, try to hire pretty women as waitresses?

Not a detail that's escaped my notice.

The idea being that men will want to come to the bar, stay in the bar, to ogle the pretty women.

He said it 'oogle.' I hate that. The damn word is 'ogle.'

Sure, I said, makes sense.

Yes it does. But something else makes more sense.

Okay. Enlighten me.

You hire pretty men.

Ah. Um. I'm not sure I get the point.

The point is this: You scour the gyms, the modeling agencies, the actors' studios. You hire a bunch of slim but muscular young men. You dress them in tight clothes. What happens?

You just opened a gay bar?

No, what happens is that the *women* come to ogle the *men*. And once the *women* start coming, the *men* follow, to try to pick up the women. Much more satisfying than ogling waitresses. The waitresses are unobtainable, for the most part, and busy anyway. They don't have time for seduction. But if a man knows that a bar will be full of good-looking young women, women self-selected for their interest in good-looking men, the good-looking men will flock to the place. And that will bring in yet more available women. And the cycle continues.

I paused to think that through. Jesus, the guy had something there.

You're a fucking genius, I said.

Raul smiled. Didn't deny it. No false humility in this one.

Well, listen, I said, I'd love to hear more, but I guess I should do my job.

Which is?

I'm trying to gather information.

About Jules?

Jules, Larry Silver, whatever.

Larry who?

Larry Silver. The dead guy.

The dead guy, he said with a wry smile. Yes. I've never heard his name before.

You don't read the papers?

No, actually.

He turned to the girl in the maid costume. She'd been waiting demurely in the corner of the room.

Diane, he said. Club soda, please.

He was almost deferential to her.

I had to admit he had some charm.

Maybe he could lend some to his brother.

Well, I said. Perhaps you could tell me something about Jules.

I wish I could. But I don't know much. When we were adopted, he was a bit upset. I guess you can understand that. We didn't understand at all, of course. We were so young. It was such a different world. To us, the whole thing was a dream. We had no capacity to understand a sad, neglected boy.

I see. That's understandable. But later?

Later he was gone. He lived in the house for a while. But he was never there. And when he was there, we never saw him. He didn't want to see us. Or his father. He wanted to be far away.

You never got to know him at all?

Not really. It's too bad. It's kind of sad, he said.

If he didn't mean it, he was a hell of an actor.

I was leaning to the latter theory.

Have you made any effort to reconcile? I asked. To help him?

He sipped his club soda.

Sure, he said. We invite him to family events. We send him presents on his birthday. But whatever we did, to him it always seemed, well, insulting. I always thought that if we pressed things any further it would only make him hate us all the more.

Us?

Ramon, me, Father.

I see.

I waited for more. I waited to see if he'd fill the silence. As so many had before him. But he was good. He was very good. The seconds ticked by. The indulgent smile never left his face.

I looked straight in his eyes. They betrayed nothing.

Another Scotch? he asked at last.

So, you haven't talked to him lately?

Who? he asked, with a slightly puzzled frown.

Jules.

No.

Has he been in contact with his father?

Not that I know of.

Raul's smile grew ever so faintly tense at the edges.

The man was thinking.

What about Ramon?

Ramon?

Is Jules in contact with him?

Raul gave out a slightly exasperated sigh.

I can't speak for Ramon. But I would be awfully surprised.

I see.

I gave the silence another chance to work.

It didn't.

Another Scotch? he asked again.

While his repertoire was highly polished, it was somewhat limited.

No thanks, I said. I've got to get going.

Too bad, he said with a small frown.

The perfect host.

I struggled out of the couch. I felt faintly foolish. I shook his hand. I thanked him for his time. He pressed the elevator button for me. With his left hand.

I took the elevator down. I nodded at the doorman. I hailed a cab.

Looks like I confirmed my theory, I said to myself.

That something might be going on.

And I don't know what it is.

76.

WE COULDN'T HAVE A FUNERAL. We didn't have a body. God knew how long the ghouls were going to keep her. Keep taking little bits of her for tests. And anyway I had to draw the line somewhere. I wasn't going to call a funeral home. I wanted nothing to do with that. Kelly would have to settle for a memorial service.

I didn't want a service, either. But my reasons were selfish. I didn't want to go through it. I didn't want to hear a hundred different ways how sorry everybody was.

I hated going to funerals. I never knew what to say. I couldn't bring myself to speak by rote. 'I'm so sorry. He was a beautiful person. He lived a full life.' But the alternatives were just as dire. Tell the truth? 'Hardly knew the guy, actually. I hear he was an arrogant sonofabitch.' 'Just here to put in an appearance, folks. Hoping to curry favor with some potential client I heard would be here.'

No, not really feasible.

Think up some original and striking way to say the obvious? Couldn't do it. Beyond my ability.

So I usually found myself shaking hands and saying nothing. Putting on an empathetic face. Feeling inadequate and out of place.

And truth be told, I simply didn't want to make anyone else go through that.

But Kelly told me otherwise.

Not everybody's a grouch like you, she said. They like a service. It makes them feel good. They come, they see old friends. They remember. It's important to people. There's a reason everybody does it, Daddy. Get over yourself.

Well, of course she was right. And I certainly wasn't going to argue the point. I wasn't going to tell my angel child she couldn't mourn her mother's death in any way she chose.

So a service there was. Complete with pomp and ceremony and a reception afterwards that set me back a cool five grand.

I could have made a speech. A eulogy. But there wasn't a chance that I could pull it off. So I kept it simple. Recited the twenty-third psalm. That was it. Nothing else.

It was perceived as eloquent. A beautifully minimalist gesture. I didn't hasten to correct the perception.

Some AA acquaintance of Melissa's buttonholed me afterwards. I'd never seen him in my life. He was dressed in denim coveralls. Paint-splattered. An artist of some type, I surmised. Or a housepainter. He came up to me. Shook my hand. It gave me the creeps. All those AA folks were past masters at the art of being your lifelong buddy the first time they met you.

That was the best version of the twenty-third I've ever heard, he said.

I resisted it. But it made me feel good. Him saying that. Apparently I'd done something right.

Jerry, he said his name was. He introduced me to a cabal of other AA folks. They were all my new best friends. Lucia, small and fat and bubbly. Ron, a tall cadaverous man with missing teeth and an enormous hand that almost swallowed mine. A brace of mismatched lesbians in threadbare suits and ties, Janice and Phoebe. The whole crowd of them would not have looked out of place on a Bowery street corner, back when the Bowery was the Bowery. Or filing out of a seedy church basement after Meeting, desperately pulling out the cigarettes they'd been forbidden to smoke inside.

I was surrounded by them. I felt like an alien among aliens.

Melissa was a special person, said Lucia.

Here we go, I thought. Cliché time.

Her jokes, Lucia said, were so subtle.

Jokes? Melissa? I didn't think I'd seen her laugh at a joke in a decade. Let alone tell one. And this coming from a tiny round woman in a polyester flower-print dress.

There was something going on here, and I didn't know what it was.

I'd call them Mel-isms, said Jerry.

The whole group laughed knowingly.

She had a unique perspective, said Jerry.

She sure did, said Lucia.

I never met anybody so sardonic, said Ron, his big smile displaying the black gaps in his mouth.

Janice and Phoebe nodded.

And her cakes, said Janice.

They were the best, said Ron.

Everybody was excited when she'd come to a meeting, said Phoebe's small voice.

There'd be cake, said Jerry.

The best, said Janice.

Mmmmm, they all said, laughing.

Cakes? Melissa had never baked anything in her life.

I looked about me. Five absurd faces. Five bodies of bizarrely varying sizes and shapes. Five portraits from the Gallery of Freaks. Talking of Melissa as if they'd known her from childhood.

I wondered if I'd stumbled into someone else's memorial service.

You were a very lucky man, to have shared her life for a while, said Ron, putting an arm on my shoulder.

They all nodded in agreement.

I'm surprised to see you don't weigh three hundred pounds, said Janice.

All that cake! exclaimed Lucia with glee.

General laughter.

Oh God, I thought. I'm dreaming. I've been transported into a David Lynch movie.

She'll be in my thoughts forever, said Janice in a tearful growl. Every day.

Mine too, squeaked Phoebe.

More head-nodding.

I needed to be alone. I mouthed a few platitudes. I turned to look for a quiet corner in which to brood.

And there was Jake.

With tears in his eyes.

Red blotches on his face, his neck.

He was almost prostrate with apparent grief.

He threw his arms around me. Buried his head in my shoulder.

I'm so, so sorry, he sobbed.

I extracted myself.

Thank you, I said, a puzzled frown on my face.

I don't know what to say, he said, removing a tissue from his pocket and wiping his eyes.

He had a stoned look.

It's all right, I said. It's all right.

Reassuring a guy at my wife's memorial service. A guy who had met her once, for ten minutes.

I wanted to run away. Never look back.

I was much relieved to see Steiglitz. Glass of wine in hand. Earnestly chatting with Kelly.

For all I hated the pompous overachiever, I could count on him not to surprise me.

Dr. Steiglitz, I said. So good of you to come.

He turned to me. The hand he proffered was shaking.

Oh God, he said, I'm sorry, Rick. I wish I could have done more.

He said it with a catch in his throat. It seemed grotesquely out of place.

I looked at Kelly. There was no enlightenment to be had there. She was playing the poised hostess, though her eyes were rimmed with red. She smiled at me. A rueful smile. Sad and beautiful.

I wanted to take her aside. To have just one moment, her to me. One moment of unfeigned grief and memory.

This outpouring of emotion for my cold and enigmatic wife, the one I had believed had not a friend in the world, was more than disconcerting. Could I really have been so wrong? So terribly, so profoundly wrong? How could the woman that I knew have kindled all these strong emotions in so varied a throng, without me having the slightest clue?

I was dizzy with it.

I needed a drink.

Fortunately, the bar was steps away.

I got myself a double. Two. I carried them to the bathroom. I locked the door. I sat on the toilet. I downed the first Scotch in two large gulps. I nursed the second. I might need to stay awhile.

Melissa had a life. She even had friends. People she had touched. People who loved her. She baked cakes. She baked goddamn cakes. When the hell did she bake cakes? Jesus, how would I know? I was never in the bloody house. If I wasn't working, or out watching Dorita flirt with macho guys at clubs, I was hanging out at the Wolf's Lair. Playing poker somewhere. Indulging my macho self. Melissa could have been doing anything. She could have gone to AA meetings every night of the week, and how would I have known? She didn't talk about them, so I'd just assumed she didn't go. Because she never mentioned friends, I'd assumed she didn't have any. Jesus. I was a fool. A dolt. A self-centered doltish fool.

And a cuckold, I remembered with a spleenish pain. Probably.

It could have been Jerry. Or Ron. Or any other ex-drunk she'd picked up anywhere.

I felt ill.

I put my head in the toilet.

It didn't hurt to be prepared.

77.

IT WAS MORNING. The sunlight hurt my eyes. Kelly came into the kitchen.

I felt like I had somehow missed the point of everything that had ever happened to me.

Kelly, I said. I have to talk to you.

I know.

Sit down, please.

She looked at me. She saw the dread. She sat down.

Kelly, I said, you know I love you?

She rolled her eyes.

Yes.

That I'll always love you, no matter what?

Yes. And me too.

She said it wearily. But she meant it, I knew.

I need to know something, I said.

I know you do.

Those people.

Mommy's AA friends?

Yes, them.

Yes, Daddy? she said with an accusing look.

Did you know about them?

Of course I did.

Why didn't you tell me about them?

Tell you about them? Did you ever ask?

I thought about that. No, I hadn't. But should I have?

She stared at me. I was the butterfly impaled upon a pin.

I was the victim.

I was the perpetrator.

Did I have to ask? I said lamely.

I knew the answer.

I tried to tell you, she said.

You did?

I did.

And?

And you weren't interested.

I wasn't?

You'd already made up your mind.

I had?

You'd given up.

I had?

You told me so.

I did?

You did. Not just in words. By everything you said and did. You didn't want anything to do with it. You'd washed your hands.

Oh Jesus. I didn't mean for you to think that.

I know you didn't. But you had. You'd washed your hands of her. She knew it. I knew it.

Oh God, I said. What have I done?

I didn't mean it that way, Daddy.

I looked in Kelly's eyes. I had to believe in them.

A sixteen-year-old child. My conscience.

Damn.

I couldn't ask her any more. I wasn't sure I wanted to know.

I sat in the living-room chair. I looked at the empty couch.

At some point, I thought, when my mind had come back into the room, we'll have to pack up Melissa's things. Or something. Maybe I could hire somebody to do it.

Kelly came into the living room. She handed me a cell phone. Melissa's.

Please, she said. Can you do something with this?

Her eyes were red.

I looked at the phone. It was just a phone. I guessed I had to cancel the service. All these things. I had to make a list. I had to find someone to make a list for me. Wasn't there some kind of organization you could hire for that stuff?

I opened the phone. I noodled absently through the menus. Calls made. Ring tones. Little bits of Melissa.

Calls received. A long list.

Strange. I'd never seen Melissa use the damn thing.

So many things I didn't know.

I wasn't sure I wanted to know them all. I wasn't sure I wanted to know any of them.

One number appeared over and over on the list. At least a dozen times.

Oh Jesus.

I didn't want to know.

I had to know.

I dialed the number slowly. As it rang, I fought a powerful urge to close the phone. Throw it away.

A male voice answered.

It was a voice I recognized.

I hung up fast.

78.

I WENT TO MY OFFICE. I ordered a tall skim latte. I distracted myself with the *Times*. I noticed it was Saturday. Well, crime is no respecter of the calendar. And anyway, what else did I have to do?

I pulled out my four-by-sixes. I couldn't spread them out without asking two nursing mothers to move to other seats. I decided against that. I just paged through the cards. Pulled out a couple of the speculative ones. FitzGibbon. Hadn't figured him out yet. A harmless liar? Cunning manipulator? Just a nut job?

Time to pay him another visit. Try to tease it out of him.

Dorita came in the door with a flourish. She was wearing a bright red jacket with gaudy brass buttons.

One thing you don't have to worry about, I said, is attracting attention.

You're too kind, she said. So, what happened with Raul?

Raul. Jesus. It seemed like a week ago I'd seen him. I had to think.

Sorry, I said, I'm a little foggy today.

Another night of drunken debauch at the Wolf's Lair?

No. Not yesterday. Yesterday was the memorial service.

As I said it I realized with horror that I hadn't even told her about it.

She raised her eyebrows.

Memorial service?

For Melissa.

Her eyebrows went up another notch.

I guess I didn't invite you.

Yes, she said. That's something I would be aware of.

And I don't know why.

You don't know why.

I don't. It wasn't a conscious thing.

It wasn't.

No. I suppose that sounds even worse.

It does. Little old me never even occurred to you, is that it?

Well, in a way.

In a way.

Okay. Yes. I didn't think of it. I can't explain why. God, I'm just so tired and confused all the time.

Dorita stopped me right there.

I wouldn't have gone anyway, she said. Tell me about Raul.

I told her as much as I could remember.

She was amused by my description. The velvet curtains. The more-than-plush sofa. The maid. Her cleavage.

That's all? she said, when I was finished.

That's all, babe. So shoot me.

My. I think I win this round.

I've already paid for it, I said. Thom, another cosmo for the lady, please.

We're in Starbucks, Ricky.

Oh, right.

Nothing else, really?

Well, the best I can say is that I've convinced myself that these phone calls to FitzGibbon's office from Jules's phone are key. Now, if we could only get someone to tell us the truth about them . . .

Yes. You seem to have failed rather miserably at that.

You are too kind, as usual.

It's just my nature.

Right. So what do you have, darling? A signed confession?

No, but a pretty good story.

I'm all ears.

I tracked Ramon down at a fashion show.

These boys do get around.

You're telling me. Anyway, there he was, in the front row. Next to some overstuffed heiress. And FitzGibbon.

They really are glued together at the hip, aren't they?

So it appears.

So how did you get close to him?

I had to call in a couple of favors. Get an invitation to the hospitality suite. They were pouring some decent wine. '89 Cheval Blanc, actually.

Very nice.

It certainly was. It's got a little age on it.

Okay, all right. Hints of honey-roasted salami, nose like Jimmy Durante. I know. I'm officially jealous. Did you get anything out of him?

I did.

I'm waiting.

Well. First thing is, they're not identical.

I figured that out already.

Well, aren't you a bright little boy, she said, taking an elegant sip of her herbal tea.

I figured *that* out already too. Can we get to the point?

Why do I need to tell you? You figured everything out already.

All right. You're smarter than me. I admit it. And a better lawyer. Can we get on with it?

Now that you've finally admitted it, yes.

And?

Didn't get a damn thing out of him. Except the fraternal twin thing.

You slay me.

Bad choice of words.

Yes. Sorry.

Say sorry to yourself.

I just did. You didn't think that apology was directed at you, did you?

Of course not. How foolish of me.

Well, tell me about it anyway.

The guy never says a word.

I've noticed that.

It was very frustrating. I tried to insinuate myself. But he wasn't having any of it.

Used all of your charms?

Well, not all of them. There's a line even I won't cross.

That's good information to have. And?

Well, I finally had to just tell him who I was. Which was a little tricky. Since I'd been pretending to be someone else.

FitzGibbon didn't recognize you?

Didn't seem so. I've only met him a couple of times at parties. And he seemed distracted the whole time. A little out of it.

Well, he doesn't strike me as a fashion show kind of guy.

Yes. It was a little weird that he was there at all.

So, you tell Mr. IQ who you really are . . .

Sort of. I said I was your assistant.

Like I said, who you really are.

Ramon didn't seem too happy when he heard your name.

Ah, my charms have been wasted on him.

And he wouldn't talk at all in the hospitality suite. He kept looking nervously at FitzGibbon. Like he was afraid Daddy wouldn't approve.

So you took him to a nice motel in the neighborhood?

No. He took me into a private room in the back.

Same thing.

Not quite.

Lap dances, at least?

If I'd asked, I presume. Anyway, the guy's not exactly a conversationalist. One-word answers. Yes. No. Maybe. I don't know. I don't recall.

I don't recall?

Those are the words.

Sounds like I'd prepared him for his testimony.

Exactly. The guy was tighter than virgin pussy.

Jesus. I hope you don't talk that way around Warwick.

Of course I do. He laps it up.

Speaking of poor choice of phrase.

I thought it was pretty good, actually.

All right. You're funnier than me too. So?

Nothing. Nada. Not a thing. Less than zero. I asked him about Jules. Doesn't know anything. No hostility. Barely knows the kid. Never heard of the victim. Loves Daddy. Works hard. Security detail. That's what he's doing right now. Has no outside interests. Except the Club. Loves the Club. Practically lives there.

That's it?

Actually, I've extrapolated quite a bit. He said less than that.

Jesus. That sucks.

It does.

Well, I think it's time to declare victory and go home.

You're such a wimp, Ricky. We need a plan.

I thought I'd pay FitzGibbon a visit.

And?

That's all.

That's all?

Listen, doll, it's all I can do to get out of bed in the morning.

Darling, you've got to get organized. What's the use of all those index cards if you don't have a plan?

Yes, well, I said. I was hoping you could help me with that. Can't I have just one day off? I'm bereaved, remember?

Right. Now I remember, she said.

It's okay, I said. You can be mad at me.

No, she said, I can't, really. Or at least I won't.

79.

I DRAGGED MYSELF out of a dark blank sleep. I looked around the bedroom. I had no idea what time it was. Hell, I had no idea what day it was.

I called Kelly. I asked her.

It's eight o'clock, Dad, she said, shaking her head. Saturday night.

Jesus, I said. That's really weird.

It wouldn't be nearly so weird if you hadn't slept all afternoon.

I think you may have a point there.

Kelly was playing Scrabble with Peter. I joined them for a while. We ordered in Chinese. It was a family sort of thing.

It felt good.

On the other hand, I thought after losing a second game, I sure could use a Scotch.

At the Wolf's Lair I ran into Jake. I thought of leaving. I wasn't in a state to deal with his mood swings.

But I needed that drink.

Jake was in his faraway mode. Or just plain drunk. Staring into space. Speaking in monosyllables. Mumbling about the evils of the world. I couldn't make out half of what he said.

I had a couple Scotches. I felt a little better. He put his arm around my shoulder. I propped him up. I was feeling charitable. He was a friend, after all. I had so few. A brother. A guy I might be able to lean on, some-day. Like he was leaning on me. Sure he was a bit of a nutcase. But hell, I had to take what I could get.

We talked poker. We had a few drinks.

Andrea might be joining us, he said glumly.

Excellent, I said, remembering the flirtatious looks I'd got, last time.

It was going to be strange to see her out of context. The poker crew didn't exist for me outside of the game.

Strange, but not unpleasant, I mused.

I caught myself. Jesus. Could I really be having such a thought?

The pure man doesn't resist temptation, I remembered from some sermon or another. He knows he's weak: he avoids it. I should go home.

Sure, I answered myself, but isn't life for the living? Melissa's gone. And she did it to herself. And me. And Kelly. And love is the best antidote. For loss. Confusion. Guilt. Longing. For anything that ails a man.

Okay, not love.

Maybe I could get Andrea to punish me. For my impure thoughts.

Hold me back. Tie me up. Please. Then do it again.

Minutes later she arrived.

Slinky, sharp, snakelike, I saw her through the haze of drink.

I wasn't going anywhere.

Jake and I were tottering. Loud. Annoying. Oblivious. She came up smiling. She could see, and I could see that she could see, that we were out of control. She seemed to relish it.

I was a better drunk than Jake. He was sloppy, incoherent. I was not entirely in control, but I could stand up fairly straight. Concoct a jest or two at the spectacle of Jake slipping off his bar stool to the floor. I raised a conspiratorial eyebrow at Andrea. She laughed.

You look like somebody famous, she said to me. I just can't put my finger on who.

Harrison Ford?

No. That's not it.

Well, I'm not famous. But the only difference between me and all those famous people is . . .

Yes?

. . . that you've never heard of me.

She laughed again.

We talked of this and that.

Jake crawled to a chair. Pulled himself up. Sat down. Put his head on the table.

Andrea put her hand on my arm.

Her hand felt warm and strong.

Let's go to my place, she said.

Okay, I said. Why not?

Jake lifted his head. Looked straight at me. There was pain in his eyes.

Shit. I was stealing his girl.

She pulled at my arm.

He put his head back down.

Damn.

He wouldn't remember anything tomorrow anyway, I told myself.

We went to her place.

As we walked, she put her arm through mine. I felt sensations that I hadn't felt in years. With Lisa it had been a tingle, not much more. This was the real thing. I felt full. I felt like a man.

My God, I interrupted myself. I haven't even buried her yet.

I started to deflate.

I pushed away the thought.

We got to Andrea's place. Fourth floor walk-up. Two tiny rooms. Kitchen at one end, couch at the other. Books and ashtrays. Dorothy Parker. Nice. We could talk.

But we didn't talk. As soon as the door closed, she was on me. She put her arms around my neck. She fastened her lips to mine. Her mouth was wet, insistent. She pushed me up against the wall. She drove herself into me. I felt her body, every curve of it. I gave myself to the sensation. I almost fainted with desire.

She dragged me to the bed. Threw me down. I tried to sit up, to bring her with me. She raised a high-heeled foot. Pushed me back down.

All right. So that was how she wanted it.

She fixed me with a wicked playful stare. She pulled her shirt over her head. Nothing underneath but her. Her breasts were exquisite things. Firm, high and pointed slightly up. She cupped them in her hands.

God in heaven, I thought. I have an erection.

She took off her jeans. She put back on her high-heeled shoes. She stood before me. Muscular. Lithe. Honey-colored. A goddess, to my hungry eyes. She turned her back. The violin.

She told me to turn over. I did as she commanded. She grabbed my hands. Crossed them at the wrists. I felt leather. She strapped my hands together tight.

She ran her fingernails down my neck. I shuddered. I moaned. Every cell in my body was singing.

Turn, she ordered.

I struggled to obey. She pushed me over. I was on my back. She opened my shirt. She ran her fingernails down my chest. I thought I would explode. She reached my pants. Undid the belt. Pulled down the zipper. Pulled them off.

She went away. Left me like that. I sunk into the bed. I closed my eyes. My body floated. This was what I'd needed, all along. I knew. I understood.

I heard her heels on the floor. I opened my eyes. She had her yellow travel duck.

It comes with me everywhere, she said.

She reached down. She put it up against the inside of my thigh.

She turned it on. It hummed and strummed against my skin.

And then it happened.

Melissa sprawled dead, or dying, on the couch. My indifference. I walked on by. Hating her. Hating it. She was dying. I walked on by.

My body shut down. The gates to heaven closed.

Andrea stood up. Her hands were on her hips. She looked at me.

You're kidding, right? she said.

Too many strong emotions, all at once. Excitement. Humiliation. Desire. Guilt. Supreme pleasure. Impotence. Anger. Guilt. I shut down.

Andrea was not the nurturing type.

Oh shit, she said. You're not kidding.

She shook her head. She turned me on my side. I didn't resist. She unbuckled the belt around my wrists. She flung it away. She picked up her clothes. She dressed quickly. She sat down on a wooden kitchen chair. Far away from me.

I think you should leave, she said.

I didn't blame her. She didn't know the story. I'd let her down. She was angry. I might be angry too, in her shoes. Her red stiletto shoes.

I'm sorry, I said again, pulling up my pants.

Yeah, she said, me too.

I buttoned my shirt. I left.

She didn't say goodbye.

80.

I WOKE UP WITH PAINS in every joint. The room was black. I'd had some awful dream. Something vague. Something fearful. It had left me tense and uncomprehending. I knew that if I went right back to sleep the dream would only start again. And I didn't want to be there. So I propped open my eyelids. I got myself a glass of water. I walked circles around the room. I lay back down. I passed right out again.

I woke.

I was afraid.

I staggered to the bathroom.

I got another glass of water.

I paced.

The whole night was like that.

Finally, the light came through the curtains. I got up. Looked at the clock. Six in the morning. I took a hot, hot shower. I cleansed myself.

It didn't work.

I was still unclean.

I made some strong and bracing coffee. I checked the porch. The *Times* was there.

It was awfully slim. I looked more closely. Monday. Shit. What happened to Sunday? I felt a moment of panic. I tamped it down. You're under a lot of stress, I told myself. I took a Valium. I took another one.

Relief. Routine. Routine was good. I drank my coffee.

I read the *Times*. I felt half normal.

Laura called.

She wanted me to come over to the morgue. Some test results were in.

I didn't want to know. Why couldn't they just let us cremate her and get it over with?

When I got there Laura was smiling. Not the nervous smile she'd had the time before. A real smile. And Harwood wasn't there.

Two good signs.

Well, she said as I sat down. It's not you.

I stared.

I'm sure you'll be relieved to hear that, she continued.

She said it lightheartedly. It was a joke. Why would I be relieved?

But I *was* relieved. I was almost overcome with relief. I was lightheaded with relief.

Concealing my confusion, I smiled and said, as playfully as I could, that I was indeed relieved, though somewhat miffed that she had ever doubted me in the first place.

I never doubted you, she said.

I should have known that, I said. It was the evil influence of our good friend Harwood, then.

I defer to your judgment on that, she replied cagily.

Okay. I don't want to put you on the spot.

We smiled at each other. We were old friends, colleagues again.

The problem is . . . I began.

Yes, I know. If it wasn't you . . .

Who was it?

That's the question, Rick. And I don't have an answer for it.

I can't even imagine, I lied.

I could have imagined many things. But I didn't want to go there.

It's not your job, Rick. Listen, I'm sorry you've had to go through all this. Detective Harwood may seem a bit crusty.

A bit?

Okay, a lot. But his heart's in the right place.

I guess I'm just going to have to take your word for that.

Harwood chose that moment to make an appearance.

He looked no less rumpled, no less yellow and no less sardonic than the last time I'd seen him.

Laura tells me you're not as mean as you look, I said.

She's entitled to her opinion, he replied, lighting a Marlboro.

I laughed.

He didn't.

So I guess you're in the clear, he said, in a distinctly unconvinced tone.

Clear of what? Having sex with my own wife?

Lying about it afterwards.

Well, I said, I suppose. Though why I'd have wanted to I don't know.

I can think of a few things, he said, expertly blowing a smoke ring and expelling a second spume of smoke through the center of it.

That's a neat trick, I said.

You ain't seen nothing.

I'll bet.

Let's get down to business, he said. We need some information.

Happy to oblige, I said. After all, you've been so hospitable.

Laura excused herself. To go cut up some dead people, presumably.

Harwood started asking questions. Many he'd asked before. I gave the same answers. Some were new. I started to catch the drift. The results hadn't exonerated me. They'd just changed the theory. Now I'd given Melissa an overdose in revenge for her infidelity.

When it seemed that he was finished, I got up to leave. He put out a hand to shake. I put out mine. He grasped it firmly. His fingers were short. His hand was broad and strong. A working man's hand.

He held mine for a while longer than seemed comfortable. He looked me in the eye.

The message was clear.

He wasn't done with me yet.

81.

I CALLED SHEILA'S OFFICE. She had a cancellation. I tried to make a joke about it. She didn't laugh. I didn't press the issue. I hailed a cab. The driver smelled of pastrami and motor oil. At last a home-grown cabbie.

He let me off across the street from her building. I stole a smoke before going in. A few minutes late, in the world of Sheila's patients, meant nothing. It meant high-functioning.

I settled into the couch with a sigh of relief.

The one predictable place in the universe, I said.

She raised an eyebrow.

I'll complain, I said. You'll say a word here and there. I'll have a revelation. I'll feel better. Until the next time I call and find you have a cancellation. Right?

She gave me a grave look. I knew her take on this. I used humor to avoid the pain. Avoid confronting problems. Blah, blah, blah.

But her look sobered me.

Okay, I said. Things are not that good.

She waited patiently. I told her the story. Some of the story. We talked about Kelly. How to make it easier on her.

I told her a bit more of the story. I told her about Harwood.

Oh dear, she said more than once, that's terrible.

I still didn't tell her everything.

You know, I said, I have these dreams.

Yes? she said, leaning slightly forward.

They're always different, yet all the same.

Yes?

They're kind of inchoate. Hard to describe. Hard to decipher, one by one. But in one sense they're all the same.

How is that?

There's always been a crime. A serious crime.

Yes?

And I'm the perpetrator.

Hm.

Usually murder. I've killed someone. And I've gotten away with it. But not completely. *I* know I've done it, for one thing. And I can't live with that. And there's someone pursuing me. Someone who knows. A man in a long black coat, sometimes. I see him on the corner. He gets into the cab behind mine. I'm never really getting away with it. Sometimes the murder happened long ago. When I was young. But the point of the dream is, I'm about to get caught.

These kinds of dreams are not uncommon, she said in a reassuring tone.

What's uncommon, I think, is how goddamn real they are.

How do you mean?

I wake up. Or I don't, really. Sometimes I wake up from the dream into another dream. In the second dream I'm waking up from the first dream. And the first dream seems so real, that in the second dream I have to ask myself if the first dream was true, that it really happened. And often it seems that it did. That I'm guilty of some horrible crime.

And then?

And then I wake up from the second dream.

And?

The same thing happens.

What thing?

It still feels horribly, excruciatingly real. I'm only half awake. I'm still guilty. It still happened. And then, after I get up, I slap myself around, I get out into the world, it follows me.

The dream?

The guilt. The reality of it. It can go on for days. I look over my shoulder. I expect the knock on the door. I see a man in a long black coat. I see accusing looks everywhere I go. I'm guilty. I did it. I'm a murderer.

That's terrible.

You're telling me, I said. Weeks later, it'll still come back to me. Now, sitting here now, I ask myself, could it be true? Is there some dark deed I've been repressing, in my past? Could it be that I've actually killed someone? Is that why I have these dreams, these feelings? Could it be the truth, trying to make itself known?

I don't think so, she said quietly.

I mean, you hear about all these repressed memory things, right? Some traumatic event, you don't even know it happened, consciously. Your father raped you as a child, whatever?

There's considerable controversy about that, Sheila said.

I know. But I can't help wondering.

You haven't murdered anyone, Rick, she said firmly.

She rarely used my name. She was taking this very seriously.

How do you know? I asked. I could have. You'd have no way of knowing.

She smiled a reassuring smile.

I know, she said. Trust me on this one.

I had no choice. I had to trust her.

I damn well couldn't trust myself.

82.

I'M STARTING TO WONDER whether there might be something to it, I said to Dorita.

To what?

Melissa.

I thought I'd changed that subject.

You had. Or you tried. Don't worry, I'm not going to get all weepy on you. I'm just beginning to wonder. For the first time. Whether somebody might have been involved. Other than her.

In her death?

Yes. I didn't give it the time of day before.

Yes?

But now that the DNA test is in.

Darling, you've got me at a disadvantage.

I do?

You do. You know what the hell you're talking about. And I don't.

I'm sorry. I'm sort of talking to myself.

Who'd have guessed?

I told her all about it. The autopsy results. The DNA tests. I told her about the service. The AA cabal. Jake. Steiglitz. All the weirdness.

I'm impressed, she said when I was finished.

You're easily impressed.

Now, darling, you know that that's not true. No, really. I'm impressed. With the whole story. It's rich. The characters are memorable. And it's a cracking mystery.

Are you implying that I'm making this stuff up?

In a delirium of grief?

Right.

No. Not exactly. It's a matter of salience.

Salience.

Yes. What appears important in one context disappears in another.

Right.

You walk by dozens of Jettas every day.

Jetta? Is that a Ford?

Volkswagen. You never even notice them.

Not me. I'm not a car guy.

And then one day you buy one of your own.

I do. Says you.

And all of a sudden.

Like lightning from the heavens.

You're noticing Jettas all over the place.

I'm still taking your word for it.

You're noticing their colors. Whether they're the same color as yours, or different. You're noting whether they're LX's, or DX's, or whatever.

I am. Because you say so.

Whether they have a sunroof.

Etcetera.

Exactly. They're salient. All of a sudden. They have some importance in your life.

Some value.

The concept does, at least.

The Jetta Concept.

Good movie title.

I was already there, I assured her.

Way ahead of me.

As always.

You wish.

And your point was?

Nothing, she said. No point. Just that all that stuff might not have seemed so significant in other circumstances.

Which tells me?

Absolutely nothing.

That's what I thought. Just wanted to check.

All right. But anyway, what we have here . . .

Is a failure to communicate?

No, darling. It's a new case.

An investigation.

The first new case for the brand-new firm of R. & D., LLP.

I like the sound of that. Research and Development.

Rick and Dorita.

Both of those things. Nice of you to put me first.

'D. & R.' lacks the essential ambiguity.

Ah. Should have known better than to see a compliment there.

Or R. & R.

Redman and Reed.

Rest and Relaxation.

Tough choice.

Well, we've got time.

We reviewed the evidence. I pulled out a bunch of blank index cards. Proceeded to defile them with new information and speculation. Lines and arrows.

The Melissa suspect card read:

> Jake;
> Melissa;
> Steiglitz;
> Ron;
> Jerry;
> any of the other AA cabal, more likely male, given
>   the fluids;
> a stranger, ditto;
> Rick Redman.

I crossed myself off the list. I'd been cleared.

I sat back. Dorita sat back. I admired the cut of her jib. I noted that her sweater was a little tighter than normal. I refrained from pulling out another index card, on which to record the observation.

Okay, she said, we've opened a new file. Let's get to work.

Where do we start?

Let's start with Jake. I don't think it's an accident you listed him first.

Really?

Really. Of all the people at the service, he had the least reason to be all sloppy and teary-eyed.

I suppose you're right. He and Steiglitz.

Maybe. I'll take your word for Steiglitz. But she was his patient.

Yes. If nothing else, she injured his professional pride.

Exactly. At least he's got some sort of excuse.

But Jake.

Tell me everything else you know about him. Maybe something will strike me that you haven't noticed.

I told her what I knew, which in the telling I realized wasn't much.

He'd never told me anything about his acting career, other than the thing about the bald-man commercial. I didn't know where he was from. We'd only really talked about poker. I told Dorita about his dark hintings at secrets unrevealed. But they could have been the rantings of someone in the throes of a near fatal alcohol overdose. In fact, that was what I'd concluded at the time. To the extent that I'd concluded anything more than that it was time to get the hell home.

He met Melissa, though, didn't you say?

Once.

I told her the story of the bookcase.

Tell it to me again, she said. Don't spare any details.

I went over it again. Melissa striding across the room with arms open. Kisses on the cheek. Jake's nervousness. Glancing at me for help. Melissa's remark after he'd left. Kind of cute, she'd said.

I fought back some emotion. It had been the last time that I'd seen her acting at all like her old self.

Not a lot to go on, said Dorita.

No. At least two things were a little odd, though. How nervous he seemed. And that remark.

Not exactly smoking guns, partner.

No. And it was also a little strange, I suppose, that she took the trouble to play the hostess. I hadn't seen her do that in years.

How many guests have you had over in those years?

Um. None. That I can think of.

Well, then.

Yes.

She was probably excited.

She was excited. As excited as she was able to get. And there's another thing.

Yes?

I told Dorita about the phone calls.

Her jaw dropped.

You're kidding me.

I'm not.

Calls from Jake? To Melissa's phone? You saved that for now?

I was struggling with it. What it meant.

What it *meant?* Tell me you're joking.

I'm not joking.

Ricky, you're in some serious denial.

It just doesn't feel right.

Feel, schlemiel. Let's deal with the facts here, Ricky. Get your brain out of neutral. Let's see what we can find out about old Jake. Start with the easy stuff. You've got wireless?

Sure.

Let's google him.

I hadn't thought of that. But if he's an actor, he's bound to show up somewhere, you'd think.

Well, yes, she said, rolling her eyes.

Jesus, I'm a trial lawyer. I've never pretended to be Rick Redman, Ace Detective.

You don't even do your own legal research anymore.

Anymore? What makes you think I ever did?

Sorry, darling. I forgot you were born with junior associates attached to your hips.

Mom hated that.

Ouch.

Let's do a search.

I googled him. Nothing. I tried the Internet yellow pages. Splurged on a couple of commercial sites that advertised that they could root out personal information on anyone alive.

Nothing. A haberdasher in Hermosa Beach. Eighty-one years old. A retired barber in Tuscaloosa.

Now that's strange, I said. Jake doesn't exist.

That's a problem.

Especially for him, I'd think.

An actor?

The invisible actor.

Odd, that.

Must have a stage name.

You'd think he might have mentioned that. I mean, don't people like to brag about who they are?

Or he's not. An actor. At all.

Or at least he's never had a real gig.

I guess that wouldn't be all that surprising. It's not like he was advertising himself as a movie star.

Leave it to me, Dorita said.

Leave what to you?

The stage name. If there is one, I'll get it.

How?

I said, leave it to me.

Her tone did not invite further inquiry.

All right, I said. I'll leave it to you.

The Jake angle seemed to be losing whatever promise it might have held.

Let's get on with Jules, I said.

Why? Aren't you anxious to keep our momentum going?

Frankly, no. I'm a little afraid of it.

Ah. I understand. Back to familiar territory.

Yes. Please.

So where are we? With Jules.

Jesus, I don't know.

Let's call Kennedy.

Why Kennedy? Why not see Jules again? Or FitzGibbon?

He's got to know stuff we don't.

I'm quite sure he does. But I'm also sure that's true of everybody. Especially my client.

Probably. But Kennedy's the most likely to give it up.

I'm not so sure. He's quite a tight-ass about these things.

Have faith, said Dorita. He hasn't had me to contend with.

83.

WE CALLED KENNEDY. We invited him out to lunch. I vetoed Michel's. Too close to the office. We'd run into someone that we'd rather not. And even if we didn't run into anybody, just being that close to the office would give me a stomach ache. We settled on the White Stallion.

When Kennedy got there he was in a good mood. His bow tie was a festive pink. We plied him with French wines and delectable pâtés. A bottle of Domaine Leflaive, 1998, was particularly fine.

It was easier than I'd expected. I had to give Dorita her due. She turned on all her charm. Which when unleashed was not inconsiderable. By the time she mentioned FitzGibbon, Kennedy was too well oiled to protest. She maneuvered him into picking up the story where he'd left it off with me.

I felt a twinge of guilt. I knew he was going to lose sleep over this, once he'd sobered up.

But hey, I thought. I'll blame it all on her.

FitzGibbon had hired Fiske & Elliot to handle the divorce, he told us.

Jesus, I said. Eight hundred bucks an hour.

We can only dream, he said.

Hey, speak for yourself, I laughed.

Anyway, they wouldn't give him the answers he wanted, so he fires them.

Seems in character, I said.

Roots around and finds some scuzzy boutique that specializes in malpractice. Committing it, I mean, not litigating it.

Gad, I said, Jack told a joke.

Oh shut up, he said.

I complied. Didn't want to interrupt the flow.

So they look at it. And they tell FitzGibbon that Fiske & Elliot were right: there's no way to get the kid off the trusts completely, unless one of the conditions isn't fulfilled. But there's a way to dilute his interest.

Jules's interest.

Jules's interest. They tell him that the law has changed over the years. 'Issue' used to mean what it sounds like it means. Your natural children. But then there were a bunch of lawsuits. Half-children. Adopted children. Whatever. And the courts began to see that the whole thing wasn't really fair. At least to our enlightened modern eyes. Adopted children are supposed to be equal in rights to natural children. So the law changed. Adopted children are 'issue' too.

Exactly, said Dorita.

Damn, I said. I knew it. I knew that word was key.

Dorita looked at me in dismay. For the second time that day.

I'm not a T & E lawyer, I shrugged.

You could have *asked* me, she replied.

So, Kennedy went on, FitzGibbon could adopt. And the more children he could adopt, the more diluted Jules's share would be. Because Jules'd have to share the capital with each of them.

Slick, I said.

Very slick, said Kennedy.

And that's just what he did, said Dorita.

That's right. He and his new girlfriend take a vacation to Spain. And they're at the bullfights. And they see these cute little urchins, selling tacos, or whatever they sell at the bullfights.

I thought it was Mexico, I said.

Spain, said Kennedy.

I think tacos are Mexican, said Dorita.

You may be right. Anyway, it's not hot dogs.

Whatever, I said.

And the girlfriend takes a shine to them. And FitzGibbon says, Hey, kids, how'd you like to come to America and be rich? And they're, wow, that's really cool, but we have to ask our dad.

A technicality, I said.

A technicality. But anyway, it turns out that Dad is right there, at the bullfight, manning the taco stand or whatever.

Not hot dogs, said Dorita.

And they ask Dad. And Dad's all for it.

Naturally, Dorita said. He's already counting the remittances from his rich American sons.

He's got six other kids. He can't feed them as it is. He sees gold at the end of the rainbow.

We would too, in his position, Dorita said.

We might. So anyway, they fly the kids back to the States, and FitzGibbon adopts them.

While he's in the middle of a contentious divorce? asked Dorita skeptically.

Unusual, I said. But it's amazing what you can accomplish when you've got enough grease to spread around.

Does Jules know about this? Dorita asked. At the time, I mean.

Sure. He can't not know. But he doesn't know the real reason. It never occurs to him.

As far as Daddy knows, said Dorita.

He's quite sure of it.

So Jules is in for a big surprise, she said.

How old are the twins? I asked.

That's the real kicker. They're the same age as Jules.

So they'll all reach twenty-five at about the same time.

Not just about. The same day.

The same fucking birthday? I said.

The same day.

Wow. What are the odds of that?

I don't know if it's odds at work here, Kennedy said.

Thanks for catching the irony, I said.

I don't know if Daddy FitzGibbon fixed that too, Kennedy continued. But it's the official version, anyway. It's on all the papers. Adoption papers, driver's licenses, everything.

My, my, said Dorita.

Now at this point, Kennedy went on, you might ask yourself, if you're a thinking person . . .

Which I'm not sure describes Rick, said Dorita.

. . . you could say, hey, it's *x* million dollars. Jules still gets one-third of it. He's still rich as hell, by his standards, right?

By our standards, too, John, I said. Unless you've got something new to tell me. Anyway, you're right. I mean, the thought occurred to me. Why would Jules care? He's getting a big pile of dough. Enough to live on comfortably.

Which doesn't make what FitzGibbon did any less disgusting.

No. Assuming his motives to be as you say.

Life and death, though? Dorita asked. To deprive Jules of the rest?

You never know.

Hey, John, I said. I really appreciate this. And don't worry about it. It stays here.

A brief look of alarm crossed his face.

Oops, I thought. Shouldn't have reminded him.

Dorita reached over and squeezed his hand. He smiled. Everything was cool.

84.

THERE WAS NOBODY IN MY OFFICE Tuesday morning. I ordered a tall skinny latte and a sesame bagel. I declined the proffer of a tiny dollop of cream cheese sealed in a minuscule plastic tub. I thought about going to see FitzGibbon. I didn't have the energy.

I went through the *Times*. I had another latte. I picked up the *Times* again. I read the stories I'd skipped the first time. I learned that a blue moon is the second full moon in a calendar month. It happens once in a while. It's not actually blue. It's just unusual. There were two blue moons in 1999, though. So not all that unusual.

I resolved to never use the phrase again. Too ambiguous.

I still loved the song, though.

I nodded off, Willie Nelson's version in my head.

I was dreaming of a girl I knew in high school. Her name was Sandra. She was soft and kind and wouldn't have anything to do with me. I was just settling into a dreamy sofa next to her at the bar in the St. Regis when I was rudely disturbed. The pointy toe of a blue high-heeled Manolo Blahnik prodded my shin. My dream attempted to work the sensation into the narrative. But it didn't take: Sandra was not given to kicking boys in the shins. I opened my eyes.

Dorita stood over me.

It's even better than you thought, she said.

What is?

The info.

What info?

The Jake info.

Oh. Well. I'm not sure I thought anything. One way or the other.

So it's even better than you didn't think.

Right. Whatever you say. Well. It'd better be good. You interrupted a good dream there.

That's my specialty.

Why did I know you were going to say that?

Incest.

You're losing me, darling.

It's incest. That's why Jake changed his name. Why Brendan changed his name.

Brendan?

That's Jake's real name. Brendan Gibbs.

Brendan? I'm going to have a hard time getting used to that.

Get used to this: he's a sister-fucker.

A what?

A sister-fucker.

I heard you. That's going to take some explanation. Meanwhile, I'm just a little taken aback by the moniker. I'd never heard that one before.

I just made it up.

You must be very proud.

I'm proud of all my children. Now do you want to hear the story, or keep trying vainly to demonstrate that you're more of a man than me?

It's a tough choice. I guess I'll go with the story. But I reserve my right to change my mind. If it's too boring.

Don't worry about that. Listen. He's born into a fairly wealthy family in southern Illinois. Some Podunk town you've never heard of. Grandpa owned the general store. Dad expanded into hardware, bought a couple of franchises. You know the deal.

I yawned.

The family's upright, respectable. Brendan's uncle gets elected mayor. His mother teaches at the local school. They give to charity. They go to church. Brendan plays piano. Gets the lead role in the high school play.

Can I go back to my nap please?

He has a sister. She's a stunning-looking girl.

Ah. Now you're talking my language. *Cherchez la femme.*

Every boy in town wants to go out with her.

But she won't have them.

Right. They're not good enough for her. She's the class valedictorian. Plays the violin. Wins the essay contest.

Way out of their league.

Right. She's very close to her family. They're enough for her.

Perhaps too enough?

You're anticipating.

That's what happens when you put the punch line first.

Guilty as charged. She and Brendan are close. They write songs together. She writes the music. He writes the lyrics.

They play croquet in the backyard.

Probably. She goes to college.

Yes.

That part I don't know anything about.

Okay.

She graduates. She comes back home. The summer after graduation. To take a rest, before she goes back to Chicago. Start her new job.

Brendan's thrilled.

A whole summer with his favorite sister.

They play croquet.

Whatever.

They play other games.

Other games.

In other places.

Dark and dangerous places.

And?

They get caught.

Ouch.

In flagrante.

Delicto?

Delicto.

Wow.

The local press goes crazy.

A gold mine.

Sells more papers than the latest crop figures.

The police beat: 'Local youth apprehended for spitting on sidewalk.'

Right. Big-time story at last.

Scandal.

Excess.

The rich brought low.

Mega-juicy.

They're all over it.

Exactly.

Daddy must have pissed somebody off, I said. Small town, prominent citizen and all that. Figure he could have hushed it up.

Or something. We'll find out.

If we want to.

We want to.

You want to.

I want to. So *we* want to.

Yes darling. So, we've got something on Jake. But what does it buy us?

The story's not over yet.

Enlighten me.

Dad shoots himself.

Dead?

Dead. With a shotgun. Can't stand the shame.

Jesus.

Mom goes off the deep end.

Locked away?

Threw away the key.

Positively Gothic.

Delicious, isn't it?

Well it would be. Except I know the guy. And I kind of like him. It's a bit of a shock.

Life is like that.

Shocking?

That too.

So then what happens?

The kids leave town. Nobody knows where. The papers keep playing it up for a while. Eventually it dies down. Everybody's dead or gone. Nothing new. They can only keep it up for so long.

That's it?

That's it.

Wow.

Yes. Very wow.

Very wow, but how does it help us?

I'm not sure it does.

But it sure is interesting, I said. I mean, there's certainly more to Jake than first appeared.

Isn't there?

And so.

And so, what other deep dark secrets might he have?

What other things might he be capable of?

Exactly.

I'm not liking this.

You don't have to. I'll do the liking for you. I'll also keep doing your job for you, she said, turning on her heel.

You could never tell when she was serious.

I didn't have the energy to worry about it.

85.

THE POKER GAME HAD GONE UPSCALE. Mike had found some rich guy, Trip Batson, some silver spoon investment banker type who thought it terribly cool to have a bunch of artistes over to his penthouse on East Seventy-ninth to play dirty poker for just enough to cover his monthly parking bill.

The table was set up with napkins in silver holders, piles of pre-counted monogrammed chips, and tiny bowls of unidentifiable Japanese gunk. And a professional dealer. The scene was pristine.

We sat. Jake asked for booze. The Philippine girl-for-hire was very accommodating. Anything we wanted. Single malt Scotch, four choices. A fine selection of wines. No beer keg, though. She was apologetic. Our host suggested that she make a trip to the corner store. Buy a few six-packs. Mike politely declined. The Scotch would be fine.

The host explained that everyone had been allotted two thousand in chips. At the end of the night, he'd do the calculations. Whoever was short would write a check.

I looked around the table. Everyone was having trouble keeping a straight face. Poker was a game of cash, not checks.

Nobody interrupted to let him know. Nobody figured it would be their issue. Any losses amongst ourselves we could handle our own way. And nobody expected to owe anything to Trip at the end of the night.

Not a problem there. Trip was your typical rich amateur player. To him the game was all hope and luck. When he won, he gloated. When he lost, he cursed the cards. He cursed a lot more than he gloated.

It should have been fun. But it wasn't. It was hard to enjoy. When I'd started going to the game, it had been entertainment, a dissolute night out with a crowd of characters I'd never get to meet at my day job. Now it was too complicated. Jake. Andrea too. I wasn't sure what to expect from her. She could have already talked. Told the others of my abject failure of the other night. Worse yet, she could choose the game itself to make the revelation. I'd never live it down with Butch.

But she just ignored me. I was nothing to her.

That was the best I could have hoped for.

Jake was a different problem. He was his backslapping self. But I couldn't see him as I had before. My guileless and charming oddball friend. Brother in maladjustment. Now I knew that his adjustment problems made mine look like a guy with a stutter looks to Steven Hawking. His mood swings made sense now. His faraway stare. Drinking himself incoherent. Dark allusions to secrets unrevealed.

He moved into aggressive mode. Aggressive and with an arrogance I hadn't seen before. Not stupid aggressive. Good aggressive. He jammed a lot of pots. He stared people down. He kept up a constant chatter. I've got the nuts! he kept exclaiming, hand after hand, laughing hyena-like and gathering in another pot as the tight and cautious of us folded mediocre hands. When he was challenged he had the cards. We knew that all that meant was that we'd chosen the wrong hand to call him on. But his rush lasted through the night. He ended up with a pile of chips that made ours look like amateur night at the bingo parlor.

After one particularly subtle move that garnered him a major pot at my expense, I leaned over, put him in a playful headlock and said, Do that again and I'll have to start playing seriously, my man.

He laughed. He punched me in the side. I twisted him sideways. We fell over and rolled on the floor. The gang gathered round, egging us on. A play fight. Butch threw himself on top of the pile. Mike poured a glass of Scotch on our heads. We spluttered up, cooled down.

When the game was over and we were waiting for the elevator, Jake turned to me.

Hey Rick, he said with childish glee, did I kick some ass tonight, or what?

You kicked some ass, Jake, I said. You kicked my ass. You kicked everybody's ass.

I did, he said, I did.

He had that faraway look again.

I fingered in my pocket a small envelope.

86.

I CALLED UP LAURA. It seemed to me she owed me one.

Her office was drab and devoid of personality. You might expect someone working in a morgue to try to jazz the place up a bit. But no. The desk was stainless steel. Just like the slabs. I suppose a little color might only have made the place worse. The contrast too extreme. But she didn't have so much as a picture of the kids on her desk.

Laura, I said, I need a favor.

Just ask, she said, and it's yours.

Well, it's a really, really big favor.

She tilted her head quizzically.

All right, Rick, spit it out. What do you need?

I need a private DNA lab.

I can refer you to several. Some of them are actually quite good.

No, I can't use commercial labs.

Why not?

Let's just say there are certain things they won't be able to do.

Laura shook her head.

I don't know, Rick. I think I see where you're heading. But that's a lot to ask.

I know. I told you that up front. It's a really, really big favor. But it's really, really important to me.

She looked me in the eye. This has something to do with Melissa, Rick?

Maybe.

Can you be a little more vague?

I'd like to tell you more. I really would. But I think it's better if I don't.

Rick. This is a little weird. I mean, I think I know you well enough to know that you wouldn't be up to something illegal . . .

That much I can assure you, I laughed. It's just that . . . well. I need this to be private. It's very important to me.

You're making it awfully hard for me to say no.

Good. Then it's working.

All right, she said, pulling over a pad of paper. I reserve the right to change my mind. But let's do this. If you have a sample you want tested, leave it in an envelope in my home mailbox. Here's the address. Don't ring the bell. Just drop it in the box. It's locked. Write any instructions on the inside of the envelope. Don't put it on a separate piece of paper. Just write it under the flap before you seal it.

My, you've got a little of the spy in you, I said.

She gave me a wry smile.

And Rick? she said.

Yes?

If this turns out to be something that's important to a case I know about . . . she paused to give me a knowing look . . . I can't keep it to myself.

Okay Laura. I understand. But let's cross that bridge when we come to it, okay?

Okay, she said, with a dubious shake of her head.

On the way home I had the car make a detour. I took the small envelope out of my pocket. I wrote some simple instructions on the underside of the flap. I sealed it, and dropped it into Laura's mailbox.

87.

BY THE TIME I GOT HOME I felt as deflated as a wineskin in the desert. I thought of going to the Wolf's Lair, to drink some of the emptiness away. I quickly thought better of it. Apart from all the self-defeating irony of the idea, it would send a message to Kelly that might as well be: Why don't we both kill ourselves right here right now? Which, come to think of it, wasn't a bad question. But not one that I wanted to inflict on my only and most precious progeny.

But I had to do something.

So I called Dorita.

Do you want to come over? I asked.

Over? To your house?

The very one, I said.

There was a long pause.

I thought of turning it into a jest. But it wasn't. And I wanted her to know that it wasn't.

Do you really think that's the right thing to do? she asked at last.

I didn't care if it was right. I just needed something. Some connection to something other than my morbid thoughts. I needed it or I was going to . . . I didn't know what. But it was going to be messy.

Yes, I said. It's the right thing to do.

What about Kelly?

What about Kelly? I echoed.

Do you think she'll be all right with that?

I don't see why not.

Ricky, Ricky. Sometimes you can be so dense. The girl's mother just died. You want to introduce a strange woman to the house? So soon?

You're not a strange woman. Wait. I take that back. You're a very strange woman. But she's met you before. It won't be that much of a shock.

I think you need to take this a little more seriously, Rick.

I really don't think she'll mind. She's not like that.

You'd better do better than think. You'd better know for sure.

I'll ask her, I said. Call you back in a few.

I hung up before she could protest.

Kelly! I called downstairs.

Yes, Dadster.

Come up here.

Okay, she said reluctantly.

It took a while, but eventually she ascended from her lair.

She looked depressed. Of course she was depressed. Stage whatever of the grieving process. Which seemed to involve never leaving the basement.

And she needed me less and less, it seemed. Another process. The growing-up one. Melissa's death just seemed to have accelerated it a bit. Not a reversible process, I knew. Nor should it be. It was normal.

Which didn't make it any less distressing.

Are you okay? I asked.

Sure, Dadster, she said, unconvincingly.

I'd like to invite my friend Dorita over.

Dorita? she asked with a cock of the head.

My friend from work. You met her in the office a couple of times. Tall. Loud.

Oh. Her. Yes.

Okay with you? I asked, as casually as I could manage.

Dadster, you gotta do what you gotta do.

She said it with enough of a smile to convince me that it really was okay. At least, enough for me to convince myself that it was.

I called Dorita back.

Come on over, I said.

You're sure?

I'm sure.

Absolutely sure?

Just get over here.

Okay. Be there in a while.

I breathed an enormous sigh of relief.

In the hour and a half it took Dorita to arrive I managed to focus long enough to run to the store, pick up some stuff, prepare a meal. I grilled some prawns, soaked first in star fruit, ginger, cognac and some other things I'd never reveal to even the most assiduous interrogator. I cooked some fragrant jasmine rice to perfection. I called up Francis, my favorite local wine merchant. He found a bottle of Château Beaucaillou 1990 hiding in a back corner of the cellar. Send it over, I said. I set an elegant table, yet discreet. No candlelight. Nothing obvious. Just nice. Pretty. Ordered.

The bell rang. Kelly was closer to the door, and turned to it with a mischievous smile.

I cringed.

Kelly opened the door.

Hi, said Dorita. You must be the angel child I've heard so much about.

Daddy! reproached Kelly.

I've just been reading Philip Pullman's latest, Dorita went on without a pause. I bet you'll love it. I've brought it with me, she said, with a questioning lilt at the end of the phrase, a little 'Is this okay, am I allowed?'

I love Philip Pullman, Kelly said.

Oh, I hope you haven't read this yet. It just came out, Dorita said, pulling the book from her bag.

No, no, said Kelly. Thank you. Thank you.

I swear I saw a little blush. On both of them.

Another new side of Dorita.

This was going to take some getting used to.

We sat for dinner. Kelly and Dorita did most of the talking. There were some awkward silences. But not too many. I poured the Beaucaillou. I allowed Kelly half a glass. She was almost seventeen, after all. I'd started hanging at the local tavern at thirteen, I reminded myself.

Hey, Kelly? I said at one point.

Yo, Dadster.

Remember when you were eight or nine, and we arm-wrestled, and I told you how amazingly strong you were?

Sure, Dadster.

That's what made you want to do wrestling, wasn't it?

She looked me in the eye. She cocked her head. She smiled.

Dadster? she said.

Yes, angel child?

You're seriously deluded.

Dorita left after dinner. Her departure was chaste. Free of innuendo. It felt good. I had deflected the demons til bedtime, at least.

88.

WHEN I WOKE, late the next morning, Kelly had already left for school. I was a little bereft. But I knew that it was a good thing.

My cell phone rang. I looked at the screen. Laura.

I have some results, she said.

I'll be there in twenty, I said.

I grabbed a cab. It had a funky smell.

Despite my haste, she wasn't there when I arrived. Called out on an emergency, they told me.

Emergency? All her patients were dead. Couldn't they wait?

I was anxious. I wanted to know. I couldn't sit still. I went out back. I had a smoke. I had three.

The back door opened. Laura stuck her head out.

Keep that up and you'll be my next patient, she said, eyeing the cigarette.

I can't think of anyone I'd rather have exploring my entrails, I said. You got something for me?

You won't necessarily like it.

Well? I said, a touch impatiently.

It's ambiguous.

Shit.

Sorry.

What do you mean, ambiguous?

We got a match. But it wasn't with the semen.

What then?

A hair.

What hair?

A hair from the sofa.

Shit. That doesn't mean anything. He's been there. He's been on that couch.

Which makes it even more ambiguous.

You can't date a hair.

Not unless you're really, really weird.

I paused. I wasn't used to jokes from Laura. I tried to keep a straight face. But I couldn't. The joke was just too goddamn stupid. I snorted. I guffawed. She smiled.

Well, I said, can you?

Within a day or two? No.

Damn.

Sorry.

Don't be sorry.

Listen, Rick, there's something else.

What?

I don't want to tell you now. I want to run a couple more things. To make sure.

Laura, come on. You can't do this to me.

Nothing serious, Rick. Just something a little strange.

Laura.

Seriously, Rick. These things come out funny all the time. Contamination and things. I just need to double-check. I'll call you tomorrow.

Laura, you're killing me here.

Rick, I went out on a limb for you. You can wait a day.

She had a point.

89.

I WENT TO STARBUCKS. I fired up the laptop. Dorita had sent me copies of the newspaper articles about Suspect Number One in the mysterious death of . . . my wife. It still didn't sound right. 'Death of my wife.' It couldn't be real. I'd found myself doing double takes every time a dark-haired woman walked by. Could that be her? May I please wake up?

The pictures were blurry, inconclusive. A high school yearbook photo. The perp getting into a car, holding his hands up over his face. Certainly a resemblance. But not enough to be sure it was Jake. I realized that I hadn't asked Dorita how she knew that this was him.

I called her up. I told her about Laura's results.

Hm, she said. Ambiguous.

Exactly Laura's word, I said. Anyway, how the hell did you track him down?

I hate to reveal my secrets.

Sure. Save it for the ADA. How'd you find him?

The Guild.

The Actors' Guild?

Exactly. They've got a record of stage names.

Isn't that confidential information?

Sure, Ricky, it's private, she laughed. As soon as I heard that, I gave up.

Sorry, darling. I didn't mean to impugn your investigative skills.

I accept your apology. Listen. I got the name. I did a search. These articles turned up. The ages matched. He's a mystery guy. Here's a mystery. It all fits. Could I be wrong? I could. But I seriously doubt it.

It would be quite a coincidence, I agreed. But I'd rather have something more concrete.

We could fly to Podunk, interview the locals. Go the whole nine yards. Or, we could just ask him.

Sure. And he'll say, 'Yeah, sure, I'm a sister-fucker. And I'm dying to expiate my guilt.'

Expiate. Nice. Are you Catholic?

No, but I've considered it. Answer the question.

There wasn't any question. But I'm telling you, if he's Brendan, we'll know. We'll know in two minutes. He's a drunk. At least, you told me he was. We'll get him liquored up.

I love you. 'Liquored up.' Who else would use that phrase?

After we get him liquored up, we spring it on him. He won't see it coming. He has no reason to think anything's cooking. We'll see it on his face. Instantly. Then, he spills it. Or he doesn't. If he doesn't, we fly to Podunk, get the goods. He does, we save the trip.

Podunk has an airport?

I can always count on you to keep your eye on the ball.

Thanks. It's one of my better qualities.

Set it up.

All right. I'll set it up. But tell me, darling. How is it that you got to be so goddamn smart?

Sex. Lots and lots of sex. It stimulates the brain.

You have no idea how depressing that is.

Don't worry, we'll fix that.

90.

I KNEW JAKE WOULD BE at the Wolf's Lair that night. It seemed like he'd moved in.

We talked some poker talk for the first few drinks. I complimented his play. He complimented mine. We talked about the others in the crew. Mike bluffed too much. You'd lose a few to him. You'd have to fold. You didn't have the cards. But you knew if you were patient you'd catch him. You'd have a big hand. You'd re-raise. He'd re-re-raise. You'd get into a bidding war. He'd never back down. It was an ego thing. You'd win more in that hand than he could make all night on your folds. Riverstreet was cagey. You had to watch him close. He had a tell or two. A twitch in his neck when he had the goods. A very slight tremor in his left hand when he didn't. You paid attention, you could make him pay. Andrea and Butch were imperturbable. You didn't look to them for profits.

This went on for an hour or two. We discussed strategy. We talked about personalities. We talked about what made a good game. We could find a better one, we agreed. Some rich guys, eager to give their money away. We could be a team. Play them like a yo-yo. They wouldn't know what side was up or down.

Drunken bravado. There was nothing like it to bond a guy to you.

Dorita got there, almost too late. We'd got so drunk I was worried that I wouldn't be able to play my role.

I didn't need to worry. She was in her element. She didn't need me. I'd set him up. She could take it from there.

She put her arm around me, asked me to introduce her to my hand-some friend. She posed. She postured. She seduced him with salacious conversation.

What is it that makes a lover? she asked. Not just a guy that can con-vince you in the bar that he's cool? A guy that can convince you later that you can't live without his touch?

Dorita put her hand on Jake's.

He didn't have a chance. A man with an ounce of ego couldn't pass up the opportunity.

He put his hand over hers. She smiled. He tried to smolder. He did a fairly decent job of it.

The fish was hooked.

We talked, we laughed. We drank. We drank some more.

Let's all go to your place, Dorita said to me.

I don't know, I said. I'm not sure I'd be comfortable with that.

Oh, I'm sorry, she said. I'm so insensitive. Jake, let's go to your place.

We flagged a cab. We all squeezed in. Dorita in the middle. I felt her long strong thigh against me.

Jake looked ready to pass out.

By the time we got to his place he'd recovered a bit. He was able to fish out his key. Only two or three tries to get it into the lock. Once we got into his apartment, black and white and stark, he was almost normal.

He made some drinks. We all sat down. He and Dorita on the couch. Me on the chair. Dorita chided him for his decorating skills, or lack thereof. He looked around, befuddled.

What's wrong with it? he asked.

Nothing that a month's remodeling wouldn't cure, she said.

Maybe you can help with that, he said.

He was looking off into the distance. I wasn't sure if it was too much drink, or just his usual vacant thing.

I don't do windows, she said. But I can recommend somebody.

That's great, he said. As long as they'll work for free.

We'll see about that, Dorita laughed. Maybe Rick'll pay for it.

Sure, I said, no problem. I'll get a second mortgage.

Dorita leaned toward Jake, cupped his face in her hand.

Jake, she said softly.

Yes? he said.

I really like you.

I really like you, too, he said, with a glance at me.

He looked scared. Asking for my permission. I nodded my head approvingly.

There's just one thing I need to straighten out, Dorita said.

What? said Jake.

His eyes were half closed.

What's with this incest thing?

Jake froze. His eyes opened wide. He looked at her. She took her hand away. He looked at me. He sobered up fast.

What the fuck? he said.

The incest thing, she repeated. I need to know about it.

Jake's eyes narrowed. His brow furrowed.

What the fuck are you talking about?

I had a second's doubt. Maybe it wasn't him. Maybe the names were just coincidence.

I'm talking about your sister, Dorita said quietly. Your sister and you.

Her face went calm, impassive. He got up abruptly. Went to the kitchen. Opened the freezer. Took out a bottle of Stolichnaya. Poured a huge glassful. Dropped the glass. It shattered on the tiles. He ignored it. Got a plastic cup. Filled it. Took a gulp. Looked at us. Shook his head.

So you know, he said.

This was almost too easy. I'd anticipated hours of sparring. Turning the screws. Letting the evidence out piece by piece, until he had no choice but to succumb.

We do, said Dorita.

Shit, he said.

He looked down at his shoes. He gulped his vodka. I looked at Dorita. She wasn't taking her eyes off him.

Jake began pacing back and forth on the kitchen tiles, mumbling to himself.

Watch your feet, said Dorita.

He looked up.

What? he asked.

He had the vacant look again.

The glass, she said.

Oh, he said, looking down again. Fuck that.

He kept pacing. He walked over the glass. It crunched on the tiles. He walked to the end of the apartment, to the window there. He stood for a while. He leaned his forehead against the pane. Far away.

My glass was empty. It felt lonely. I went to the kitchen for a refill.

All right, said Jake.

He came back to our end of the room. He pulled an armchair over, facing Dorita. He sat down.

I'll tell you the story, he said. But first I need to know who you are. What the fuck do you care about my life?

He was talking directly to Dorita. It was as though I wasn't there.

We were just curious, Dorita said. We did a little search. We found some newspaper articles.

Curious? he said, his voice rising. Who the fuck are *you*? I just met you tonight.

Rick was curious, she said. We were talking. He said he met this actor guy. I did an Internet search. Nothing came up. It seemed you didn't exist.

He curled his lip.

I exist all right, he said.

That seems clear enough, she said. But nothing came up. We thought it kind of strange. For an actor.

I never said I was a *successful* actor, he said, with a mirthless chuckle.

Silence.

So I checked with the Actor's Guild, she said. And I got your real name. Did a search. And there it was.

But why do you care? he asked, a note of pleading in his voice.

I don't, Dorita said. But Rick does. Rick likes you. And Rick's my friend. He wants to help, if he can.

Help? How the fuck can you help me? he asked, with an angry look at me.

I don't know, I said. All I know is that you're living with a secret. And that isn't good. It warps you. It makes your life hell. Believe me. I know.

Yeah, he said, with a sneer. I know you know.

What does that mean? I asked.

He paused. He looked straight at me. He seemed to be weighing his options. He shook his head.

You know what I mean, he said.

No, I don't.

Silence.

All right, he said at last. Whatever. You know about me. You read all that bullshit in the papers, anyway.

That's why we're talking to you, said Dorita. We know what's in the papers is never right.

Who the fuck *are* you? Jake asked her again, half angry, half resigned.

He looked at me for help.

I'm Rick's friend, she said calmly.

Friend?

My only friend, actually, I said. Other than you, I added quickly.

He softened.

Okay, he said. Will you let me explain?

We maintained an expectant silence. The moment was excruciating. One wrong word and he could clam up. Throw us out. Disappear.

It's not like they said in the papers, he said.

Dorita nodded. I nodded.

She was eight years older than me, you know.

I noted the past tense.

The whole thing was stupid beyond belief.

We waited.

She was twenty-two. I was fourteen. I mean, imagine.

He shook his head. We waited some more. I reminded myself that he was an actor, self-described.

We loved each other, he said quietly.

We waited.

Not that way, he said. Jesus Christ. Not that way.

Not the way the papers said? asked Dorita.

Not that way, he repeated. We loved each other so much.

Tears appeared in his eyes.

So what happened? Dorita asked gently.

My dad, he said, choking on the word.

Your dad?

He was an operator. A political guy. He could never get enough of it. Power. Influence. He wanted to be the big man in town. I mean. I didn't see it then. I see it now. But it was so stupid. It was just a little town in the middle of nowhere. Why the fuck did he care?

He stopped again. If he wasn't overcome with emotion, he was doing a bang-up job of faking it.

And? asked Dorita, almost whispering.

And he got tangled up with this developer. Ryan. Josh Ryan. A big fat asshole. I don't know all the details. I don't want to know.

It started coming out of him in a rush.

Ryan was a big shot. He'd come over to the house. Dad wanted us to like him. To treat him good. He'd give us instructions before Ryan got there. Say this. Say that. Make him happy. We all hated his guts.

Ryan?

Yeah. The guy was so full of himself it made us sick.

Us?

Me, Randy, Mom. We hated the fucker.

Randy?

Short for Miranda.

Okay.

And then one day, Randy's off at college, Mom and Dad are talking. On the patio, in the back. And there's shouting and screaming. And I hear stuff breaking. And I run out back there. And Dad's on the ground. And Mom's standing over him. And she's got a big flowerpot in her hand. And she's about to smash it over his head. And I yell out, and I run over, and I grab her arm. And she screams, and starts crying. And Dad gets up. And he slinks back into the house. And Mom's crying.

Jake/Brendan's eyes filled with tears.

I'd never seen her cry before, he said. Never.

We waited.

He looked up at us. His eyes were red.

You're sure you want to know all this? he asked.

Only if you want us to, said Dorita softly.

He gazed at Dorita. He looked at me. Or through me. He continued.

I don't even know what set it off. Some stupid deal my father brokered for this guy. Somebody tried to screw somebody. Maybe they were all screwing each other. Probably. I don't know. And Mom knew it before Dad. She was trying to tell him. To warn him. And he wouldn't listen. But later he finally figured it out. And Ryan and my dad ended up hating each other.

Making it unanimous, I said.

Right. And nobody was happier than Randy. We didn't have to pretend anymore. Because Ryan had been hitting on her. He got the idea that she was his property. Dad was his, and if Dad was his, so was Randy.

Gross, said Dorita.

Beyond gross.

Jake paused. He wiped his eyes. He looked exhausted. Excuse me, he said. He went to the bathroom.

Dorita looked at me. I looked at her. We heard the water running. She shrugged. I shrugged. We weren't sure.

I hope he doesn't throw himself out the window, she said.

There's no window, I assured her.

Jake came back.

What more do you want to know? he asked, looking at me.

Dorita cut in before I could respond.

As much as you want to tell us, she said gently.

Jake took a deep breath.

Ryan was a major-league prick, he said. He wanted to get back at Dad. For whatever. And at Randy. For disrespecting him.

How had she disrespected him? I asked.

Not marrying him.

Marrying him?

He wanted her to marry him. It was like an arranged marriage thing, in his head. Dad owed him. He was going to take Randy. As payment.

Jesus, I said.

Yeah. And before the big fight, Dad was almost on his side. It was a sick situation. But it got sicker.

Jake wiped sweat from his forehead. We waited.

I don't know how he did it. But he got a picture. Must have had some PI guy or whatever. He got a picture.

What was in the picture? Dorita asked.

Randy. Naked. And me. On the bed. In her room.

Were you naked too?

No. I was in my track shorts. Listen, I know it sounds bad. It looked bad. He gave it to the paper. But it wasn't what it looked like.

We waited.

Jesus. I never told anybody this.

What? said Dorita gently. What didn't you tell anybody?

That I'm gay, he said.

I almost choked on my Scotch. This was not where I'd thought it was going.

Nothing wrong with that, Dorita said.

No. Not here. Not now. But then. And there. You didn't tell people that. You might as well just kiss your life goodbye. So when the picture came out. What was I going to do? We loved each other, Randy and me.

He looked at me with pleading eyes.

But not like that, he said. She was the only one who knew. About my . . . thing. We shared everything.

His eyes misted up again.

I was trying to reconcile this revelation, if that was what it was, with the Jake I knew. The poker-playing, backslapping, hard-drinking guy. I thought back. Yes, I could see it. It could be. All that angst. All those hints of deep dark secrets and the unfairness of the world. The drinking. It all fit.

Though it fit some other theories too.

We were in her room, he said. I was her kid brother, for God's sake. She knew what I was. She knew she could be free with me. She knew she could share anything. God.

His voice choked up.

We waited while he composed himself.

She was always very self-conscious. Sure, she was the star. The valedictorian. The girl the guys all wanted to take out. But it never was enough for her. She wanted more. She wanted to be a *real* star. Out in the world. Somebody at the college had approached her. Asked her to model. That was going to be her start. She was going to the big time. But she was still so insecure. She never thought of herself as beautiful. It didn't matter how many guys asked her out. Drooled over her. She never believed it.

We smoked a little dope, he continued. We stole a little gin from Daddy's stash. We were pretty wasted. I was trying to convince her she was beautiful. She thought she was too skinny. A bag of bones, she said. I laughed at her for that. Look, she said. Look at me. She was out of control. She took off her dress. She had nothing underneath. She liked to be that way. Nobody ever knew but me. She could sit there in church, and only she and me would know.

He broke down. He cried. Dorita went to him. Put her arms around him. He melted in her arms. She looked at me. She raised her eyebrows. I shrugged. Damn.

Once he'd calmed down a bit he went on.

So she's standing there in front of the mirror, naked, and she's yelling, 'Look at me, I'm nothing.' She was hysterical. I'd never seen her like that. I was trying to calm her down. And I guess that's when the bastard took the picture. He was at the window. He had to have been there. Next day a bunch of reporters show up. Jesus.

He told us the rest of the story. The police. The newspaper stories. Daddy found dead with the top of his head on the bedroom wall. Mom breaking down, inconsolable. Catatonic. They took her to the hospital. She never spoke again.

Their lives were ruined. They couldn't even look at each other. It was all too painful. They got the hell out of town. He went to Chicago. She went to L.A. They didn't talk. They didn't write. They needed to expunge, erase, forget the ugly past.

Jake, I said when he was finished. There's something that doesn't make sense to me.

What? he said.

He was tired. Resigned.

You said you were gay.

Yeah?

When Dorita was hustling you, tonight?

Yeah.

You weren't acting like a gay guy.

He looked at me like I was stupid.

I was trying to impress you, Rick, he said.

Oh man. What else had I missed?

I found out soon enough.

Mom died, last year, he said. And I thought about it all. I thought to myself, I said to myself, we were all we had. Randy and me. I had her. She had me. We didn't have anyone else. Back then. And I still didn't have anyone. Anything. I had this stupid acting thing. It was going nowhere. Auditions. Humiliation. Building bookshelves.

He gave me an ironic smile.

I smiled. I nodded my head.

So I decided to look her up. I'd find her. It wasn't that hard. I knew where she'd gone. I called some people. I traced her from L.A. to here.

And?

And I wasn't sure. I wasn't sure if she'd want to see me. I didn't know what kind of life she'd built here. How deep she'd buried the past. So when I found out she was married, had a kid, had a life, I figured I had to go slow.

Of course, Dorita said.

Of course, I echoed.

So I checked it out.

Reconnoitered, I said.

Right, he said. And I found out you hung out at the Wolf's Lair.

Right, I said slowly, puzzled at the change of subject.

He looked at me. He spoke directly to me.

I figured I could get to her through you, he said. Gradually.

I stared back at him. What the hell was he saying?

He saw my confusion.

Jesus, he said. You didn't know?

Know what? I said.

My stomach turned over.

I thought you knew, he said. I thought that was the point of all this.

Knew what? I asked.

Though by then I knew.

Melissa, he said. Melissa was Randy.

Oh my God, said Dorita.

Oh Jesus, said Jake. I thought you knew.

91.

I WAS SHAKING. I had to get away. I told Jake I was sorry, I had to go. I had to think about this. He said he understood. His eyes said something else. He looked lost, afraid. I didn't have the energy to deal with that.

I had a million questions. Had he contacted Melissa before the day he'd come over? Since? Did he know anything about her death? About who might have . . .

I couldn't ask the questions. It was already too much.

We went to Trois Pistoles, Dorita and I. I ordered onion soup and a bottle of cheap Burgundy. I ignored the soup. I drank the wine. I chain-smoked cigarettes.

Well, I said gloomily, that explains the phone calls, doesn't it?

It sure does.

They were talking. He probably came over. How would I know? I'm never in the goddamn house.

Dorita wisely said nothing.

I changed the subject. I talked about books, movies. I couldn't bear the thought of silence.

We talked about meds. I gave her my list. She gave me hers. Zoloft for depression; lithium so the Zoloft didn't make her manic; Inderal for the tremor induced by the lithium; Clonodine for the sweating and Nexium for the nausea brought on by the Zoloft; Klonopin for the panic attacks, which she occasionally confused with the Clonodine, with unfortunate effects; Provigil to stay awake because all that other stuff induced narcolepsy; Seroquel to get to sleep.

Wow, I said. You are one crazy babe.

That's why you love me, honey.

Somewhere into the third bottle of Burgundy we started talking about her. She'd never opened up before. She didn't then, either, really. But she said a few things. Enough for me to know that she hadn't had it easy. That she had her monsters too.

Dorita pulled her chair around to my side of the table. Put her arm around my shoulder.

We'll get through this, she said.

We?

You and me. Together. We'll get you through it.

Damn, I said. I don't feel sad enough.

What *do* you feel? Dorita asked softly.

I hung my head. I wasn't going to say it.

You need some good old-fashioned comfort, she said.

We're on the third bottle already.

Not that kind.

I looked at her. Oh dear. She'd read my mind.

Please don't say what I think you're going to say, I said.

Okay. I won't say it. Let's just do it.

Please. I really don't think that's a good idea.

Why not? she asked.

More reasons than I can count. You got a couple hours?

Sure.

I was afraid you'd say that.

Come on, Ricky. If you've been truthful with me . . .

You know I have.

. . . which I have no reason to doubt, you haven't done it in years.

Not for lack of trying.

Sure. Not for lack of trying. Once in a while. But you can't keep on like that. There's a lot of life left on those old bones.

I was silent.

Well, isn't there?

No comment.

Getting cagey, are we? Come on, Ricky, it's written all over your face. You hate it. You want to get out of this thing. You want to live again.

I thought awhile. She was right, of course. I couldn't cling to the martyr thing forever.

I can't argue with that, I said.

Well, we agree on that much. So what's wrong with your best friend taking care of you?

Precisely that. Because you're my best friend. Because if we do it, God knows what will happen then. You're not only my best friend. You're really my *only* friend. And what if I lost that? Where would I be?

Darling. I'll always be your friend. No matter what. You know that.

I looked into her eyes. They were sincere, I had to admit. They radiated sincerity. I felt a warmth creep up my body, from my toes, that I hadn't felt since . . . well. I'm not sure I'd ever felt it before.

Okay, I said. I'll think about it.

Think about it? These moments come but once, my neurotic friend. Whatever makes you think the offer will stay open while you think? There's a lineup for these favors, darling, she said, turning to the crowd at the bar.

Next! she called out.

Heads turned.

Jesus, I whispered. Keep it down. This is bloody blackmail.

Yes it is. And if I were you I'd fork it over pronto. The consequences could be dire.

I couldn't really argue with that, either.

All right, I said. I'll try.

Try. I'm not at all sure that will be enough. But I guess I'll take my chances.

Your chances? Maybe I'm missing something, but it seems to me that *I'm* the one taking all the chances here. Jesus, do you understand the enormity of what I've just learned?

Ricky, she said in a soft voice, what in God's name makes you think that *I'm* not taking any chances?

Had I not known her better, I'd have thought that her eyes had tears in them. I felt a fool. Again.

Oh God, I said. I'm sorry.

It's okay. I'm used to it.

Her smile was warm and giving.

Let's go to my place, she said.

I'd like to. But Kelly.

Let's go to your place then.

But Kelly.

Don't worry about Kelly. I'll take care of her.

We went to my place. Kelly was out. I called up Francis, told him to send over the Grande Dame 1988. I'd asked him long ago to save it for me. For a special occasion. One that never seemed to come. I pulled out the handblown Riedel glasses that I'd bought in Germany, years ago. Before they'd made the wine press highlights, started mass production. I'd tried the new ones since, the ones they sold all over now, at reasonable prices. They didn't have the same effect for me.

Kelly came home. She saw the champagne glasses. She looked at Dorita. Dorita winked. Kelly looked at me.

She shook her head.

Okay, she said. I get it. I'll go to Peter's.

And off she went. Without a backward glance.

My God. What had I done?

Dorita took me to the bedroom. She took me to my own bedroom. She pressed me up against the wall. She kissed me. Gently, yet with passion. I fell to my knees. I kissed her stomach. She laughed. She pulled me up, and to the bed. She undressed me, slow and gentle. She undressed herself. I watched, transfixed. All these years of coveting. Of sublimation.

And I wasn't disappointed. Those breasts I had so long imagined, full and languorous, impossibly imposing on her slim and muscular frame. Her legs, finally revealed from toe to waist, long and strong and graceful. Her stomach smooth and cool as ivory. She laid it all out for me.

And I was afraid.

She was utterly desirable and smooth, exquisitely constructed. I knew, I knew beyond certainty, that even had I been a normal man, with normal lusts and fully functioning libido, I'd be in so much awe of her that I'd be utterly unable to function.

But she took care of that.

She lay down beside me. I was exposed. She was radiant. She put her head on my shoulder. She asked me to read to her. I chose Dylan Thomas. I read poems of rage and defiance. 'Do Not Go Gentle into That Good Night.' 'And Death Shall Have No Dominion.'

Rage, rage against the dying of the light, I read.

And it gave me the power.

And she was gentle, and giving, and warm, in the face of the rage. She stroked me softly, like a whisper in the night. We lay by candlelight.

Her mouth hovered and touched and rose again to attack with abandon my most sensitive, my grieving places.

She was a miracle.

I came alive.

She devoured me.

And when it was over, we lay back. We smiled. We touched. We held each other.

For the first time in memory, all felt right with the world.

92.

IN THE MORNING I WAS CONFUSED. Confused and disturbed. But Dorita was there. So I couldn't call Sheila.

I had to get out of the house. I had to get Dorita out of the house. Before Kelly came back. Before my head exploded.

Time for a change of scenery, I said.

We went to Starbucks.

Okay, Dorita said once we'd settled down with our coffee. Enough with the sentiment. It's time to get to business.

Damn, I said. You always want to ruin my fun.

It's my job.

You and the rest of humanity.

Heaven doesn't exist in a vacuum.

True. You need a little hell. To spice it up.

So, back to business. Question one: Do we believe him?

I don't know. I haven't thought about it. I've been trying not to think about it.

That's not the answer. Think.

I thought.

If he's lying, he's a damn good liar.

Oscar material.

Which belies his lack of success in the field.

True. Very true.

Let's proceed on the assumption that he's legit.

We can do that. We can also check it.

You want to go to Podunk?

Not today. I just meant we can always do that if we have to.

Sure. We can do that.

Okay. So, let's assume he's foursquare.

Let's.

And the physical evidence bears him out.

At least it's not inconsistent.

Correct. He was in the house. Behind your back, he hugs her. They're overwhelmed to see each other. He leaves a hair behind. Follicle attached.

Sure. He was next to her on the couch when I came back from the kitchen.

Another detail you left out.

I did?

You did.

Sorry. Anyway, it fits.

We need to look at other suspects then.

I'm not sure that 'suspects' is the right word. But the . . .

Semen. You can say it.

I don't want to say it. But I guess you can.

We thought for a while.

It has to match somebody, I said.

Who?

That's the million-dollar question.

Sixty-four thousand, I think it was.

Let's not quibble. Who's next on the list? The twins?

That's the other case, darling.

Right. Just testing.

The AA guys.

A possibility.

But messy.

A smorgasbord of suspects.

And they all seemed so sincere, you said.

Not in any way conclusive.

Of course not.

Let's remember Occam's razor.

The simplest explanation is usually the best.

Not quite.

Right. The simplest explanation *that explains all the facts* is the best.

Dorita looked steadily into my eyes. She didn't say a thing.

It was a challenge.

I thought. I pondered. In my head I shuffled the index cards.

One popped out.

Jesus, I said. You're right.

He was the last man she was seen with.

Other than me.

You've been cleared.

He's weird.

So you've said.

She was in his thrall.

It appears.

The last time Kelly and I picked her up from the hospital, two or three months ago?

You never told me about that.

When we were leaving?

Yes?

He hugged her.

Well, that's not necessarily unusual.

Maybe not. But I remember thinking there was something strange about it.

Yes?

I don't know. I couldn't put my finger on it. It made me uncomfortable.

We sat in thought.

And then there was the day I came home, I said. Her last relapse. And he was on the couch with her. Holding her hand.

That couch seems to get a lot of action.

She lived on it. He told me he needed time with her alone.

Jesus H. Christ.

That was *my* reaction, at first. But then, I figured it was just a therapeutic thing. That my reaction was just paranoid. Insecurity. That he was helping her. And I could never help her.

Damn your neuroses, Ricky.

And then, when I came back into the living room, he couldn't get out of there fast enough.

Hmm. You'd think he'd want to talk to you and Kelly for a while, no?

Sure. Explain the situation. Reassure the family. Though he never was that kind of guy, I have to say. With him it all seemed to be about power.

Dorita gave me the under-the-eyebrows look.

Yes, I said. Yes. Damn. It fits.

It does appear to.

Jesus, I just remembered something else, too. That night, when he was at my house? When I went up to Kelly in the dining room? One of the first things she said was that Melissa had been asking for him.

Asking for Steiglitz?

Steiglitz. Everything fits. Goddamn everything.

It does appear to.

Let's check him out. I'll do it. Damn. I don't even have to. I *know* it was him.

Whoa, said Dorita. Slow down. Let's make a plan.

I don't need a plan, I said. I know what to do.

She raised her eyebrows.

Trust me on this one, I said. Did I single-handedly win the Case of the Red Car Door?

You did. I have to admit it.

So trust me.

93.

I CALLED STEIGLITZ'S ASSISTANT. The good doctor was at the clinic in Westchester. He'd be free after five.

What to do til then? I was jumping out of my skin.

My cell phone rang. Laura.

I think I know what you're going to tell me, I said.

Really?

Yes. But go ahead.

It's really strange, Rick. Which is why I wanted to double-check. But the hair?

The hair. Yes. I know. It's a close match to Melissa's.

Rick, how in God's name did you know that?

I have my ways, Laura. Anyway, thanks for the help. Really. You've been great. Gotta go.

I hung up.

Distract me, I said to Dorita. Or I'm going to have to do something antisocial.

Why should today . . .

Yeah, yeah. Come on. Distract me.

We've got to break the Jules logjam, she said.

Jesus, you're right. Less than a week. Shit.

We talked it through. Everything we knew. We couldn't find a weak point to attack. We couldn't find a pattern that felt right.

FitzGibbon, I said.

You said that before.

You've got a better idea?

No.

Then let's go.

Maybe Dorita could add a frisson to the mix. Unsettle him a bit. Who knew what might come out?

We took a cab. It smelled of apple cores and filth.

As it happened, the twins were there. Both of them. Our first dual sighting. Ramon looking tight and edgy. Raul smooth and well tailored.

They didn't look a bit alike.

Pleased to see you, Raul said.

Sure.

I considered asking FitzGibbon if we could meet in private. Get him alone. But I thought better of it. It would be interesting to see the interaction of the three. We might learn more by watching than by anything the cagey bastards had to say.

If there was anything to learn. I still wasn't convinced that Jules hadn't chased Larry Silver to the alley. Stove his head in.

Nice of you to make the time to see us, I said.

Sure, said FitzGibbon, with a quizzical glance at Dorita.

My colleague, I said. Dorita Reed.

FitzGibbon rose and bowed elaborately.

Have we met before? he asked.

We have, said Dorita. Good to see you again.

FitzGibbon nodded uncertainly. Sat down. Ramon scowled. I began wondering if the expression had been tattooed on his face at birth.

We're not sure how much progress we've made, I said. But there are a few issues we'd like to talk to you about. That might lead somewhere.

Okay, said FitzGibbon.

These trusts, I said. I understand that they were set up by your father?

Yes, he said warily. Ramon leaned forward. Raul lit a long slim cigarette. He looked unconcerned.

And they were intended for the benefit of your children?

Ye-e-s, he said, drawing it out.

The part that speaks to your 'issue,' correct?

That's right, he said slowly.

FitzGibbon looked at Raul.

Ramon's scowl deepened.

And you also know that there are conditions that have to be fulfilled before your children get the capital, right?

FitzGibbon looked confused.

There are some conditions, interjected Raul.

I looked at him. He looked as placid and content as always.

One of which is that they not have been convicted of a felony, correct?

That's one of them, yes, said Raul.

Which is an interesting coincidence, I said.

Excuse me for a moment, said Raul pleasantly. I'm not sure I understand. How did you get this information? It was my understanding that you couldn't handle that matter. You had a conflict, or something.

Oh dear. An inconvenient detail.

The phone rang. Raul picked up the phone. He listened.

Yes, he said. I understand.

I looked around for Ramon. He wasn't there.

Raul leaned over and whispered something in FitzGibbon's ear.

Then he turned to me.

Excuse me, Mr. Redman, he said, but something has come up.

Pardon me? I asked.

Terribly sorry, he said. We must attend to it right away.

He nodded toward the door.

I looked at FitzGibbon for help. He was gazing out the window.
I looked back at Raul. He was looking steadily at me.

His Look said: Get the hell out of here.

Well, perhaps we can speak later in the day? I asked.

Perhaps, said Raul. We'll let you know.

Ramon returned. He parked himself in front of FitzGibbon's desk, arms crossed. Obscuring my view of the Patriarch.

I looked at Dorita. She looked as frustrated as I felt.

I couldn't just leave it at that.

Listen, I said, I don't know what's set you guys off, but I'm just asking a few questions. We've learned a few things. Things that may lead to other things. We're working for *you*, Mr. FitzGibbon.

I craned my neck to try to get some eye contact with the Patriarch. Ramon shifted to block my view.

Our job is to clear Jules, I said to FitzGibbon, trying to project my voice through Ramon's midsection. Surely you want to help us any way you can?

I really think it would be better if you left, said Raul.

Calm and cool.

I looked at Dorita.

She shrugged.

We left. What else were we going to do? Start a fistfight?

Wouldn't be prudent.

Ramon followed us out the door. Into the elevator. He followed us to the lobby. He followed us into the street.

Dorita and I picked up the pace once we got outside. Ramon fell behind. I looked back. He was going back into the building.

Well, I said, there goes what little was left of my career.

And mine.

Shit.

FitzGibbon's probably on the phone to Warwick as we speak.

Or the Bar Association.

Or both.

Damn. We may have gotten Kennedy in trouble too.

Jesus. You're right.

And we didn't even get to the phone calls.

Let's get a drink.

When we had found a suitable watering hole, we sat down and looked at each other.

What's done is done, said Dorita.

I suppose, I said.

That was really something.

If we didn't know before that there were some guilty consciences around that place.

We sure do now.

Looks like the whole bunch of them are in on it.

In on something. The question is, on what? We still don't have a sliver of evidence tying any of them to Larry Silver. Other than your esteemed client, of course.

Our client, I said. In any case, you'll be tracking down the slivers this afternoon. While I continue the investigation of our friend Dr. Steiglitz.

Dorita sighed, rolled her eyes.

I'll see what I can do, she said. Call me later.

You can count on me, I said, without conviction.

94.

THREE HOURS UNTIL THE STEIGLITZ APPOINTMENT. I tried not to think about my now-defunct career. I wondered whether I should warn Kennedy.

Of course I should.

But I couldn't bring myself to call him.

I looked for some sand to bury my head in.

I flipped open the laptop. Twenty-first-century sand.

I googled Steiglitz. Eighty-eight hits. The guy got around.

He published a lot of papers. Gave a lot of speeches. Was heavily involved in politics. Hung with movie stars and models.

There were some lawsuits too. You can't be a doctor in the United States of America and not get lawsuits. I counted nine. That didn't seem to be a huge number, for a prominent addiction specialist. But medical malpractice was not my field. I made a note to check with Terry O'Reilly.

Terry was an old law school buddy who did a thriving malpractice business. He made a hell of a lot more money than I did, and wasn't half as smart. He'd asked me more than once to join him. I'd been tempted. All that dough. But I knew I could never bring myself to be an ambulance chaser. Too seedy. I knew they justified it as a crusade for the little guy. But that's not how I saw them. Extortionists, they were to me. Find a victim. Drag out the boilerplate. Fill in the blanks. File the complaint. Wait for the settlement. Take thirty percent. Buy a new Bentley.

I didn't want any part of it.

But that didn't sour my friendship with Terry. He was a good guy. And a better golfer. We didn't talk business.

Most courts had websites. On many of them you could access the pleadings. The briefs, the motion papers. Some even had transcripts of trial proceedings. It took me a while, but I managed to track down some information on each of the nine Steiglitz cases. A couple were what you'd expect. Some poor depressive finally succeeded on his fourteenth suicide attempt. Great. Let's sue everybody. Steiglitz was named in the complaint, along with every other doctor, nurse and orderly and the hospital involved. Plaintiffs' lawyers liked to cast a wide net. Haul in as many insurance companies as they could. Spread the pain. Make settlement more palatable. Take their thirty percent. Buy another yacht. Upgrade the summer castle in Bordeaux.

A couple of the other cases were also routine. Bad reaction to drugs. Sue the drug company, the doctor who prescribed it. The pharmacy. The maker of the bottle it came in. Whatever.

One caught my eye, though. *Jane Doe* v. *Steiglitz.* No other defendants. Records sealed.

Interesting. It was very rare that a judge would agree to seal the records. Litigation in America was supposed to be open, public. Justice in secret was justice denied. Where minors were involved, or rape victims, their identities could be protected. Here, the 'Jane Doe' on the caption indicated something of that sort. But the whole file sealed? Well. Must be something there worth finding out about.

I called Terry. He commiserated about Melissa. I brushed it off. I'm okay, I said. Let's play golf.

It's the middle of winter, Rick.

Right. You know a Dr. Hans Steiglitz?

Sure. Big mover and shaker in addiction. Had him as an expert witness once.

Really? Not a client though?

Not a client. Why, you want to sue him?

Not yet. Just wanted to find out something about him. He treated Melissa.

Ah. Finally you're coming around.

I didn't say that.

I can hear it in your voice. He's like all the rest. All talk and fucking up everything he touches. You want to sue him?

I said no. I want to find out some stuff. You think you can help me?

Depends on what it is.

I told him about the sealed file.

Damn. That's a tough one.

I'm not asking you to steal the file. I've got other guys for that.

He laughed.

Just ask around. See if you can find out what the case was about. It could be nothing. I don't know. I just need to know enough to see if it's worth following up.

Sure. But it'll cost you two strokes on Sunday.

It's the middle of winter, Terry.

Right.

Like I said. A good guy.

95.

IT WAS RAINING. My stomach was hurting. My scalp was tingling. I knew these feelings. They were the same ones I got on the way into court. Butterflies, but worse. Stage fright, but more extreme.

It was too much. I had to have a cigarette to calm it down. I had to have a lot of cigarettes to calm it down.

I asked the driver if I could smoke.

Sure, he said. No problem. Then I can too.

Relief. It was a long ride out to Westchester. Smoke-free, it would have been interminable.

So many times I'd been there. The first, the second time, I'd paid attention to every detail. I'd talked endlessly with the staff. I'd read and reread the pamphlets. I'd wanted so badly to make it work. To get the old Melissa back.

By the third or fourth trip the cynicism had set in. Going to the clinic after every new relapse became a depressing routine. There was nothing I could do. It was up to her. If she didn't really want to stop, it wasn't going to happen. They told me that. But it still was hard to take. The helplessness.

I'd begun to wonder whether it really was possible. To slay the Monster.

The well-manicured grounds came into view, discreetly separated from the surrounding stately homes by a rustic stone wall.

It all looked gray in the rain.

My heart went cold.

Not a bad thing, actually, for the job I had to do. Squeezing information from a reluctant witness. No room for extraneous emotion.

Steiglitz showed me into his office. It was expansive, elegant. Just like he was. Or thought he was. He was his usual slick and unctuous self. His handshake was firm and dry. It lasted just the right amount of time to convince you of his genuine sympathy. He didn't sit behind a desk. He ushered me into an armchair. Pulled one over for himself. Just two guys sharing their feelings. Open up. Share. Let's make it all feel better.

The first task was to make him comfortable in his assumptions.

I told him that Melissa's death had made me do some hard thinking. That I'd finally realized it. That I too had a drinking problem.

He was solicitous. He questioned me gently, but extensively. My drinking habits. A little family history. My motivations. My rationale.

That part required no mendacity. Fact was, I was getting out of control. I was more and more needing several drinks just to feel normal. I had the shakes in the morning. I was up to eight double Scotches a day, easy.

Yes, I had a problem.

In fact, so convincing was my story that I almost decided to admit myself into the clinic, right then right there.

Steiglitz did not approve. Too many bad associations with the place, he said.

That, I couldn't argue with.

My cell phone rang. Terry. I apologized to Steiglitz. Took the call. Terry told me what he'd found. Not a smoking gun. But maybe enough. Enough to make an educated guess.

I hung up the phone. Apologized again.

No, no, said Steiglitz, not a problem.

He carried on where he'd left off. I should find a group in Manhattan I'd be comfortable with. He'd suggest a few. I could try them out. See if there was one I would respond to. They weren't all clones of twelve-step hell. There had to be a group or two for cynical, successful guys like me. Guys who weren't going to put up with the usual quasi-Christian pabulum.

Sure, I said. Sounds good. I'll try that. Thanks.

I did not get up to leave. I pulled the silent thing on him. I looked him in the eye.

I knew that if I was right about him, he'd be drawn in. A guiltless conscience would just say, 'Well, I'm glad we've made some progress.' Would get up, put out his hand. Whatever. Indicate the audience was over.

Well, he said, I'm glad we've made some progress.

He got up. Put out his hand.

Damn. The guy was good.

There's something else I want to talk about, I said.

Oh, he said with a broad smile. Of course. I didn't mean to be rude. He sat back down.

That's okay, I said. I understand. You're a busy man.

Well, I guess I am, he said expansively, with a touch of pride. But I can always spare some time for an old friend.

An old friend? Too big a stretch.

The first crack in the facade.

I wanted to ask you about something I came across, I said.

Yes? he said, his head cocked to the side in a simulacrum of interest.

Jane Doe.

Jane Doe?

Yes. Jane Doe.

I'm afraid I'm at a loss.

Jane Doe, I repeated once again. It's a name the courts use to mean 'anonymous.' When there's a confidentiality order. When to make the name public would cause so much harm that the public's right to know is secondary.

Silence.

Do you follow me? I asked.

Yes, he said. His smile had stiffened.

You've got a Jane Doe case, don't you?

I do?

You do.

Ah.

I was waiting for him to call Security. Have me thrown out. I could see him calculating the consequences. If Jane Doe were nothing, that's exactly what he'd do. Call my bluff. Throw me out. But if there was something there, throwing me out would only delay the inevitable. He'd go for damage control.

I had a big edge. He didn't know what I had in my hand.

I didn't know what he had either. But he didn't know that.

And his next move was going to tell me.

And what is it you'd like to know? he asked, as affably as he could manage.

The fish was on the hook.

I dropped the pretense. I put on my poker face. Impassive. Unreadable. I looked unblinking into his eyes.

What's the big secret? I asked.

He paused. He considered his options.

I'm not at liberty to say, he said.

How's that? I asked evenly.

As you said, there's a confidentiality order. I'd be in contempt of court.

I see. But otherwise, you'd be happy to share it with me, of course?

That re-raise he hadn't expected. He paused again. Looked at his cards. He didn't have the nuts, that was sure. Did he have something he could call with? Re-re-raise? Did he have enough to beat a bluff?

No, he said, I don't think I would.

Why not?

Because I have an obligation to my patients. To keep their affairs private.

Even those who sue you? I asked, ignoring, for the moment, the interesting choice of noun: affairs.

Even those.

He sat up straighter. He thought he was getting the upper hand. He was reading me for a bluff.

He was good. He was very good. If I was going to get anything out of him on this cold damp afternoon, I had to take it all the way. I had to tell him what he was holding.

If I was wrong, the game was over.

But it wasn't really a bluff. It was a semi-bluff. Terry would get me something. I'd win this one in the end.

But I didn't want to wait. I wanted Steiglitz right then. I wanted to watch his tan go white. I wanted to watch him squirm. I wanted to make it hurt.

Hell, what did I have to lose?

I re-re-raised.

Even those who sue you for sexual misconduct? I asked.

It was only a moment. But it was the decisive moment. The microscopic, instant straining at the corners of his eyes.

I'd got him. I'd figured his cards.

I think this conversation's gone far enough, he said.

Okay, I said with a friendly smile. I understand. Patient confidentiality. I wouldn't want to make you breach your patient's trust.

Just two professionals understanding each other, we were.

He didn't move. He didn't say a thing.

There's just one other thing, I said.

Yes? he said, with a distracted air.

He was deflated. I saw it in his shoulders. He was resigned to it.

It was going to be worse than he thought.

I wondered, I said, if you might not mind giving a DNA sample.

Pardon me?

A DNA sample.

Whatever for?

Well, I said. I think it's time for me to lay my cards on the table.

He stared at me. His jaw was clenched.

There was an autopsy. Of course, you know that.

An autopsy?

Of Melissa.

The muscles in his jaw let loose. His mouth hung open, just a bit, as though about to speak. But he didn't.

And there was a curious result.

He gathered himself. He got up from his chair. He went to the window. His back was to me. He looked out at the rain.

Semen, I said. There was semen.

He said nothing.

It wasn't mine, I said to his silent back.

And it's been remarked, I continued, that you were the last man she was seen with. Other than myself. Before her death, that is.

He slowly turned around. His eyes were full of tears.

A most peculiar sight.

He walked slowly back to his chair. Sat down. Looked straight at me.

All right, he said. You know.

I do now.

He looked startled. It dawned on him: he'd been outplayed.

He shrugged.

She was a very special woman, he said.

I know that. I married her.

I wanted to spit at him.

You don't have to do a DNA test, he said.

I know that too, I said with conviction. Now.

But you don't think . . .

I don't think anything. I want to know. I plan to find out.

He sat in thought. He looked up. He looked me in the eye.

Her death was exactly what it seemed, he said.

He'd recovered some of his poise. His gaze was level. His voice sincere.

But that was not enough for me.

How do you know that? I asked.

I don't know that. But I knew *her*.

My eyes narrowed.

I swallowed hard. I didn't want to ask the next question.

But I had no choice.

The game had gone that far.

They said there was evidence of – I hesitated at the word – forcing.

He didn't flinch. He shrugged, apologetically.

I'm sorry, he said. I know how it sounds. But you understand, I'm sure.

I did. I didn't want to. But I did.

Show me who's a man, she'd say.

I hung my head.

I heard his voice from far away.

I was her . . . well, I was more than her doctor, of course. But the end was inevitable.

I said nothing.

You knew that, he said. You know that.

My body lost a fraction of its tension. There was truth in what he said.

I looked into his eyes.

He didn't look away.

We were two men in a room.

Two men alone.

96.

I'D HAD THE FORESIGHT to have the car wait for me. I got in.

What was I going to do?

Nothing. I wasn't going to do anything. What was there to do?

My forehead felt like bent nails.

A few Scotches at the Wolf's Lair would help, I thought.

I was right.

Four Scotches in, my cell phone rang. I didn't feel like talking to anyone. I ignored it.

Thirty seconds later it rang again. I was about to pitch the phone at the men's room door when I noticed the number: Dorita. Shit. What did she want now?

I answered.

Rick, she said, breathless.

I'm busy, I said.

Something's happened.

I'll call you back.

FitzGibbon's dead.

Jesus Christ. How? What?

We don't know yet.

Jesus Christ. Where are you?

There's a meeting tomorrow morning. Be there.

Where?

The office. Ten o'clock. The real office.

The real office? I'm not allowed to go to the real office.

It's a new and different world, Ricky. Be there.

Where are you?

There's nothing to do right now. Be at the meeting.

She hung up.

I tried to make sense of the news. I couldn't get my mind around it. I tried to remember why FitzGibbon was important to me. The fat blowhard. What did I care? Steiglitz, on the other hand, I couldn't get out of my head.

I tried to stop thinking altogether.

I was more exhausted than I thought a man could be.

I staggered home.

I wasn't sure I could negotiate the stairs.

I didn't try.

I fell into the armchair. I slept.

The sleep was deep and dark and dreamless.

When I awoke the sun was streaming through the window. It hurt my eyes. I turned over. My head hurt. My back hurt. My right elbow hurt.

I heard Kelly come into the room.

Daddy? she said.

Yes my angel, I mumbled into the cushions.

What's going on?

I turned my head. I squinted into the barbarous light.

Steiglitz. Shit. What was I going to do?

My instinct was to tell Kelly the truth. The whole truth.

So help me God, I thought.

I thought again. She was so abominably young. I couldn't inflict this nightmare on her.

Nothing, I said, I just didn't have the energy to climb the stairs.

Oh, she said. Okay. I'll make some coffee.

You *are* so impossibly good to me, I smiled weakly.

I know, she said. Don't get too used to it.

I dragged myself to my feet. Took a quick shower. Put on some clean clothes. Went to the kitchen.

Kelly was pouring the coffee.

I found myself enjoying the sharp rich stimulating scent of good Jamaican Blue. The quiet company of Kelly.

Maybe life was worth living after all.

The phone rang.

It was Dorita.

Get the hell over here, she said.

I looked at my watch. Shit. Ten o'clock.

97.

AT THE OFFICE EVERYTHING SEEMED QUIET. Calm. Orderly. Misleading.

In the conference room were Warwick, Shumaker and Dorita.

Warwick looked stricken. Angry and stricken. Shumaker looked like Shumaker. Imperturbable. Dorita looked as nervous as I'd ever seen her. She was smoking. In the same room with Warwick.

Things had come to this.

Seriously? I asked.

Dead seriously, Dorita said.

Warwick and Shumaker nodded glumly.

The rest are on their way, said Shumaker.

The rest of the partners, I deduced. The whole ugly crew. Coming in on a Saturday. Jesus. This was big. This might be the end of the firm.

What the hell happened? I persisted.

We don't know, exactly, Shumaker said in his even tone. We're awaiting a report from the DA's office.

Nothing? I said. We know nothing?

First indications are suicide, Shumaker said.

Warwick shook his head.

Jesus. Warwick was screwed. Hell, the whole firm was screwed. Fifteen million a year out the window.

He fell from the thirty-third floor, said Dorita, instantly rendering my thought both comical and just plain bad.

Jesus, I said. Fell? Jumped? Was pushed?

We don't know anything yet, said Dorita.

Has anyone talked to Jules? I asked.

Warwick gave me a withering look.

Why? he asked. You think the kid did it? You want to do this pro bono now?

He had a point. I'd sort of forgotten that Jules's defense was a paying job. And our paycheck had just hit the road. Hard. Still, could we just leave Jules high and dry?

Has anybody talked to the twins? I asked.

Warwick threw up his arms.

They're at the police station, said Shumaker.

I looked at Dorita. She gave me a tiny nod. She knew what I was thinking.

I excused myself. Went to my office. I was a little surprised to find that it was still there. I called Butch. He wasn't available. I paged him. I knew he'd call back.

While I waited I reflected on the fact that Warwick hadn't physically attacked me as I came in the door. FitzGibbon, it appeared, hadn't called him to complain about our conversation of yesterday.

You would have thought he'd have called the minute we'd left. Two partners of the firm to whom he entrusted millions' worth of business, violating his trust? Practically accusing him of murder? It's a wonder he hadn't put out a hit on me.

Damn, I thought. For all I knew he had.

I needed to know the time of death.

Dorita came in just as the phone rang. It was Butch.

Butch, I said. I knew I could count on you.

Sure, Rick. No problem. But I can't talk.

Two quick questions, Butch. You in on this FitzGibbon thing?

Sure. Everybody's in on it. It's the biggest thing around here since Rockefeller.

Okay, just two things. Then maybe we can meet later.

Sure thing, Rick. But I don't know when. I'll have to call you.

All right. First thing, were the twins there?

When he fell?

Right.

Seems they were.

Okay, second thing. Exact time.

Ten thirty-four, he said.

They were at the office at ten thirty at night?

You said two questions, Rick.

Okay, Butch. That one was rhetorical. Didn't count. Call me when you can.

Will do.

I looked at Dorita. I nodded my head. The twins had been there. Ten thirty-four. In his office. I presumed his office. It was on that floor. And hours after we'd left.

All those hours to call Warwick.

But he hadn't.

Something had come up, Raul had told us.

It must have been something big.

So, Dorita said. Theories?

We spooked him into it.

Fear. Or remorse. Or both.

Ramon pushed him.

Raul pushed him.

They didn't want to wait for their inheritance.

A time-honored motive.

Jules pushed him.

Hm. Not with the twins there, he didn't.

He's in cahoots with the twins.

There you might be stretching it a bit.

He got drunk and fell.

Unlikely.

Too much of a coincidence?

It's hard to believe that it didn't have something to do with our conversation with him.

Yes. The problem being.

That if it did, it doesn't eliminate even one of the theories.

Exactly.

All we've got are theories.

Well, we still have our jobs.

Today.

Tomorrow?

Unlikely.

I just had a great idea, I said.

Yes?

Let's have a drink.

Rick?

Yes?

You've got a problem.

Thank you.

And anyway, do you think we should be letting time go by? Cold trail and all that?

It won't take long, I said, fishing in the cup of pencils on my desk for the small key that opened my bottom desk drawer.

You're kidding, right?

Would I kid you? I asked, pulling out a half-empty – well, in the circumstances half-full – fifth of Scotch and two small glasses.

Dorita made a face. But she drank hers down.

That felt good, I said, relishing the distraction of a good gut-burn.

Can't deny it.

Hey, I said, pouring myself a refill. I never got an answer. Has anybody talked to Jules?

He's at the station too.

They picked him up on this?

Well, wouldn't you? Closest blood relative? History of animosity? Suspect in recent murder?

Yeah, I guess so. Jesus, why didn't he call me?

Maybe he doesn't know your number.

He knows my number.

Maybe he doesn't want to see you.

That doesn't make any sense.

Anything make sense around here for the last month?

You've got a point there.

I usually do.

The little moron. Who else is going to help him?

I can't answer that question. Not enough information. It does, however, betray a rather excessive amount of self-regard.

Damn, I said.

What?

I got a call last night. Just before yours. I ignored it. Probably that was him. Calling from the station.

Could be.

I'm going down there.

Not without me, you aren't.

I didn't mean to imply otherwise.

Okay. Give me a few. I've got to make a couple of calls. Cancel a few things.

Dorita left. My chest felt tight. I thought about Steiglitz. Shit. I didn't want to think about Steiglitz. I didn't want to think about anything.

I eyed my empty shot glass. It looked lonely. I reintroduced it to some mediocre Scotch.

98.

WE FLAGGED A CAB. It smelled strangely of pickles. Dill, I thought.

I took that to be a good sign.

At the station there was a mob. Television trucks and vans lined the entire block. Reporters were shoving microphones into any face that moved.

The obligatory beefy boy in blue blocked the entrance to the station.

I'm Jules FitzGibbon's lawyer, I said.

Says who? he asked.

His cynicism was concealed under a thick layer of cynicism.

Says me, I said.

That ain't gonna do it, he said, standing his ground.

Butch Hardiman in there? I asked.

Butch? Maybe, he said.

Ask him, I said. He'll vouch for me.

He looked at me impassively for a moment. He took my name. Turned to a diminutive female cop.

Charlie, he said, come here.

She came over.

Hold these guys right here, he said. I've got to check something out.

Okay, she said. She stepped between us and the door. She put her legs apart. She put her arms on her hips. Right next to the gun.

We amused ourselves watching the police-cruiser flashers' red, white and blue turn the mob scene outside into a patriotic disco party.

Mr. Beefcake came back. He whispered something to Charlie. Charlie stepped aside. Mr. Beefcake gave us a nod. We stepped in.

Butch was waiting for us just inside the door. He didn't look happy.

Butch, I said. Why didn't somebody call me?

It's a zoo in here. I'm not sure you were the first thing on anyone's mind.

You've got a point. Where's Jules?

Last I heard he was in with Donegan. Give me a sec.

He went through the swinging doors to the back of the precinct house.

Donegan? Dorita asked.

I know him a bit, I said. He's a lifer. The kind of guy was born with a police-issue .38 strapped to his waist.

Ouch. Poor Mom.

I think you used that one already.

It's still funny.

Right. He's a big guy, with a bigger head. Not too bright, but dogged as hell. After twenty years they finally made him detective. He outlasted them.

Sounds charming.

Actually, he's an okay guy. I think.

I guess we'll find out.

Butch came back through the swinging doors.

Donegan says you can come back, he said. But the kid says he doesn't want to see you.

What?

That's what he says.

Did he give any reason?

No. Just said he doesn't want to see you.

A tiny tattooed thing flung itself around my neck, cried out, Mr. Redman! I'm so glad you're here!

I pried its arms off me. Asked it to calm down a bit.

Dorita raised her eyebrows.

Dorita, I said, this is Lisa. Lisa, my friend Dorita.

Friend? said Dorita.

Pleased to meet you, Lisa said, more demurely than the circumstances called for.

She held out a hand. Dorita took it.

The same, I'm sure, said Dorita, with a jaundiced glance my way.

They tell me Jules doesn't want to see me, I told Lisa.

Oh God, she said. He's been so weirded out by all this. He doesn't even know what he's saying. I'll go talk to him.

Okay, I said. I'd appreciate that.

She pushed through the swinging doors, back to the inner sanctum.

So, said Dorita, that's your little temptress.

Yes, indeed. Captivating, isn't she?

Other words come to mind.

Tiny and tattooed?

Sure. That, and way too young for you.

Oh, I don't know. She's legal. That's my bottom line.

I was afraid of that.

Lisa came out and beckoned to us.

We followed her back.

She seemed to know her way around the place.

She led us to an interrogation room. In the room were Donegan and Jules. Jules didn't look up. The front of his white T-shirt appeared to be streaked with blood.

Jules, I said, what happened to you?

Nothing, he said, without looking up.

He's been cutting himself again, Lisa whispered.

It's none of their goddamn business, Jules barked at her.

I looked at Donegan. He shook his head. It was clear that he was overmatched.

Can I have a few minutes alone with my client? I asked him.

Sure, he said, they're all yours.

On his way out he gave me a subtle shift of the head. Come out here for a second, it said. I followed him out.

Just thought you should know, he said. The kid's been . . .

I know. I saw the shirt. He does that.

You didn't see what's under the shirt. This kid isn't playing around. We got somebody watching. Just in case.

Okay. I got you. Listen, they haven't charged him or anything, have they?

Nothing new, anyway.

Donegan left. Gave me a wink on the way.

I had no idea what it meant.

When I got back into the room Lisa was sitting next to Jules, her arms around his neck.

Jules didn't react.

Jules, I said, I'm so sorry.

What about? he asked, with hooded eyes and a disturbingly calm air.

Your father. Look, I know you didn't always get along.

He snorted in derision.

But it's always tough, no matter what.

It's not tough. Nothing tough about it.

I looked at his blood-streaked shirt.

He didn't follow my lead. He looked steadily at me.

Jules, I said. I think I understand. I just want you to know that we're here to help you. If we can. Anything we can do.

Who's the we?

Oh. I'm sorry. This is Dorita. She's my partner. She's helping me out on your case.

My case? he asked with a sneer.

The Larry Silver case, I said gently.

I'm not worried about that.

That's good. That's good. Listen, Jules, what have they been doing with you here? Do they think you're a suspect in your father's death or something?

I don't fucking know what they're doing. They picked me up. They brought me here. That fathead cop's been asking me all kind of shit. Where I was last night. Where I was this morning. Where I was when I was born. All kinds of shit.

Did they arrest you? Read you your rights?

Nah. They asked me to come down. But they did it like if I said no they'd make me.

Then you can leave anytime you want, you know.

Sure, I know that.

Okay. And you don't have to talk to them.

I got nothing to hide.

That may be true, Jules, but they can twist things around. You shouldn't be talking to them. Especially without a lawyer. What did you tell them?

I didn't tell them shit.

About where you were last night. What did you tell them about that?

I told them the truth.

And what was that?

I was with Lisa.

She smiled and nodded at me.

Where?

Around.

Where around?

All over around. Here, there. Everywhere.

Jules. I'm trying to help you here. You don't have to play these games with me. I thought we got over that.

That was before.

Before what?

Before you started fucking with Lisa.

Jules! Lisa cried out.

I don't know what you're talking about, Jules, I said, with as much outrage as I could muster.

What are you talking about? echoed Lisa.

Never mind what I'm talking about, he said, looking straight at me. Just get the fuck out of here.

His look was not one that allowed for negotiation. I nodded at Dorita. We got up. I glanced back as we went out the door. He was still giving me the hairy eyeball. She was still clinging to his neck.

We went out front. We asked for Butch. It took a while.

Butch, I said when he finally appeared. Can you find out for me what's going on with Jules? Is he being treated as a suspect or something?

Everybody's a suspect, he said. Until the case is closed.

Yeah, yeah. I know that. But seriously?

I can't really say.

He gave me an apologetic shrug.

I looked around. The room was packed with cops. Reporters. Guys in raincoats. Folks whose function there I couldn't place. I gave Butch the benefit. Even if he wanted to tell me something, he couldn't do it there.

99.

WE WENT TO THE BAR across the street. The joint was crawling with reporters, technicians, hangers-on, scandalmongers. We found a relatively quiet spot in the back.

That's one fucked-up kid, I said.

Sure, said Dorita. And you'd be Mother Teresa on Valium in his situation.

Hey, I'm not judging. He's got a lot to deal with. But all the same. What's with this self-mutilation thing?

We all have our means of coping.

I guess.

Just because his is visible.

I suppose you're right.

Lung and liver lesions.

Not visible.

More deadly.

Can't argue.

Don't try.

Won't.

Okay, what now?

I don't have a clue.

Give up?

Right. Like you have that bone in your body.

I need two, she said. One for me and one for you.

Don't worry about me. I got a bone.

I'm not touching that one. Let's get back to the question.

Let's get hold of Butch. There was stuff he wasn't telling us.

Can you get him out of there?

I'll try.

I paged Butch. I didn't expect an immediate response. I didn't get one.

We felt helpless. We ordered another round.

Dorita asked about Steiglitz.

Later, I said.

She insisted.

I gave her the short version.

She wanted more.

Later, I said.

I changed the subject. I talked about basketball. Could the Knicks pick it up? Not just make the playoffs, but go far? Go all the way? That was a bit much to ask. But please, could we have a team that was fun to watch?

My cell phone rang.

Butch? I said.

Yo.

Can you get away?

Give me half an hour.

White Stallion?

I'll be there.

We're buying.

You're all heart.

Dorita put her hand on my knee. I felt electric pulses up my thigh. In spite of all the ruckus, my libido still was operational. Thank the Lord for small mercies.

We made our way to the White Stallion. Butch had beaten us there. He was drinking a beer at the bar. He looked exhausted.

Man, I said, you look exhausted.

What you see is what you get, he said.

Sorry, man. I don't want to add to your troubles.

Nothing next to yours, he said with his big smile.

Hey. Don't worry about that. I'm coping.

He looked at Dorita.

I see, he said.

Nice to see you too, Dorita said.

I changed the subject fast.

So Butch. Can you fill us in? What the hell is going on over there?

Chaos. Chaos is going on over there. Nobody's in charge. FitzGibbon was a big fucking cheese.

I think we knew that.

And now everybody's pointing fingers. Why didn't they follow up the Jules thing properly.

They're making a connection?

They don't know if there's a connection. They don't know anything. Problem is, everybody figured Jules was a lock for this Larry Silver thing. No point in wasting resources on it. But now they don't know. They're afraid somebody's going to find something they missed. The press is all over it like blackflies in North Bay.

North Bay? You been up there?

Nah. Just sounded good.

Good call. Okay. They have anything to make them think there's a connection?

How should I know?

I thought you were plugged in.

Plugged in to what? The circuits are all shorted out, Rick. The breakers are blown. It's dark in there.

Jesus, Butch, I never knew you were such a mean man with a metaphor.

I have my moments.

Listen, Butch, I said. Are the twins being held?

Not that I know of. Questioned.

Are they suspects?

Don't know. Really, I don't. Like I said, it's chaos in there.

Can you get us in to see them?

That's a tall order. That's a very tall order.

That wasn't the question.

You're right. Okay. I'll see what I can do.

Much obliged, I said, raising my glass.

Hey. I owe you.

I still didn't know what for.

Butch called minutes later. By the time he'd got back to the station house higher powers had intervened. Shut the place down like the Baghdad Green Zone. We were going to have to wait til the twins got out of there. Try to find a way to get them to talk to us.

I knew enough to leave that part to Dorita.

100.

I WENT HOME to get some sleep.

I didn't get much.

The phone rang. Dorita.

We've got an audience, she said.

Good work.

I know. Be there in an hour.

Where?

The Park Avenue Palace.

I'm on my way, I said.

I drank two cups of coffee. I grabbed a cab. It smelled of clove cigarette smoke.

I almost gagged.

When we got to the Palace, Ramon was at one end of the living room, Raul at the other. A detail that did not escape me. I asked Ramon to join us at the sofa end of the room. He walked reluctantly over, perched on some kind of uncomfortable over-carved antique. Raul remained seated on his throne.

Raul, Ramon, I said, choosing the order deliberately, I know it's a rough time.

Ramon looked at me impassively. Raul searched assiduously in his pockets for something. A lighter, it turned out. He lit a Marlboro Light.

You know I'm here for Jules, I said. He's my client. I still have an obligation to do the best for Jules. You understand that, right?

Raul nodded. Ramon remained impassive.

I know you must be very tired. We just have a couple of questions for you. You've probably answered them already, more than once. But we weren't there. So I hope you'll indulge us for a few minutes.

Please, said Raul with his charming smile. Ask away.

Ramon said nothing.

I turned to Raul.

Truffles, I said. What's your position on truffles?

His smile went a little crooked.

I'm not sure I understand you, he said.

Epicurean delight? Or Frog fraud?

He paused a second to figure that one out. Then the charming smile came back.

I think some thinly shaved white truffles can add to a dish, he said with a small chuckle.

Interesting, I said. I incline more to the Frog fraud theory. I mean, think about the taste, in isolation.

Kind of root-cellary, said Dorita.

Precisely, I said. You know, if potatoes were as allegedly rare as truffles, I bet we'd be paying ten dollars an ounce for them, too.

Maybe so, said Raul, chuckling. Maybe so.

Ramon looked confused.

I was beginning to peg him as the stupid one.

I was feeling good. I'd established some rapport.

I wasn't fooling myself. This Raul was a slick one. He might well have had his own reasons to seem cooperative. But that was just fine. I could use that.

Guys, I said, making sure to include some eye contact for Ramon. I need your help.

Whatever we can do, said Raul.

Ramon said nothing. Still trying to figure out that truffle thing.

Can you tell us what happened with Mr. FitzGibbon yesterday? Everything you can remember?

We did tell the police several times already, Raul said, shading the smile into apologetic mode.

I understand. I know it's a pain. But I often find that people remember different things when they're talking to civilians. The police set up a certain dynamic.

Ah, said Raul thoughtfully. An interesting notion.

With more than one application, I said. But we can discuss that later. Do you mind going over it again once more?

No, not at all, said Raul.

I almost believed him.

Fire away, I said.

We were working.

I'm sorry to interrupt so soon, I said, but what exactly were you working on?

I directed my question at Ramon. I was still searching for a way to co-opt him. He was like a Sphinx, I'm tempted to say. But he was more like a brick.

We were working on the plans for our new club.

I see. You're starting a new club of your own?

That's the plan.

Okay, you were at Mr. FitzGibbon's offices, working on the plans for your new club. Was anyone else there?

No.

I glanced at Ramon. His scowl appeared to have deepened, just a bit.

Where in the building were you?

We were in a conference room, on the same floor as Mr. FitzGibbon's office.

I noted the incongruous use of the patronymic. I also remarked that Raul, though speaking in the plural first person, never took his eyes off me. Never looked at Ramon. To include him in the conversation. To gauge the degree of consent he was getting for his collective pronouncements.

And he was there too?

Who?

Mr. FitzGibbon.

In his office, yes. He had some deal he was working on. Some takeover thing.

Was it normal for him to work that late?

Sure. All the time. He never stopped working.

Okay, I said. So you're working. He's working. Then what?

Then we heard the sirens.

The sirens?

Ambulances. Police. Fire trucks.

He'd jumped?

Apparently. Raul's smile had turned sardonic. But we didn't know that yet.

I'm sorry, I said. I just wanted to make sure what you were talking about.

Raul looked at me like a lizard looks at . . . well, like a lizard looks at just about anything.

Then what happened? I asked.

We went to his office. To see what was going on. There are no windows in the conference room, where we were. His office isn't far away. He wasn't there. The French doors, the doors to the balcony, were open. We went out, to look down into the street. To see what was happening. There were an awful lot of sirens. We thought there might have been a terrorist attack or something.

I see.

I looked at Ramon.

He nodded his grudging assent.

And then?

We still didn't know where Father was.

So it was 'Father' now.

We looked down. And then it started to occur to us. What might have happened.

Raul was slowing down. He was in grieving son mode. I looked at Ramon. He was staring at the floor.

I'm sorry, I said. I know this isn't easy. Can you tell me what happened then?

We found the note.

There was a note?

They both looked at me.

You didn't know about the note? asked Raul.

I do now. What did it say?

Raul hesitated.

The police asked us not to tell anyone that, he said.

I understand, I said. Where was it?

On his desk.

Handwritten?

No. It was a printout.

A printout?

Of an e-mail.

His suicide note was a printout of an e-mail?

Yes.

For the first time, they both looked uncomfortable.

I let the silence sit for a while. Raul looked straight at me. His gaze was steady, but his confidence was wavering. I could feel it. Ramon was looking at his shoes.

Who was it to? I asked.

The e-mail?

Yes.

We can't tell you that.

The police asked you not to tell me that?

They asked us not to tell anyone.

Ramon nodded at his shoes.

Had Mr. FitzGibbon said anything to you yesterday, any other time, that might help us understand why he did this?

They both shook their heads. An almost convincing display of dismay.

Well, said Raul, we appreciate your concern.

Our time was up.

Dorita and I exchanged glances.

We needed that note.

101.

I HUNTED DOWN BUTCH. I got him on his cell phone. I asked him what he knew about the note. The e-mail. Not much, he told me.

Who was the e-mail addressed to?

I don't know.

Can we get a copy?

Whoa, Rick, he said. That's a tall order. That's a really fucking tall order.

I know, Butch. I hate to push it. You've been so great. But I think we're on the verge. One last piece of the puzzle. That's all we need. I just know this is connected to Larry Silver. I can feel it in my bones.

Dorita raised her eyebrows.

I ignored her.

If this doesn't crack it, I said, I won't ask any more favors. Promise.

Crack what, Rick? The guy threw himself out a window.

Maybe, I said. Maybe not. And whether he did or not, there's still the 'why' of it. You know that.

There was a note.

So what? Anyone can type a note.

Yeah, yeah. I know. It's not that I don't want to do you the favor. You know I want to do it for you. But I'm not sure it's possible. Shit. I don't think I can get near it.

Can you at least find out what's in it? Can you ask around?

I'll see what I can do, Rick.

You're a prince, man. I'll buy you a beer.

You're all heart.

I know. It holds me back.

I told Dorita what Butch had said.

Next step is to track down Jules, she said.

Maybe we should give him some time to settle down.

I'm not sure there's time now.

Why not?

I don't know. It's a feeling. People are dying.

One person died.

Two, counting Larry Silver.

Okay, two.

Things come in threes, Ricky.

And I thought you had such a scientific mind.

Everything in its place, darling. I'm not saying I'm right. I'm just saying I have a feeling.

Let's go with your feeling, I said. There's not much else to go with.

I knew you'd see it my way.

I knew you knew that.

I guess you win then.

Finally, I said. Hey, don't you think the way to Jules goes through Lisa? And isn't she the weak link? Why don't we try her first?

I'm not sure I agree that she's the weak link. Just because she's a woman? Is that what you're saying? I mean, we're dealing with a guy who slices up his gut with razor blades.

Good point. But I've dealt with both of them, and I'm telling you, he's a tough nut to crack. She, on the other hand, seems to be constantly on the verge of breaking down, telling me something. Just my feeling.

Now *you've* got a feeling?

Yup. One of my very own.

My, you've become so sensitive in your old age.

It happens.

So it's your feeling against mine?

No. I figured my reasoning was so compelling you'd be obliged to agree.

Ah, I'm quite sure you're wrong about that. But I'm willing to do it your way, if only to create the illusion that you've finally made a contribution to the enterprise.

I'll ignore that.

Suit yourself.

Where we'd find Jules, we'd no doubt find Lisa. Of course, they'd be together. An inconvenient detail. Back to Plan A.

We went to the loft.

We looked at the alley on the way.

It looked like an alley.

We rang the bell.

We were buzzed in. No questions asked. All of a sudden everybody seemed to want to talk to us.

I put it down to my natural charm.

Saw you from the balcony, Jules said when he opened the door.

He was sullen, but not overtly hostile. His anger seemed to have played itself out. Something about getting out of the police station, maybe.

Lisa was there, preparing drinks.

Hi, Lisa, I said.

Hi, she replied, without turning around. Familiarity or contempt, I wasn't sure. Perhaps a bit of both.

You got a lot of nerve coming here, Jules said in a flat voice.

You let me in, I replied.

I did, he shrugged. You got me there.

It was time for tough love. Nothing else was working.

Listen, Jules, I don't know what you were talking about at the station house. 'Fucking with Lisa.' I haven't been fucking with Lisa. We just talked once. Before you got here.

Sure.

Let's get this cleared up. I don't need *you* fucking with *me*. I don't need you at all, actually. We don't have your father to pay the bills anymore. I should send you back to the public defender. But I'm not like that. I finish what I start. I'd think you might appreciate that a bit. And *you* sure as hell need *me*. What the fuck else do you have?

He seemed to think about that.

I don't need shit, he said.

Fine. That's your attitude, good luck to you. Have fun in Sing Sing.

I got up to leave. Dorita gave me an exasperated look. Setting up to play good cop.

She didn't have to.

Okay, okay, said Jules. Sit the fuck down.

He shrugged. He spread his hands. A gesture that could be taken as a small show of humility. A reluctant welcome.

I sat down.

What? he said.

What what?

What you want to know?

Lisa came over with the drinks. Scotch for me. Cosmo for Dorita.

Oh, said Dorita, my favorite. Thanks. How did you know?

Look at you, said Lisa. It was a cosmo or a Tom Collins. I had a fifty-fifty shot.

Dorita was speechless. It was a rare and disconcerting sight. Though not unpleasant, in its way.

You've been a bartender, I said to Lisa.

Sure, she said. I've been everything.

I turned back to Jules.

What we'd like to know, I said, is everything you know about your father's death. Every detail. God is in the details.

Ain't no God.

It's just an expression, Jules. Try not to be so literal-minded.

I'll work on it.

Good. Now, can you tell me everything you know?

I don't know shit.

Jesus, Jules. This is getting a bit boring. Do you always have to say that?

I say the truth. Sorry you don't like it.

You're telling us you don't know a single thing that might shed any light on how your father died?

Nope. Don't know shit.

Jules. You and I both know that's not true.

What the fuck do *you* know?

It was time to pull a bluff. Nothing else was working. Ingratiation. Intimidation. Subtlety. The kid was too messed up to respond to the usual techniques. I had to take a chance. Go with a hunch. A stab in the dark. If it didn't work, I'd find a way to recover. Turn it into a joke. Whatever.

I know you were there, I said.

It stopped him cold.

He stared at me. Lisa came over and sat next to him. She put her arms around his neck. She didn't look at us.

I stared back at him. I waited.

The fuck you say? he said at last.

You were there, I repeated.

Where?

I laughed. I didn't elaborate. The room had grown cold.

Get the fuck out, he said. Get the fuck out of here.

That again? I said. It's not going to work, Jules. I'm here to help you. You can't seem to get that into your head. I'm your lawyer. I need to know the facts. And I might leave here, but I'm not going away.

We'll see about that, he said.

He said it with an intensity that I felt as a physical blow. My body tensed. What door had I opened here? What rock had I turned over?

It was a threat. A physical threat.

He got up. Started walking toward me.

An immediate physical threat.

Okay, okay, I said. We're leaving.

We got the hell out of there.

Where in God's name did you get *that?* Dorita asked once we were safely in the street.

I don't know, I said. It just came to me. I didn't think it out. He was just so fucking calm about everything. And this is a kid who cuts himself. It didn't make sense. There had to be something more. And why wouldn't he tell us where he was? Why wouldn't he take the opportunity to show he didn't have anything to do with his father's death? He knows he's a prime suspect, with all that anger in him. And then it hit me. The phone calls. Raul and Ramon were using FitzGibbon's offices. The phone calls didn't have to be to FitzGibbon. They could have been to Raul, or Ramon. So I took a stab. What the hell.

I'm in awe.

About time.

So, my little genius, what were the phone calls about?

I haven't figured that out yet. But I feel close. I feel really damn close.

102.

I WENT HOME. I had to see Kelly. Make sure she was all right.

She seemed to be all right.

I met Dorita at the White Stallion.

Where to from here? she asked.

The eternal question.

It may be eternal, but it still needs an answer.

The weak link. Where's the next weak link?

Let's think about it.

I'll need a Scotch for that.

Why did I know you'd say that?

Because you're brilliant.

True, true.

Almost as brilliant as me.

Hah. One lucky guess and suddenly you're Albert Fucking Einstein.

Winners make their own luck.

We'll see.

It really all seems to revolve around the three brothers, doesn't it? I said.

Can't deny that. And Jules isn't talking.

You are correct, ma'am.

Raul is too damn slick.

Right.

So that leaves Ramon.

Who never says a damn thing.

True enough. And you have to wonder why.

Because he's too smart to say anything?

Contrary to the evidence.

Because he's too damn stupid.

Correct. At least, an excellent working hypothesis.

Okay, and that buys us?

A weak link.

Waiting to be broken.

We toasted the stupid twin. We made a plan. We had another drink. We were oiled for battle.

Dorita called Ramon's cell phone number.

Ramon, she said. Dorita Reed. So nice to hear your voice.

I rolled my eyes. Surely he wasn't *that* stupid.

She glared me down.

We've been making some inquiries, she said into the phone. We'd like to talk with you about a couple more things. Any chance we could have a few minutes of your time?

I watched her listen.

I see, she said. I understand. But Ramon, I really think you should make the time.

She listened some more.

Ramon, she said. You need to think carefully. We've got some information. Something you really need to hear.

She listened.

She smiled a sneaky smile at me. She'd got the fish on the hook.

She hung up.

The Club at eleven, she said. The VIP room.

Wow. Can we get lap dances?

If you fancy a lap dance from a guy named Bruce.

I'll consider that.

Hey, we have time for another drink.

Two, at least.

Fancy that.

103.

BY THE TIME WE GOT TO THE CLUB we were buzzed and pumped. Or pumped and buzzed. I wasn't sure. I was too buzzed.

Igor met us at the door. It seemed like old times. He escorted us to the VIP room. I had to admit they'd done a nice job. Plush seats of various sizes were scattered about, in a calculatedly random way. Huge glass tubes with a passing resemblance to giant lava lamps stretched from floor to ceiling. They were all aglow with a purple velvet light. It suffused the room. Strange things were happening inside them. Things that looked different from every angle and distance. Posing here and there were largely naked men and women, each as dark and delectable as crème brûlée.

Ramon was at the back of the room. Seated at the only couch that had a full-size table associated with it. The business nook.

We sat down. Each on a mushroom-like stool that sank with our weight into a comfortable cup. Whoosh. Immediately we were transported. Into the world of the spoiled and dissolute.

The spoiled part was new to me.

It was early enough that the music wasn't cosmically loud. We could talk.

Hi, said Dorita.

Hello, said Ramon, with his usual defensive air.

Good to see you, I said, extending my hand, not without a frisson of dread.

Well founded, it turned out. I got the limp, wet hand again. I had to force a smile.

He sat impassively.

Dorita took the lead.

Ramon, she said. We've been talking to people. Looking around.

He said nothing. His face betrayed not an atom of reaction.

Funny thing, she said. We talked to Jules.

His left eye twitched.

Turns out he was there.

There?

When Mr. FitzGibbon died.

He didn't take his eyes off her. I detected a tightening of the muscles in his neck.

We were kind of wondering, Dorita went on, what you might be able to tell us about that.

And maybe, I added, why it was that you and Raul seem to have forgotten to mention it.

He didn't say a thing. He flagged one of the girls. She brought us drinks. Ramon a Perrier.

Dumb. But careful.

Well? Dorita said.

He still just stared at her.

Damn. I was right. We were talking to a brick.

Dorita bore down.

Ramon, she said. The silent treatment's not going to do it for you. You were there. Raul was there. Jules was there. Somehow Mr. FitzGibbon managed to throw himself off a thirty-third-floor balcony despite the presence of the three of you. Somebody's going to have to explain it. If it's not you, it'll be one of the others. I'm not sure you want that.

Ramon furrowed his brow. It made him look angry and mean. But I was beginning to understand. It was just his natural condition. Confused.

Do you agree? asked Dorita, soft and understanding.

I . . . I don't.

You don't agree?

I don't know.

Dorita tried again. She repeated the whole thing, in words of one syllable.

Ramon thought for a while. If it could be called thought.

I can't tell you anything, he said.

Why not? asked Dorita. Are you afraid?

That got him animated. He sat up straight. He glared at her.

Ramon, I said. I need a minute with you.

I took him aside. I whispered in his ear.

Where's the bat? I asked.

What?

The baseball bat.

He stared at me. I caught a hint of understanding in his gaze.

The cops never found the murder weapon, did they, Ramon?

I don't know what you're talking about, he mumbled.

Then how do I know it was a baseball bat?

Silence.

You might want to ask yourself that, Ramon.

He turned and left the room.

I sat back down next to Dorita.

Buy me another drink, I said. He might be a while.

You sure you don't want Bruce over there? she asked. I might be able to swing you a discount.

Not tonight. I'm a little Bruced out.

Ah, too bad. That's quite a Bruce they've got.

I can see that. And yet I'll pass. Just this once.

What did you say to Ramon? she asked.

I asked him where the baseball bat was.

What baseball bat?

The one that killed Larry Silver.

I never heard anything about a baseball bat.

Neither did I, but I have the crime scene photos. Shape of the wound. Sure looks like a baseball bat to me. So I took another stab.

Keep that up and I might actually start admiring you.

Careful what you ask for, I said.

How'd he react? she asked.

Before I could answer, Igor appeared.

We looked at him. He looked at us.

Mr. FitzGibbon is indisposed, he said.

I'm shocked to hear that, I said. Please wish him a speedy recovery for us.

Thank you.

Listen, Dorita interjected, can we talk to you for a moment?

Igor gave her a lizard eye. Blank and ready to catch a fly.

We're dealing with a murder case, she said. It's a very serious business. I'm not sure that you want the Club to be tainted with this kind of thing.

Igor maintained his professionally neutral expression.

I only have one question, she said. And all I'm asking is for one honest answer. You could lie to us. But the consequences might not be pleasant, if you do.

His stare was no less blank.

So here's the question. Did Ramon say anything to you back there? Anything other than that he was 'indisposed'? I'm not asking for anything more. Anything else you saw or knew or heard before. I'm only asking you about tonight. Right now. What you heard. What he said.

Damn. The babe was good. Giving him an easy out. Even if Ramon hadn't actually said anything back there, the guy could say he had, tell us what he knew that way. Without implicating himself, taking any risk. Nice move.

Igor still didn't respond.

Listen, I said, lurching into bad-cop mode. We can call our connections, have the cops descend on this place like flies on shit. Trust me, it won't be pleasant. And it won't be good for business. Your boss won't be happy. But we'll make you a deal. You tell us what Ramon said, we won't make the call. Deal?

It's got nothing to do with me, he said.

We understand that, said Dorita. No problem. You tell us what he said, your name won't come up.

Igor looked at us each in turn.

We waited.

He only said one thing, he said at last.

Yes? said Dorita.

He said, 'Fucking Veronica.'

'Fucking Veronica'?

Yes.

As in, 'that fucking Veronica'?

Right.

That's the whole thing? she asked.

That's all he said? I echoed.

That's all.

Dorita looked at me. I looked at her.

Veronica.

Jesus Christ on a stick. Why hadn't we thought of that before?

104.

FITZGIBBON'S ONE TRUE LOVE, said Dorita once we reached the street.
The twins' adoptive mommy.
Jules's stepmom.
Cherchez la stepmom?
Damn, she said. How blind have we been?
The one person we've never talked to.
Who's connected to everyone.
The linchpin.
The hub of the wheel.
The cliché of the week.
How stupid could we be?
Blind.
We're giving Ray Charles a run for his money, she said.
You couldn't have come up with something more original?
It's been a tough day.
I can't argue with that. So, where the hell is she?
The sixty-four-million-dollar question.
Thousand.
Whatever. We find her, it's all over. I can feel it in my bones. To coin a phrase.
Her husband just committed suicide, I agreed, and not only hasn't she showed up, nobody's even mentioned her.
If it smells like a fish.
Then it's fishy.
Exactly. I guess.
Okay. Where's Veronica?
Unfortunately, we can't ask FitzGibbon.
We could try, I suggested.
I'm not into the séance thing anymore.
Me neither. He could have killed her.
Committed suicide out of remorse.
Certainly the simplest explanation.
They had an argument.
Not inconceivable.

She told him she's found a new man.

Bronzed, half her age, I mused.

Looks good in a Speedo.

She flaunts him.

FitzGibbon flies into a rage.

Throttles her.

Or, more in character, hires somebody to kill her.

Ramon? I asked.

Could be.

Mr. Security.

Yes. And that might explain why everybody's acting so weird.

They're all in on it?

Well, at least they all know, she said. How could they not know? Mom vanishes one day? We've hardly heard a word about her from anyone. Jules's hated stepmom. He'd want her gone. The twins' adoptive mom. Maybe they hated her too.

Who knows?

Or at least it would be convenient for them if she were gone.

Eliminates an heir, doesn't it?

Heiress.

Right.

A whole new bag of motives to play with.

It feels like Christmas.

Who's been naughty and all that.

Right. Okay. Where to start?

Fire up the laptop, she said.

Good timing, I said, as Starbucks hove into view.

First I called Vinnie Price. Woke him up.

Jesus, he said, is it that important?

Yes, I said. And anyway, that's an inappropriate question.

He laughed.

I asked him to get what he could get on one Veronica FitzGibbon, née . . . née what? We had no clue. Man, what artful detectives we were turning out to be. Veronica FitzGibbon, then.

Check it out, I said. Get what you can get.

I fired up the laptop.

There was some gossip column stuff on the Internet. She'd had a tiff with FitzGibbon. Public stuff. Yelling and screaming. Cutlery. Glassware.

The usual. She'd decided to take a cruise. Get away from it all. FitzGibbon. The big city. The stress. The pollution.

Interesting, I said.

Très, said Dorita.

Skipped town.

Apparently.

We tracked Veronica through some personal data sites. Not strictly legal. She'd left the country, all right. A Norwegian cruise ship. Off to the Caribbean. From there to Europe.

Vinnie Price called back. There was a credit card trail. She'd spent a bloody fortune along the way. She'd boarded a ship for the return journey. From Marseille.

Then the trail vanished.

Not a sign. No more credit card receipts. No nothing.

I asked Vinnie where the credit card bills went to.

FitzGibbon, he said.

Interesting.

Just because we didn't have anything after Marseille didn't mean there wasn't anything there. It was hardly likely that we'd found all the traces in two hours. Maybe she'd maxed out the credit card, switched to another one. Or cash. But it was curious. Tracing her movements had been so easy. It was like trailing a moose through city streets. A big, wealthy moose. And then, nothing. She vanished.

Dead, said Dorita.

You think?

I do.

Those bones again?

They're very good bones.

I've never denied it. Cheekbones, especially.

You're too kind.

I am. And it certainly fits the evidence. Still.

Still?

It fits the receipts, I said. The official trail. And there's a whole lot else it fits. Such as FitzGibbon. They have an argument. She takes off. The whole thing's on his tab. He's getting the bills. She's the love of his life. He gets all misty every time her name comes up. She disappears. All of a sudden, no more charges to the card. No trace of her. She's supposed to be back. She isn't. He doesn't call the cops? He says nothing about it to me? To anyone? It doesn't compute.

Unless he killed her.

Killed himself in remorse.

Like I said.

Like I said.

Okay, let's not fight about it. We'll divvy up the spoils later.

But that would mean the twins were in on it too.

Plausible.

Otherwise, wouldn't *they* have raised the alarm?

He could have had some cover story.

She joined the Carmelites.

The ones with the vow of silence?

Right. Except they sing.

Singing nuns? Wow. Sure. Mucho plausible. I'll check out the singing nun sites on the Internet.

Let's hold off on that for a minute, I said.

I'm holding.

Let's remember, Ramon was the source.

So even if he didn't do it himself, he knows something.

Well, not necessarily. It came through Igor, remember?

True. But let's stick with the simple explanation.

For now.

For now.

But.

But what?

But if what Ramon knows is that FitzGibbon had killed his wife, why wouldn't he just come out and tell us? FitzGibbon's not in any position to exact retribution now.

A good point, Dorita said.

And we can't ask him, I said. FitzGibbon, that is.

Another dead end. So to speak.

Another fucking brick wall.

Okay. But we're farther down the road than yesterday.

Maybe. One more dead body that we can't explain. What a triumph. We had one. We had two. Now we have three.

Told you so.

How did I know you were going to say that?

And they're all connected.

How do you know that? I asked.

I don't. But they have to be. It's just too much of a coincidence. All these bodies piling up. There's got to be something connecting them.

I think we're into the realm of speculation here, counselor.

Maybe so. But let's make it informed speculation. Where haven't we looked? There's got to be a dusty secret hiding in some corner somewhere.

Another one.

Something too obvious to notice, maybe.

Just like the last one.

The data's piling up. There's a pattern in there. There has to be. We've just got to find it. Write the new stuff down.

Watson and Crick, I said.

That's us, she agreed. Write it down.

I took out some blank cards. I wrote the new stuff down. I was surprised. Ten new cards. Jesus. A lot of new data.

I sorted the new cards into the deck. I spread them out. We looked at one card after another. We generated a lot of blank looks between us. We had another drink. We thought about stuff. Loose ends. Weak links. Where to go to next.

I pulled a card. Two names.

I tossed it to Dorita.

We talked to them already.

That was then. This is now.

Good point. We have more material.

Time passes. Attitudes change.

Right, she said. Let's give it a shot.

Fine. You go see the girlfriend again.

Sarah.

Cherchez la femme.

If you insist.

Me, I'll go home. I've got to get back to Kelly.

What, you're not going to go try to get something more out of your junkie friend?

Serge? Are you kidding? We'd be lucky just to find him alive. After Sarah you can go *cherchez la junkie* too, if you like. I'm going home.

Your French is so bad it's giving me a hernia.

So go herniate. Hey, I like that. 'Go herniate.' I think I'll use that. Next time I run into Warwick.

Dorita laughed. She leaned over. She kissed me. Her mouth was soft and yielding.

The contrast with her personality was striking.

105.

KELLY AND I BAKED BREAD. We watched old episodes of *Family Guy*. The place was warm. We made some Chinese soup. We loved to make Chinese soup. I tried not to remember that it was four days til the preliminary hearing.

We laughed. We ate. We joked.

The investigation could wait. Who was I fooling, anyway? I was no investigator. I was a dad. The little shit probably did it anyway.

My cell phone rang. It was Dorita.

Where the hell are you? she asked.

Home.

Still? Jesus. I should have known. I'm coming over.

I'm not sure ...

See you in a few.

Damn.

Dorita's coming over, I said to Kelly.

Okay, she said.

You're sure? I asked.

Sure I'm sure, she said. Why not? She can have some soup.

I couldn't read her.

By the time Dorita got there we were working on the sorbet. Chocolate walnut.

We'd kept some soup warmed on the stove.

Dorita didn't look to be in a soup and sorbet mood.

I've got it, she said.

You've got it, I replied. Great. Have some soup.

You're kidding. Didn't you hear me? I said I've got it. I've got the last piece of the puzzle.

Okay, okay. What is it?

Here's the scoop. It took me awhile, but I tracked her down.

The girlfriend?

Sarah.

Sarah. Right. And?

Quite a number.

I think you said that last time.

I may have. Anyway, it still applies. And I got something, darling. Something good.

You've outdone yourself.

More than I can say for *your* day's work.

I can't deny it. You win this round.

Just wait. I think I won the whole damn war.

I'll gracefully concede.

You'd better. Or I'll . . .

She looked at Kelly.

Okay, said Kelly. You can stop there. I'm going to Peter's.

Sorry, I said.

Don't worry about it, Dad, she said, heading for the door.

I wasn't entirely sure what she meant.

All right, I said to Dorita. Can we get to the bloody point?

The point is, said Dorita, that it had nothing to do with poker.

Meaning?

Larry supposedly went to Jules's place to collect on a poker debt. You remember that, don't you, lunkhead?

I love you too. Yes, I remember it. Haven't managed to verify that there even was a game, though.

That's probably because there wasn't one. Poker had nothing to do with it.

Nothing?

Nothing.

Now that *is* interesting. What did it have to do with?

Larry knew something.

Yes?

Sarah didn't know what. But whatever it was, Larry thought it was going to make him rich.

A shakedown?

Precisely.

Yet more interesting. What did he know, exactly?

You're not listening. She didn't know. He didn't tell her. But it was something big. Something really big.

Well. I'm not sure that you've exactly busted the case wide open here, darling. I'm not even sure you're right about the poker thing.

What do you mean?

So Larry had something on Jules. Why couldn't it be something to do with poker? Some scam they pulled?

You really know how to keep your eye on the ball, don't you.

Okay. Right. Doesn't matter, does it. Whatever it was, it does throw a new light on things.

Whoa. Slow down. Let me catch up with you.

Oh, shut up. Have some sorbet.

She had some sorbet.

Okay, I said. Larry knew something. Who can tell us what Larry knew?

Jules, for sure.

He wouldn't even tell me the truth about the poker game, the telephone calls. I don't think. He's either hiding something, or he's built himself a very thick wall.

The twins?

Maybe. But we still don't have anything concrete to connect them to Larry Silver.

Lisa?

Lisa. Yes. How could she not know?

It explains her protectiveness.

Well, it's not clear that needs explanation. But yes. And, she's definitely a weak link.

Maybe the only one we've got left.

Let's go for it.

We've got to get to her away from Jules this time, though.

Yes.

I'll take care of that.

I knew you would.

106.

WE AGREED TO MEET at the White Stallion. Dorita would have Lisa with her. If she didn't, we'd have to go to Plan B. Whatever that was.

I got there early. I drank only mineral water. It was a sacrifice I was willing to make. Just this once.

I amused myself by taking notes on the other patrons. Pretending they were suspects. Writing down my observations on index cards. Hell, maybe I'd write a book.

I was intrigued by a tall, thin guy, with a cowboy look. Pointy boots. Well-worn jeans. Deeply tanned face, lined with a road map of serious living. He was rolling his own cigarettes from a leather pouch.

A guy more out of place in New York City would be hard to find.

Then I noticed that he was talking to himself. Quietly. But angrily.

Ah, I corrected myself. He fits right in.

I was about to interrupt his conversation, to glean more details for my index card, when Dorita arrived. And there with her, looking small and lost, was Lisa.

Hey, I said to Dorita.

You know Lisa, she said.

Hi Lisa. Good to see you.

Lisa looked at me with pleading eyes.

Hi, she said softly.

I've filled Lisa in, said Dorita. She's here to talk with us.

She gave Lisa a motherly smile.

Dorita was a woman of many guises.

Let that be a warning to you, I thought to myself.

We moved to an isolated table. Lisa had a gin and tonic. This was good.

Dorita chatted with Lisa. I listened. Dorita was going with the girl stuff. Stuff Lisa could relate to. Nipple piercing. That kind of stuff. They both seemed quite sophisticated in the area.

This gave me pause.

But hey, it was working. Lisa was warming up.

In fact, it was ridiculously easy. In Lisa's world, somebody engaging and warm, somebody who spoke your language and also cared about what you had to say, was so rare that it came as a revelation. You embraced it, you followed it. Or you didn't. And if you didn't, the memory would haunt you forever. The opportunity lost. The warm forgiving world you'd been invited into once, just once, gone in a puff of arrogance born of insecurity, misplaced anger, stupidity.

So, if you cultivated that. If you nurtured the fear of missing that moment. You could make someone like Lisa do whatever you wanted.

Which was where the cults came from.

So we used that thing. The sad and ugly weakness of the lifelong victim.

Did the ends justify the means?

I left that for the philosophers. Well, the real philosophers. We needed some goddamn answers.

I watched with admiration as Dorita pulled Lisa into her orbit. They laughed. They commiserated. They nudged each other. They made jokes at my expense. I was sitting in as surrogate for the male.

And then Dorita sprung the trap.

And what about Veronica? she asked, out of the blue.

Lisa looked at me. At Dorita. She looked as scared, as helpless as a rabbit in the clutches of a hawk. I felt bad for her. But I also was elated. In her face was the proof. That we were on to something. That the damn thing might be solved. Right here. Right now.

I looked at Dorita with admiration. She ignored me.

Lisa, she said quietly. You're not answering me.

Lisa looked at her with a new and sudden loathing. Her face went hard.

Fuck you, she said.

Veronica and Larry Silver, said Dorita. They're connected. We know that, Lisa. Lisa, save yourself. It's not right, what Jules's done to you. Lisa, he's taken over your life. He's made you his accomplice. It's not right. You have your own life to live.

But we'd lost her.

Fuck you, she spat again.

She grabbed her bag, her sad, incongruous canvas bag, a cartoon drawing on it. Lisa Simpson. She ran out of the bar.

I looked at Dorita.

We seem to have hit a nerve, I said.

Dorita nodded. She didn't look happy.

I knew what she meant.

We sat in silence for a while. We sipped our drinks.

I'm not sure I liked the way you were talking about my client, I said.

He's not your client anymore.

Yes he is. He hasn't fired me yet. He just hates me.

Dorita rolled her eyes, went into another funk.

Okay, she said finally. What does it mean?

Let's start with what's absolutely clear. Veronica's at the center of this.

Yes.

Ramon. Lisa.

Yes.

I think it's safe to say that the best working hypothesis is that Jules killed Larry Silver after all. But not over poker winnings. Because Larry Silver showed up to blackmail him.

Because Larry Silver, somehow, knew something about Veronica.

Exactly.

And where to go from here is the question. Tell the cops?

I don't think I'm quite ready to do that. Like I said, Jules is still my, our, client. Until he officially fires us. Or we fire him. We're not doing this for the cops. We're doing this as part of our obligation to our client. Sure, we suspect he's guilty, now. But we don't know that for sure. And even if we did, unless we knew that someone else was in imminent danger, we couldn't tell them. Even if we wanted to.

So let's keep going. I mean, the preliminary hearing's in two days.

It is?

It is.

Goddamn. I was even more right than I thought.

Must be a novel feeling for you.

107.

WE SLEPT ON IT.

I slept on it at my place.

Dorita at hers.

It seemed like the right thing to do.

In the morning we met at Starbucks. Being at the office helped me think.

We reviewed the bidding. We chewed over the alternatives.

We listed the candidates. We weighed the options.

We chewed the fat. We crunched the bones.

We picked the lint off the jacket.

We ditched the metaphors.

We sat in silence for a while.

Butch called with some news. The preliminary autopsy result on FitzGibbon. Death caused by the fall. No doubt about that. No signs of pre-fall trauma. Though after a fall from that height, it was hard to tell.

No surprises there, I said.

No.

Doesn't rule out being pushed.

No, it doesn't, he said. And also . . .

Yes?

The blood work was awfully weird.

Out with it. You're killing me here.

All kinds of shit. Mescaline. LSD. Meth. Whatever.

What the fuck?

Yeah. That's what we all said.

This was the big cheese on the mayor's antidrug task force, for Christ's sake.

Exactly. And anyway, just not the type in general.

Man. Another fucking curveball. Wait a minute.

I pulled out a blank index card. Filled it with scribbles.

Okay, I said, listen, we need you now. We need you on the team. I know you've got your job to do. I'm not asking you to compromise your job. But we need you. Come over and talk to us, anyway. We've got to make sense of all this shit. We're just about there. I know it. But the last step, this is going to be heavy. We need your brain. We might need your muscle, too.

He hesitated. I argued. He wavered. I persuaded.

He came to Starbucks. It started all over again. He had a duty to the force. He couldn't just become a cowboy vigilante. He wasn't Clint Eastwood. He had a job. A mortgage. Why couldn't we just go to his boss with the stuff we got from Sarah? They'd follow it up. Hell, it was dynamite.

Besides the problem of our obligations to our client, which he understood, it wasn't dynamite, yet, I explained. It was the scent of dynamite. We still didn't have a shred of real evidence. We had suppositions. Educated guesses. Okay, highly educated guesses, veritable Ph.D.s of guesses. But still guesses. Odd behavior. Conflicting statements.

We wore Butch down.

He shook his head in resignation.

Okay, he said. But on one condition.

Shoot, I said.

When I say the word, we call it in.

I looked Butch in the eye. There were not many people I could trust. Trust not only to not betray me when the chips were down. But to have the judgment to know when they were. But Butch was one of them. We needed him. He was a man of action. Action was coming. I could feel it in my bones.

The choice was elementary.

Okay, I said. You're the man.

All right, he said.

Plan time, said Dorita.

The weakest link, I said. It's worked so far.

I'll give you that, she said. But are there any left?

By definition, I said. However strong the weakest link, it's still weaker than the rest.

I knew that philosophy degree would come in handy one day.

What makes you think this was the first time?

Just a wild guess.

Okay, kiddies, said Butch. Let's get to the point.

I had a thought. A very good thought. I was proud of my thought. I decided to string it out. For maximum effect.

Why, I asked, did Lisa run?

Because she knew something, said Dorita.

That she didn't want to tell you, added Butch.

And?

They looked at me.

That's not a sufficient explanation, I said. She could have just said nothing. Denied. By running, she told us we were on to something. Why did she run?

Ooh, said Dorita, you're so sexy when you're being mysterious.

Just the Socratic method. You brought me back to undergraduate days, with that philosophy remark.

All right, Monsieur Descartes, can we get to the goddamn point?

Lisa knows something, I said.

Right.

She didn't want to tell us.

Correct.

And.

And.

And she knew that if she stayed with us, she *would* tell us.

Exactly.

Ah.

So.

So, she's still the weakest link.

Bingo, said Butch.

Oho, Monsieur Descartes, said Dorita. If you keep this up, I might even start respecting your intellect.

You keep threatening.

All right, children, said Butch, let's go grab the little bitch.

I prefer to think of her as misguided, said Dorita.

Whatever, I said. Let's grab her.

By force? asked Dorita.

Why do you think Butch is on the team? I asked.

Wait a minute . . . said Butch.

Just kidding, I said.

But we do have to get her away from Jules again, said Dorita. And persuasion isn't going to work this time.

Let's figure that out when we get there, said Butch.

I couldn't agree more, I said. But first, I think I'll finish this tall skinny latte.

Butch and Dorita got up.

Okay, I said. Just kidding. Let's go.

108.

THE CAB SMELLED HEAVILY of spilled beer and ashes.

I had another thought.

Butch, I said. The note. Did you find out anything about the note?

Jesus, he said. I totally forgot.

You're kidding.

No, I'm not. Christ, man, you were badgering me so bad I couldn't think straight. I'm turning into you.

Okay, I'll take that as a compliment. What did you find out?

I couldn't get a look at it. I'm not officially on the case. It's locked up. They're guarding it like Bush's IQ scores.

Sure, I said. I get that. But what did you find out?

I talked to some guys.

And?

It wasn't a handwritten note. It was an e-mail.

We knew that. To who?

To whom, said Dorita.

To whom?

To his wife.

Veronica? Dorita and I said in unison.

Jesus, said Dorita. Get out an index card.

I already had one in my hand.

Whoa, I said. This is a blockbuster.

Might just blow us out of the water, said Dorita.

All right, said Butch. It's time to let old Butch in on the fun.

I had forgotten, in all of the excitement, that we hadn't shared with Butch everything we knew. We explained the Veronica angle.

Butch whistled. Perhaps in admiration. Perhaps not.

Listen, I said, this is definitely weird. But let's put it in context. All it really adds to what we know is that FitzGibbon *thought* that Veronica was still alive.

Pretty feeble, said Dorita. We've got to think this through.

The cab pulled up at Jules's building.

Sure, I said. I'm with you. But right now, we're here.

Shit, said Dorita. Shouldn't we hold off on this?

Forget it, I said. Damn the damn torpedoes. If we can get Lisa to talk, the rest won't matter.

I don't know, said Dorita.

Let's do it, said Butch.

A man of action, I said. I admire that. Dorita, you're outvoted.

She wasn't happy, but she went along.

We rang the bell.

No answer.

We rang again.

No answer.

I looked at Butch.

Aren't you a cop? I asked.

Sure, Rick. I'm a cop.

Then can't you just bust down this door? Isn't that what cops do?

Hate to break it to you. But no. Not without a warrant.

Jesus. Why does the law always have to interfere with our fun?

Damn, we were having a good time. I was thinking of asking Butch to join the partnership. R. & D. & B., LLP. It had a ring.

Speaking of which, the door buzzed. I threw myself at it, pulled it open just before the buzzing stopped.

We made our way upstairs. The door to Jules's loft was open. We peered in. We didn't see anybody. I called out Jules's name. Lisa's. No answer. I looked at Butch. I was nervous. Maybe it was time to call in the troops.

Butch went into trained cop mode.

He pulled a gun I hadn't known he carried.

Of course he has a gun, I thought. He's a goddamn cop.

He crouched. He slid into the room. He checked behind the door. He silently reconnoitered the downstairs area. It didn't take long. Nobody there. No perps. No bodies. No nothing. Not even a mouse. He looked at the balcony above. He looked at me and raised a questioning eyebrow. Where's the staircase? he was asking. I pointed to the corridor across the way. Butch slid across the room. He vanished. Dorita and I exchanged worried glances. My heart was pounding. Uncertainty was worse than death. If they shot you, you were gone. Nothing more to worry about. If you had no clue, all you could do was cringe.

Butch wasn't cringing. Neither was Dorita. She took off her black Blahnik pumps, set them lightly on the floor. She slid off after Butch. I tried to grab her arm, hold her back. She shook me off. She vanished too.

I felt like a coward.

Hell, I *was* a coward. Better get used to it.

I was guarding the entrance, I told myself. I was taking on the dangerous job.

I closed the door as quietly as I could. I stood guard.

I waited. I lit a cigarette. I didn't hear a thing. The fear became certainty. I ought to call the cops. I didn't have the skills for this.

Dorita appeared on the balcony. That she was standing up, not hunched over in danger mode, conveyed a message. She motioned me to come up.

I took off my shoes. That seemed to be the protocol. I crossed the empty space. It seemed interminable. I found the stairs. A wrought iron spiral thing, tucked out of view. I climbed it slowly. I thought my heart would burst. At the top, I found Dorita. She shook her head at me.

You wimp, she whispered. Come here.

She grabbed the back of my neck. She kissed me.

The unexpected kiss is the best.

She led me down a corridor. She stopped at an open door. She nodded me in.

Inside, Butch was crouched on the floor, next to a foam mattress stained with blood. In the corner of the room cowered Lisa. Her face was in her hands. On the mattress, cross-legged with his back against the wall, was Jules. He had on the same T-shirt as I'd last seen him in. Still streaked with blood.

I took a closer look. Not streaked. Soaked. Wet with it. A long curved knife lay loosely in his hand. Butch was carefully examining Jules's torso.

Entrails.

Shit. The little prick had finally done it. Disemboweled himself. Hara-kiri.

I could only hope he'd landed in samurai heaven.

I looked at Lisa. I looked at Dorita.

Get her out of here, I whispered.

Yes, boss, said Dorita.

She went to Lisa. Put her arms around her. She whispered something in her ear. She lifted up the tiny girl. She led her out.

Butch looked up at me. I nodded.

Sure. Call in the troops. What the hell. I didn't have a client anymore.

We had some time with Lisa before they got there. She was shaking, sobbing, but not out of control. She was a tough little thing, after all was said and done.

Dorita took her downstairs. I poured us all a drink. Fuck regulations. I wasn't a cop. Gin and tonic for Lisa. A double Scotch for me. Dorita had to settle for a gin and tonic too. I didn't know how to make a cosmo. Not the time to ask for the recipe.

I brought Butch a beer. He shook his head no thanks. Oh yeah. He was a cop.

Dorita sat with Lisa on the couch. She had her arm around her shoulder.

Lisa, Dorita said quietly. We need to know what happened.

I know, said Lisa, barely audible.

We know it wasn't you, Dorita said. We know you did whatever you did out of love. We can see that.

Dorita looked up at me reprovingly. Lest I have a different notion. Lest I interfere.

Lisa closed her eyes.

I just want to go to sleep, she said.

I know, said Dorita. I understand. And you can. You can go to sleep. But first you have to tell us. Tell us what happened.

Lisa opened her eyes. She looked at Dorita. Dorita looked into Lisa's eyes. Lisa slumped back into the sofa. The sharp edges softened into resignation. She nodded her head.

Veronica, she whispered.

Dorita and I looked at each other. There it was again.

What about Veronica? Dorita asked.

Lisa took a deep breath. She straightened her back. She looked at us.

Veronica's dead, she said.

Okay, said Dorita softly. How did she die?

I killed her, said Lisa.

My poker face broke down.

I didn't have an index card for this.

Lisa looked at me, at Butch. She shrugged.

I didn't mean to, she said.

I'm sure you didn't, said Dorita. Can you tell us how it happened?

That day you came over, said Lisa, looking at me. She was tied up in the back room.

The words caught in her throat.

The room we just found you in? asked Dorita.

Jules and me were fighting.

That time, I said.

Right, she said. And then, just after I went upstairs, Veronica got the gag out of her mouth. She started shouting.

That's why you put on the music, started yelling at Jules? I asked. To drown out her shouting?

Yes, she said quietly.

Jesus. Veronica had been right there. In the loft. And I hadn't even thought about her. Thought about finding her. Talking to her.

Cancel my job interview with the CIA.

And then what happened? asked Dorita.

She put her hand on Lisa's, gave it a reassuring squeeze.

I went into the back room, said Lisa. I was scared. I was so scared.

She sobbed a sob or two.

She pulled herself together. She took a deep breath.

I got the duct tape, she said. That we'd taped her to the chair with. And I wrapped it around her face. To stop her screaming. And when I'd wrapped her up I went into the other room. I lay down. I put a pillow over my head. I couldn't stand it any more. I was trying to protect Jules. I was just trying to protect Jules.

We could hear the sirens coming.

She struggled to contain the tears. She took a deep breath. She looked at me apologetically.

What was the argument about? I asked.

About Veronica, she said. I told Jules we had to let her go. It was so stupid. The whole thing was so stupid. But he wouldn't do it. I told him we could go to Mexico. Wherever. Just get away. But he wouldn't listen to me. He wanted to . . .

Wanted to? asked Dorita.

Get revenge.

Against whom?

His father. Mr. FitzGibbon. God, he hated his dad so much. It was like, it was like a sickness. Like he was crazy with it.

And how was he going to get revenge? By killing Veronica?

Sort of, she said.

A crowd of blue shirts appeared in the doorway. They were led by a tall detective with a hawk nose and tiny black eyes. I thought I recognized him. From some hooker bust a few years ago. I'd been hired to help out some john with connections to a senator.

Butch leapt up to intercept the horde. Lisa looked up. No reaction registered on her face. She was beyond reaction.

Butch conferred with Detective Nose in a hushed and urgent voice. The Nose kept glancing up at Dorita and me. I saw him note our shoeless feet, raise an eyebrow.

It was clear what was going on. Butch was trying to explain that we were getting a full confession. Learning everything. And any little upset of the balance might tip Lisa over. Into silence.

Dorita was whispering into Lisa's ear. She was crying again.

Butch won the argument. A couple of uniforms with evidence kits quietly went upstairs. The rest backed off. Including the Nose, though not without a baleful glance in my direction. Butch closed the door and sat back down across from me.

Dorita was still talking quietly to Lisa. I couldn't hear what she was saying. Butch put ten fingers up, then five. Fifteen minutes. Detective Nose was giving us fifteen minutes.

Dorita, I said, as softly as I could manage.

She looked up impatiently.

Fifteen, I whispered.

She nodded.

How was he going to get revenge? Dorita asked, getting Lisa back on track.

I don't know the whole thing, said Lisa. But they were going to get control of everything, somehow.

Get control? asked Dorita.

They? I asked.

Of Mr. FitzGibbon's money. He was doing it with Raul and Ramon.

Dorita looked at me. I looked at her. The phone calls.

I don't know how, exactly, Lisa went on. He was using Veronica to get to his father. And Raul and Ramon were, like, there. With his father, all the time. They told Mr. FitzGibbon that his wife was kidnapped. That he had to play along, pay the ransom, or she'd be dead. That they might come after him, too. The kidnappers. So Ramon had to be with him every second of the day. Ramon never left his side. Unless Raul was there to take over for a while. But Ramon was the security guy, supposedly. So it was almost always him.

I looked at Butch. He got up quietly. He went out the door.

Dorita looked at Lisa, still with the kindly air. Let's go back a little bit, she said. How did Veronica die?

She . . . she suffocated, said Lisa.

Suffocated?

From the . . . the duct tape.

Okay, said Dorita, taking Lisa's hand again. It's okay. We know you didn't mean that to happen.

I didn't, sobbed Lisa. Oh God, I surely didn't.

Surely. It dawned on me that Lisa, for all her punked-out trappings, hadn't always been a street kid. She'd come from somewhere. She had a family. A dad. A mom. Whoever they were. What they'd been through.

They hadn't seen anything yet.

So when I came over the second time? I began to ask.

When I sat on you? she anticipated, with a tearful sneaky smile.

Right.

I wanted to distract you. To keep you from looking around. Seeing something. Before Jules got there.

Damn. I wasn't irresistible after all.

Besides, she said, you were kind of cute.

That was better.

That sneaky smile gave me something to think about. This little girl was far from helpless.

Seeing what? I asked.

I don't know, she said. I was afraid, that's all.

I looked at my watch. We were running out of time. Butch came back in. He gave me a Look. I knew what it meant. We weren't getting an extension.

What about Larry Silver? I asked.

Oh, him, she said with a sneer. That fucker got what he deserved.

How's that? I asked.

Jules needed somebody to do the actual snatch, she told us. He couldn't do it himself, of course, because Veronica knew him. Jules knew Larry from the streets. He knew Larry was a mean and angry guy. Somebody who could be violent. And he was stupid. Jules thought he could control him. So he got Larry to do the job. When Veronica got back to New York, Larry grabbed her, brought her to the loft. Blindfolded, so she wouldn't see Jules. He paid off Larry. Two thousand bucks.

And that was the beginning of the end.

Because Larry wasn't going to settle for a lousy two thousand bucks. On the day of his murder, as we knew by then, Larry hadn't come to the loft to talk about a poker debt. He'd come to shake down Jules. They'd gotten into a fight all right. That much was true. But after they were lying there exhausted, Jules had to find a way to make sure Larry didn't leave angry. He couldn't risk that. So Jules started to negotiate, at some point managing to put a call in to Raul, who sent over Mr. Security with a baseball bat. Jules gave Larry some cash. Promised more. Larry wasn't the sharpest knife in the drawer. Left the loft happy with his victory. Put one over on that little prick Jules, he was no doubt thinking. Until Ramon grabbed him by the neck, dragged him to the Dumpster.

The baseball bat did the rest.

But Ramon unfortunately left Larry's body where it could easily be found. And when the police figured Jules as a suspect for Larry's murder right away, the whole thing started to unravel. It was a fucking disaster.

They'd barely had time to get Veronica out of the place before the cops showed up. Took her to the empty loft upstairs.

And then Veronica's death. From then on it was damage control.

Funny, I thought. This didn't jibe with Jules's sudden calm and arrogance, the fourth time I'd gone to the loft.

So, I hazarded, why did Jules . . . do what he did? Upstairs. Just now.

I couldn't think of a nice way to put it.

The tears welled up in Lisa's eyes again. He'd always been obsessed with the samurai thing, she told us. He'd played with the idea many times. And the night before, it seemed that he had some kind of breakdown. Or maybe it was a revelation. He finally figured out that everything was coming apart. Raul was going to let Jules take the hit for Larry Silver's murder. Or pin FitzGibbon's death on him. Get rid of him some other way. Whatever. Maybe just have him hit by a truck. Jules had become irrational, afraid. He'd lost his inner Superman. He'd heard the buzzer ring when we'd arrived. He'd looked out over the balcony, seen who it was. When he saw us, he figured the end was coming. He took the honorable way out. As he saw it, anyway.

Jesus. I was batting four hundred. Five times I'd been to the loft. Twice people died. I was the Grim fucking Reaper.

As my watch ticked off the final seconds, Dorita asked Lisa why she didn't get out of it at some point. Call the cops. Or at least get the hell out of there.

She couldn't get away from it, Lisa explained. Not only was she so involved that she couldn't get out, she was actually enjoying it. She'd gotten caught up in the whole James Bond thrill of it. Nothing in her life had ever been so vital, so close to the bone. She felt alive. Free, in a complicated kind of way.

Alive by death, I thought. Nice.

Which was the cue for the door to slam open, the Nose to stride back in. He didn't have a compromising air. Enough with the goddamn lawyers. This was going to be his investigation. Butch rose to meet him. Detective Nose brushed him aside.

Lisa Mueller? he said.

She looked up at him with a defiant air.

You're under arrest for the murder of Veronica FitzGibbon.

Sure, she said, her hard edge back again. No sweat.

We'd lost her.

On the way out Butch asked one of the CID guys whether they'd found Veronica.

In the other building, the guy said.

What other building?

The one next to the alley.

109.

THE SCENE WAS GUARDED by yellow tape and blue uniforms. A skinny cop with a bad facial condition pointed me and Butch to a dark staircase at the end of a narrow hallway.

Down there, he said. But be careful. They're dusting for prints.

Okay, we said.

The staircase was dimly lit by small orange bulbs. We went down slowly. At the bottom they'd set up high-powered floodlights. Every dust ball and dead cockroach was starkly lit, outlined by a harsh shadow.

Careful, shouted one of the CID guys.

I looked down. I'd almost stepped on an evidence kit.

Sorry, I said.

Butch grabbed my elbow.

Just follow me, he said.

Butch conferred a moment with the guy who looked to be in charge. Nodded his head a few times. Beckoned to me. Led me to the farthest reaches of the basement space. Past lines of storage spaces. Each was about four feet wide. Made of ancient spruce laths floor to ceiling, lashed together with chicken wire. The cubicles were endlessly deep in broken tricycles, rusting roller skates, old high chairs. The doors were held shut by a potpourri of dime-store locks. They looked just about secure enough to keep out a paraplegic rabbit.

Perpendicular to the end of the row was a high tin-covered door. I recognized it right away. The inside image of the door in the alley.

I felt sick. I'd never gotten around to checking where it led. Had I only followed through with my intuition, then . . . what? I might have found a corpse? Well, maybe I shouldn't feel so bad. Maybe if I had, FitzGibbon would have been spared the ignominy of throwing himself out of a thirty-third-story window – or being pushed – the thought reminded me that we didn't have all the answers yet.

Would that have been a contribution to the collective welfare?

I thought not.

So maybe it was okay that I was such a solipsistic fool.

Or maybe not.

Time would tell.

In the meantime, Butch led me forward. Took a left at the metal door. We ducked down. Peered into the crawl space. The one in which, until a moment earlier, the rotting remains of the good Veronica FitzGibbon had reposed.

It was dark.

It was ordinary.

In the way that extraordinary places often are.

110.

AFTER OUR TOUR of the grotto we picked up Dorita. She had stayed behind. Not having a strong desire to look at dead bodies.

We retired to the closest eatery. I had a double Glenmorangie, straight up.

There are still things we don't know, said Dorita.

I can't argue with that, I said.

Me neither, said Butch.

There's stuff that Lisa didn't know, I said.

Couldn't know, said Dorita.

Stuff that only Ramon or Raul can tell us.

You want to talk to them, good luck, said Butch.

I knew what he meant. I knew what Butch's little trip outside the loft had been for. They'd probably picked up the twins before we'd even finished talking to Lisa.

If you're with us, I said, you'll try to get me in.

You're going to have to go through the ADA, he said.

Russell Graham? No sweat. I'm tight with him.

Sure, Butch laughed. I knew that.

Hey, I said. Let's give it a shot. We've got some leverage, you know. I've got something to trade.

Yeah?

Information. If nothing else.

True, Butch said. It's worth a shot. Come down with me. I'll try to get him to talk to you.

We grabbed a cab.

It smelled of success.

Butch called the ADA from his cell phone. Gave him the goods. It took some doing, but he got the up-and-coming Russell Graham to agree to see me. He'd give me ten minutes to talk him into it.

At the station house Butch led me into the back. He told Dorita to wait outside. She didn't like it. But there were only so many civilians we could throw at the ADA all at once.

He was waiting in a small room. It smelled of mold.

I didn't have a dog in the fight, I told him. I didn't have a client anymore. I just wanted to get to the bottom of the whole thing. Finish the job we started. See justice done. Which put me on their side now. And I could do it faster than they could. I knew these guys. I knew what buttons to push. And anyway, I had a lot of information. Some maybe they had already. But I was willing to wager they didn't have it all.

The ADA wasn't exactly enthusiastic about it. But he knew that I knew stuff he wasn't going to get anywhere else. So he cut me a deal. They were still working on Raul. He wasn't talking. They hadn't gotten to Ramon yet. They'd give me twenty minutes with him. But the cameras would be on. I needed to know that. No funny shit. They were letting me in solely for their purposes. To see what I might get. After the twenty minutes were up, I had to be debriefed by the ADA. Give up every squib of information I had. Not just whatever I got from Ramon. Everything.

It felt like a deal with the devil.

I took it.

Ramon was sitting in a stark and empty room. Four metal chairs. A flimsy table. Him. Me.

I sat down right next to him.

Hey, Ramon, I said. I hear you're in deep shit.

He gave me the patented Ramon blank look.

I leaned in.

Listen, I said. We got a good situation here. You know what it is?

The brick wall stayed brick.

We got a dead guy, Ramon, I confided. You hear me?

He looked at me with a flicker of interest.

I feigned shock and dismay. I leaned back. My mouth fell open.

You mean they didn't tell you?

He gave me a wary look.

Shit, man. You really *don't* know. Those pricks. Jules. Jules killed himself. Stuck a knife into his gut. Hara-kiri. You know, that Japanese shit? You know that shit?

He nodded warily.

Yeah, I said, shaking my head. He was some fucked-up sick kid.

Ramon showed a glimmer of assent.

So anyway, I said. That means two things. I know you figured this out already. Because you're a sharp guy. But let me lay it out for you. Can I lay it out for you?

He nodded slowly, twice.

Two things, I said. One, I don't have a client anymore.

Ramon allowed himself a half-smile.

So I'm in the market for a new client, I said, slapping him playfully on the arm. If you get my meaning. But more important, I said quietly, leaning in to whisper into his ear, like I said, we got a dead guy. We stick the dead guy with it all.

I leaned back. I gave him a triumphant grin.

Whadya think? Is that rich, or what?

He looked at me. I looked at him. I kept grinning. My face hurt.

Yeah, he said. That's good.

I knew you'd see it that way, Ramon, I said, with another conspiratorial lean in his direction. You're a smart guy. But then we gotta get our story straight. If we're going to pin it on Jules, we gotta make sure everything fits.

Sure, he whispered, looking at the one-way glass. I know that.

Don't worry, I said. We just keep our voices low, it's okay. Listen, I whispered, that's where I come in. I'm a lawyer. I know how their minds work. You give me the stones, I build the wall.

I got the blank stare again.

I gotta have the facts, I said. What really happened. So I know where the weak points are. Then I make up the story. A story that fits whatever evidence they might find. There's a million stories in the big city. We got to pick the right one. Can't have any holes in it.

Ramon said nothing. I could see the brick in his head struggling mightily to turn itself into a brain. To figure out what was going on.

Hey, I said. I know what you're thinking. What's in it for Rick Redman? That's an easy one. You're going to get the money, right? You're inheriting the dough. And I need a client. I need a client can pay the bills.

He still said nothing.

Anyway, I said, you got two choices, right? You sit here. You say nothing. The cops come back. They grill the shit out of you. You don't say nothing. I know you won't. You're a tough guy. But then what happens?

He didn't respond.

I'll tell you what happens. They're pissed. You don't say nothing, they draw one conclusion: guilty as charged. So they charge you. They shake down everybody and his dog. They turn over every rock. Because they don't like you. They don't like you at all. They get very, very serious when somebody doesn't help them out. They're vindictive bastards.

I thought I saw a glint of understanding in his eyes.

You know what happens then, don't you Ramon?

Silence.

Don't you?

Silence.

I'll tell you, then. I go to Raul. You don't take my offer? Raul does. And you're high and dry, man. You think Raul's going to protect you? When he knows he can pin it on a dead guy and you? You know Raul. He's a slick motherfucker. He could talk his way into Fort Knox.

Silence. A slow shaking of the head. Hard to interpret.

Think about it, Ramon. When you were there, after Mr. FitzGibbon went over the balcony. You guys saw the e-mail. It pointed to Veronica. What's the first question they'd ask? Where the hell's this Veronica? Why didn't you just get rid of it? Why didn't you throw it away, delete it from the computer?

He gave me a stony look.

Because Raul told you not to. If it'd been sent somewhere, they'd get it eventually. And they have ways to figure out what's been deleted. That if you deleted it, they'd know. You'd look bad. Raise suspicion. Right?

He said nothing.

Anyway, what the note said wasn't so bad for you. Suicide. Better than murder. Maybe you'd get away with the Veronica thing, Larry Silver. Pin it all on Jules.

Silence.

That's what he told you. Am I right? Or am I right? Is he a smart sonofabitch, or is he?

Slowly, painfully, Ramon got it.

Yeah, you're right, he sighed.

He'd finally figured it out. He was fucked, either way. He had to trust me. It was his only chance.

I don't know that much, he said.

What do you mean?

It was Raul. It was Raul and Jules. They cooked the whole thing up.

Tell me about it, I said.

He talked.

111.

WE GOT TOGETHER in a big, anonymous room. Bright fluorescent lights. Hard wooden chairs. Linoleum. I insisted that Dorita be there. The ADA asked Butch to stay. They were probably taping the meeting. I didn't care. Maybe I'd ask for a copy afterwards. For the movie. The one about my stunning legal career.

Well? Russell Graham, ADA, asked with a skeptical air. Did you get anything?

You weren't watching? I asked, surprised.

Something came up. Lee was there, he said, nodding to the beady-eyed detective.

The Nose had a name.

Couldn't hear a thing, he said.

Okay, I said. Here it is. As best I can figure it.

As I started putting it all on the table, Russell Graham gradually lost his stiff and wary air. Moved on to surprised. Impressed, even. Sidled up to warm and cuddly. He even started contributing to the discussion.

Collectively, we put it all together.

Jules, it was obvious, was a hell of a lot more sophisticated than he let on. He knew Raul for what he was. Somebody for whom other people's feelings and values didn't exist.

Well, Dorita interjected, takes one to know one.

You're talking about Jules, I presume? I replied.

As opposed to?

Me, for instance.

Sure, she said. Whatever gets you through the night.

We got blank looks from the rest of the crowd. They didn't seem to be entirely tuned in to the Rick and Dorita show.

Like your average rich psychopath, I surmised, Raul hadn't had the need or opportunity to break the law. To go over the line. The club stuff kept him busy. Decorating the Park Avenue pad. He'd got his ego stroked enough that he hadn't needed to go anywhere else for it.

But when Jules came to Raul with his scheme, Raul couldn't resist the idea of all that easy money. As he saw it, Jules was taking all the risk. He and Ramon could maintain plausible deniability all the way.

They'd snatch Veronica, Jules proposed. Raul could find out her itinerary easily enough. Jules would arrange the grab. They'd tell FitzGibbon that Veronica had been kidnapped – that much, of course, would be true. The kidnappers wanted ransom, but were crazy, fanatical religionists, and couldn't be trusted. They might even come after FitzGibbon himself. They had to be dealt with very carefully. Ramon, Mr. Security, would deliver the ransom, which quite naturally would then disappear, along with the kidnappers. But FitzGibbon would get Veronica back. He'd be happy. To him, it would have been worth the price.

Raul bought it. Putting one over on the old man. The prick who had the gall to make him work for a living. He couldn't resist. And with Raul came Ramon. As always.

And when FitzGibbon fell for the scam too, he fell for it like Hepburn for Tracy. They'd read him well. Veronica was his one true love. That much of what he'd said was true. He'd been heartbroken when she'd left. It had eaten him up. He wanted her back in a desperate way. And then, by happenstance – or maybe by design – I wasn't sure how much credit to give the three little shits – he had an enemy to blame for her absence, instead of himself, in the guise of the dastardly terrorist kidnappers.

FitzGibbon having a paranoid streak to begin with, they hadn't even needed to prompt him to circle the wagons. It was only natural to rely on family in a crisis. By means of which Ramon could make sure that FitzGibbon never had any second thoughts, or if he did he didn't act on them. No surreptitious phone calls to the cops. No midnight doubts about the whole outrageous scheme. Because Ramon was always there.

Ramon himself, of course, couldn't be trusted to decide anything.

Too damn stupid. So Raul kept him on a very short leash. On the other hand, Raul was sure, he could count on Ramon not to betray the plan. He knew that from a lifetime's experience with his brother. Raul had always been the smart one. The charming one. The one who could get them what they wanted. Ramon followed Raul like a well-trained hound. And Raul, in his hubris, his absolute self-regard, had no doubt at all about his ability to control everyone: Ramon, FitzGibbon, Jules and, when it came down to it, me as well.

The Larry Silver thing had thrown a big wrench into the plans. When Ramon called Raul to report on his successful mission, Raul told him to leave the body there, where it could be easily found, three blocks from Jules's place. Then they'd have something to hang over Jules, if they needed it later. But that, it turned out, was a big miscalculation. Raul didn't know the neighbors had called the cops about the noise. That the cops would make the connection.

Once the cops were all over Jules, Raul figured he'd be sorely tempted to cop a plea by implicating the twins. So Raul, pulling the double switch, convinced Jules that he had a plan to make sure Jules wouldn't get pegged for the murder. Said he had some homeless sucker he'd frame for it. That way, Raul controlled the situation from every angle.

Hence Jules's sudden calm and arrogance, I said. If he believed Raul, he figured he was bulletproof on the Larry Silver thing.

I wonder about that, though, said Butch. I can't see Jules buying that story.

Yeah, I said. He was a wily little fucker. Much more probable that Raul told Jules he was going to pin it on Ramon. Told *Ramon* the homeless guy story.

His own twin brother? said the ADA.

I wouldn't put it past him, Butch said.

I wouldn't put it past him to actually do it, either, I said.

After all, said Dorita, Ramon actually *did* kill Larry Silver.

Didn't even have to frame him, really, I said. Just needed to make a phone call.

And *that* was a scheme Jules would have no trouble believing in, said Dorita.

And then Veronica. At first it must have seemed a total disaster. But Jules didn't see it that way. He just revised the plan. Because, apart from

Jules's emotional motivation, which was real and, truth be told, under-standable, now there was an even bigger pot of gold at the end of this particularly twisted rainbow: control of FitzGibbon's corporate empire. With Veronica out of the way, and Jules disinherited, the only thing standing between the twins getting the whole damn thing was FitzGibbon himself.

And we had to believe, though we'd never know the details, that Jules had some plan to take it away from them.

Yes, I mused, it makes perfect sense. The two little geniuses, Jules and Raul, each no doubt believed that in the end he'd outwit the other.

But something doesn't jibe, said the Nose. Why would Jules hold her in his own place? Maybe he could prevent her seeing him, but she'd hear him, wouldn't she? You told us Lisa had to make a bunch of noise to pre-vent you from hearing Veronica. It had to work the other way too. She must have heard Jules talking. Wouldn't she know his voice?

And even if she didn't, the ADA said, she'd have overheard enough to figure out who he was.

I was thinking the same thing, I said. But there's an explanation.

Which is? asked the ADA.

There's only one way it all makes sense, I said. Jules never intended for her to live. His plan was never to just get the ransom. That was the lure. To get Raul and Ramon on board.

He intended all along to kill her, said Dorita.

And engineer FitzGibbon's death as well, I said. Daddy was the real target. Right from the beginning.

Jesus, said Butch. Nicely done.

And, remarkably enough, the little prick had almost gotten away with it. But in any Byzantine scheme, there are always imponderables. Stuff you can't predict. Lisa. The weak link.

Raul didn't even give her a thought, Dorita said.

Actually, I said, we don't know if he even knew she existed.

Good point, said Butch.

Jules saw the danger, though, I said. Hence his clumsy attempts to scare me away from her.

Didn't work, said Butch.

Not lucky, said the ADA.

Not lucky enough, I said.

We talked through the rest of it. The whole thing could have come unraveled much earlier, of course. FitzGibbon was a hard-headed, and sophisticated, man. Controlling. As the thing dragged on, he started questioning Raul's tactics. He wanted his Veronica back. He started talking about going to the cops. So Raul went to Jules, who had another brilliant idea. Or, more likely, it had been his plan all along. He began supplying the twins with psychotropic drugs. Whatever came to hand. Mescaline. Psilocybin. LSD. And Raul began spiking FitzGibbon's food and drink with the stuff. Those things are hard enough to deal with when you know you're taking them. For FitzGibbon, it must have been utterly disorienting, terrifying. He started to question his own sanity. He became more and more afraid, and Raul played on his fear, kept him off balance, and malleable.

In spite of their efforts, though, FitzGibbon had continued to display signs of suspicion, and, ironically enough, it seems that he really *had* become enamored of me.

Must have been the drugs, Dorita interjected.

No doubt, I said.

FitzGibbon had gotten increasingly insistent that I be hired to help with Veronica and the kidnappers. The twins didn't for a minute think that FitzGibbon had figured out the scam – he was too far gone by then for that – but they were terrified that somehow, some way, FitzGibbon was planning to communicate to me the fact of the supposed kidnapping. To get me on the team. And they couldn't take the chance that somehow I might stumble onto what was going on. On at least a couple of occasions Ramon had caught FitzGibbon trying to call me, and managed to cut off the call in time.

And I didn't pick up the calls, I said.

You've lost me, said the ADA.

I kept getting these calls on my cell, I told him. 'Private number.' I ignored them. If I had answered the phone the first time, one time . . .

Hindsight is a wonderful thing, said the Nose.

I was starting to like the guy.

So, I said, the twins increased the dosages. And by the time of the fashion show that Dorita showed up at, FitzGibbon was basically a shell of his former self. An automaton. Incapable of forming an independent thought.

The drugs also explained his so-called suicide, we agreed. He had started to have hallucinations, terrible dreams. Fears and paranoia way beyond anything he'd known. And that had led, as a train wreck leads to twisted metal and death, to his plunge from the thirty-third-floor balcony. Whether the little monsters had planned for it to happen then, or in that way, we didn't know. Most likely FitzGibbon just did them a favor, spared them from having to give him a little push over the railing.

But before he jumped, he felt compelled to leave one last word for Veronica, whom he still believed, or hoped, to be alive. The e-mail.

I guess I can see it now? I said to Russell Graham.

The ADA pushed a printout across the table:

sorry doll i can't really explain it's so weird but doll you were right i've been unfair to Jules i wish we could have worked it out

i love you both

Eamon

112.

I WENT TO THE OFFICE. The real office. Well. It didn't seem so real anymore. I took my index cards with me. I closed my office door. I spread them out on the floor. I put into one pile all of those that made sense, in light of everything we'd learned. I put in another pile those that didn't.

The second pile was empty.

I walked the length of the thirtieth floor. I acknowledged nobody. Lest I be deterred from my intended task. I strode past Cherise without a glance in her direction. I arrived at Warwick's office door. I did not knock. I walked right in.

He was on the phone. He looked up at me, mouth open. This was just not done. He mumbled something into the phone. Pressed the hold button.

Redman, he said testily, I'm on an important call. Please speak to Cherise. I think I have an opening at three.

Fuck that, Warwick, I said.

His face turned a shade of pink I hadn't encountered before. His mouth twitched. He was searching for words.

Don't waste your breath, I said. I quit. Oh, and by the way. Go herniate.

I turned and walked away. I left his door open.

In the background, fading into the history of my former life, I heard Warwick's whining voice.

Something about burning bridges.

Hah, I said to myself. Some bridges are better burnt.

My last official act was to invite Dorita for lunch. Michel's, I suggested. I was hoping to see Warwick show up, planning to flatter some overstuffed prospective client. Maybe I could bribe a waiter to piss in his soup.

Dorita arrived. She was wearing a flowing silk thing in a pale peach color.

My, I said. You've gone pastel.

A momentary loss of judgment, she said. Don't worry.

That's a relief. I was just about to recommend a good therapist. But then I remembered you already have three.

Speaking of therapy, what the hell did you just do?

I quit. I told the fucker off. And please don't say anything about burning bridges.

Wouldn't dream of it, she said.

Anyway it's done. And I'm quite convinced that my next project's going to get me through it. At least until we set up shop as R. & D., LLP, Ace Detectivists.

Don't hold your breath. One of us still has a real job.

You have my deepest sympathy.

Speaking of jobs, did you hear about Steiglitz?

No.

He's selling his clinic. Going to Africa.

Gone safari on us?

No. For good. He's joined Doctors Without Borders.

My, what a little guilt will do for a man.

I guess you'd know. So, what are you going to do? Dealer at the Taj? Live on tips?

Close, but way better. I'm opening my own room.

You're opening up your bedroom for public viewing?

Hadn't thought of that, actually. Maybe I'll do that too. But no. A poker room. I found this amazing space in Williamsburg.

You're kidding, right? Tell me you're kidding.

I am not.

Isn't that illegal?

Depends, I said. On who's watching.

113.

THE CALL FROM LAURA CAME.

Rick, she said in her official tone.

Laura, I replied.

I was calm. I knew what was coming.

The final report's coming out tomorrow, she said.

Okay.

I wanted to give you a heads-up.

I appreciate that.

It won't come as a surprise to you.

Nothing would come as a surprise to me. I'm all surprised out.

She paused.

Okay, she said. The bottom line is, involuntary overdose. Self-inflicted.

Right.

I can give you the details.

No. No. I can read it tomorrow.

Okay. But if you change your mind.

No. I won't. It's okay.

All right, then.

All right.

I hung up. I sat back. I was suffused with a most confusing calm.

I paid a memorial visit to the Wolf's Lair. I ordered soda water.

Double? asked Thom.

Sure, I said. Let's go crazy.

Another double soda water later, Jake came through the door.

We shook hands.

We stood awkwardly. I wondered whether I should call him Jake or Brendan.

Have a seat, my man, I said at last.

We sat side by side at the bar. I felt no imperative to speak. I could have asked him all those questions about Melissa. Filled in some of the remaining blanks. But I didn't.

Let her rest in peace, I thought. Leave her with her mysteries.

So, he said. Anything new going on?

I told him I'd quit drinking.

He was impressed. Said he might try that too.

I told him about the poker room.

He liked it.

Hey, he said, the World Series starts in two weeks.

Shit, I said. I'd forgotten all about that.

The World Series of Poker. Vegas. Lights. Cameras. Action. Millions in prizes. Side tables full of overstuffed rubes. Babes in bikinis.

I looked at him.

He looked at me.

I'll make the reservations, I said.

114.

I WOKE UP BEFORE DORITA. She was on her stomach, sleeping softly. I crept out of bed. I stood and gazed at her. I was not worthy. That such a creature would share my bed. Might share my life. Damn. I apologized to God for all my whining. I was a lucky man. Even if it ended here, I was a lucky man.

I rustled up some eggs and Emmental. I scoured the nether regions of the fridge for half an onion, the odd dried-out mushroom. I pled guilty to bad housekeeping. I turned the detritus into a passable omelet.

I brewed a pot of Jamaican Blue. I went upstairs. Kelly was still asleep. I let her snooze. She deserved it.

Dorita had awoken on her own. She was in the shower. I snuck in. She had her back to me. I kissed the nape of her neck. She leaned back into me. My shirt got wet. I didn't mind.

Come downstairs, I said. I've thrown a little breakfast together.

Mmmm, she said. You sure you don't want to join me for a while first?

Darn it, I said. Had I only known. But the omelet's getting cold.

She turned around to face me. A full frontal excess of perfection. My knees went weak.

Have it your way, she said. I'll keep this for myself.

You cruel, wanton witch, I said. You dare to make me choose between warm omelet and you?

I do. And you can brave the consequences of your choice.

I'm all for free will, I said. But sometimes you just can't stand on principle.

I threw off my clothes. I eased into the shower stall. I slithered up.

Other stuff transpired. Suffice it to say that by the time we reached the kitchen the omelets had congealed. We popped them in the microwave. They were chewy but retained a hint of flavor. We left some for Kelly, still slumbering innocently in her room. Unaware of the Wagnerian events unfolding in her home.

115.

I CALLED SHEILA.

Come over, she said. I'll make some time.

When I got there I was momentarily mute. So much had happened. I didn't know where to start.

Shall we talk about Melissa? Sheila suggested.

I don't know, I said.

And I didn't. I didn't have anything to say.

I can't get my mind around it, I said.

Yes, said Sheila, indulging me. I'm sorry.

I wish *I* were.

Rick. You don't mean that.

I do. Sort of. I mean yes, I'm sorry. I feel bad. Of course I do. But somehow it doesn't feel like it's supposed to feel.

How is it 'supposed to feel'?

I didn't have an answer.

Do you feel guilty? she asked finally.

Guilty, sure. I'll never stop feeling guilty. Guilty for what I did.

What did you do?

Nothing.

Oh, come on, Rick.

Not nothing. But not enough. If I'd done enough, she'd still be alive.

I hesitate to use the word, but isn't that a little . . . arrogant?

Arrogant? How so?

You ascribe to yourself the power of life and death. Rather grandiose, don't you think?

I thought about that.

Ah, I said. Yes. I see.

I told the Steiglitz story, the story of the AA crowd. All the secrets. How helpless I'd felt. Drowning in a tide of revelations.

Oh dear, she said.

Yes, I said. Oh dear.

Silence.

But there's a silver lining, I said.

I'm so glad to hear that, she said, brightening.

I told her about Dorita.

She's saved my life, I said. She's perfect. Radiant. The answer to my prayers.

Sheila looked somber.

I was taken aback. I'd expected her to share my excitement.

Rick, she said.

It suddenly occurred to me that she'd used my name three times. A new record. Jesus, I thought, I must be really messed up.

That's great, she said. It really is. And I hope it works out for you. But you need to be careful. Manage your expectations. There are no magic bullets in this life. We've talked about that.

I felt a pain in my lower back.

Sure, I said. But that was in the context of momentary pleasures. Ecstasies. Escapes.

Are you sure this is any different?

I paused. I shrugged. I thought. I struggled.

No, I said at last. I'm not sure. I can't be sure. But it sure feels like it.

How did it feel those other times? Those other times that you felt close to bliss. Did it feel different?

No, I said slowly, carefully. Not different. But it went away. As soon as I left the room. It vanished. Or soon. Within a couple of hours. Days, anyway.

The glow faded.

It did.

Well, Rick, this might just be a bigger glow, mightn't it? Just taking a little longer to fade?

I was silent. Damn, I thought, I'd been like a kid in a candy store.

Like Melissa? she suggested. Like the first few months with Melissa?
I pondered. I struggled. Well, I thought. There it was. Real life.
Candy melts, I said.
She knew exactly what I meant.
And if you eat too much of it? she asked.
You get sick.
Or sick of it.

116.

ON THE WAY HOME I stopped at the Wolf's Lair.
I needed a drink.
Hey Thom, I said.
Rick! said Thom. Good to see you.
Good to be here, I said. Give me a double.
Soda?
Morangie.
Thom raised his eyebrows. Poured the Scotch.
The brass rail felt cool and right on my hand. The warm mahogany
of the bar.
I sat and thought.
I thought about Melissa.
What was I thinking when I thought about you?
I couldn't remember.
Another double? asked Thom.
Twist my arm, I said.
Anything for a friend, Rick.
Yes, I thought.
Anything for a friend.

ACKNOWLEDGMENTS

To Max, Tess and Lana for putting up with my frequent absences while I wrote this thing and for being fabulous and funny. Dr. W. for the inspiration and keeping me (relatively) sane. Arielle, Danny, Thom and Jason for the inspiration. Sam for believing in me. Charlotte for believing in me and introducing me to Sam. And Kendall for being the best editor a fellow could ask for.

And, of no less importance, to everyone I forgot to mention.

And to Dylan, for being so strong, and inspiring so many with his strength. Rest in peace, my son.